LUCK & CHANCE

BEYOND THE REALM OF WISDOM

A PORTION OF BOOK PROFITS WILL GO TO
SUPER TYPHOON HAIYAN / YOLANDA
VICTIMS IN THE PHILIPPINES.

THIS NOVEL IS THE KARMA OF THE DEAD
MANIFESTED TO HELP THE LIVING.

LUCK & CHANCE

BEYOND THE REALM OF WISDOM

BY

ELLIOTT B. ADDISON

ILLUSTRATIONS BY JOSEPH BOGINSKI

PRIMEWORLD MILLENNIUM

NEW YORK

PRIMEWORLD MILLENNIUM CORPORATION

Text copyright © 2014 by Elliott Bennett Addison

LUCK & CHANCE: BEYOND THE REALM OF WISDOM
Publishing Rights © Elliott Bennett Addison

Cover Design and Illustration: Joseph Boginski

Text Design and Layout: Elliott B. Addison

Typography: Elliott B. Addison, Mark Xu (許嘉瑋), Eliz Schutte

The characters and events portrayed in this book are fictitious. Any similarity to real persons, living or dead, is coincidental and not intended by the author.

The Primeworld Millennium Corporation
Trade Paperback Edition February 2014

ISBN – 13 - 978-0-9911771-0-3

ISBN – 10 - 0-9911771-0X3

[1. Fantasy – Fiction. 2. Action and Adventure – Fiction. 3. Magic – Fiction. 4. Saga – Fiction. 5. Bildungsroman / Coming of Age – Fiction. 6. Philosophy – Fiction. 7. History – Fiction. 8. Secret Societies – Fiction. 9. Schools – Fiction. 10. Science – Fiction, 11. Colleges – Fiction 12. USA – Fiction. 13. New York – Fiction. 14. Philippines – Fiction. 15. Transmedia – Fiction.]

Printed in the U.S.A

COLLECTOR'S EDITION
First edition, First Printing
February 2014

10 9 8 7 6 5 4 3 2 1

Dear Pam,

May you find some Zen enlightenment through this novel series.

Elliott Addison
March 29, 2014

"*Luck & Chance* is riveting. I was hooked from the first chapter. I can't wait to read more of the series."

Eliz Schutte, age twelve

"This novel is a work of brilliance. It kept me at the edge of my seat at every turn of the page. A coming of age story filled with drama, it leads us through the characters' exciting lives."

Shanshan Chan / 陳珊珊, age thirteen

"Elliott Addison's *Luck & Chance* series is the manifestation of wisdom into form, of imagination into action, and of mythology into reality, inspiring adventures of the mind and spirit."

Adam Heller, High School English Teacher

"Filled with memorable episodic mosaics and a powerful yet lyrical narration, Addison's *Luck & Chance* is a literary heavyweight in its own right.

Jie Xiu / 修潔

ACKNOWLEDGMENTS

I'm one lucky guy! God has granted me a wonderful opportunity to write this *Luck & Chance* saga. Joy and excitement have filled my every moment in this endeavor. I am grateful for the privilege to work on this project.

Through Mother, I inherited the love of books and writing. Thank you Mother for all your love and sacrifices. You are my Rock of Gibraltar. I love you.

I thank Benjamin, my brother, for his continued moral and financial support, without which this novel would not have been written and completed. Thank you, Benjamin, for opening many doors of possibilities for me. You have done it again!

Genevieve, thank you for your warm and hearty reception of the Prologue. Your encouragement gave me the impetus to go forward with the *Luck & Chance* saga series.

Richard Croghan, my indefatigable high school teacher, thank you for lighting my candle in many crucial moments in my life and showing me the way forward.

Loida Nicolas Lewis, thank you for your business acumen and guidance to ensure the commercial success of this novel.

Thank you Jie Xiu (修潔) and Naal Desravines for your foreword contributions. You have distilled the message of *Luck & Chance* for the readers.

Joyce Ann Davidson, thank you for encouraging me in my literary journey.

I thank Yanhuey Olive Chiu (邱燕惠), Naal Desravines, Eliza Dixon and Christopher Mueller for assisting me in selecting the music inspiration pieces for the many chapters in this book.

David Stawar, thank you for being my Webmaster, designing and implementing an awesome website.

Joseph Boginski, you have fantastic artistic talent! Your book cover encapsulates the key elements of the novel – with your personal twist.

For the editorial reviews, comments and corrections, I am grateful to Joseph Boginski, Francis Burgweger, Jr., Richard Croghan, Joyce Ann Davidson, Naal Desravines, Ann Core Greenberg, Adam Heller, Jan Kardys, Megumi Kobayashi, Carmel Legault, Buttercup Mayer, Beth Marie McLoughlin, Rachel Menti, Valerie Sprague, Jie Tan (譚潔), and Jie Xiu (修潔). I very much appreciate their time, patience, thoroughness and diligence.

For my Beta Group consisting of young adults, I thank Jordan Abbassi, Shanshan Chan (陳珊珊), Thomas Dougherty, Matthew Dougherty, Daniel Lu (魯晨曦) and Eliz Schutte. They have given their valuable and honest feedback to my manuscript.

I give Eliz Schutte special mention for suggesting the use of Footlight MT Light as the primary font for the novel, which makes it easier reading for the eyes.

Mark Xu (許嘉瑋) and Candice Xu (徐純琪), thank you for helping me with the Chinese font and text set-ups. Now, the readers can more easily find the Chinese music inspiration pieces.

I thank all my friends (you know who you are) for their enthusiastic support, cheering me on in this journey. I will need all your continued encouragement and support for the rest of the epic fantasy series.

Please pray for me and for the success of the saga novel.

THE DEDICATION OF THIS BOOK IS SPLIT TEN WAYS:

TO GOD,
FOR GIVING ME ALL I NEED,
IN MY JOYS AND IN MY SORROWS,

TO MY MOTHER,
FOR GIVING ME LIFE,

TO MY BELOVED BROTHER,
BENJAMIN,
MY BENEFACTOR,

TO GENEVIEVE,
MY ONLY BEGOTTEN DAUGHTER,

TO SUPER TYPHOON HAIYAN / YOLANDA VICTIMS
IN THE PHILIPPINES,

TO THE POOR,
MAY THEY RECEIVE ABUNDANCE,

TO THE WEALTHY,
MAY THEY HAVE CONTINUED SUCCESS
AND NOT FORGET THE POOR,

TO ALL STUDENTS,
MAY THEY ENTER
THE BEST UNIVERSITY OF THEIR CHOICE,

TO ALL IMMIGRANTS,
MAY THEY PROSPER
IN THEIR COMMUNITIES,

AND TO YOU,
THE FAN OF *LUCK & CHANCE*,
WITH ALL MY LOVE.

FOR

READERS OF ALL AGES

AND

FROM ALL NATIONS

I share these memorable and
magical adventures of Luck and
Chance and their years at the
International School for Brainiacs
Squared (ISBS) in *New Joy Sea*,
USA – so that you can be the
wiser.

All descriptions of artwork,
architecture, documents and historic
figures are accurately depicted.

CONTENTS

FOREWORD

ONE

The wait is over for the millions of avid Harry Potter fans, young and grown-ups, desperately waiting for the next riveting epic fantasy fiction series. Filled with memorable episodic mosaics, Elliott Addison's *Luck & Chance: Beyond the Realm of Wisdom* provides a powerful yet lyrical narration. It is a literary heavyweight in its own right.

With an original literary architecture, Addison's textured novel is written with lucidity, warmth and wit. It appeals to readers of all ages seeking wisdom and a life enhancing experience in this ever-changing world. It encapsulates much wisdom unfolding through the many characters in *Luck & Chance*.

Luck and Chance are two Eurasian boys raised in an orphanage. Deserted by their mysterious parents, they grow up under dubious circumstances in Manila, Philippines.

Brilliant and breathtaking, the novel introduces a fascinatingly unique world in which the twin brothers are entwined in each other's fate and destiny, seeking a way to break away from their miserable past. They embark on a journey fraught with danger in search of their mysterious origin, while charting a new course in their lives. There are tiny, funny creatures seeking their true essence. Tragic betrayals with unintended consequences and epic battles loom behind the scenes

The twins' journey to the mythical International School of Brainiac Squared (ISBS), in *New Joy Sea*, U.S.A., a very special college where they are caught up in many secrets, mysteries and magic of a different kind. They make new friendships and uncover betrayals. Their search for their own identity and purpose makes this a compelling read as any Hogwarts adventure. The readers will be intrigued by the distinctive differences based on Addison's unique world of Luck and Chance. ISBS reflects a complex social structure which traps the protagonists in a morass of danger, paralleling myriad issues plaguing our modern world.

This first novel of a fantasy series draws the reader into an intricate and complicated web of suspense, intrigues, struggles, love, and magic. Yet the gradual revelations and peeling away of secret layers surrounding the dark forces and their schemes to destroy Marcus Blundermore, one of the ISBS Grand Masters, and his forces, do not overshadow the brothers' grand mission to be Magi – the wisest of the Master Magicians. All the while, they are being pulled into a larger looming conflict. Although plagued with the pain and sorrows of the real world, the twins hold the beacon of light in dealing with the perplexing oddities in their lives, and gain a deeper understanding of themselves.

In addition to being a captivating adventure story, Addison's novel is a psychological and intellectual thriller. The story is like a puzzle box, permeated with riddles, myths, and deep philosophical points which will cause the reader to delve into his or her own issues in life.

Addison is gifted in dissecting the questions of life. His book is much more than fantasy. His tale imbeds numerous layers of subtexts and symbols for the readers to explore and mull through. This much is certain: his blend of fantasy and philosophy has been highly successful and powerful.

This first novel in what promises to be an exciting fantasy series, *Luck & Chance: Beyond the Realm of Wisdom*, features skillful plotting, exquisite prose style, imaginative ethereal landscapes as well as challenging ideas for the readers to reflect. Addison deserves much credit for tackling ideas of this depth and magnitude in this novel within the context of the new magic of science and technology and for his ambitious re-imagining of myth and theology. This novel is as entertaining as it is instructive.

Friends have known Addison as an accomplished investment banker, fluent in five languages, well-traveled through thirty-seven countries and a man of vast knowledge in multiple fields of finance, the arts and sciences. His determination and passion to write a book that will speak the voice of wisdom to young generations is neither surprising nor totally unexpected. He draws on his rich imagination, his extensive global experience and his passion in writing a fantasy book series for this important purpose: to charge the younger generations and all readers to dream and fulfill their true passion. His prose flows with life and far exceeds our expectations.

In exploring the eternal questions in *Luck & Chance*, Addison discusses the tenets of key world religions and beliefs, and explores the esoteric meaning of the universe, history and life. This, he draws from luminaries, such as Nicolaus Copernicus, Leonardo da Vinci, all the way to modern-day paradigm-shifters, such as Albert Einstein and Steve Jobs. These personalities have impacted our modern world. They will be felt within the novel. Addison's novel develops a compelling argument for the existence of magic and miracles within the context of science and technology, fate and destiny, religions and beliefs.

Addison maintains his faith in the greatness of humanity and in each person, despite individual frailties and shortcomings. He cites the greatest explorers who missed their mark by thousands of miles. Yet, despite their enormous miscalculations, they were propelled to greatness for their willingness to take a chance in life. Their willingness to leave behind the known and to venture into the unknown is still impacting us to this very day.

The book is heavily populated with unforgettable characters which the reader will fall in love with and want to re-experience them over and over again. Besides Luck and Chance, the reader will meet the sophisticated and wealthy twins: Engima and Choice. There are the funny, tiny *Moldivian* friends from a mythical South Asian island: Buff the Monkey and Lotto the Pirate, Little Princess Indira and Magus the Elephant. There are the three Grand Masters: Marcus Blundermore, Aurelius Primus and Abigail Daneuve. There are arch villains like Gul, Z-Aster and Datu Villani, who imbue the novel with sinister and malevolent schemes. The characters are so vivid, they jump off the pages into real life.

The reader will feel the tears and sorrow, the joy and redemption. Through the characters' blunders, improprieties and mistakes, he or she will learn and appreciate the pretty and the ugly in this world, yet never give up in the pursuit of one's own true passion.

A likely literary classic, this novel concludes with a looming war between the forces of Marcus Blundermore and Datu Villani. It contains the basic exposé and clues to an overarching intricate storyline at ISBS and beyond involving the protagonists, their friends and their foes. How will the war unfold? With so much action yet to come, this is good news for fantasy readers of all ages: children, teenagers and grown-ups alike.

The anticipation will build. The suspense will intensify.

Let us welcome Elliott B. Addison into our presence. Let this great modern tale begin!

Jie Xiu / 修潔
New York City, NY
February, 2014

FOREWORD

TWO

"A revolution is coming — a revolution which will be peaceful if we are wise enough; compassionate if we care enough; successful if we are fortunate enough — But a revolution which is coming whether we will it or not. We can affect its character; we cannot alter its inevitability."

Robert F. Kennedy

Luck & Chance: Beyond the Realm of Wisdom is an inspirational literary gem that narrates the journey of humanity through its heroic characters, coursing through life's trials and tribulations to fulfill their destiny. Those memorable characters battle the forces prevailing at every moment of their lives. In the process, they help us uncover the meaning of and the very purpose of our existence and the true essence of our being.

Luck & Chance: Beyond the Realm of Wisdom is a masterful devotion to wisdom, often forgotten but not lost. It is a treasure chest of amazing storytelling, and mind-bending collection of vignettes that speak to the heart and soul of our humanity. This novel is mesmerizing, intriguing and amusingly entertaining, while taking license to colorful treatments of names, places and things to deliver a balance and compelling chronicle.

The first book of a novel series, it broadens our horizon in spite of how we view ourselves, promoting our responsibilities to one another and to our world. Chosen by Providence to be the Warriors of the Light, Luck and Chance lead us on a poignant soul-searching chase, seeking to bring awareness to the treasure of the inner self and to awake the consciousness of our humanity.

The twins' destinies may not be identical. Though Fate has stricken them with matching strife, as eternal companions, they are the oracles of each other's conviction. They are ordained by their undeniable will and foresight to survive. Fate lays the foundation for Destiny. As a consequence of Fate, we may inherit an existence born in bedded roses of chaos, a life drenched in waters of ravaging rivers, fraught with the uncertainties of circumstance. Regardless of our fate, we must endure the thorns of daily living. How we overcome our situations depends on our choices. How we trounce our nature and its many contentions will determine our destiny.

There wouldn't be Destiny without Fate. There wouldn't be Fate without Destiny. They are a set of interlocking dyads. There are many more. Chance depends upon Luck to manifest. Without Chance, Luck would not evolve. Coexisting as one, they must overcome all of the challenges set before them throughout their journey. We all know Luck and Chance well and possibly too well. We are incredibly exposed to them as they are to us. They are ever present at various junctions of our lives.

We are at this juncture as a result of those unexpected challenges, the Enigma(s) we have overcome (or not), and the Choice(s) we have made, contingent upon the Luck(s) we have had, and the Chance(s) we have taken (or not). Through paradoxical interplays of dyads such as Luck and Chance, and Enigma and Choice, their stories compel us to reflect deeply and seek answers from within.

They drive us to liberate ourselves from the mundane, and strive for the higher purpose of our lives. Against what seem insurmountable odds, they provide us with a guide to overcome our Fate. In so doing, we achieve our Destiny.

Luck & Chance: Beyond the Realm of Wisdom is a delicious appetizer to the upcoming epic adventure series. This inspiring story channels us along twisting themes and startling plots in an enchanting voyage of Luck and Chance engaging Fate and Destiny, in their struggles for Life against Death.

It provides us with a transcendent blueprint to appreciate our profound ability to transform our lives and establish a new paradigm. It sustains us with vital courage, determination, intelligence and enthusiasm to achieve and celebrate our Ascension toward and beyond the Age of Wisdom. It corrals us toward a new field of singularity and mystical adventures into Oneness, a new territory chartered, where only a few have ever been.

What is Destiny without Fate, Choice without Enigma, and Luck without Chance? What is Life without The One?

Luck & Chance: Beyond the Realm of Wisdom is a spicy nectar, at times sweet and other times bitter, a serendipitous tonic from the Valley of Kings, Queens, Knights, Magi and Genies.

It is a fairy tale which seems all too real, a grand bargain open to all who are moved to journey across the realm of the unexpected. It renders a portal to Life, unrestricted by form and deities, an avenue to freedom branded by adversities, a pathway to Truth and Light, to Luck and Chance Beyond the Realm of Wisdom.

Naal Desravines
Bronx, NY
February, 2014

FOREWORD

THREE

It was during the weekend of October 10, 2010 when the story of *Luck & Chance* hit me. I was driving down to Washington, D.C., to visit my mother, who was eighty-four at the time. The idea of *Luck & Chance* came to me in those long hours of driving.

Upon returning to Stamford, Connecticut, I outlined the *Luck & Chance* saga series and proceeded to write the Prologue. During the year-end holiday season of 2010, I met up with my daughter, Genevieve, at the Grand Central Station in Manhattan. Down by the food court, I read her the Prologue. Her warm and hearty reception gave me the impetus to go forward.

The novel series is a labor of pure joy and love, bringing me closer to my true destiny as a writer. I have never been more alive. Every thought, every word is the result of a close communion with God and with humanity.

On Christmas Eve, 2013, I completed *Luck & Chance: Beyond the Realm of Wisdom.*

With gratitude, I offer this novel to God, through Jesus Christ, for the many blessings He has showered me.

May this novel provide hope and encouragement to many.

A greater power dwells within each of us. If accessed and cultivated properly, it will unleash our true passion toward remarkable achievements, changing the face of the world and the way we live. Knowledge is power. Wisdom is divine. I hope all readers can tap on to their internal well of wisdom to find their personal gift, which is greater than themselves.

Interestingly, this novel is written with a high level of musicality. The chapters in the novel have an eclectic collection of music as inspiration. Each of the music inspiration pieces has provided me a unique emotional and cultural envelope to that particular chapter. Likewise, I hope that by listening to the accompanying music inspiration pieces, you, the reader, will achieve a more intense and complete reading experience of this novel. When a different music inspiration piece is applied, each chapter will evoke a different emotional and cultural tone and texture.

Hence, this novel is *innovative* and *one of a kind*. This is an important cross-media world-building project. Within the realm of transmedia through the access of the Internet, this saga novel interfaces with the best rendition of the music video pieces.

There is a mindful synchronization of the literary narrative with the music inspiration pieces. Through this multiplatform storytelling technique, the reader will attain a broader and richer emotional and cultural range of experiences in the novel. There are selections of classical music and operatic arias, Broadway hit songs, contemporary rock, hip-hop and rap hits, and blockbuster movie soundtrack hits. There are selections of classical guitar music, piano music, Spanish music, French music and Chinese music, etc. Each reader is free to track a specific music genre throughout the novel – or just choose and mix a variety of music in whichever way. Songs from all continents are represented, entailing twenty-one languages. The reader will have myriad of choices.

Also, each reader can choose specific music inspiration pieces *beyond* the list presented in the book, to give each person *that* unique experience beyond time, beyond place. The music inspiration selected will render each reader a *concert* for the ears, for the heart and for the soul.

You will swoon. You will rock. You will laugh. You will cry. You will be transformed.

Enjoy! You will never enter the same river twice.

As entertainment, this saga novel is ideal for the whole family to experience together.

Let us now enter into the world of *Luck & Chance*.

Elliott B. Addison
Stamford, CT
February, 2014

LUCK & CHANCE

BEYOND THE REALM OF WISDOM

MYTH IN REALITY

MUSIC INSPIRATION

AIR
ORCHESTRRAL SUITE, MOVEMENT NO. 2
JOHANN SEBASTIAN BACH

THE CIRCLE OF LIFE
(ENGLISH & ZULU)
LION KING
ELTON JOHN & TIM RICE
SINGERS
LEBO M & CARMEN TWILLIE

A LOVE BEFORE TIME
YUE GUANG AI REN
月光愛人
(ENGLISH & CHINESE MANDARIN)
CROUCHING TIGER HIDDEN DRAGON
TAN DUN / 谭盾
SINGER: COCO LEE / 李玟

GET LUCKY
DAFT PUNK & PHARNELL

LOCKED OUT OF HEAVEN
BRUNO MARS

GLORIA IN EXCELSIS DEO
GLORIA
(GLORY TO GOD IN THE HIGHEST)
(LATIN)
ANTONIO VIVALDI
OSPEDALE SANTA MARIA DELLA PIETÀ
ORPHANGE IN VENICE, ITALY
ALL GIRLS CHOIR

*   *   *

*A*las, the saga continues…for life lasts eternal.

Luck was Luck because he was often lucky.

Chance was Chance because he took chances.

They were twins; intertwined with each other in the events of their lives which were sometimes joyful, sometimes sad, at times pathetic, at times poignant, often perplexing, often paradoxical. They had moments of mischievous genius and of tragic stupidity. Irony would be the cosmic joke, for them and for us all, including me.

Luck and Chance were a happenstance, oh so random, oh so incomprehensible.

*   *   *

*O*nce upon a near present time, on a miraculous May morning in Manila, the sky was clear azure blue. But the air was hot, hot, hot.

Flap. Flap. Flap. The embattled Piaf the Stork was about to pass out. "Almost there!" She clucked, while her beak was tightly clamped on her enormous orange bundle, with a big knot tied around her neck.

"To land or not to land?" Piaf was giving up. "Gotta land. Or else I'll die." She was dazed with exhaustion. "China can wait. I won't be able to make it to China."

Piaf extended her wings, glided, and descended toward Manila Bay. "Gotta live. Tomorrow's another day." She was angling for a good spot to land. "Easy now. Easy landing."

Organ music bursting with Bach rose from the chapel of Misericordia de Dios Orphanage, run by the Franciscan nuns, outside Manila.

Through the chapel windows, Wawa, a young Spanish nurse from Catalan, caught sight of a magnificent white stork with its bundle of joy, about to land on the orphanage courtyard by the sea. "Oh my gosh! It's true!" She gasped in amazement. "Dios mio! Did I just see a stork?"

Ducking low, Wawa, together with Nanny Claire Bonsens, her young French intern, scurried out of the orphanage chapel while Mass was still going on.

The two young nurses dashed out the rear side doors of the chapel toward the courtyard, wild with excitement.

Piaf flapped wildly as she descended near the garden pond which was covered with big lotus leaves. Two stems of pink lotus blossoms swayed in the welcoming morning breeze.

Gently, ever so carefully, she landed, resting her bundle lightly on the grass.

Upon landing, Piaf scouted the area, making sure it was safe. "This place better be good!"

The two young ladies giggled with joy as they approached Piaf's *special delivery. Taking some crackers out of her pocket, Wawa broke them into small pieces, and threw them in Piaf's direction.*

Heading toward one corner of the courtyard, Claire pulled out the garden hose and began filling up a wooden tub. "Come! Drink up! This should cool you down."

Sensing Claire's friendliness, Piaf slowly ambled over to the tub for her first gulp of water after these exhausting hours. As she drank, she kept a guarded eye on the orange bundle.

Wawa approached the garden tub, oh so gingerly, so as not to frighten Piaf in any way. With loving kindness, she fed Piaf morsels of crackers. She tiptoed toward Piaf's bundle and untied it, oh, so carefully. The big coarse cloth had the Pin of Piaf clipped onto it.

"Well heavens!" Wawa exclaimed. Inside the bamboo basket laid a pair of Eurasian twin boys. A square kerchief enveloped each of their tiny chests down to their tummies. One in red; the other in yellow.

On the first child's red kerchief was sewn the word: LUCK. Luck had wondrous large eyes. A gold medallion was hanging down his neck, resting on his tummy. The medallion had a triangle embossed on its face, with a large white pearl embedded in the middle of it.

On the second child's yellow kerchief was sewn the word: "CHANCE". With only one eye open, Chance looked around, like a One-Eyed Jack. Also, a gold medallion was hanging down his neck. The medallion had a circular laurel embossed on its face, with a large white pearl embedded in the middle of it. The medallion also rested on his tummy.

4

Wide eyed with wonder, Wawa and Claire marveled at the two babies.

And that was how Luck became Luck; and Chance, became Chance!

*   *   *

Over their tender years, Luck and Chance relished Wawa's frequent recounting of their arrival into this world of Light and Darkness.

*   *   *

CHAPTER 1

TROUBLE IN THE MALL

MUSIC INSPIRATION

WE ARE THE CHAMPIONS
QUEEN

CHEERS
干杯
(CHINESE MANDARIN)
MAYDAY / 五月天

JAI HO!
(YOU ARE MY DESTINY)
(ENGLISH & HINDI & URDU & PUNJABI)
SLUMDOG MILLIONNAIRE
SAJID WAJID, A. R. RAHMAN
GULZAR, TANVI SHAH
SINGERS
SUKHVINDER SINGH, TANVI SHAH,
MAHALMI IYER, VIJAY PRAKASH

I GOTTA FEELING
BLACK EYED PEAS

RUN
(CHINESE MANDARIN)
HIT-5

CORRE!
(RUN!)
(SPANISH)
JESSE & JOY

STAYING ALIVE
BEE GEES

*　　　*　　　*

In every person, in every soul, high or low, contains the universe. Each person, each soul, has a story screaming to be told. Each, so moving yet so baffling. Each, a tantalizing tale. Each, an enigma.

*   *   *   *

Last night, Luck and Chance came face to face with the Devil – without seeing her face.

Now at seventeen, the twins had just survived a deathly ordeal with a neurotic woman gone berserk. Having imprisoned the twins in her dungeon, she ranted curses mixed with hysterical wails of anger. Her evil laughter echoed in the dead of the night. The maniacal screams of a delirious woman continued to ring in the twins' ears.

Touched by Fate, the twins would never be the same.

*   *   *

It happened yesterday late afternoon, in the upscale Makati Shopping Mall at the outskirts of Manila, where they were shopping for their shoes. The twins had no idea that by nightfall, their view of the world would forever change.

"Here, enjoy your new rubber shoes. You guys really got a great bargain – just because I love you both. I just don't know when I will see you both again." At forty, Mama Margarita, a matronly saleslady, slid two shopping bags over the counter. She had dark complexion, with two big eyes, thick lips, and pudgy cheeks resembling a Jamaica mama. "Good luck with your college years in America!"

She knew Luck and Chance well, having sold them numerous pairs of footwear over the years since they were ten. She had watched them grow to their present state, so full of promise, so full

7

of potential, with a bright future ahead of them.

Luck cheerfully picked up the two smart-looking shopping bags. "These will take us to our American Dream! After college, we'll make boatloads of dough!" He let out a boisterous laugh.

"Whoever gave you *that* idea – going after the American Dream?" Mama Margarita teased.

"I saw the movie *Citizen Kane*." Luck shot back. "It turned my light bulb on. Someday, I want to be a mogul." He exuded a triumphant smile, like a hero boxer having won a prize fight, as he pranced around the shop, jabbing left and right with his fist. He could see himself a boxing champion.

Not to be outdone by his twin brother, Chance blurted his favorite novel. "*The Great Gatsby!* It's a great novel and a smashing movie. Someday, I want to be *the* great Gatsby – without getting shot and dying alone!"

Such were the dynamics of the twins: outdoing each other, the reality of sibling rivalry.

Mama Margarita had become long-time friends to the twins and the thought that she would not see them for a long while just made her feel sad. "My dears, when are you leaving the Philippines? I will miss you both so very much."

"Very soon!" Full of energy, Luck cut in like a huffing Tasmanian devil, shuffling and skipping around, this time, imitating a prize fighter's butterfly footwork in a shadow boxing dance. "Flitter like a butterfly. Sting like a bee. Someday, I'll be famous!" He gave out a thunderous laugh, bobbing his head here and there. "There, knock-out left-right hooks!" He thumped his chest, then raised both his fists, singing: "WE ARE THE CHAMPIONS!"

Excited with his new gear, Chance had a change of mind. "I'd like to wear these *now*. Is that OK?"

"But of course." Mama Margarita was happy to oblige.

"Me, too!" Luck liked his brother's idea.

Sitting on a chair, Chance slipped out of his worn out leather shoes and proudly put on his golden rubber shoes.

Luck did the same. He put on his new pair of red rubber shoes.

Mama Margarita helped put their beat up leather shoes into the shopping bag. "You both look so spiffy!"

Curious, she asked Luck: "So, who's your hero?"

Luck broke into a mischievous smile. "You *really* want to know?"

"Sure!" Margarita nodded.

Without any hesitation, Luck declared: "John D. Rockefeller, Jr.! The *only* son of John D. Rockefeller, Sr., the great oil baron, the richest man of his time. He had lucky genes. Fated to be rich. Rockefeller, Jr. came to this world with a silver spoon in his mouth. I wish I was born into a rich family."

"You want to know *my* hero?" Chance cut in.

"And *who* is that?" Mama Margarita was delighted that Chance liked his new pair of rubber shoes.

Test walking his footwear, Chance paced around the shop. "Christopher Columbus. The man who dared to take *chances* – daring to venture into the New World. Columbus's biggest error ushered his greatest accomplishment. He miscalculated the distance from Spain to India – missing his mark by a long shot.

His total gap extended beyond the length of continental USA, the whole Pacific Ocean and the breadth of China. What an error! Just imagine! Yet, what a triumph! Such is the irony of history."

Chance laughed, mystified by Columbus's mistake and his greatness. "Columbus impacted lives by the millions – for the better – even up till today. Thousands of families immigrate to America yearly. Students from all over the world flock to American universities for higher education. International business people head to America to do deals, make money, and be very successful. All because of Columbus – a man who erred and failed to reach India by thousands of miles." With Columbus as inspiration, Chance fancied himself coming to America and giving himself a *chance* in life.

Looking at his watch, Chance tugged at Luck. "We better get going. We still have lots of errands to run."

"Good luck to you two!" Mama Margarita gave Luck and Chance a winner's high-five. "Get rich in America! When you do, don't forget your Mama Margarita!"

It dawned on her that she had an aunt in Queens, New York. "Feel free to contact my Aunt Colada in Queens, if you should need any help." She went to her handbag, pulled out her little address book and wrote down her Aunt Colada's contact details on a small slip of paper. This she gave to Luck. "My Aunt Colada is the sweetest lady." Then, Mama Margarita gave each of the brothers a bear hug, each lasting like an eternity.

As he prepared to leave the shop, Luck, once again, shuffled, pranced and bobbed, punching the air like a boxer, this time in his new pair of rubber shoes. "WE ARE THE CHAMPIONS!" He chanted.

"Luck, you are so goofy funny!" Mama Margarita laughed.

*   *   *

Who were Luck and Chance? They could be any parent's children. But this was not to be.

Both fair in complexion, the identical twins were blessed with mesmerizing almond-shaped brown eyes. Only Chance wore square silver-rimmed eyeglasses. Cheery, the youngsters were exquisitely handsome, debonair, and boyish, with waves of cascading black hair cropped at the brow lines. Six feet tall, slender and buff, they looked slightly younger than their age. The girls in high school were crazy about them.

Highly rational and very smart, the twins used their intellect to understand their personal worlds. They were both inquisitive to the whys and how-comes of the human predicament. They excelled in the exploration of the human psyche and the spiritual realms. Avid existentialists, their mantras were: "Will I?" or "Won't I?"

They couldn't be easily distinguished by appearance. Rather, their character, behavior, and proclivities provided the distinctive clues as to who was who.

A rambunctious lad, Luck was *the* extrovert, easily attracting unwanted attention with his signature laugh. He loved pulling pranks on his friends and teachers and often got away with it. His joviality could disarm the strictest disciplinarian.

A born leader, Luck was the more confident and optimistic of the two. Charming and self-assured, he would lead classroom discussions, be the center of attention and embrace action. A wise-ass, he commanded a wacky and irreverent sense of humor and was more willing to laugh at Life and Circumstance. A wily

11

maverick, he had a streak of naughty mischief and subversive humor in his blood. He delivered pranks like a provocateur *par excellence*. Because of his propensity for mischief, his friends called him reckless. Due to his tendency to say or do something without full consideration, they nicknamed him: Reckless Luck.

Luck was the salesman of ideas and outcomes. Laughter was his friend – given his habit of boisterous laughs. A socializer and party animal, he was a magnet of friends because of his irreverent yet golden tongue. Witty and eloquent, he would flit here and there like a hummingbird, moving from one stimulating idea to another. With an inborn sense of music and rhythm, he often outshined others in any social crowd, especially in lighthearted arena of play and banter.

His main advantage was his resilience toward adversity, and as such, an invaluable asset. Buried deep within him, he commanded a mysterious strength that could repulse an army of thugs.

Luck's constant was his aspiration for a *better* life: seeking the fullness of the American Dream, a dream spawned in his heart years ago through the books he read and through the movies he watched. He was young, like the early morning dew of spring.

His loyalty toward friends was unbreakable. Over the years, his utmost loyalty was to his twin brother, Chance. Luck knew what he wanted, whereas Chance loved to noodle on ideas, brood on alternative perspectives, with a conspiratorial slant.

An intriguing character, Chance was a master of speed – a speed that could be lethal. Curious and adventurous, he was an insightful observer of the world around him, with a wholesome decorum about him. He would gladly assist an old lady snagged in the middle of crossing the unruly traffic streets of the Greater Manila Area, an urban zone of over twelve million.

12

Shy and introspective, ever questioning and oftentimes agnostic, Chance was a thinker, a seeker of truth. He sought to understand the underlying and hidden truths hidden behind illusions. For him, the world had no top, no bottom; it just kept on turning. What was top, what was bottom depended on his state of mind: his personal perspective. More serious, with the pensive look of an introvert, he tended to be analytical, observing the situation at hand, figuring out what was happening before deciding which actions to take. Often, he knew the right answers, but somehow, he remained ambivalent, curious of other angles.

A dreamer and an intellectual explorer, he would mull on somewhat off-beat perspectives. He questioned the whys of events, the motivations of people's actions, and the validity of certain conclusions. He was most interested in the metaphysical, delving into the ambiguous world with questions for which there might be no clear answers. Spiritual, he pursued age-old questions of what Life was all about, why he was here and where he was going.

He had an excellent taste and natural love for the arts. The shallowness of "beautiful" people bored him. Despite his lack of interest in politics, he had a deep sense of justice.

Physically, he had these weird vulnerabilities. His ears would easily turn red, registering his momentary embarrassments. Worst of all, his nostrils would invariably flare when he lied. It was all on his face, betraying him. He knew it, too. He had no defense.

Chance was part poet, part philosopher, part geek. He had a knack for creating opportunities – for better or for worse – often undefined, still seeking to form meaning. Chance had yet to find the object of his true desires. Unsure of himself, he would suffer the uncertainties of his own ambiguities and vague hesitations. He had this indescribable way of being that could be exasperating, fraught with disjunctive ideas striving for synthesis. Thus, his classmates nicknamed him: Brooding Chance.

These twins were so lucky to be alive despite being so shortchanged by Fate.

*   *   *

Having done their shopping, there was lightness to the twins' feet as they emerged from the shoe store. If there were wings on their shoes, they would fly to the skies like Hermes. Full of confidence, they were excited to be finally heading to America for college.

At the door step of the shop, amidst the crowd, the twins noticed two tall hulking men, both around six and a half feet tall and in security uniforms. The men's heads and faces were heavily tattooed, their eyes menacing. They were heading toward the direction of the twins from the right.

The twins headed out the store and made a sharp left in the opposite direction and merged into the crowd.

With a backward glance, Chance noticed the skull-heads were approaching them ever so near through the crowd. Being astute and vigilant, Chance's sixth sense told him that these skull-heads were singling them out for trouble. "Hurry, Luck. Looks like they *are* after us."

A little uneasy, they quickened their pace, as they pushed their way through the swarming crowd of shoppers at the mall. "I have a *bad* feeling about this." Chance could feel trouble brewing.

*   *   *

More hoodlums than security guards, Johnny Dangerous and Double Trouble were two gigantic brutes. They both had eyes that would make any intrepid martial arts master cower in trepidation. Their shaven heads were heavily tattooed, marking them as the soldiers of Death. They were mean monsters that mercilessly broke anyone's bones at their boss's command.

A muscular gangster, Johnny Dangerous had a fierce gaze of a hungry *cayote*, ready to tear up his weakest preys. A school dropout, he did not achieve much in life. His only choice was to be the personal bodyguard of his boss: the Witch of the Catacombs, the preeminent entrepreneur in the Philippines – with a very dark side. Well known for her voracious greed, she circulated in the highest echelon of Philippine society.

Over the years, Johnny Dangerous was promoted as the top lieutenant of her personal army of goons. In this capacity, he attended numerous high-end events, occasionally rubbing shoulders with the who's-who in Philippines. This was glory enough for him, making his day. His craftiness earned him the nickname: Sly Fox.

His alter-ego was Double Trouble, a massive hulk, weighing around three hundred fifty pounds. With neither brawn nor brain, he could only rely on his weight and his size to earn a living. Because of his size, he sweat profusely, and his was stinky sweat. He was the Witch's top bouncer, ensuring no unsavory characters gatecrash her many parties. He often pitied himself, thinking he was condemned to this trade because he had no other skills. A police flunky, he was let go because he could not run fast. This became a problem with chases.

Initially, he felt lucky to be hired by the Witch of the Catacomb – all because he was her driver's nephew. Over the years, he got promoted to second in command of her goons – because he caught two bullets for her in two attempted assassinations on her life. He felt stuck in Life because of sloth and gluttony. Every day, he lived at the edge of Life and Death. That was his fate.

By thirty-two, he had a litter of ten kids. In his family, someone had to make a living. It had to be him. To his family, he was Double Trouble because he could be trouble to others and to himself. He had an explosive temper and high blood pressure. A bad combination. His colleagues called him: Broken Fridge.

*   *   *

Today, Johnny Dangerous and Double Trouble had an important mission: to capture Luck and Chance. Someone had tipped them off that the brothers would be in this mall today.

As the two skull heads were about arms-length from the twins, Double Trouble blew a whistle while Johnny Dangerous shouted thunderously: "Shop lifters! Stop them!"

The brothers broke off into a zig-zag run, crashing into retail kiosks in the middle aisle of the mall. Wigs and mannequins went flying. The twins hurled flower vases and perfume bottles like lethal projectiles toward the two marauders.

This was the part of the job Double Trouble hated most: the chase.

Highly trained in the martial arts of *kung fu* (功夫) since seven by their Uncle Antikweetee, the twins leapt over the mall railings like flying dragons down to the second level of the mall. After landing, they headed for the nearest escalator. No sooner, from the crowd, *twelve* different skull heads, with chains and police clubs in hand, emerged at the first level escalator, whose steps were ascending upward toward the second level. The twins had to scramble back up from the descending steps of the escalator.

Back on the second level of the mall, Luck and Chance, back to back, took on defensive stances, crouching like threatened tigers, ready to pounce, as they faced pure Evil. Then, between flips and summersaults, the twins ran up walls and railings, bounding sideways across display windows, attempting to outrun the marauders. They grabbed umbrellas, canes, and golf clubs at shop fronts, whipping them like weapons at the six gangsters. Hurling vacuum cleaners and chairs at their attackers, the twins thought they could make headway and escape.

From one of the café kiosks, Chance threw cups of scalding coffee at the skull-heads, yelling: "Hot tea, coffee or me!"

From the stairways, *twenty four* more muscular hoodlums emerged, with a panoply of weapons, pushing their way wildly through the crowd, thrashing merchandize against glass windows.

Between leaps and rolls, forward summersaults and backward flips, the twins fought ferociously against a total of *thirty six* skull heads.

Running past the fruit kiosk, Luck grabbed pineapples and threw them at the skull heads.

Watermelon & Durian

Having difficulty deciding between a watermelon or a stinky durian, Luck playfully chanted, swaying his hips from left to right, while his forefinger pointed alternately between the watermelon and the durian. "Eenie, meeny, miney, mo!" As his forefinger ended up at the durian, he picked it up and smashed it over the head of one of the marauders.

In close hand to hand combat, Chance managed to kick one of the skull heads in the groin.

"Oh! Nasty!" One of the meanies collapsed on the floor, doubling up and cringing in pain.

Amidst wildly swinging chains and police clubs, the twins were completely outnumbered and outmaneuvered – by a total of *thirty eight* thugs, which included the initial two. Luck leapt, delivering a split flying kick, hitting *two* of the gangsters squarely at their chests.

Meaning business, Double Trouble fired three shots. Pow! Pow! Pow! Nearby store display windows shattered. A commotion broke out as store owners rushed to shut down their stores. Terror stricken, salespeople ducked behind counters. Shoppers dashed for the nearest mall exits, screaming in panic, in sheer terror.

Over time, two of the strongest skull-heads managed to pin down the twins in head locks. Although pinned to the ground, the twins continued to struggle.

"Don't you make any stupid moves or you're dead meat. You guys are under arrest." Johnny Dangerous snarled at the twins. Two other skull-heads violently handcuffed the pair from the back.

This was a fight the brothers could *not* win.

Simultaneously, two other gangsters tied the ankles of the twins tightly together, hollering: "You're headed for jail! One wrong move and you're both dead."

The skull-heads quickly hauled the pair down the stairways, passed the bewildered crowd, which was too stunned to get involved. The skull heads dashed toward a nearby unmarked van, whose motor was running, ready for a speedy getaway.

By this time, the brothers knew they were being kidnapped. Kidnapping was a rampant occurrence in Manila.

Why is this happening? Luck was bewildered.

For Chance, the unfolding event was surreal. *Dang! What have we done?*

Four of the skull-heads threw the teens into the van. With brute force, one of the skull heads violently gagged the twins with dirty socks, while another gangster blind-folded them with duct tape, while yet another hoodlum hooded each of them with stinky burlap bags – tying a noose around each of their necks.

As the van took off, the twins were plunged into total darkness. A convoy of six vans followed behind. The twins rolled inside the van as it swerved and careened through the city traffic. They could not comprehend the why, the how, and the wherefore of their perplexing predicament.

Minutes later, the van came to a screeching halt at *La Casa Sin Numero*, an elegant mansion at Forbes Park, a ritzy neighborhood in the residential compound of Makati at the suburbs of Manila. The doors at the back of the van swung open. The rough and mean hands of the skull-heads dragged the twins along a stony gravel path.

Two German shepherds by the garden barked wildly, causing a commotion amongst neighborhood dogs.

The twins heard clinking of keys and a creaky door opened. They tumbled down a narrow path of stairs into an echoing, dank dungeon, which smelt of urine and poo.

Inside, the kidnappers resumed to punch and kick the pair – punishing them for putting up a ferocious fight moments ago.

Vengefully, Johnny Dangerous hit Luck over the head. "This is what you get for messing with us!" Plat! Luck fell, hitting his head against the damp floor, as his brain went numb.

Later, the gangsters chained the twins up against the cold, stony walls – their arms outstretched. Likewise, the skull- heads untied and spread the twins' legs apart, clamping their ankles with shackles which were attached to the wall.

"Thank your Maker that you are still alive!" Double Trouble hissed, as the gang of goons headed toward the door. Bang! The wooden doors slammed shut. Clang! The twins heard a second door from the outside being bolted.

Silence ensued, except for the ticking of a wall clock and the twins' desperate heaving. As the hours passed, still gagged and blindfolded, the twins felt faint, suffocated, at times close to passing out.

Luck could not figure out *his* quandary. *Why this? What is happening? What got me here?*

Chance wanted to understand *his* situation. *Why me? What now?*

*　　*　　*

CHAPTER 2

THE SCREAM

MUSIC INSPIRATION

BAD ROMANCE
LADY GAGA

ELYSIUM
GLADIATOR
HANS ZIMMER & LISA GIRRARD

FEARLESS – OPENING TITLE
WU SHU JING SHEN
武术精神
FEARLESS
SHIGERU UMEBAYASHI

THE BOXER
PAUL SIMON & ART GARFUNKEL

DON'T CRY
GUNS N' ROSES

BACK TO LIFE
(PIANO)
GIOVANNI ALLEVI

*   *   *

Sometime after 3:45 A.M., the dungeon door suddenly burst open.

All the twins heard was a woman's seething foul mouth: "Tonight, you both will die! Maggots! You'll meet your Maker!" She let out a manic laugh. In this instant, she had become a demon from Hell. "Know that I am GUL!"

She flicked her lighter and a gushing sound of gas and fire can be heard from the furnace. Menacing clanking of metal instruments hit the cement floor. Waves of intense heat filled the dungeon.

The brothers sensed something awfully *sinister* was about to occur.

Ever the rebel, Luck struggled to free himself – but in vain.

In shock, Chance shuddered, terror shooting up his spine.

Half mocking, half foreboding, Gul murmured at the twins' ears: "I've been waiting for *this* moment! Every sin has its retribution! It's payback time! Oh! CRAZY LOVE!"

Shock and fear seized Luck, as his shirt was ripped open. Gul checked his medallion which gave away his identity. "Are you Luck?" She growled. He unknowingly nodded. Gul grabbed a searing hot branding iron, and dangled the tip of the iron near his hooded face.

Terrified, Luck felt the raging heat. *She is going to deface me!*

Then, she plunged the branding iron onto his chest, holding it in place, branding him.

Luck's eyes receded to the depths of their sockets. "AAAAAAAAGH!" A muffled scream burst out to no avail.

Not missing a beat, Gul picked up the second iron meant for Chance. She dangled the tip in front of his hooded face, enjoying the ritual of torture.

Feeling the intense heat, Chance turned his face from side to side, at times almost ramming his face straight at the hot iron.

Then, Gul violently ripped open his shirt and sank the second branding iron hard onto his chest. "WAAAAAAAAA!" Chance

22

gave out a long muffled scream.

Zsssss! The sizzle of burnt flesh filled the air.

Grinding their shoulders against the walls and writhing in shock, a chorus of screams from the twins, mixed with Gul's diabolical cackles, pierced and shattered the deathly silence of the night. Between their shrieks, the brothers felt their lungs bursting. Excruciating burning pain shot into their chests, forever branding their flesh and their souls: their new reality.

"KNOW THIS TRUTH: WE'RE BORN; WE EAT; WE POO; AND WE DIE ALONE!" Gul ranted, at times shrieking in crazed madness.

Between groans of agony, thoughts of impending death overtook the pair.

In this moment of existential despair, Luck gave out a primal wail that reverberated throughout and beyond the dungeon walls.

"AAAAAAAAGH!"

Strangely, a heavy weight bore down on Gul as she struggled with a fearsome invisible force. Fighting to maintain her balance, she keeled to one side. Then, she was violently wrestled to the ground by this invisible force.

Loud clanks of heavy metal smashing upon the cement floor rang through the dungeon.

Inexplicably, her face was pressed down and squashed against the cold cement floor, her nose broken. Excruciating pain shot up her head. "YAAAAAAA!" Her nose bleeding, Gul screamed in pain as her head was repeatedly banged against the cement floor, her cheek bones bruised and her face practically gashed. "Let me go! No more! Stop! Ugh!" This was the *strangest* phenomenon: she was struggling with an enemy she could *not* see.

In the dizzying daze, the twins heard a wall clock striking four. Ding! Ding! Ding! Ding!

"Oh, no! No......" The twins heard Gul's gasps as her footsteps quickly receded to the other end of the dungeon, followed by a loud slamming of a heavy wooden door.

A cock crowed from outside the dungeon – at the garden of *La Casa Sin Numero*.

Deathly silence descended, except for the desperate heaving of the twins and the tick-tock of the wall clock.

Ever defiant, Luck writhed in pain, refusing to admit that Death had come to claim him. *I'm too young to die! There's no dignity in Death! WHY DO I DIE?*

Weak, fainting and in shock, Chance shook his head from side to side, resigned to death. *Oh Death, knock me out of my misery! I can't take it anymore. Let me die! WHY DO I LIVE?*

*   *   *

Tick tock! Tick tock! Tick tock! Tick tock! The monotony of the wall clock ticked the time away. Nearly an hour passed.

In the meantime, the twins could only let out muffled grunts to each other, unable to communicate very much.

Crash! The brothers heard a crashing sound of keys hitting the cement floor outside the dungeon door, arousing barks from the two German shepherds outside by the garden.

Then, there were sounds of keys maneuvering the keyhole. There were several tries. Someone was yanking the door open.

The brothers sensed Death returning to finish them off. Creepily, the wooden door creaked open. The pair heard footsteps heading toward them.

Oh no! Not again! Chance's heart pounded wildly. *Here's Death coming! This time, there would be no reprieve. Not again!* He braced for his inevitable death.

Hurried footsteps headed toward them.

Unrelentingly, the German shepherds at the garden barked their heads off – joined by a chorus of dogs from other adjacent houses.

Once more, totally tensed up, the twins writhed against the wall, trying to kick whoever was approaching. But the leg shackles restrained them.

Instead, someone gently touched the twins' numbing arms and quickly untied the noose around each of their necks. "Shhh... It's Auntie Claire Bonsens." The brothers heard a low hushed voice amidst the barking of dogs outside in the garden.

She took off their stinky vomit-filled burlap hoods.

Ah! Air! Mixed with the smell of urine and feces in the dank dungeon, there was a disgusting foul odor of Death.

She unwound their blindfolds and then, the duct tape.

In the dim light of dawn, the pair could barely focus their eyes.

A surge of relief overtook the twins. The brothers recognized Nanny Claire – if only vaguely. "I'm the French nurse – your Wawa's *best* friend." A nervous wreck, her voice was quivering. Her hands shook uncontrollably. During their toddler years, she had visited the pair often during weekends at Misericordia de Dios

Orphanage. Each of her visits with them was punctuated with fun and games.

With a bunch of keys in her hands, she struggled to find the right keys to unlock the thick iron cuffs around their wrists and the shackles around their ankles.

Finally, one by one, each key engaged its lock, unlocking it. And the twins were freed.

Claire ungagged them.

"Auntie Claire!" Relieved but in an utter state of shock, Luck gripped Claire's arms, ever grateful for her rescue. "Why are you here?" Stunned and puzzled, Luck could *not* understand her presence.

"I've worked here for the longest time. I heard your screams a while ago. Terrifying! But I was too scared to come down – not knowing what was happening. No time for explanations! We have to run! NOW!" She insisted in her husky voice, which was drowned out by the crazy barkings of the dogs in the garden.

Still dazed, Chance felt as though he was being jostled out of a nightmare. "What's happening?"

"No time now! I'll explain later. Let's scram!" Claire ordered sternly. "Gul's on your case. Better be gone! Fast!"

At thirty-eight, she had the strength to half-drag the brothers toward the dungeon door, through the narrow hallway leading to the backdoor, then into the shrubs outside. Two German shepherds snarled at the twins – but quieted down upon seeing Nanny Claire. After passing the backdoor gates, she released her grip on the pair and made a dash for the house van, with the twins closely following behind.

26

"Where do we go?" She started the car engine.

"To our Aunt Juliet's house. She is our Missing Mama's younger sister. We've lived there these past seven years." Luck sat on the passenger's seat beside Auntie Claire, while Chance sat at the back seat.

"Make sure your Aunt Juliet dresses up your wounds when you get home. You don't want any infections." Nanny Claire admonished, as she put the pedal to the metal and sped away.

The night had surrendered its darkness to the breaking dawn. The twilight morning gave way to the first glimmer of daylight. Between turns and swerves, Claire drove the van into the breaking dawn.

Thanks to Claire, the brothers were saved.

The dawn killed the night. The dawn aborted the twins' possible deaths. The dawn gave them back their lives.

Luck and Chance knew, deep in their hearts, a grand bargain had been struck. From here on, they would view the world differently – having experienced Hell and having survived to tell about it.

They had come face to face with the Devil – without seeing her face. There must be a reason that they were spared – to be given another *chance* in life.

*   *   *

"Who is Gul?" Perplexed, Luck looked at Claire with dismay, as she drove them to their Aunt Juliet's home. "Why us? What have we done? I want to leave the Philippines. The sooner, the better." Luck did *not* want another encounter with Gul. He wanted to be far, far away from her. Right now, his main concern

27

was his safety. *America! That is my escape!*

Realizing how perilously close he was to Death, like a pent up dam bursting, Chance broke down into a painful sob. "What have I done? Why did *this* have to happen to me? I've done nothing wrong! Why was I born? I *never* asked to be born into this miserable world!" He cried as if the world was coming to an end. "I want my Missing Mama! I miss her so! I *can't* stand it here anymore in the Philippines!" Hysterically, he wept. "I want to *get out* of this Hell! It's too much. I can't bear it anymore. I can't believe it would turn into this! Is this what life is all about? Hoooo... Hoooo..." Years of pain and solitude roiled into cascading waves of pitiful and sorrowful sobbing. He was inconsolable, wrapped in self-pity, feeling so very alone, so very abandoned in this world.

Claire had to turn the van onto a side street and stop at a secluded corner to calm Chance down. She got out of the van, got onto the back seat and sat beside him, stroking his back gently. "Cry. Chance, cry it out. Don't store it all inside. Let your pain come out. You are in no way responsible for tonight." For a moment, her eyes also welled up, herself almost breaking into tears. His cries tore into her heart. "Let go. Let go of tonight. You have *everything* ahead of you! Only the best will come to you."

Chance continued to weep profusely. Minutes passed. Slowly, between sniffles and hiccups, he quieted down. His hair wet with sweat, with tears smeared all over face, still devastated, Chance turned worriedly to Claire. "Auntie Claire, am I living on borrowed time?"

*   *   *

CHAPTER 3

SHADOWS FROM THE PAST

<u>MUSIC INSPIRATION</u>

THE LAST EMPEROR - THEME VARIATION 1
THE LAST EMPEROR
RYUICHI SAKAMOTO, DAVID BYRNE, CONG SU

RETURN TO THE PAST
HUI DAO GUO QU
回到过去
（CHINESE MANDARIN)
JAY CHOU / 周杰伦

HOTEL CALIFORNIA
THE EAGLES

NEVER SAY NEVER
JUSTIN BIEBER & JADEN SMITH

YOU EXIST IN MY SONG
WO DE GE SHENG LI
我的歌声里
(CHINESE MANDARIN)
QU WANTING / 曲婉婷

LAUDAMUS TE
GLORIA
(LET US PRAISE YOU)
(LATIN)
ANTONIO VIVALDI
OSPEDALE SANTA MARIA DELLA PIETÀ
ORPHANGE IN VENICE, ITALY
ALL GIRLS CHOIR

*   *   *

Over the years, Fate would hold sway over Luck and Chance, imposing certain preordained outcomes.

We, for our part, knew Luck and Chance all along, for they had always been with us. For without them, where would we be?

Did Luck and Chance know their own origin? Were they cast upon this world because of some accident? Thus, this quest for the Truth of their origin drove Luck and Chance face to face with their past.

*   *   *

Today, soaked in sweat from the suffocating humidity of this tropical June morning, the twins disembarked from a jeepney – a discarded American relic of a World War II jeep, now converted to a ubiquitous icon of Philippine transportation. Presently, the twins were a block away from the orphanage by the sea.

Built in the seventeenth century, the orphanage's massive façade rose up with an understated dignity against the backdrop of the majestic Manila Bay.

Philippine Jeepney

Haggard, deep in anxiety, the brothers trudged down the *cul-de-sac* toward the back entrance of Misericordia de Dios Orphanage.

"Twelve years have gone by real fast. Five years at the orphanage. Five years with Missing Mama. Seven years with Aunt Juliet. But our best years were at the orphanage." Chance remembered the comfort and happiness he had experienced there in the orphanage. Twelve years had flown by – since they left the orphanage!

The orphanage was a bastion and a sanctuary for innocent souls. It protected newborns from the circumstances which drove them there in the first place. It provided these infants Hope and a *chance* in Life amidst uncertainties. Destiny was content with this arrangement. All would be fair in love and hate – except for the children in the orphanage.

Luck's usual swagger had gone limp. He pursed his swollen lips. "We had our best years here."

Today, all the innocence in the twins' eyes was lost. This morning, they returned to seek the *truth* of their origin and the *reason* for their present circumstance.

Earlier, while tending to their wounds, Aunt Juliet had suggested to them to visit Wawa. Otherwise, the twins would *never* know the history of their past. Wawa would have the answers, Aunt Juliet advised them.

Silently, they approached the guard-house, making their presence known. At twenty-eight, Bozo the Guard, his fierce eyes bulging, queried the boys. Wearing a short-sleeved khaki shirt, Bozo had dark olive brown skin, with a whistle hanging down his neck. His face was pockmarked with acne scars.

"What's your business here today?" Intimidating, Bozo scanned each twin from head to toe.

Luck marshaled his courage. "We'd like to meet with Wawa, please."

After getting some satisfaction with the twins' answers, Bozo registered the boys and buzzed for Wawa, now the Director of the orphanage. "There are two youngsters here for you." Bozo announced tersely over the intercom.

"Who are they?" A woman's voice blared from the guard's intercom.

"Luck and Chance, Ma'am. They want to see you."

At forty-three, Wawa's fair skin shone brightly. Being Catalan, she had her college nursing at the University of Barcelona in Spain. Later, she completed her master's degree at the Columbia University School of Nursing in New York City. Committed to delivering excellent health care, Wawa began her nursing career at the General Hospital of Madrid.

At twenty-six, young, idealistic and eager to see the world, she volunteered to serve in the Philippines, in time dedicating her life to providing transformative healing and education to poor and abandoned families in the greater Manila area. During her first three years, the transition was arduous for her, since she had to learn Tagalog to interact with the local Filipino communities. Wawa possessed a force for Goodness – especially for the newborns and toddlers sequestered in the orphanage under her care. She stood for sense and decency in life. Through Wawa, many lives were changed – for a *chance* to a better life. *This* was her mission. The rest she left to God.

*　　　*　　　*

"I'm coming right away!" Wawa sounded excited over the intercom.

"Luck and Chance?" Wawa's heart leapt! *Oh! That's a surprise!* Waves of joy mixed with sorrow and pity seized her. *They've returned! It has been so many years! Merciful God, thanks for keeping them safe!* "Ah, these pitiful boys!"

Excited, she rushed down the stairs to the rear entrance hall, incredulous at what was happening. "Am I dreaming? Can all this be true?"

*   *   *

CHAPTER 4

FLASH MEMORY

<u>MUSIC INSPIRATION</u>

BECAUSE I LOVE YOU
(PIANO)
YIRUMA

CROUCHING TIGER HIDDEN DRAGON
TAN DUN / 谭盾
CELLIST - YOYO MA / 馬友友

THE MOON REPRESENTS MY HEART
月亮代表我的心
(CHINESE MANDARIN)
TERESA TENG / 邓丽君

ENDLESS LOVE
MEILI DE SHEN HUA
美丽的神话
(CHINESE MANDARIN)
THE MYTH
SUN NAN / 孙楠
HAN HONG / 韩红

ENDLESS LOVE
MEILI DE SHEN HUA
美丽的神话
(CHINESE MANDARIN & KOREAN)
THE MYTH
JACKIE CHEN / 成龙
KIM HEE SUN / 金喜善

DADALHIN KITA SA PALASYO KO
I WILL BRING YOU TO MY PALACE
(TAGALOG)
REGINE VELASQUEZ

LATIKA'S THEME
(HINDI)
SLUMDOG MILLIONNAIRE
A. R. RAHMAN

LES PARAPLUIES DE CHERBOURG
(THE UMBRELLAS OF CHERBOURG)
(FRENCH)
MICHEL LAGRAND
SINGERS
CATHERINE DENEUVE & NINO CASTELNUOVO

O BABBINO CARO
(OH MY BELOVED FATHER)
GIANNI SCHICCHI
(ITALIAN)
GIACOMO PUCCINI
SINGER: AMIRA WILLGHAGEN (9 YEARS OLD)
HOLLAND'S GOT TALENT
(DUTCH WITH ENGLISH TRANSLATION)

UN BEL DÌ VEDREMO
(ONE GOOD DAY, WE WILL SEE)
MADAMA BUTTERFLY
(ITALIAN)
GIACOMO PUCCINI
SINGER: MARIA CALLAS

THE PRAYER
(ENGLISH & ITALIAN)
CELINE DION & JOSH GROBAN

*　　*　　*

An act, once made, is irretrievable and eternal, marked with its unintended consequences.

*　　*　　*

"This is amazing!" Director Wawa raced down the stairs.

All the while, her thoughts reverted to *twelve* years ago – to her good friend, Missing Mama, when the brothers had just turned *five*.

Writhing with guilt and regret, Missing Mama had been deeply troubled by her pregnancy involving the twins. At that time, Wawa, a young nurse at the orphanage, convinced her to continue her pregnancy to full term. Wawa viewed the twins as deserving of life. They deserved a *chance* in this world. No force could thwart their reaching to full term: their existence would be safeguarded – here in the orphanage.

Wawa viewed Luck and Chance as karmic necessities to this life – for Missing Mama and Phantom Daddy.

Wawa flashed back to that clear morning twelve years ago…

*   *   *

Still the mother, Missing Mama scurried into the orphanage. At forty-three, she was tall and skinny. Missing Mama viewed herself a victim of Circumstance which wrenched her heart. For her, life was unpredictable and unforgiving. All these years, she blamed herself. So she ran away, far away. Only to return after five years. It was time to return: to face reality.

"…toiled for so many years…for *this* day!" Missing Mama panted excitedly. From her knapsack, she took out a wad of cash and plunked it on Wawa's office desk. "Wawa, here is my payment for their food and board for their five years here. Shame, shame, shame! But I've finally paid my dues for my CRAZY LOVE!"

"Now I want my boys discharged. *Today.* I want them now!" Beaming with pride, she looked at her twins with much anticipation.

Wawa clasped Missing Mama's hand. "Glad you came today. Tomorrow would have been *too late*. For some time, a rich woman in black has been inquiring about adopting the twins."

36

Staring at Wawa, teardrops rolled down Missing Mama's cheeks.

Wawa was at once relieved and awed with Missing Mama's decision. A day's delay would irrevocably alter everyone's destiny.

With the papers signed and formalities completed, the twins were released to Missing Mama. Between sobs of joy and sorrow, Missing Mama took out two smart looking sets of cowboy outfits, complete with cowboy boots and hats from her knapsack. One set was brilliant red for Luck; another set, bright yellow, for Chance.

"You have mothered my boys for these five years..." Gazing at Wawa, Missing Mama's eyes welled with tears of gratitude. Scooping the boys up into her arms, she hurried out of the orphanage onto the busy Roxas Boulevard to hail a jeepney.

Meanwhile, the brothers wailed and cried their heads off, desperately reaching out their tiny hands toward Wawa. The twins barely knew Missing Mama, who was carrying them away. Here, they were being wrenched away from Wawa, their proxy mother for the past five years. "Wawa... Wawa..." They cried and cried non-stop.

After a moment's hesitation, Wawa raced out of the orphanage to catch up with Missing Mama. Hugging Luck, Chance and Missing Mama one last time, Wawa whispered, "Luz, call me anytime, if you need help. You can always count on me!" With that, Missing Mama climbed onto the jeepney with the twins.

Wawa had admired Missing Mama's courage and determination. *May God bless Luz and her twins!* Wawa shook her head as she watched the jeepney speed away, stirring up a cloud of exhaust smoke behind it. Then, the jeepney merged with the ongoing traffic, lost in the cacophony of tooting horns, cars cutting off each other into the urban chaos.

That was the last time Wawa ever saw Missing Mama.

*   *   *

CHAPTER 5

AT THE GATES OF TRUTH

MUSIC INSPIRATION

FALLING LEAVES RETURN TO THE ROOTS
落叶归根
(CHINESE MANDARIN)
LEEHOM WANG / 王力宏

A LONG ROAD HOME
FEARLESS
SHIGERU UMEBAYAHSI

BABY
JUSTIN BIEBER

IT MIGHT BE YOU
STEPHEN BISHOP

FEARLESS - ORIGINAL THEME MUSIC
SHIGERU UMEBA

BUHAY
(LIFE)
(TAGALOG)
FREDDIE AGUILAR

*   *   *

So, what is Truth?

Truth is the perpetual Now, linked to its Past and tied to its Future. Truth is; as it was; and as it will be.

Perception of Truth is Reality relative to its beholders.

*   *   *

For the twins, standing by the gates of the orphanage, the few minutes' wait felt like eternity. The brothers came here for a rendezvous with the truth of their past, a past they could *not* understand all these years. This was the moment they were waiting for. The moment was now. They wanted clarity. They wanted answers. They wanted the whole truth.

Luck spat out his chewing gum into a trash can twenty-five feet away. "Good distance. Not bad. Now, let's rehearse our questions: why are we here?"

Chance nodded and proceeded with their practice drill. "Why were we in the orphanage — for five years? Why did Phantom Daddy disappear? Where is Missing Mama? Why did Missing Mama *suddenly* leave the Philippines?"

In front of Misericordia de Dios Orphanage, the twins looked dissipated, still shaken from last night's harrowing deathly terror. "Know that I'm GUL!" Her growl kept reverberating in their heads.

Chance persisted with a few more questions. "Who is Gul? What is she all about?" The ordeal he endured last night had severely tested his soul.

Suddenly, an excited welcoming coo burst forth as the orphanage doors swung open. "My, my! How you've *grown*!" Wawa bellowed, as she bounced out of the orphanage doors with her flowing pastel blue nursing gown fluttering in the wind, her arms flung wide open. Her face beamed with joy, her white nurse's cap windblown as she ran toward the boys. She was clothed with the strength and dignity of the Divine.

"This is so incredible!" Wawa bear-hugged the two youngsters, as they grimaced bravely. Their chest wounds stung.

"You're back!" She was beside herself as she looked at them with all her love; for, at the very core of her being, she possessed the spiritual delight of Love. As she locked her eyes on Luck and Chance, her whole being exuded Happiness.

Over the years, she had often wondered about them. How she had yearned to see the twins again, after these twelve years! In their five years in the orphanage, she had given the brothers *all* her love.

"I can't believe my eyes!" Her excitement made her cheeks all the rosier. "You're both so grown up! One day you were toddlers. Another day, you are adults. I can hardly recognize the two of you. Now, who's Luck? Who's Chance? You both look so alike. It's so uncanny!" She cracked up with laughter.

Luck was not so enthusiastic. "We may look the same, but we are not the same."

"You two can truly throw me into a tizzy!" Wawa looked confounded like a lost goose. "Now, who's Luck?"

"I am." Luck raised his hand.

"And I'm Chance."

"Chance wear glasses." Luck put on a fake smile. "It's *that* easy."

"My Pooh-Pooh!" In her irrepressible expression of endearment, Wawa vigorously squeezed both of Luck's poor cheeks – as she was fond of doing this when he was a toddler. "You must love this... confusing people." Wawa pretended to be stern.

Luck brushed back his hair, pointing to the right side of his forehead, revealing a good-sized mole. "See, I have this mole by

41

the right side of my forehead. Missing Mama once said it makes me smarter."

"You've got busted lips! Were you in a fight?" Wawa frowned, expressing concern. "Since you were a toddler, you love getting into fights. Reckless Luck, you! What is it this time? What happened?"

"I'll tell you later." Luck was reluctant to start out with Wawa on a down note. Thus, he continued: "To help our friends, we wear our stringed necklaces, each with our unique medallion."

From underneath his shirt collar, Luck pulled out a thick red stringed necklace, which was hand-rolled by Missing Mama years ago. "The red stringed necklace was supposed to bring good luck and drive away evil. See my gold medallion. It's embossed with a triangle." Luck thrust his medallion toward Wawa. "It's real gold." In his heart, Luck wondered why the necklace and the medallion had lost their charm last night. He was baffled. *What kind of a talisman is this?*

Taking his turn, Chance took out his thick red-stringed necklace from inside his shirt collar, displaying his medallion. "Mine is a gold medallion embossed with a circular laurel."

"Yes, I have seen these before!" Pensively, she recalled the first day she saw them. Upon seeing these medallions, Wawa believed: *Luck and Chance, they have truly returned!*

"You can still *fool* people. You can swap necklaces. Luck, you can wear Chance's eyeglasses. You can trick people. You think you're smart. Huh!"

"No, you'll ultimately find out." Luck had a grim look on his face, betraying the terror he lived through last night.

"We're marked men. We're dead men walking." Chance mumbled, his eyes welling up. The deathly ordeal he and Luck endured this past night kept flashing before him. Dread was written on his face. He could *not* understand the Evil he encountered last night.

Detecting Chance's gloomy expression, Wawa peered into his eyes, fishing for a clue, seeking an answer. "It looks like something really *awful* happened."

"Wawa, let's do this later, please..." Luck pleaded.

"O.K. Let's go in. You boys look famished!" Wawa relented.

*   *   *

CHAPTER 6

GLIMPSES INTO THE PAST

MUSIC INSPIRATION

LA CAMPANELLA
(PIANO)
FRANZ LISZT
YUNDI LI / 李云迪

CASTLE IN THE CLOUD
LES MISÉRABLES
CLAUDE-MICHEL
ALAIN BOUBLIL & HERBERT KRETZMER
SINGER: CHARLOTTE DE LILLA

LONELY DAYS
BEE GEES

YOU AND ME
NI HE WO
你和我
(ENGLISH & CHINESE MANDARIN)
CHEN QI GANG / 陈其钢
SINGERS
LIU HUAN / 刘欢 & SARAH BRIGHTMAN
BEIJING OLYMPICS 2008
北京 2008

A LITTLE LOVE SONG
XIAO CHING GE
小情歌
(CHINESE MANDARIN)
SODA GREEN / 苏打绿

FAIRY TALE
TONG NIAN
童年
(CHINESE MANDARIN & ENGLISH)
MICHAEL WONG / 光良

STARRY NIGHT
XING KONG
星空
(CHINESE MANDARIN)
MAYDAY / 五月天

CORDELIA'S LALLABY
(PIANO)
CARLY COMANDO

PI'S LALABY
(TAMIL)
STORY OF PI
MYCHAEL DONNA
BOMBAY JAYASHRI

I STARTED A JOKE
BEE GEES

MY FAVORITE THINGS
THE SOUND OF MUSIC
RICHARD RODGERS & OSCAR HAMMERSTEIN II
SINGER: JULIE ANDREWS

HALO
BEYONCÉ

CHILDREN'S STORY
SLICK RICK

NAUGHTY BOY
LA LA LA & SAM SMITH

YOU RAISE ME UP
JOSH GROBAN

GRATIAS AGIMUS TIBI
GLORIA
(LET US THANK TO YOU)
(LATIN)
ANTONIO VIVALDI
OSPEDALE SANTA MARIA DELLA PIETÀ
ORPHANGE IN VENICE, ITALY
ALL GIRLS CHOIR

*   *   *

What role would Fate play in a Tale of Love? Would it be a momentary happenstance or luck sublime?

What role would thought and planning play in the pure ecstasy of the heart? In the spontaneity of the Moment?

*   *   *

With eagerness, Wawa led the twins through the orphanage doors. They rushed down the hallways, then turned a corner and paused briefly at the nursery section.

The force of Life could be felt here, a force that would defy treachery, betrayal, malice, disappointment and remorse. Because of Wawa, no evil could befall her residents in the orphanage.

"Come, see!" Wawa urged, pointing toward the cribs inside the nursery. The pathway to Life had begun here for the brothers. The scent of newborn babies filled the air.

In this orphanage nursery, there were newborns up to six year olds. There were sixty cribs of different sizes. For the twins, the place was *déjà vu*. They saw the newborn babies, quivering as they stretched and yawned, their tiny little hands helplessly grasping thin air, exuding the faintest of strength.

Luck and Chance peered through the glass windows into the nursery, at once conjuring up memories of their past. Yes, they were here before.

*   *   *

"I separated the two of you toward different ends of the nursery, so that there wouldn't be any confusion, for the five years you both were in this orphanage." Wawa could not contain her excitement. "Luck, you were at the far corner at the *right*, near

46

that big window facing the garden courtyard." Wawa whispered. "Do you remember?"

Memories of years past rushed back to Luck. He felt the lonely solace of the nursery, which was at the same time secure yet distant.

He remembered, when he was around four, Wawa would bathe him in the big stainless steel square sink with soothing warm water running from the faucet. He played with his yellow ducky, floating in the huge basin. He loved splashing water all over himself and on Wawa, as he let out excited yelps. Wawa would play with him, dry him off, put on his soft cotton pajamas, and tuck him into bed. She would place a little teddy bear underneath his arms and kiss him on his forehead. He would know that it was time to sleep. He would watch Wawa pick up another kid and disappear behind the swinging doors, most likely to give the kid a bath like she did to him. He remembered lying there for a long time, alone, cuddling his teddy bear, rocking his head from left to right in a rhythmic self-lullaby, until he slipped into his solitary slumber.

*   *   *

"Chance, you were at the *far left*, near the other big window, close to the orphanage chapel." Wawa whispered tenderly. "Do you remember?"

Nodding, Chance remembered those years with Wawa.

"Chance, do you remember our late afternoon outings across the Roxas Boulevard toward Manila Bay? You were barely two. Each time I put you down on all fours on the seawall ledge to face the bay, you would automatically turn away from the sea and face the land. It was as if there was a magnet pulling your face away from the sea. That was really funny. You were like a human compass." Wawa burst out laughing.

Chance let out a shy laugh. "Yeah! I must have been afraid of falling over the seawall ledge into the raging waves." He remembered being terrified by the roaring waves, which looked menacing. *Funny how the waves and seawall looked far less threatening now.* At two, the seawall ledge was like a pathway, around three times his length. Now, the seawall ledge looked more manageable, just three times the length of his feet.

*   *   *

Inside the nursery, it was bedlam. The twins gazed intently at the babies' and toddlers' faces. Some toddlers were hollering at the top of their lungs.

Other younger babies were quietly sitting inside their cribs licking and playing with their assortment of toys.

In the big playpen, there were colorful wooden alphabet blocks of red, yellow and blue. Outside the playpen and strewn on the floor were plastic pewter kings and queens, magicians, wizards, knights and bishops, horsemen, swordsmen, witches and henchmen. Scattered all over the floor were red knights, green knights, black knights and white knights.

On a table by the wall was a perpetual Christmas nativity scene of baby Jesus with His parents, Mary and Joseph, and the three Magi from the East.

"Do you remember?" Wawa reminded the twins.

"You told us the story of the first Christmas: the virgin birth of Jesus Christ." Chance enjoyed not only the story of Christmas but the experience of it: the colors, the carols, the gifts, the joy!

"That was the biggest Miracle of all." Wawa beamed with delight. "And I told you the story of the Three Magi from the East, bearing gifts of gold, frankincense and mirth. These were the three wise men: Melchior, a Persian scholar; Caspar, an Indian scholar; and Balthazar, an Arabian scholar. They were also known as the Three Kings of the East."

The twins nodded. They had enjoyed her Bible stories while they were toddlers.

Wawa continued: "Following a star, the Magi came upon the manger of baby Jesus in Bethlehem. Upon seeing the child Jesus, they knelt down and adored Him, presenting Him with gifts. Jesus was their epiphany. Then, I asked what you want to be when you grow up?

"I said I wanted to be a Magi." Luck responded almost automatically.

"And why?" Wawa prodded for more elaboration.

"Because we want to have the gifts of the Wise Men to give to Jesus." Chance finished Luck's thought.

Wawa chuckled, as the twins busily eyed the other children in the nursery.

One fat toddler was standing like a Sumo wrestler, with one leg over the rail, wanting to climb out of his crib. His face was round. His tight and undersized t-shirt revealed a puffed up tummy, his belly button showing.

"This kid is a riot! He can finish two bowls of rice each meal. His name is Jumbo." Wawa laughed cheerily at her own joke.

Another baby was sitting like a meditating Buddha, drowsing off, fighting to stay awake, nodding his sleepy head back and forth, until he toppled over, still half-asleep, oblivious to the noises nearby. "His name is Double Chin." Wawa whispered.

The brothers chuckled at the children's funny gestures.

*   *   *

At the far section of the nursery, where the young toddlers and older kids assembled, the twins caught sight of the Magician, his face painted in thick white, emanating a big smile. He wore a mime artist's black tights, with a bright star-spangled blue overcoat. Mixing pantomime, robotic dancing and magic, he performed with skill and grace.

"Oh, the Magician is visiting today for his monthly performance." Wawa noticed the twins watching the Magician's performance. "His magic routine has changed little, except for some variations. But the effect is the same: intoxicating!"

For the brothers, it was a nostalgic sight.

As toddlers, the Magician had intrigued them. They had learned to trust the Magician in his lure, in his transparent fantasy, and his enigmatic gestures. His magic had encapsulated the experience of wonder into pure fantasy. The implausible results had been genuine surprises. A real thrill to watch!

With his blindfold on, the Magician flicked a *white* string of pearls and rolled it into a ball of pearls with his left hand, which closed into a fist – with the *white* pearls inside his *left* fist. Then, with a magical motion, he appeared to have pushed the string of white pearls into his *right* fist with his left forefinger. After a magical gesture, very slowly, he pulled out the string of pearls from his *right* fist.

This time, the string of *white* pearls were transformed into *pink* ones, looped around another string of *black* pearls, which was, in turn, looped around a string of *grey* pearls! And so on – to the wonderment and cheers of the toddlers.

The twins vaguely remembered watching this same performance many years back, when they were mere toddlers here at the orphanage. This was their first encounter with the Pearl String Magic.

Then as now, the brothers were mesmerized by the Magician, who kept pulling long unceasing loops of differently colored pearl strings, one string looped over another. *How did he do it?*

Magic! The toddlers and the kids watched with awe, their mouths wide open, wowing at the sight – but not knowing the *meaning* of the Pearl String Magic. Nonetheless, they enjoyed the spectacle thoroughly.

For all these years, Magic never left the orphanage.

For a moment, the brothers were lost in the Magic, which had left an indelible lightness and gaiety in their souls during their time there. Then as now, they had not grasped the *meaning* of the Pearl String Magic.

There, the Magician stood, his face transfixed in a broad silent grin – signifying Mystery.

"Let's go," Wawa tugged insistently at Luck. "I need to feed you boys."

*   *   *

CHAPTER 7

A TASTE OF INNOCENT JOY

<u>MUSIC INSPIRATION</u>

SWEET CHILD O' MINE
GUNS N' ROSES

TIME AFTER TIME
CYNDI LAUPER

IF I NEEDED SOMEONE
THE BEATLES

WHAT MAKES YOU BEAUTIFUL
ONE DIRECTION

ROCK BOX
RUN-DMC

WAKA WAKA
(THIS TIME FOR AFRICA)
SHAKIRA

HUNGARIAN RHAPSODY, NO. 2
(FUNNY PIANO)
PIANISTS – VICTOR BORGE & ZHAHAN ARZUNI

DOMINUS, DOMINE
GLORIA
(GOD TO GOD)
(LATIN)
ANTONIO VIVALDI
OSPEDALE SANTA MARIA DELLA PIETÀ
ORPHANGE IN VENICE, ITALY
ALL GIRLS CHOIR

*　　　*　　　*

They all walked briskly down the hallway, made a few turns, entered the dining hall and settled in the orphanage's VIP dining room.

An elegant grandfather clock stood at the center of the dining room's main wall.

For the youngsters, the reality of the Past rushed back through the familiar smell of the kitchen: the garlicky smell of fried rice; the mouth-watering scent of sautéed fish with ginger; and the aroma of stir-fried mixed vegetables. Ah, the delicious smell of noonday meals!

A sumptuous lunch was served in stainless steel trays. Everyone had the same menu of chicken soup, sautéed tilapia, an assortment of vegetables, and a mound of fried rice.

As soon as the delicious taste of chicken soup touched Chance's palate, a thrilling excitement shot through him. The taste of chicken soup confirmed that he had returned to the origin of his past. For a brief illusory moment, the precious essence of innocence rushed back – those days without time, without worries, without fear. An exquisite happiness flitted through him: *I love this orphanage!*

For Chance, this brief illusory moment melded the Past and the Present into one, defying all the vicissitudes of his life.

Each mouthful gulp was so tasty. It seemed as if he had *never* left the orphanage, a place where Wawa's presence, attention and love permeated so completely. Memory and experience were now one – glued by the delicious taste of chicken soup which Wawa fed him so lovingly over his five years at the orphanage.

Drink was lemonade in plastic cups. For dessert, there were small pieces of chocolate. Lastly, there were fortune cookies.

All munched their food with gusto, with Wawa recounting her days with the boys of years past.

Lunch was yummy.

The twins could not wait for Wawa to finish her stories. She loved to yak.

Once upon a time while they were four, after meals, they had this ritual: cracking open fortune cookies and reading their fortunes.

Eager to crack open his fortune cookie soonest, Chance mentally complained that Wawa was eating her words rather than her food. *Geez! Wawa is taking forever to eat. You're too busy reminiscing about the Past – finding ways to playfully embarrass us. Blah, blah, blah.*

Luck and Chance loved this fortune cookies ritual. Years back, as little boys, they would anxiously wait for all the nurses to finish eating their meals so they could get the nurses' fortune cookies. This was their game with Wawa, and occasionally, with Claire Bonsens, when she visited the orphanage during her off days.

At long last, Wawa finished her meal.

It was fortune cookie time!

Luck burst out laughing as he read his fortune: *You are the crispy noodle in the vegetarian salad of life!*

With a frown, Chance read his fortune: *It is by those who suffer that the world is most advanced.*

His brows curled up: first the right brow; then the left brow. Soon, he was doing the wave with his left and right brows – like

54

two dancing earthworms squiggling above his eyes. Wawa saw this and let out a yelp of a giggle.

Wawa's fortune was this: *Knowing others is intelligence; knowing yourself is true wisdom. Mastering others is strength; mastering yourself is true power.*

"Now, who said that?" Luck asked.

"Lao Tzu (老子)!" Jumped in Wawa.

*   *   *

CHAPTER 8

THE GOOD NEWS

<u>MUSIC INSPIRATION</u>

MAYBE
(PIANO)
YIRUMA

TUPTIM
ANNA AND THE KING
GEORGE FENTON & ROBERT KRAFT

LETTER OF THE WEEK
ANNA AND THE KING
GEORGE FENTON & ROBERT KRAFT

GOOD TIME
OWL CITY & CARLY RAE JEPSEN

BRANDENBURG CONCERTO, NO. 3-I
JOHANN SEBASTIAN BACH

DOMINE, FILI UNIGENITE
GLORIA
(TO THE LORD, THE ONLY SON)
(LATIN)
ANTONIO VIVALDI
OSPEDALE SANTA MARIA DELLA PIETÀ
ORPHANGE IN VENICE, ITALY
ALL GIRLS CHOIR

*   *   *

*T*his was a popular Chinese saw.

Once there was a farmer. One day he broke his leg. He lamented: How unlucky I am!

Over the weekend, a war broke out and the army general

came to town to conscript for soldiers. Upon coming to the farmer's house, he found the farmer lying in his cot with his broken leg; the army general found him unfit for battle and left him. The farmer was spared.

The farmer exclaimed: I am so lucky!

*   *   *

So, what is Luck? And what is Chance? Is it but a frame of mind? A context that can change so whimsically?

Why can context change the meaning of events? And so radically?

*   *   *

The twins knew they were lucky, making it to the top ten percent of the graduating class – with flying colors. Luck had the better grades. Multiple choices often stumped Chance due to his ambivalence with *nearly* similar answers – his major drawback.

For college admissions, Luck scored high in Calculus and Chinese Language & Chinese Culture Advanced Placement Exams. On the other hand, Chance scored high in Statistics and Biology Advanced Placement Exams. The pair were precocious in their intellectual maturity.

With hard work and perseverance, the brothers graduated with honors in their class from Ateneo de Manila University, High School Department, one of the prestigious private schools in the Philippines, catering to the *crème de la crème*.

This school had produced national leaders and heroes, such as, Jose Rizal, the national hero of the Philippines in its fight for independence from Spain.

Since its founding over a hundred fifty years ago, Ateneo prided itself in urging its students toward greatness, self-sacrifice and heroism. Such calls resonated deeply in the hearts and souls of many, including the twins.

There was no enmity between the brothers. They knew they were among the best of the best. Their destinies would be intertwined like two peas in a pod. As they venture forward, the world would be their oyster. Or so they thought.

*   *   *

For the twins, their recent graduation day was a lonely event, with no relatives attending their commencement.

Seven years ago, Missing Mama abruptly departed from the Philippines. With no explanations. The twins, then ten years old, were taken in by Aunt Juliet, Missing Mama's younger sister.

No one bothered to discuss Missing Mama's sudden sojourn overseas with the boys. In fact, none of their close relatives in Manila knew her whereabouts. It was a painful mystery the boys would bear for these past seven years.

So the brothers grew up amidst Aunt Juliet's benign neglect.

Over the years, Uncle Romeo, Aunt Juliet's husband, turned into a cold, taciturn man who chain-smoked all day. He showed little sympathy for the twins.

Aunt Juliet, an over-solicitous husband-fearing wife, made sure to please him and most importantly, to dote on their only son, Nero Montago – an eighteen year old spoiled brat.

*   *   *

On their graduation day, the no-show from Aunt Juliet's

family left the pair feeling deeply disappointed. There were no gifts, no family celebrations, no family recognition. Nothing.

Chance felt the world was unfair to him. For that whole day, he pouted.

Luck comforted Chance. "We have been more fortunate than most. The school principal, the key department heads and our academic mentors took pictures with each of us. That's huge! Real trophies! We're the only kids in our graduating class heading for America to attend college. This should be considered a great reward. A vindication."

Not for Chance. He was inconsolable. Aunt Juliet and her family's absence from their graduation was the ultimate betrayal. A final let-down.

*   *   *

The brothers wanted to leave Aunt Juliet's home, to escape from her often cold and pathetic treatment. They yearned to get an education abroad for a better future. These objectives gave impetus to the twins to give it their all to go abroad.

As lunch was coming to an end, Wawa glanced at her big manly watch. "Oh my! How time flies!" She knew she would soon have to go to attend to her next appointment.

"So, what brought you two here today?" Wawa finally popped the question that she had been dying to ask the twins – a question the brothers were too shy to raise.

"We're headed for America! We'll be attending the International School for Brainiacs Squared. ISBS!" Luck declared proudly.

"Wow! Congratulations! You'll get an *excellent* education

there!" Wawa was visibly impressed by their achievement.

With glee, Luck showed Wawa his ISBS admission letter, which was stamped with a red seal, laced with two red ribbons. "Auntie Wawa, ISBS is a *most* reputable school." Luck could not contain himself. "It admits only the most brilliant and most promising students from all over the world. Its curriculum and training there are groundbreaking. Bottom line, ISBS curriculum is structured to be relevant, to address today's world problems. Its training is iconoclastic! Here, best solutions and actions are valued above all."

Wanting to be heard, Chance jumped in. "Yes, its students are driven toward action. Its graduates join top multinational corporations. Or, various government agencies. When we graduate, we'll be very much sought after! Many of its graduates are renowned in solving the world's many intractable problems and serious crises. We'll make a difference in the world. Auntie Wawa, we'll make you proud of us."

Wawa smiled at the brothers and cleared her throat. "Yes. ISBS is a very *special* school. *A magical school!*" She winked knowingly at the twins.

"How do you know?" Chance scratched his head – incredulous, that Wawa would know this.

"I'm not as dumb as I look!" Wawa scowled.

"Luck researched the top American colleges. ISBS is our top choice."

"So you two want to be Magi! Soon you two will be great – and *very* famous!"

Luck felt triumphant and gave out a broad grin. "We got

scholarships! Plus we got room and board fully paid for! And we got part-time jobs for pocket money! It's an offer even a dummy would not pass up." The brothers gave each other a hearty fist bump.

"Yes, it is all because of Luck!" Chance was exuberant.

"If I'm not mistaken, I believe Marcus Blundermore, your *uncle*, is the current President of ISBS." Wawa teased. "Is this a coincidence or what?"

The youngsters nodded in the affirmative, with a silly smile streaked across their faces.

"Aren't we lucky!" Happily resigned to this fact, Chance raised his hands in sublime surrender. "Uncle Blundermore – that *alone* is a great reason to choose ISBS!"

Luck beamed.

Wawa nodded approvingly. "When you were here in the orphanage, Blundermore used to come here and visit the two of you near your birthday – showering you both with gifts!" She remembered divvying up their gifts, putting some away to distribute to the twins over other special days of the year.

"You both will be in good hands." Wawa was pleased with their choice. "Even if you both stay in the Philippines for college, getting a good job in Manila would be a challenge. Here, getting a good job is tied to good social connections. Your job prospects will be bleak, regardless which Filipino university you attend." This much Wawa knew. "In America, you will have a future. Over there, you will at least have a fighting chance." She was so proud of them.

Deep in her heart, Wawa was feeling bittersweet. *Is this a flash in the pan? One moment I see Luck and Chance – after so many years. Another moment, they will be gone. When will I ever see them again? God, why are You so stingy? Is this Your cruel joke?*

*   *   *

GUL'S MARKS

MUSIC INSPIRATION

BECAUSE
THE BEATLES

PHANTOM OF THE OPERA – THEME SONG
ANDREW LLOYD WEBER
SINGERS: SARAH BRIGHTMAN & MICHAEL CRAWFORD

BELLE
(THE BEAUTY)
NOTRE DAME DE PARIS
(FRENCH / ENGLISH)
LUC PLAMONDON & RICHARD COCCIANTE
SINGERS
GAROU, DANIEL LAVOIE, PATRICK FIORI,
HELÈNE SEGARA & JULIE ZENATTI

ANG BUHAY NGA NAMAN NG TAO
(A PERSON'S LIFE)
(TAGALOG)
FREDDIE AGUILAR

AT WORLD'S END – THEME SONG
PIRATES OF THE CARIBBEAN: AT WORLD'S END
HANS ZIMMER

*   *   *

Even as Luck was reveling at the idea of going to ISBS, Chance was silently lamenting on the quandary the twins were in, especially after last night's terrifying close encounter with their own death. "There's nothing keeping us here. There would be no turning back now. We leave or we die." Chance shook his head, downcast. "We *have* to leave the Philippines – far away from Evil. Never to return! "

"Why?" Wawa asked disconcertedly.

"We've been warned. We're doomed here. We're living on borrowed time!" Chance squirmed on his seat, unable to bear the dread churning within him.

"How so?" Wawa was now concerned. The good cheer of moments just past turned deeply disturbing, as if the Devil herself had just entered the room.

"A monster of a woman from Hell! She wanted to finish us off. Luckily, Nanny Claire rescued us." Chance gasped, suddenly finding his throat tightening and going dry. It was as if he was re-living those moments when a stinking burlap sack was put over his head, with a noose tightly tied around his neck. He felt his head spinning in some inexplicable swirl of vertigo.

"Huh!" Wawa shuddered at the sight of Chance turning white as a sheet.

"That's one of the reasons why we came here." Chance could not go on.

Luck's voice, too, was trembling. "She was a witch, spelled with a capital B. Her goons chained us up against her dungeon walls. She wanted to finish us off! We were as good as dead!"

"What did she do?" Wawa cut in.

Luck glanced at Chance for his permission. Chance nodded.

"This dreadful thing." Slowly, Luck lifted his t-shirt. He carefully removed the long gauze wrapped several rounds around his chest by Aunt Juliet this morning. At the final round, he felt a vicious sting as he peeled the woolen fibers of the gauze from his fresh wound.

Then, there it was! Just by the left side of his chest, there was a ghastly red-bluish wound, the letter "L", seared into his flesh.

Likewise, Chance lifted his t-shirt, gingerly removing a long gauze. And lo! Just by the left side of his chest, there was a hideous red wound, the letter "C", seared into his flesh.

"Holy smoke!" Wawa screamed in a ghastly shriek of terror. "Awful Hell!" Each of their wounds was fresh, wide open, displaying its heinous mark.

*   *   *

Tick tock! Tick tock! The tick-tock of Time from the grandfather clock in the VIP room was the only audible sound.

At this moment, the dining room dimmed into an eerie darkness – with the twins' brandings emitting evil energies. A whiff of evil wind blew across the room, fluttering the curtains, warping Time and Space within the dining room into a twilight zone of hell. Then, just as suddenly, the atmosphere in the room returned to normal again.

*   *   *

"Jesus-Mario-Sep!" Wawa crossed herself, terrified. "What evil spirits have befallen you!" Wawa froze, agog in fear.

"You see, we can't hide our identity." Luck confessed with dismay.

Moments later, Wawa came through to herself, bewildered. "So, *who* did this? You have not answered me!

"GUL!" Luck blurted out.

Wawa was speechless.

Fear flashed thru Chance's face. "We're too young to die. We want to live."

An interminable silence descended upon the room.

"Gul – who is she? Why us? Why did she want us dead?" Luck insisted to know.

"We asked Aunt Juliet early this morning. She told us *you* have the answers." Chance gave Wawa a searching look. "She was quite distraught, too."

Wawa gave the boys a sorrowful look. "Gul is a sad and ugly tale. I am so sorry. You two have been dragged into her ire... Into trouble's lair... You shouldn't be..." Suddenly, putting her hand over mouth, Wawa stopped herself from talking. *This tale is too grim for the boys.*

* * *

CHAPTER 10

QUERY INTO THE TWINS' ORIGIN

<u>MUSIC INSPIRATION</u>

WHERE IS ARMO?
THE LAST EMPEROR
RYUICHI SAKAMOTO, DAVID BYRNE, CONG SU

TELL ME WHY
THE BEATLES

LOVE THE WAY YOU LIE
EMINEM & RIHANNA

A QUIÉN QUIERO MENTIRLE?
(TO WHOM I WANT TO LIE)
(SPANISH)
MARC ANTHONY

NO REPLY
THE BEATLES

BRAVE
SARA BAREILLES

*　　　*　　　*

This morning, while tending to their wounds, Aunt Juliet suggested to the brothers that today was a day no better than any for the twins to visit with Wawa, the holder of the keys to their secret past.

Once they leave the Philippines, the pair might never return and never had the chance to know the truth of their origins.

*　　　*　　　*

Luck focused on the main purpose of the twin's visit today. "That's why we're here. Why were we at this orphanage for five years? What happened?"

"Where's our Missing Mama? Our Phantom Daddy?" Chance butted in.

"Why did they leave the Philippines – each of them so suddenly?" For seven long years, Luck wanted to know.

"Why not take us with them?" Chance hoped a curtain of truth could be opened.

"Why just disappear? With no explanation?" Luck's lower lip throbbed with pain..

"Aunt Juliet told us you'll have the answer." Chance peered into Wawa's eyes. "She said you know the truth."

There was a profound silence.

Hesitantly, Wawa responded: "Truth is a double-edged sword. It cuts both ways. Truth. It is an alluring yet treacherous snare. Truth can be a trap where many have suffered and died trying to seek it. And even when they have obtained the truth, they cannot handle it. Many are left wishing they have not insisted on knowing the truth."

Three hearts throbbed impatiently. Two young hearts beating for the truth; one old heart trying to shelter them from the brutal Truth.

"Why open the gates of the ugly Past where it serves no purpose except for sorrow and pain?" Wawa was not too keen to push open the gates of the Past. *These kids are too young. They don't know what they are getting into.*

Barely audibly, Wawa whispered: "LOVE! With its twists and turns...like so many things in life."

A pause.

"Your parents left the Philippines...each for their own reasons. You see, they didn't want any harm to befall either of you." Her words were punctuated by the cadenced ticking of the grandfather clock.

Chance pressed on. "But why such mysterious departures for the Missing Mama and Phantom Daddy?"

Wawa's mind swirled into a whirlpool of confusion. *To tell or not to tell?*

"LOVE... Love gone awry... for all its inexplicable reasons." Wawa found herself saying words she did not fully understand. *Now, why did I say this? This is stupid.*

"Is that the truth?" Luck was bewildered with the answer.

"Is that all?" Chance uttered in disbelief. "It's too simplistic." Chance could *not* accept Wawa's answer.

"Yes. That's Life: IT IS, AS IT WAS, AND AS IT WILL BE." Wawa said firmly, pursing her lips, resolved that the less said, the better.

"In that case, Life has been pretty cruel." A sense of futility surged through Chance's total being, disappointed that he could not learn more.

"We only had five years with our Missing Mama." Luck lamented.

The silence in the room was deafening.

"Don't dwell in the dark Past. It's over with." Wawa looked at the twins with the tenderness of a mother. "Live in the Present. That's all we have. Find happiness in *this* moment. Nowhere else. Can you try that?"

Softly, Wawa showered the twins with these loving words. "Make time to play and see the brighter side of your life. Focus on what's *working* for you – what's positive in it. If something is not working in your life, rework it or let it go. In trying moments, say this: 'I *love* myself. Now, what should I do?' Be mindful with what's *right* for you. Choose and practice *loving* behavior. *Love* yourself! Can you do that for me? For yourself?"

His eyes welling, Chance nodded, appearing to agree.

"Anger won't do." Wawa put her arm around Chance's shoulder. "It will only eat you up and poison your soul. In time, it can destroy you. Look at the future. You have everything ahead of you! Now finish your lemonade."

*   *   *

Changing the subject matter, Wawa reminded them. "Do you remember Father Legazpi? He is your Uncle Blundermore's best friend. He is now the Cardinal of Manila. He misses you both."

The twins nodded.

"While both of you were here in the orphanage, he never failed to visit you every Saturday. He loves you both so very much. When we were toddlers, we used to ride with him at the backseat child carrier of his bicycle in Luneta Park!" Chance remembered the happy times with Fr. Legazpi. Often, he took the twins to Luneta Park, the most famous park in Manila, not far from the orphanage. There, Luck and Chance took turns at the backseat child carrier of Fr. Legazpi's bicycle, their hands

70

gripping his shirt, as he rode around the Grand Stand by the sea – the sun beating on their faces against the warm sea breeze.

"He would love to see you both. He still comes here to the orphanage every Saturday. By the way, when do you leave for America?" Wawa took out her smartphone to take notes.

"Soon." Chance was thinking of Uncle Antikweetee, Missing Mama' elder brother. "Our Uncle Antikweetee will be giving us our plane tickets very soon!" His anticipation rose, knowing that they would be getting their plane tickets any day now.

*   *   *

"By the way, have you both been confirmed in the Catholic faith? It would be great to be confirmed before departing for America." Being religious, Wawa wanted to make sure the twins received the Catholic sacrament of Confirmation.

The boys shrugged.

"Return tomorrow. I'll arrange to have Cardinal Legazpi, the Cardinal of Manila, get you both confirmed. Be here at 11:40 A.M. tomorrow." Wawa punched an appointment into her smartphone.

The twins' eyes brightened as they rose to take their leave, glad at the prospect of once again meeting their Fr. Legazpi, their priest, their grown-up friend: a man of compassion.

Wawa kissed the two youngsters. "God loves you!"

As she parted ways with the twins at the main orphanage door, Wawa shook her head sadly and muttered, visibly exasperated. "GUL DIABOLICA! She strikes again. *But why? Why now?*"

*   *   *

CHAPTER 11

THE ALTERED STATE
OF
MARIA CLARA PRISMA

MUSIC INSPIRATION

ROLLING IN THE DEEP
ADELE

STAY
RIHANNA & MIKKY EKO

HERE COMES THE RAIN AGAIN
EURYTHMICS

GONE WITH THE WIND – THEME SONG
MAXIMILIAN STEINER

TAKING HER HAND
HOUSE OF FLYING DAGGERS
SHIGERU UMEBAYASHI

LOVERS – TITLE SONG
HOUSE OF FLYING DAGGERS
SHIGERU UMEBAYASHI
SINGER: KATHLEEN BATTLE

PEONY PAVILLION
HOUSE OF FLYING DAGGERS
SHIGERU UMEBAYASHI

GIVE ME A REASON TO FORGET
WRONG PERSON
CUO DE REN
错的人
(CHINESE MANDARIN)
ELVA HSIAO / 萧亚轩

GEI WO YI GE LI YOU WANG JI NI
给我一个理由忘记你
(CHINESE MANDARIN)
A-LIN / 黄丽玲

IT'S OK TO BE LONELY
JI MO JI MO JIU HAO
寂寞寂寞就好
(CHINESE MANDARIN)
TO HEBE / 田馥甄

TOO BAD IT'S NOT YOU
KE XI BU SHI NI
可惜不是你
(CHINESE MANDARIN)
LIANG JING RU / 梁静茹

BAKIT NGA BA MAHAL KITA
(TAGALOG)
ROSELLE NAVA

*　　　*　　　*

*W*hat would become of a person whose dearest wishes in Life were crushed? How could one overcome one's disappointments? How could one make a way in Life? Where could one turn in a world without Love?

This would be a tale of Maria Clara Prisma, a woman of poignant pathos.

Why? What convoluted betrayal would weave such an inglorious outcome? Why was Fate so unkind?

*　　　*　　　*

Two nights ago, just past midnight, Maria Clara Prisma downed a bottle of Chianti to drown her sorrows of the Past. In time, the effects of the wine swept her into a state of drunken stupor.

She dialed her phone. "Johnny Dangerous! Come over here! Bring Double Trouble with you! Right away! This is important!"

All the while, Claire Bonsens was busily preparing Maria Clara's midnight dinner.

Minutes later, the two top goons showed up.

Maria Clara threw the eight by eleven pictures of Luck and Chance on the kitchen table. In a drunken frenzy, she shouted her orders. "I want you to grab these two bastards. The sooner the better! Mobilize all our goons! In fact, our whole army!"

She grabbed the kitchen knife from Claire's hand and hysterically, stabbed at each of the pictures, over and over again, bellowing: "These two are scumbags – good for nothing maggots! They only cause me so much heartache. They are goners! Now go get them! Bring them to me *alive*! Failing this, you two will be fired. I mean it!"

Claire shuddered as she sliced up pieces of chicken. "Who are they?"

"Luck and Chance!" Maria Clara screamed. "They will soon be history!"

Claire knew them! "No! This can't be!" She dropped her cleaver, CLANG! as it hit the floor.

She had spent much time with the twins while they were newborns till they were five – and during her day-offs with Wawa over those five years while the twins were at the orphanage.

Completely upset, Claire fled the kitchen.

*   *   *

Since *that* fateful day many, many years ago, Maria Clara had turned into the Witch of the Catacombs, where every night would be Halloween. Even the powerful dared not mess with her lest they draw her ire.

Many of her unfortunate victims, real or not, met brutal and unnatural deaths, their remains entombed in the Catacombs of *Intramuros* in Old Manila.

* * *

In her youth, she possessed the radiance of Hope and Goodness. Herself a legend, Maria Clara Prisma reigned as the pre-eminent beauty queen, graced with wealth and power. Raised in a prominent family in Cebu City, her world expanded upon arriving in Manila. She was a pageant queen: Miss Cebu. Later, she became Miss Philippines. Then, she won the *Miss Universe* title. This would change her life big time.

A *prima donna*, Maria Clara flaunted her beauty as a seductive tool of financial connivance. No doors could deprive her from access into the board rooms of preeminent companies, domestic and international.

However, deep inside, she ached, tormented by a rotten void of unrequited love. Over the years, it had consumed and devastated her. Love was a realm beyond her reach.

As she climbed to the top echelons of Manila high society, she used her beauty like a trump card.

Here in Makati at the suburbs of Manila, she managed her global enterprise: *Los Heuvos Locos,* the world's largest poultry and egg hatchery business. Crazy Eggs!

Through *Los Heuvos Locos,* she extended her global reach.

Over the years, she bought into electric utilities, the metro light rails and expressways, with Get-Out-of-Jail-Free cards in her pocket. Yes, she, too, was in the mining business: *everything is mine, mine, mine!* She was the quintessential mining queen.

She could sing the most touching melodies. She could orate and win her audience's hearts. She charmed the public with her high fashion wardrobe consisting of innumerable Maria Clara dresses, made of fine *jute*, a delicate pineapple fiber. With her high shoulder arched sleeves and long shimmering skirt, the effect was stunning and most seductive. Her Maria Clara dresses showcased her personality: conspicuous extravagance.

At the vortex of the very rich and powerful, she projected a happy and powerful face. One would think she was happy and content, but that was mere camouflage.

Fate had left her demoralized in spirit. Over the years, the weight of disappointment gnawed away the optimism within her. Fate was *not* kind to her.

*   *   *

Ironically, beauty would plague her like a cruel curse.

Far from being optimistic and joyful, she became *strangeness* personified. Two weeks before her appointed wedding day. For no reason, her betrothed disappeared from her life. Since *that* fateful day of being jilted by her lover, her life underwent a visceral metamorphosis. Since then, she ached and was tormented by a rotten void of unrequited love. Over the years, this Great Disappointment consumed and devastated her. Love was a realm beyond her reach.

Over time, the forces of perennial Good and Evil roiled her very being, convoluting her personality and character into a monstrous chameleon as changeable as day and night. Now, she was the embodiment of disjointed personalities and emotional neuroses which waxed and waned depending on the time of day and her stress levels.

So like clockwork over a twenty-four hour cycle, she would evolve incessantly in her malady of the soul. At dawn and at dusk, hers would be a personality and character in turmoil, with neither reason nor rhyme: sometimes blowing hot; sometimes blowing cold.

By day, the splendor of her beauty and grace outshined all beauties. At noon, benevolence, understanding and kind heartedness would reign supreme. As day turned to night, Maria Clara Prisma's soul would enter the gates of Hell.

After sunset, she would be a sad eclipse of the heart. As night deepened, a seething, vindictive, and pure evil would exude from her very soul. Her demons would churn their ugly force, and Maria Clara would become Evil incarnate.

From midnight onward till prior to dawn, malevolence would be her very essence. Malice and hate, mixed with the obsession for vengeance, would dominate her soul. She would sink into a bottomless pit of insanity, tormented by the ruthless punishment of unrequited love. Over the years, it had consumed and devastated her. Love was a realm beyond her reach.

*   *   *

At fifty-five, this was her daily soliloquy, her daily canticle:

> *To men who taunt me only by with their grinning faces, when I discover that they have neither hearts, nor spine, nor souls, when they open to me a perspective of flatness, triviality, imbecility,*

77

*coarseness and ill-temper – I'll be the very Devil all
men shall dread. Let him wish that he has never
been born.*

*But to the noble and sincere gentleman, the soul
mate of fire and the character that bends but does
not break, at once supple and stable, tractable and
consistent, loyal and true – I am ever tender and
faithful. He will wish that he lives forever.*

Oh, where is such a man of my heart?

The forces of these thoughts wrenched her heart on a daily
basis, raising her soul to virtue in the splendor of day, then,
casting her into a monstrous demon during the darkest of night.

*   *   *

Over the years, in her travels or in conferences, she would
encounter men that appeared to resemble her lover. Her heart
would skip a beat. She would gasp. But to no avail. Her lover
remained a phantom in her dream: that ideal man that never was.

Often times, in the deep of the night, her anger devolved into
hate for everything that had a tinge of her lover. In recent
sleepless nights, she would utter in rage: "Vengeance will be
mine!" Her attitude toward the twins had turned into a
murderous obsession. She wanted the brothers dead.

Gone were the days when she hoped she could use the twins
as pawns to lure her lover back. She had tried to adopt them – for
the love of him. But that was then, when they were at
Misericordia de Dios Orphanage…many years ago.

Now, devoid of Hope, Luck and Chance had become the *very*
object of her revenge – the targeted victims in her quest for

vengeance over cheated love.   Maria Clara seethed. "They shall
never leave the Philippines – and shall never set foot in America.
NEVER!"

*   *   *

CHAPTER 12

AT THE GATES OF HELL

<u>MUSIC INSPIRATION</u>

ON THE FLOOR
JENNIFER LOPEZ & PITBULL

UNBREAK MY HEART
TONI BRAXTON

TOTAL ECLIPSE OF THE HEART
BONNIE TYLER

QUEEN OF THE NIGHT
DIE ZAUBERFLOTE, K 620
(THE MAGIC FLUTE, K 620)
(GERMAN)
WOLFGANG AMADEUS MOZART
ROYAL OPERA HOUSE COVENT GARDEN
SINGER: DIANA DAMRAU

IF THERE WAS A DAY
RU GUO YOU YI TIAN
如果有一天
(CHINESE MANDARIN)
LIANG JING RU / 梁静茹

BUY AND SELL LOVE
AI QING MAI MAI
爱情买卖
(CHINESE MANDARIN)
MURONG XIAO XIAO / 慕容晓晓

TEARS
HUI HU XI DE TONG
会呼吸的痛
(CHINESE MANDARIN)
LIANG JING RU / 梁静茹

ONLY TEARDROPS
EMELLE DE FOREST
EUROVISION 2013 WINNER

BRING ME TO LIFE
EVANESCENCE

*　　　*　　　*

*S*uch is the Mystery of the Human Condition. We are born.
We grow up. We fall in and out love. We get rich or poor.
We grow old. We get sick. Then, we die – ALONE. The
Human Condition has not changed over the millennia.

Can we overcome our human condition? Can we change
it? How?

*　　　*　　　*

Last night, just past 3:00 A.M., Maria Clara Prisma returned to her
mansion, *La Casa Sin Numero.* She knew her goons had captured
the twins and had shackled them in her secret Dungeon of the
Catacombs. Prisma would have the final say. On this night of the
super moon, she would complete her revenge: she would liquidate
them.

*　　　*　　　*

A High Priestess of Darkness, Maria Clara wore a hooded
black robe with an appended purple cloak to implement her black
deed. With a flickering sinister candle *floating* ahead of her –
leading the way, she entered an incense-filled cellar of Darkness.

She proceeded to perform an abbreviated Black Mass for the
consecration of her evil deed. Throughout, black candles lit the
room. On a make-shift altar laid a host. *"Ave, Satanas! Veni,
Rege Satanas!* Oh, King of Darkness, unsheathe your sword.

Tonight, the hour has come for *my* deliverance. Let vengeance reign! *In nomine Dei nostri Satanas Luciferi Excelsi!"* Intoning, she called upon the Power of Darkness. Before long, she was deep in a full-fledged trance of the Spirit of Darkness. The Powers of the Deep were nigh. Now, drenched with sweat and in wild frenzy, she yelled profanities as she kicked open the wooden doors of the adjacent Dungeon of the Catacombs.

*   *   *

Now a Witch of the Catacombs, she approached the twins. They were chained against the dungeon wall. "Tell me: Where's your Phantom Father? Tonight, you both will die! Maggots! You'll meet your Maker – I'll see to it!" She screamed at the brothers. In that instant, she became a demon from Hell, the Devil personified. "Know that I am GUL!"

The foul smell of Death permeated the air.

She turned up the furnace into full blast, putting into it the branding iron rods she prepared for each of the twins a day ago. A fierce gushing sound of gas furnace fire and heat filled the putrid air. She also had a long Spanish sword in the furnace. By her foot was a huge ax.

Gul declared: "LIFE IS A SWIRLING EDDY OF DESPPAIR SPECKLED BY FALSE HOPES IN AN EVER DARKENING UNIVERSE!"

She gave out a devilish laughter; the sum of her rage now focused on the twins. "Let's see who gets the last laugh!" She spat at the twins.

The branding iron rods were glowing red hot. The process for the grand execution was set in motion. "All is fair in love and hate! Vengeance is mine! Nothing can stop me now!" Gul ranted curses with wild fury mixed with wails of deathly anger.

She dangled the branding iron in front of Luck's hood. For a moment, she wanted to brand his face.

Gul was now keen for the kill. "All the suffering over the years for this moment!"

With cruel roughness, she ripped open Luck's shirt – to confirm her victim's identity. Her eyes wide open, she checked Luck's medallion which identified him as Luck. "Are you Luck?" She growled. Luck unknowingly nodded. Gul's blood boiled. The moment had finally arrived. All the shame, all the hurt, all the anger merged into this moment. At the height of her fury and delirium, she grabbed the searing triangular-headed branding iron for Luck and plunged it onto his chest, holding it firmly in place. Hissing smoke rose from Luck's chest. The branding was completed.

"AAAAAAAAGH!" A muffled desperate scream burst out to no avail.

Gul's heart pounded. Her head throbbed. Her whole body shivered. She picked up the second iron with a circular branding head. Tauntingly, she dangled the branding iron in front of Chance's hood. "Feel this heat!"

She likewise ripped open Chance's shirt and sank the branding iron hard onto his chest. "WAAAAAAAA!" An excruciating muffled scream filled the air.

"Ah, Vetruvian! This is double revenge! Your bastard sons will now pay the ultimate price of *your* betrayal! It's all your fault. No sin goes unpunished! It's payback time! Oh, CRAZY LOVE!"

Gul felt a dizzying orgiastic zing and spasmodic release run through her whole body. Wincing with diabolical glee, Gul watched the twins grind themselves against the walls, writhing with pain.

"KNOW THIS TRUTH: WE'RE BORN; WE EAT; WE POO; AND WE DIE ALONE!" Gul shrieked madly.

Amidst the wails, Gul reached for the long sword for the kill. But as she raised the sword, she felt a strange and powerful grip wringing her wrists.

"Huh! What's going on?" Strangely, a heavy weight bore down on her. Bewildered, Gul struggled with her sword, which swung from left to right on its own – as if someone was wrenching it off her hand. At this moment, she was wrestling with an invisible foe. An invisible someone was squeezing her tight. Her whole body was wrung into inexplicable immobility, as she staggered and struggled in place. Then, she felt an ever tightening suffocation as her eyes were bulging. She could *not* breathe. Someone had her in a head-lock, squeezing the life out of her. "What...What the Devil is going on..." She groaned in pain, dropping her killing sword upon the cement floor. CLANG! She was being wrestled down to the floor, her face repeatedly being smashed against the cement slab by an invisible force – an inexplicable *ch'i* (氣).

Amidst the chaos, the wall clock struck four! Ding! Ding! Ding! Ding!

"Oh, no! No......" Gul gasped, coming to from her crazed stupor. Her conscience reawakened. The hour had struck. A painful remorse gripped her heart. *Oh, no... What am I doing?*

She could *not* go on with her plan. As the last ding-ding of the wall clock was striking four, a strange clarity of mind and conscience returned to her. *How can I do this to the boys? I shouldn't have done this...*

She swung violently, wrestling herself free from the invisible force gripping her wrists and neck.

She threw her cloak over her head. Still screaming, she sped toward the dungeon door and slammed it behind her.

Now, a cock crowed victoriously, announcing the arrival of dawn.

*   *   *

As Prisma stumbled into her bedroom, she caught a glimpse of herself in the mirror. Her sinister face looked deathly pale, practically devoid of life.

"Am I a ghost? Have I come to this?" She was stunned by her own appearance – her face badly bruised and bloodied, with a black eye and a broken nose.

"How could I do this?" Panting hysterically, Prisma crashed onto her king size bed, her whole body shuddering with agitation. "Why is this happening?" She gasped in confusion, her soul in torment.

The first faint light of dawn broke through her window. As the hours progressed toward the morning, Prisma had only pity and sorrow for the two brothers and herself. She could have ended it all! But it was *not* to be. She just could *not* do it.

"I, too, have kids." Prisma sobbed hysterically. "Why am I in this state? I just don't know *how* things are going to turn out."

*   *   *

CHAPTER 13

UNCLE ANTIKWEETEE

MUSIC INSPIRATION
LISTEN TO YOUR HEART
ANNA AND THE KING
GEORGE FENTON & ROBERT KRAFT
SINGERS: DHT

WHAT A WONDERFUL WORLD
LOUIS ARMSTRONG

ON STRANGER TIDES – THEME SONG
PIRATES OF THE CARIBBEAN:
ON STRANGER TIDES
HANS ZIMMER

ALAALA
MEMORY
(TAGALOG)
FREDDIE AGUILAR

**I DON'T WANT YOU TO BE LONELY
WO BU YUAN RANG NI YI GE REN
我不愿让你一个人**
(CHINESE MANDARIN)
MAYDAY / 五月天

*   *   *

So who has primacy?

Luck or Chance?

This ageless question will be answered through this magical journey beyond the Realm of Wisdom.

Luck preferred to seek clarity from the myriad of circumstances Chance had experienced. Luck would pursue the certainty of positive outcomes whereas Chance would present an existential narrative which would be neutral to all concerned.

Luck would lay hold of a propitious moment, call it a win while he was ahead, declare the reasons of his own victory and call it a day.

Chance would claim mastery over the sea of cosmic probabilities, where all possible permutations exist. Yes, it would be Chance to display the whole panoply of possibilities to Luck's amazement.

*   *   *

Clip clop! Clip clop! Clip clop! Clip clop!

The cadence of the horse was rhythmic, as Luck and Chance gripped for dear life on the arms of the seat of their *calesa,* a Spanish style horse buggy. Pot-holes galore pockmarked the cobblestone streets. It was surprising that these streets in *Intramuros* were still navigable at this state of disrepair. Interestingly, the syncopated cadence of the horse sounded more like the irrevocable beckoning of Fate unbeknownst to the twins, soon to unleash its irresistible force.

*   *   *

The *calesa* bounced its way through the narrow cobblestone streets of *Intramuros,* the heart of Old Manila, the soul of Old Philippines. The Spaniards built this fort to establish Manila as its capital and maintained its four-hundred years rule in the Philippines. That was how the Spanish culture was implanted in this country.

Calesa

During the reign of King Philip II of Spain, and under General Miguel Lopez de Legazpi, the Spaniards completed building this fort in 1606, establishing Manila as the capital of the Philippines. During the Spanish period, *Intramuros,* meaning "within the walls," was considered Manila itself, the seat of Spanish power and influence in the Philippines for around four hundred years.

It was built to protect the seat of the Spanish government from foreign invasions. *Intramuros* had massive impenetrable walls. There were rampant rumors of stolen treasures hidden within its walls.

As *Intramuros* was highly historic, lots of tourists came here to savor Manila's past.

Over the recent decades, the *Intramuros adobe* rock walls were blackened by soot and pollution.

*   *   *

Soon, the twins arrived in front of their uncle's antique shop: Antikweetee World Enterprises (AWE). Its storefront displayed exquisite Spanish armory and swords, knives and daggers of various styles, big and small, native Filipino weapons and myriad of Spanish medieval works of art.

After paying the *calesa* driver, Luck pushed open the heavy metal doors of the shop. In the process, a clang announced someone had entered the store.

Every time the twins visited AWE, they could not help but marvel at the elegant Spanish swords hanging by the walls.

This time, Luck and Chance came to visit Uncle Antitweetee to pick up their plane tickets for America.

* * *

Uncle Antikweetee was Missing Mama's elder brother. At fifty-nine, he was an uncle every kid would love to have. Very smart and hilariously funny, he had introduced the pair to the magical excitement of the different eras, Past and Present, within and beyond the Philippines. For him, *imagination* was paramount in materializing one's dreams and fantasies into one's own reality of the Present. A Master of the Past, he knew the essence of the eternal Past. He would learn from it. Then, he would *transcend* it. With that, everything would be alright.

Through him, the twins learned about the American Dream — a dream which would harness and put focus on the brothers' recent years of striving.

* * *

As the pair were growing up, he dramatized the landing of Ferdinand Magellan, in full costume regalia of a Spanish admiral, at the Island of Mactan, near Cebu, where the world navigator was killed by the local leader Datu Lapu Lapu. A *datu* must do what he must! For Datu Lapu Lapu was the *datu*, the king of his clan.

The twins relished Uncle Antikweetee's colorful tales of King

89

Arthur and the Knights of the Round Table, related palace intrigues, the rise and fall of chivalry, battles and conquests in the name of the king and God.

In recent years, Uncle Antikweetee contributed to the twins' decision to go to America and specifically to ISBS. "There, you will learn Magic!" He would often remind the twins – when it came to the topic of ISBS. He was familiar with the college application process in America. He helped guide the pair with their college selections, narrowing their three top choices and three safeties – for nothing in Life was guaranteed. He also assisted them with their application essays. Without Uncle Antikweetee's help, they would not have come this far. Even if Uncle Blundermore was their uncle, there was no assurance of admission to ISBS. Being a graduate from ISBS himself, he had special insights into that very school. This made the crucial difference.

As the twins entered AWE, they proceeded slowly, knowing it would most likely be their last visit for a long, long time. They browsed the main antique items in the shop.

Inside the shop, there were elegant Spanish swords hanging on the walls. At the corner, there was the panoply of Spanish armory of the *conquistadores*. At the end of the store were collections of iconic Christian paintings, such as those of El Greco of Toledo. One of these paintings was El Greco's *Maria Magdalena*, a close disciple of Jesus Christ.

There were sculptures of saints and ornately carved altars. At the far end of the store was *the* huge aged wooden cross of General Miguel Lopez de Legazpi, the famous Basque Spanish *conquistador* from Acacuplco, the founder of Manila. This shop looked like a mini-museum, storing the rich treasures of the Past.

As they walked toward the back-end of the shop, they asked a saleslady for the one and only: Uncle Antikweetee.

"Is he there?" Chance dreaded the thought that Uncle Antikweetee might be out of town on business. If so, their trip to *New Joy Sea* might be delayed, jeopardizing their much awaited attendance of the ISBS Freshman Week events.

Worst, Gul might send her goons back to finish them off.

*   *   *

CHAPTER 14

THE MAGICAL GIFTS

<u>MUSIC INSPIRATION</u>

TICKET TO RIDE
THE BEATLES

BILLIE JEAN
MICHAEL JACKSON

I'LL FOLLOW THE SUN
THE BEATLES

BENEDICTUS
REQUIEM MASS IN D MINOR, K 626
(LATIN)
WOLFGANG AMADEUS MOZART

*   *   *

Would the divine gifts of self-knowledge, oracular foreknowledge and heightened perceptions help Luck and Chance overcome the obstacles of Life and make the correct choices?

Could any magical powers alter outcomes?

*   *   *

"Boo!"

Crap! Luck instinctively leapt backward, landing, feet first, onto the sales counter.

Chance was already in his defensive stance, ready to deliver a blow.

From behind a post where a fully armored knight stood, Uncle Antikweetee jumped forward from nowhere, brandishing his sword, slicing an impressive double X on the air. "How do you like my *dos equis*!" Uncle Antikweetee laughed so hard he could barely stand up. "Fooled you!" He bellowed heartily. "I've trained you well. Ten long years of *kung fu* martial arts training! Now you can move Heaven and Earth!"

Through his patient training, the twins came to trust their uncle. The brothers learned that with singular focus and concentration, they could break the most indomitable cement blocks, manifesting the astounding Magic of Physics.

Uncle Antikweetee loved to wear his colorful pirate's costumes. Today, he was wearing a Spanish pirate's outfit with a long red kerchief wrapped around his head and a thick belt and buckle to match. He had two uneven braids dangling from each side of his mischievous face. This was his way to entertain potential customers as they browsed through his shop. It was a fun way to break the ice with prospective customers or amuse visiting tourists. He was a cultural heritage unto himself.

He marched noisily toward the twins in his worn out Spanish boots.

Still recovering from last night's harrowing ordeal at Gul's, the brothers were *not* amused by their uncle's antics.

A hulk of a fellow, Uncle Antikweetee was a happy-go-lucky chap. As a master of his trade, customers just loved his glowing personality and kept returning for his weird pranks, if for nothing else.

"Welcome to my humble abode!" Uncle Antikweetee motioned the pair to his make-believe pirate's cellar.

"Hold all the calls," Uncle Antikweetee hollered instructions to his assistant as he closed the thick wooded cellar door behind him.

Dimly lit, the cellar wreaked with the smell of tobacco. Boxes upon boxes of recent shipments were piled up in one corner.

*   *   *

As the twin brothers sat down in his cramped and disheveled cellar office, he flipped out two plane tickets. "These are for you, boys. Plane tickets to America!"

Uncle Antikweetee lit his cigar. "Your lives will forever be changed. Not a moment too soon!" His thick greyish and flipping moustache could not hide his beaming pride.

"Jack be nimble; Jack be quick!" And he burst out laughing, holding the plane tickets up in the air.

The pair eagerly dove forward and snatched their plane tickets from their uncle's hand.

Their spirits lifted and, for a moment, last night's terror dissipated.

"We'll be flying *Jet-Orange!*" Luck and Chance were thrilled. "Booya! Uncle, that's awesome." Luck and Chance gave each other a huge smacking high five.

The twins were most thankful. They were now one step ever closer to realizing their dreams: leaving the Philippines for America. They could clearly feel one door closing with another one opening up.

"I thought you'd like that," Uncle Antikweetee beamed. He thought such a flight would be a proper reward for the brothers.

They had worked so hard, hoped so fervently, and achieved so brilliantly in high school for a chance to attend a top university abroad.

Jet-Orange was the niftiest airline catering to young international travelers.

The pair had heard that flying *Jet-Orange* was like being in a theme park on air. Each route had its own theme. And for each season, the flight theme would likewise change.

Uncle Antikweetee took out two red packets from his shirt pocket. "For each of you!" Uncle Antikweetee offered. Amongst the Chinese, red packets contained good luck money, given to youngsters during special occasions.

"Whoa!" Elated, the twins were beside themselves. "US$888! This is huge!"

Luck gave Chance an exploding fist bump.

"This should tide you over until each of you land yourselves some part-time jobs." Uncle Antikweetee was delighted to see the radiant smiles on the twins' faces.

"Over these years, I can't imagine how much ISBS has changed! I wasn't as academically driven as your Uncle Blundermore. Books were not for me. I'm the happy go lucky guy. I'd rather see the world. But I enjoyed my years at ISBS." A whiff of nostalgia seized Uncle Antikweetee as he reminisced of his years at ISBS.

"We'll keep you updated with the latest events at ISBS! What are e-mails for?" Luck exclaimed.

*   *   *

"So what do you know about Magic?" Uncle Antikweetee threw a question at the brothers.

"*Hocus pocus!*" Luck blurted.

"*Abracadabra!*" Chance did not want to be outdone.

Uncle Antikweetee sucked on his cigar, wondering how and where to start. He blew out puffs of circular smoke which slowly vanished in the air. "You see, in the beginning, there was Magic, which was with LOGOS, the Source of All. And Magic *was* LOGOS. Through Magic, all realities were made. In Magic was Life – the essence of the world. To all that *believe* in Magic, Life *becomes* magical and is born of the Source. Magic permeates the universe. Magic is real. Are you with me?" Uncle Antikweetee chuckled heartily.

"That sounds beautiful!" Luck was enthralled by the promise of Magic.

"Magic is meant to be good." Uncle Antikweetee blinked at the pair. "Magic is alive in our deepest subconscious, which holds our strongest heartfelt desires. Whether we are aware or not, we create our realities through manifesting these heartfelt desires. This is the core of Magic. Through our consciousness, we conjure the magical possibilities of our realities. Our personal magic becomes manifest in our inner values and beliefs and executed in our choices – the outcome of which becomes our reality. Even being able to have a choice and seeing the manifestation of that choice is Magic itself. Get that, my dear fellows."

The whole cellar was fogged up with cigar smoke.

With Uncle Antikweetee's powerful words, Luck and Chance were overcome with wonderment. Magic, that was a new philosophy – a new theology.

Uncle Antikweetee maintained the focus of his exposition. "Through meditation and training, we bring our deepest desires into consciousness. Over time, we realize that we bear full responsibility for everything we have created in our lives. The world we live in right now reflects the cumulative effect and outcome of all human desires over the millennia."

"How do we find Magic?" Chance inquired.

Uncle Antikweetee raised his brows and stared directly at Chance. "You want to find Magic? Magic is not something you find. Rather, you connect with it, because it is all around you. It is a phenomenon you tap into through your very self. If only you open your eyes and look for the signs!"

*   *   *

Then, Uncle Antikweetee swirled his swivel chair toward his metal safe, bent down slowly, and carefully turned the knob of the safe. He took out an ancient wooden box. "This is Magellan's spherical compass." He gestured toward Chance. "This Magic Compass helped Magellan cross the world's most treacherous seas. It helped him navigate through what is now known as the Straits of Magellan in South America. He was a great man because he was willing to take chances – to prove a point. And, oh, did he try."

Uncle Antikeetee reached out for Chance's hand.

"Hold this compass." Uncle Antikweetee handed Chance Magellan's Magic Compass. Gently, Uncle Antikweetee cupped his hands over Chance's hands and gave this benediction.

"From now on, Chance, you are the proud owner of this

Magic Compass – by the power of *your* parents, Vetruvian Mann and Luz Blundermore." Uncle Antikweetee proceeded to intone the Magical Canticle of Vetruvian and Luz. "It is yours. For the Magic Compass to work, you must be earnest and true to yourself and your passion. As long as you are alive, this compass will be linked to you and your soul. And yours alone. It will only work if your heart is pure, noble and virtuous. Your quest must be for a higher purpose *greater* than yourself. Foremost, you must embody: INTEGRITY, for this Magic Compass to work." Uncle Antikweetee completed the Canticle for the Magic of Vetruvian and Luz.

"This Magic Compass always points to the True North and can work wonders. Keep it close by, especially in times of peril. When you come to a fork in life, consult your Magic Compass. It will help you make the right choice." Uncle Antikweetee handed the Magic Compass to Chance.

"You see, this spherical compass has four pointers – pointing to the North, the South, the East and the West, by whichever way. This *red* pointer always points to the True North. This compass will guide you to your True North – your Polaris. This Magic Compass knows your heart's deepest wishes. It will direct and guide you. Tell the compass exactly *what* you seek. Your dreams. You must be clear. In effect, you're dialing up the Universe for guidance. This compass will *speak* to you. As you get closer to your target, it will glow red – like the red nose of Rudolph the Reindeer. When you are nearest to your designated target, the whole needle will be *blinking* bright red. As you drift farther away from your target, the lower pointer will glow emerald green. The farther you are from your designated target, the fainter the green." Uncle Antikweetee instructed Chance about the magic powers of the compass. "For this compass to work its Magic, you *must* have Integrity. Without Integrity, nothing works. Remember that." Uncle Antikweetee gave Chance the longest stare. Then, with a gentle voice, he coaxed Chance to take a closer look of the Magic Compass. "Interestingly, inside the sphere, you will notice a suspended, floating *square mirrored cube* from which the four pointers jut out. This mirrored cube reflects images around you. It can reflect light. It can reflect darkness. It is a reflector that can help you win great battles. This is a mirror cube that *sees*. This mirror will *save* your life. You need to learn to read your Magic Compass. It will not work for others."

*   *   *

"Now, you." Uncle Antikweetee pointed at Luck. He swirled his seat toward his safe and took out a tubular bamboo encasement, which measured around eighteen inches long.

Carefully, he fished out an aged parchment scroll from the tubular encasement. "This is the world map used by the famous Captain James Cook, the Admiral who sailed the Seven Seas." Slowly Uncle Antikweetee unrolled the parchment scroll. "This is a Magic Map."

Luck and Chance stared at the Magic Map.

"This Magic Map has changed the world, especially in the Pacific and in Australasia." Uncle Antikweetee laid and spread out the Magic Map on his table. "This Magic Map gives answers to your questions through RIDDLES. You have to decipher the riddle correctly. Then, you have to make the right choices. It requires brains and actions to solve problems at hand. Right actions are key. This Magic Map will help you."

"Look here," Uncle Antikweetee continued. "There are numerous pictographic icons displayed around the peripheral border of this Magic Map. See this Heart? Through riddles, it will provide you with answers to your *true* feelings and emotions. See this Brain? It will help you brain-storm through issues. See this Stomach and Guts? It will make you feel and check your guts, whether a decision taken is right or wrong. See this Nose? It will help you sniff out a situation. Does it stink? If so, there must be a *rat* somewhere. Just press the icon, write out your question or issue, and it will lead you toward the right direction through riddles."

Luck dared not chuckle or smirk, much less to laugh, lest he offend Uncle Antikweetee. He found the Magic Map most amusing.

Uncle Antikweetee reached out for Luck's hand.

"Place your hands on this Magic Map." Uncle Antikweetee instructed Luck. Once again, he intoned the Magical Canticle of Vetruvian and Luz, finishing with these words:

"For this Magic Map to work, you must embody: COURAGE. Though this Magic Map answers *your* questions though Riddles, if and when interpreted correctly, it will be your answer sheet to life's many issues. Ask your questions carefully. Ask the right questions. You'll get great answers. All you have to do is write your question here in the center of the Magic Map with your finger, and the Riddle will appear. This Magic Map will not work for others. This Magic Map will work wonders. Keep it close by, especially in times of peril.

"This Magic Map will give you the best way to go from Point A to Point B." Uncle Antikweetee advised Luck. He rolled the Magic Map and slipped it back into its tubular bamboo encasement.

"Luck, this is for you." He handed the tubular bamboo encasement containing the Magic Map to Luck. "This Magic Map will give you tremendous powers over your opponents and enemies."

*   *   *

"Whoa! This is not all." Uncle Antikweetee once again swirled his chair toward the safe. He bent over and took out a rectangular box and a leather pouch.

He opened the box. Inside was a red crimson head band.

"Luck, through this Head Band of Heightened Perceptions, you can read into the minds of other people. You read their actual thoughts and their plan of action." Uncle Antikweetee whispered. "This Head Band is made especially for you, Luck. Your parents left these for you."

Softly, he whispered: "Give me your hand, Luck." He intoned the Magical Canticle of Vetruvian and Luz, finishing with these words: "For this Head Band of Heightened Perceptions to work, you must embody: UNDERSTANDING."

Luck solemnly put the Head Band around his head. He put them on, looked at his uncle, and could read Uncle Antikweetee's thoughts. *"I understand the hardships you have gone through. I'm proud of your diligence. You will go far. Very far. All the very best!"*

It was an ethereal message which Luck felt deep within his soul. Luck embraced Uncle Antikweetee tightly. "Thank you, Uncle. I love you."

*   *   *

Uncle Antikweetee opened a leather pouch. Inside was pair of

101

transparent acetate dice: one with red pips and the other in black pips.

"Chance, these Oracular Dice of Life will help you deal with your life options. The dice with the red pips is called '*Yes*'. The dice with black pips is called '*No*'. At critical moments in your life, these dice can help you in your decisions. Just shake the pouch gently, like so, to the East and to the West, to the North and to the South – all the while concentrating on the question at hand. Then put your hand into the pouch and see whether you get a '*Yes*' or a '*No*'. It is all very binary. Through your choices, you write your own Mini-Myth. In the final analysis, each of us is the *author* of our own life and myth. Now, be a master author of your own Mini-Myth." Uncle Antikweetee whispered. "Chance, these Oracular Dice of Life are made especially for you. Your parents left these for you."

Uncle Antikweetee gave the Oracular Dice to Chance.

Chance held and gazed intently at the Oracular Dice of Life. "Chance, these Oracular Dice of Life are yours. Give me your hand." One last time, Uncle Antikweetee intoned the Magical Canticle of Vetruvian and Luz, finishing with these words: "Foremost, for the Oracular Dice of Life to work, you must embody: HOPE."

After the incantation, Chance placed the dice in the pouch and started shaking it. He closed his eyes, concentrating on his first question. Aloud, he asked: Will I be successful at ISBS? He prayed, as he continued to shake the pouch. *Oh, please, I want to be successful!*

Slowly, he put his fingers into the pouch and pulled out a dice: it had the red pips. *Yes!*

There was a wild cheer amongst the three. "This is wild, Uncle! Thank you so much! I love you, too." Gently, Chance hugged Uncle Antikweetee.

"All these are given to each of you by your parents. Use them well. The world will be better because of the two of you. Each of you must live out your true destiny. Each of you must be responsible for creating and writing out your own Mini-Myth: *how* will you live your life; how will you *make* your mark; how do you want to be *remembered*? Let the Magic of your character unfold your destiny!"

*   *   *

Finally, Uncle Antikweetee gave each of the twins a huge rectangular leather attaché. "These are made out of genuine Italian leather." He grinned, as he bit into the leather handle, to prove that it was real leather. "I got these in Milan. Just for the two of you."

Luck's huge square attaché had this monogram: WOBM, which stood for Winston Odysseus Blundermore Mann, his legal name.

Chance's huge rectangular attaché had this monogram: BPBM, which stood for Brandon Perseus Blundermore Mann, his legal name.

The brothers gathered their gifts and happily put them away into their respective brand new leather attachés.

"For your sakes, make sure to keep these gifts close by or at a secure place. Don't ever hand these to strangers. Yours will be the greater loss!" Uncle Antikweetee gave the twins a parting wink. "Be great! Make me proud. Make our family proud! Oh, send my best regards to Uncle Blundermore when you see him!

Will you? He misses your mother. He has been good to you two all these years! *Believe* in Magic! As you believed in the Magic of Physics, believe in the Magic of Belief. And Magic will happen to you! Magic is everywhere – if you only look and perceive. Get an excellent education at ISBS! Come back as *wizards* – nothing less!"

*   *   *

Clip clop! Clip clop! Clip clop!

Luck and Chance heard the cadence of horses outside the streets.

"I guess it's time for you two to roll. Remember, you have the whole future ahead of you. Hitch your aspirations toward a purpose *greater* than yourselves. Courage, young men! Courage! Have a great journey!" With that, Uncle Antikweetee kissed the pair on the forehead and blessed them.

*   *   *

CHAPTER 15

AN UPDATE

FROM

NANNY CLAIRE BONSENS

MUSIC INSPIRATION

HOW CAN I NOT LOVE YOU
ANNA AND THE KING
JOY ENRIQUEZ

DANZA KUDURO
(DANCE TO KUDURO)
(SPANISH & PORTUGUESE)
DON OMAR

TELEPHONE
LADY GAGA & BEYONCÉ

MALAGUEÑA
(CLASSICAL GUITAR)
ERNESTO LECUONA
GUITARIST: MICHAEL LUCARELLI

* * *

Could Circumstance define the person?   Or could the person define the Moment?

How would this interplay of Circumstance and the Moment work in the lives of Luck and Chance?

Luck and Chance would permeate our lives.   We might think we already know them.

Really?

How much of this knowledge was based on circumstantial evidence, or a fleeting intuition, or a momentary burst of Wisdom?

*   *   *

Early that afternoon, as Nanny Claire Bonsens went about her afternoon errands, she stopped by Shangri-La Hotel, a luxurious five-star hotel at Makati of Greater Manila, to make a discrete phone call to Wawa.

Furtively looking behind her to make sure no one was trailing her, she entered one of the hotel's fancy phone booths. She placed a phone call through to Director Wawa, once her comrade-in-arms at Misericordia de Dios Orphanage. She did not want to use her personal smartphone lest this call be traceable.

*   *   *

Some seventeen years back when she was twenty-one, like Wawa, Claire worked at Misericordia Orphanage as a nurse intern.

Claire was also an alumnus of the Columbia University School of Nursing in New York City – a common affiliation binding the two in deep friendship. For a few months, she also took care of the newborn twin brothers. Then Claire was hired away by Maria Clara Prisma to be nanny to her newborn twins: Enigma and Choice.

Nanny Claire was from Chinon of central France. She spoke beautiful French of the Loire region. For this reason, Maria Clara chose Claire to be the nanny to her twin girls. She wanted her twin daughers to speak fluent French.

Wawa and Claire frequently met to catch up with each

other's lives. Today, the world of Wawa and Claire was turned upside because of Luck and Chance.

*　　　*　　　*

Wawa picked up the call. Claire could not be more eager upon recognizing her voice. "Luck and Chance – "

"I know – I met them today." Wawa could not help herself, their voices crisscrossing.

"Oh, Gul got homicidal! *Oh, c'etait tres terrible!* It was horrible! Gul went crazy last night! She had the twins chained against the dungeon wall – outstretched like Leonardo da Vinci's Vetruvian Man!"

"*Dos equis* the two were!" Wawa sounded distraught.

"She tried to kill the twins early this morning!" Claire recounted all that had transpired.

"How come? Why now?" Wawa could not understand.

"Gul had an epileptic seizure this morning. In her delirium, she kept calling the names of Luck and Chance and blabbing nonsense!"

"Then what happened?"

"I jabbed her with the largest syringe and gave her a heavy dose of tranquilizer to knock her out. Gul will be sleeping for the whole day." Claire could not stop smiling at her own heroic.

There was so much to say, so much to catch up with, so much happening – all at once.

"Today, the twins have been traumatized." Wawa reported. "They showed me their heinous brandings! Terrifying!"

"Definitely!" Claire cuddled her phone, trying to muffle her own voice by covering the mouthpiece with her other hand. "Gul's been acting up for the past few days... ever since she got a list of new ISBS entrants for this coming school year. This morning, on her bed was the list of new entrants to ISBS. She punched holes through the names of Luck and Chance with her mail opener. Ominous! Gul's fury is *not* over yet."

"Oh my..." Wawa was at a loss of words.

"What should I do?" Claire sounded anxious. "When Gul awakes, she'll ask about the whereabouts of the brothers. What should I say? I'm a dead duck!" Claire shuddered at this thought.

"Escape!" That was the first thought that came to Wawa. "Leave! You are in danger!"

"Where can I go?" Claire suddenly realized how precarious her own predicament was.

"Come to the orphanage. I'll get you a job here! Now, run!"

"I'll get my essentials. I'll be right there!" Claire hung up the phone and made a mad dash for her own escape from Gul. Dashing out of the hotel, Claire hailed a taxi for Gul's residence. "*La Casa sin Numero.* Forbes Park." She directed the taxi cab driver who nodded politely. Everyone knew how to go to *La Casa sin Numero* – even without instructions.

A heaviness of heart gripped Claire. *I'll be paying a very high price for this. I'll miss Enigma and Choice. I've raised these two girls for these seventeen years. Now, just because of Luck and Chance, I'm losing my Enigma and Choice! This is so sudden! The choices of Life are so cruel!*

In effect, Claire was leaving everything behind: seventeen

years at Gul's and plus the twin girls she raised and held so dearly in her heart. With this thought, a deep sadness descended upon her.

*   *   *

Upon arriving at *La Casa sin Numero,* Claire ordered the taxi cab driver to wait by the driveway. "I'll be right back!"

The two German shepherds in the garden barked. Claire motioned them to stay quiet which they did.

Claire entered from the backdoor. The whole house was quiet. *Gul must still be sleeping.*

She tipped toed toward her room, and hurriedly packed her meager belongings into two suitcases and dashed back out to the waiting taxi cab.

*   *   *

This was a brief note Claire left for Maria Clara.

GOOD-BYE!

Doña Prisma,

I'm leaving for France on a family emergency.

I don't know when I will be back again – if ever.

You need to know this: You are the craziest woman I've ever met. You are cruel, sick and hopeless!

Regarding my last paycheck, you can shove it up your wazoo!

Adieux!

Claire

*   *   *

CHAPTER 16

SUMMONING THE CARDINAL

<u>MUSIC INSPIRATION</u>

THIS BOY
THE BEATLES

CAN'T BUY ME LOVE
THE BEATLES

LIVING ON A PRAYER
BON JOVI

I DON'T WANT TO MISS A THING
AEROSMITH

I WANT TO KNOW WHAT LOVE IS
FOREIGNER

LA CHANSON DES VIEVUX AMANTS
(THE SONG OF OLD LOVERS)
(FRENCH)
JACQUES BREL

LE TEMPS DES CATHEDRALES
(THE AGE OF THE CATHEDRALS)
(FRENCH & ENGLISH)
NOTRE DAME DE PARIS
LUC PLAMONDON & RICHARD COCCIANTE
SINGER: BRUNO PELLETIERS

*   *   *

*T*he glory of the One who moves all things,
  Permeates the universe and glows,
  In one part more and in the other less.

The Divine Comedy, Paradiso, Canto I, Dante Alighieri

*   *   *

Where are the gods when human souls reach out to embrace the other in the spirit of Love?

Love seems to have its own force, its own logic, its own volition. It is a miracle beyond wisdom, a miracle beyond being. It is an enlightenment of the consciousness and of the soul. Love is a state of being fully alive: a state of being fully human. Love conquers all.

*   *   *

Late that afternoon, Director Wawa returned to her office to delve into the files of Luck and Chance. That day was a whirlwind. She never imagined that she would see the twins face to face, after all these years.

After reviewing their files, fingers half trembling with excitement, she phoned Cardinal Augustin Legazpi's rectory, which was situated beside the Manila Cathedral.

*   *   *

Years back, young Augustin Legazpi was trained as a Jesuit priest at the Ateneo de Manila Seminary.

The Society of Jesuits was founded by St. Ignatius of Loyola, who was once a knight in the Basque Country of Spain. On May 20, 1521, during a battle with the French in Pamplona, Spain, a cannon ball landed between his two legs, seriously wounding him.

During his recovery, he read *De Vita Christi* by Ludolph of Saxony. As a result, he was fired up to lead a self-denying life for Christ, emulating the heroic life of St. Francis of Assisi. At this time, he learned a method of prayer called Simple Contemplation, which was eventually incorporated into his Spiritual Exercises.

112

Later, St. Ignatius of Loyola founded the Society of Jesus. Its priests, the Jesuits, had a knack of living in this world while *not* being part of it. They excelled in profound spirituality and in community service. Over time, they played an important role in evangelization, by building renowned universities throughout the world. They had the reputation of being the crack troops for Christ.

From a cannon ball landing between his legs to his founding of a religious order. What a miracle of God! What Divine Magic!

Fate landed a cannon ball between St. Ignatius's legs. Luck made him recover in the hospital. Choice made him dedicate himself to the Lord. Destiny made him create the Society of Jesus. That was the generosity of the Lord!

That was *agape!*

*   *   *

Sincere in his love for God and his wanting people to love Him, Augustin Legazpi joined the priesthood. As a Jesuit, he led a life singularly devoted to serving God and humanity. He radiated a spirituality that was neither holier-than-thou nor condemning. He developed a compassion and grace in his way of life. Priesthood was his commitment and obligation to God, a way to reach, discover, add dimensions and experiences in serving Jesus Christ – and most of all, to cleanse his karma.

Ever searching for the perfect Jesuit *magis*, he strove for the quintessential interior attitude reflecting the "ever more and more giving spirit" of St. Ignatius. *Ad Majorem Dei Gloriam!* For the Greater Glory of God! That was the Jesuit motto he lived by, to achieve "the more universal good" with creative fidelity in serving God. His mantra was: talk less; do more. He realized that for all decisions made, no matter how personal or private they might appear at first glimpse, they have implications for the wider community – now and for time to come. Yes, he wanted to achieve the *perfect* Jesuit *magis. Ad majorem Dei Gloriam!*

At sixty and strikingly handsome, Augustin Legazpi was recently promoted to Cardinal of Manila – the Primate of the Philippines. This was an office of Mystery and Magic: a pastoral office that could offer Hope to the hopeless. With zest and dedication, as the servant and comforter of hurting people, he advanced the healing mission of the Church in this archipelago nation. Cardinal Legazpi understood the world, having mastered spiritual politics and political spirituality. He embraced the squalor and sorrows of the poor. In his own way, he changed the world for good – alleviating poverty amongst the indigent and providing solace for the suffering. Most of all, he had worked hard to banish the poverty of the heart.

While he was from the Legazpi family, one of the richest oligarchies of the Philippines, he chose the life of a clergy. The Legazpi family was linked to the earlier Miguel Lopez de Legazpi, the famous Spanish *conquistador* who founded Manila.

*   *   *

"The Cardinal's rectory." The operator picked up the call.

"His Most Reverend, please. It's urgent." Wawa was surprised by her own choice of words. "This is Director Wawa Esperanza of the Misericordia de Dios Orphanage."

"Please hold." A calm gentle voice of a young man came through the line.

Moments passed.

At last, the warm voice of Cardinal Legazpi registered over the phone. "Hello there! Wawa de Barcelona!"

"You won't believe this." Wawa could barely restrain herself. "Luck and Chance visited the orphanage today! They've returned."

"They have?" The Cardinal's ears perked up. "Now, that's news to me. How are they?"

"They're lovely boys. Just turned seventeen. The good news: they've just *graduated* from Ateneo de Manila High School. They will be attending the International School for Braniacs Squared — ISBS — in *New Joy Sea.*"

"That's fabulous!" Cardinal Legazpi was enthralled. He was pleased the boys would be going ISBS. "This is a school famous for producing Adepts, Brainiac Knights and Magi."

"The kids will be in good hands." Wawa felt elated. "You know that Blundermore is the President of ISBS."

"Of course, I know." Cardinal marveled at the turn of events. "I've met Blundermore several times — every time he visited the Philippines."

"Are you alone?" Wawa dropped her voice a notch lower, just to make sure no one would overhear her and to make sure no one was spying on the Cardinal on the other end of the line.

"Yes, I'm alone. Why?"

*   *   *

Before her call, the Cardinal was just reading and meditating on *Paradiso*, Dante Alighieri's final book compendium. Written between 1318 and 1321, Dante's *Paradiso* was the last of three books of *The Divine Comedy*. Herein, Augustin meditated on the four cardinal virtues of Prudence, Fortitude, Temperance and Justice. He contemplated on the three theological virtues of Faith, Hope and Love. His mind concentrated on the impact of human action and its consequences in this life and the afterlife. As he focused on Beatrice, Dante's spiritual companion and guide to Heaven, the Cardinal's mind meandered to the woman he once loved.

*   *   *

There was sadness in Wawa's voice. "Bad news. Gul Diabolica was up to her antics again. Last night, she kidnapped, tortured and branded the twins – on the chest! *Muy horrible!*"

"Oh, no!" The Cardinal could not believe his ears. Over the years, he had come to love the twins. "But she should *not* harm the boys!"

Bewilderment and despair fell upon the Cardinal. *She promised she would do no harm to the twins... That was the deal.*

"She almost *killed* the twins..." Wawa whispered.

Consternation and panic jolted Legazpi, as if a dark sword pierced his heart. "The boys are *off limits!* Gul surely *crossed* the line! She is not playing fair! This is totally unfair to the boys!"

Anguish filled his soul. *Oh, God! Where are You?*

Then, pure horror seized him. "The *Illuminati!* This is their *modus operandi!* Gul is an *Illuminati!*" This much, he knew about her.

"The *Illuminati?*" Wawa could not follow.

"Yes. The *Illuminati* is a nefarious, subversive and

conspiratorial group. Its goal is to rule the world. It was founded in Bavaria, Germany, in 1776 by Adam Weishaupt. Very anti-Church and anti-monarchy. So, in 1785, Charles Theodore, the Elector of Bavaria suppressed and wiped out the secret society. So, its members infiltrated in German Masonic Lodges. And also the Scottish Masonic Lodges. Subsequently, the *Illuminati* crossed over to America through the Freemasons. Now, they are worldwide. Operating in the shadows."

"But why Luck and Chance?" Wawa could not understand.

"Because, she viewed them as her *personal* enemies. She has displaced her own Great Disappointment upon the twins." The Cardinal shuddered, knocking Dante's *Paradiso* off his desk and onto the floor. Bang! "She wanted them dead! So first, she branded them! Do you understand? Then, the kill!"

"Shh... Nanny Claire Bonsens rescued them." Wawa wanted to comfort Augustin. "She is the nanny of Enigma and Choice. Claire works at Gul's." By now, Wawa was hyperventilating. "My God! These boys are so lucky to be alive!"

Augustin gave out a sigh of relief. *True, it can be much worse.* "Wow...Gul...a victim of a nasty forlorn love. Ah, the pains and consequences of forlorn love!" For a while, the Cardinal was speechless. Groping for words, he whimpered. "How life has wrought so much suffering to people's souls. Gul *cannot* forgive. She *cannot* love. She is stuck. Vengeance *wreaks* her heart. All for what? Gul has no life. Just suffering. She's gripped by unrelenting pathos. All her beauty and wealth cannot buy her happiness – cannot buy her love. That's her tragedy."

"Gul recently found out that the twins were going to ISBS. This drove her crazy! Can you believe that?"

117

"Some heartbreak don't heal, ever. They fester, metastasize like cancer and devour the whole body and soul of a person. Now, she's gone crazy. I'm afraid this is what happened to Gul."

A past heartache stirred within Cardinal Lagazpi – a sorrow that never left him no matter how hard he tried to get rid of it.

Wawa continued with her reporting. "Augustin, this morning, the boys came here to inquire about their Missing Mama and their Phantom Daddy. They wanted to know why they were placed in the orphanage for five years."

"What did you tell them?" Cardinal Legazpi was incredulous with this sudden turn of events – all in a day's events.

"Nothing… Just the word: LOVE." Wawa hesitated.

"Ugh!" The Cardinal did not say much.

"This was all I could muster. It's so inadequate!" Wawa protested gently. "I didn't know where to start with them."

"Some things are better left unsaid." The Cardinal assured her. "They are too young to understand."

"Love… That changed my life." Augustin had been through that road. "Once, I was in love. Deeply in love. With a most beautiful lass. The rose of my heart! Years after graduating from ISBS, I proposed to marry her. In the end, my love for this woman almost destroyed me."

Waves of pain swept through Cardinal Augustin Legazpi. *Ah, Love! Why is Love strewn with thorns? What do I know about Love?*

Wawa was taken aback by this confession from the Cardinal.

"Her parents disapproved of me." There was sadness in his voice.

"But why?" Wawa was bewildered. Confused. "I can see a real promising young man in you. After all, you have the looks and the brains. You are from a distinguished family."

"You must be kidding. That's the paradox! I have the wrong family name. This was my sin. I was born into a wrong family." Augustin's lineage did not prevent him from suffering the turmoil of the heart.

"But you are a *Legazpi*! The *most* prominent family in the Philippines!" Wawa protested.

"Precisely! Our two families were and remain up to this day the most implacable rivals in business and in politics. Each of our parents disapproved – vehemently." Augustin sounded exasperated. "My life was mired with paradox and contradiction. That's how I decided to be a priest. To escape it all! Ah, CRAZY LOVE!" He sighed, as he recalled episodes of his own bad romance.

"Ugh! Thank you for sharing." Wawa felt privileged for his confidential commiseration. She did not realize that Augustin was once smitten.

"Twists and turns... That's the Mystery of Life. All happy persons are alike. They are happy because they believe in the possibility of happiness. It's really an attitude, which makes or breaks a person. We are created for happiness because it is within each of us. All unhappy persons are unhappy in their own ways. For some, unhappiness comes from lack – from the poverty of the soul. For others, it comes from superfluity. The most painful cause of unhappiness is Circumstance. How we are trapped by Circumstance! How Life treats each of us so differently!" Augustin sighed, groping for the right words. "Even I am *not* spared! Oh, God help me!"

There was an awkward pause. The thought of Gul pained him. *From Maria Clara to Gul! What a fall!* Now he saw the foibles of Gul's life turning into a dastardly disaster.

"The boys will be heading to America any day now – possibly sooner." Wawa honed in on the reason why she called Cardinal Legazpi. "You need to administer the sacrament of Confirmation to them."

"When?" His voice lightened up. He was eager to be together with the brothers. He had not seen them for some time.

"Tomorrow, at noon."

"Tomorrow it shall be."

As he hung up the phone, the Cardinal could only shake his head at the thought of Gul, Vetruvian, Luz, and the twin boys. *All bets are off! This time, Gul has gone too far. How can she! She will have to pay the price! The truce is off! She has gone too far. The Devil has returned to sow turmoil.*

*   *   *

CHAPTER 17

CONFIRMATION

MUSIC INSPIRATION

ORA
(PRAY)
(PIANO)
LUDOVICO EINAUDI

BRING HIM HOME
LES MISÉRABLES
CLAUDE-MICHEL
ALAIN BOUBLIL & HERBERT KRETZMER
SINGER: COLM WILKINSON

VENI CREATOR SPIRITUS
GREGORIAN CHANT – HYMN H-VIII
(COME, HOLY SPIRIT)
(LATIN)
RABANUS MAURUS
SCHOLA GREGORIANA MEDIOLANENSIS
CONDUCTOR: GIOVANNI VIANINI

SANCTUS
REQUIEM MASS IN D MINOR, K 626
(HOLY)
(LATIN)
WOLFGANG AMADEUS MOZART

ARABIC ORTHODOX CHANT
(ARABIC)

RUSSIAN ORTHODOX ANGELIC SONG
(RUSSIAN)

AGNUS DEI
REQUIEM MASS IN D MINOR, K 626
(LAMB OF GOD)
(LATIN)
WOLFGANG AMADEUS MOZART

CANON IN D MAJOR
PACHELBEL

PANIS ANGELICUS
(THE BREAD OF ANGELS)
(LATIN)
CÉSAR FRANCK
ARRANGED BY: JULIAN SMITH
SINGER: CHARLOTTE CHURCH

AVE MARIA
(HAIL MARY)
(LATIN)
DI FRANZ SCHUBERT
SINGER: LUCIANO PAVAROTTI

MARCH OF THE TEMPLARS
(LATIN)
GEORGE ALLEN

JERUSALEM
WILLIAM BLAKE / HUBERT PARRY
KING'S COLLEGE CHOIR, CAMBRIDGE

*   *   *

Where is God when human souls reach out to embrace their destiny? Destiny seems to have its own force, its own logic, its own volition – intertwined with the hearts of men.

What role would Fate play in this tale of Luck and Chance? Ah, Fate, you're so beguiling and unfathomable. Show me your hand.

What role would thought, planning and actions play in this Game of Life? How would this Game of Life unfold?

*   *   *

Before setting out for their journey, Luck and Chance would have an appointment to receive a divine commission. Through the sacrament of Confirmation, the brothers would be touched and marked by the Divine.

*   *   *

At high noon, *Sanctus* filled the air at the chapel of Misericordia de Dios Orphanage as Cardinal Augustin Legazpi celebrated High Mass. Wawa beamed heartily to no end. Beside her was Nanny Claire Bonsens.

Today was the brothers' day of Confirmation, a Catholic sacramental rite, making them soldiers of God and full members of the Church while granting them the outpouring of the Holy Spirit along with His gifts. This was a rite which would make their union with the Church more perfect, bestowing sanctifying grace and strengthening the union between individual souls and God. The youngsters were fortunate enough to have this rite administered for them by the ebullient and famous Cardinal Legazpi, the Cardinal of Manila, one of the highest Catholic persons in the Philippines.

*   *   *

A dashingly handsome Filipino-Spanish *mestizo*, Cardinal Legazpi had remained fit and displayed a sophisticated demeanor, which made him very popular with his Manila archdiocese and with Rome.

Today, he wore a pair of rimless spectacles revealing a set of beaming eyes, so full of vitality and humor. Solemn and dignified, Augustin donned his Cardinal's regalia for the High Mass. The Mass was the central act of worship in the Roman Catholic Church, viewed as the source and summit of the Christian life.

In the silence of his preparatory prayers, he beseeched the Lord to spare Luck and Chance from any further harm from Gul and to keep them safe from Evil.

Augustin led the orphanage chapel congregation in the recitation of the Nicene Creed. Then, there was the renewal of the baptismal promise for the deepening of grace.

Cardinal Legazpi blessed the twins. This sacrament of Confirmation would make the twins soldiers of the Light, fighters of Truth and protectors of what is good in humanity. "My child, what name do you choose?" Cardinal Legazpi asked Luck.

Luck pondered for a moment. He could feel the love of God showered upon him over the years up to this moment. Amidst the poverty of the spirit, God's love somehow came through and sustained him. God had come through in Luck's winter of hurts with magical solutions. Luck was thankful for the many opportunities God had provided him. Faith had saved Luck. Faith had given Luck courage. Faith in God's eternal mercy had blessed Luck with consolation.

"Fidel." Luck whispered, his heart burning with the fire of the Holy Spirit.

In turn, Cardinal Legazpi asked Chance. "My child, what name do you choose?"

Chance recalled the many trials he had endured, especially over these past years, how he had called upon God for succor and guidance amidst confusions and setbacks. When neither relatives nor friends offered comfort and love, he felt God's love in events and serendipities. In his moment of desolation and despair, He sent down angels in the most unique of circumstances. In his darkest moments, God made good His promise with His Love. For this, he was grateful.

"Amadeus." Chance murmured, his eyes turning red, his heart moved to the core. "FOR THE LOVE OF GOD!"

"My child, do you reject Satan and his legions and their evil deeds?" Cardinal Legazpi asked each of the twins.

"Yes, Father." The twins nodded in the affirmative.

"Will you, Luck and Chance, be God's staunchest soldiers for the Good of Humanity?"

"Yes, Father." They both affirmed

Cardinal Legazpi blessed the pair, anointing them with holy oil on their foreheads and palms. He thereupon laid his hands upon Luck, intoning:

"My child, by the ministry bestowed to me by the Church, and in the name of the Father, and of the Son and of the Holy Spirit, I confirm, you, Luck, as the soldier of Christ. O Holy Spirit, come upon Luck and bestow upon him Your special gifts and powers so that he will spread and defend the Faith by word and action as a true witness of Christ, to confess the name of Jesus Christ boldly and never to shy away from the Cross. Receive the Spirit of Wisdom and Understanding, the Spirit of right Judgment and Courage, the Spirit of Knowledge, the Spirit of holy Fear in God's Presence. Guard what you have received. God the Father has marked you with His sign; Christ the Lord has confirmed you and has placed His pledge in you, and the Holy Spirit has come to dwell in your heart."

Likewise, Cardinal Legazpi laid his hands upon Chance, intoning the same incantation.

*　　　*　　　*

For Catholics, in the sacrament of the Eucharist, the miracle of transubstantiation occurred, whereby Jesus Christ, body and blood, soul and divinity, was truly present in the host and in the wine – despite their appearing the same. At this moment, Cardinal Legazpi, bowing deeply, repeated the words of Jesus at the Last Supper, telling his disciples to do *this* in remembrance of

Him. "Take this, all of you, and eat of it: for this is My body which will be given up for you." He then consecrated the host.

Once again, he bowed, took the chalice and he said: "Take this, all of you, and drink from it: for this is the chalice of My blood, the blood of the new and eternal covenant, which will be poured out for you and for many for the forgiveness of sins. Do this in memory of Me." He then consecrated the wine. Through this Eucharist, Catholics receive the Divine Miracle of Jesus's real Presence.

During Communion, Pachelbel's *Canon in D* filled the air. This was followed by Shubert's *Ave Maria* in Latin.

As the High Mass ended, the chapel bell rang. The choir and congregation sang William Blake's *Jerusalem* amidst thundering organ music. Wawa, the nuns from the Franciscan convent and the attending nurses working at the orphanage, clapped with joy. *Gloria in excelsis Deo!*

Through this sacrament of Confirmation, Luck and Chance were embraced by the Magic of God.

*   *   *

CHAPTER 18

LUNCH WITH THE CARDINAL

MUSIC INSPIRATION

THE RICE FESTIVAL
ANNA AND THE KING
GEORGE FENTON & ROBERT KRAFT

(EVERYTHING I DO), I DO IT FOR YOU
BRYAN ADAMS

O MAGNUM MYSTERIUM
(O GREAT MYSTERY)
(LATIN)
MORTEN LAURIDSEN

DON'T STOP BELIEVING
JOURNEY

WHEN YOU BELIEVE
WHITNEY HOUSTON & MARIAH CARREY

*　　　*　　　*

To sin is to commit cosmic treason, to disrupt the natural flow of nature, to violate the universal law of Truth.

Sin causes many unspeakable consequences, disrupting one's karma and those of others.

*　　　*　　　*

After their Confirmation, the twins joined Cardinal Legazpi for a private lunch at the orphanage's VIP room. Just the three of them. Still with his scarlet *biretta* on, the Cardinal was now in his red-trimmed black cassock.

As they sat down, Cardinal Legazpi beamed proudly at Luck

and Chance. They were very special to him. Since they were born, he made it a point to visit them weekly on Saturdays at the orphanage. As toddlers, they had an ineffable impact on Augustin, then a priest. Through them, he felt God's mysterious hand engineering his transformation toward a deeper understanding of the spiritual dimensions of life, more precisely his own *karma*. *Look, these two abandoned twins heading for ISBS! How else can one explain God's mercy and grace!*

With warm compassion, he looked at the brothers. Today would be his last chance to have a real sit-down talk with them. He had a message for them.

"Are you a believer?" With a twinkle in his eyes, the Cardinal asked Luck.

The Cardinal briskly turned to Chance, directing the same question at him. "Are you a believer?"

"Believer in what?" Raising his querying brows, Chance did not know where the Cardinal was going with this question.

"Do you believe the *power* of thought and the spoken word – how these can alter reality?" The Cardinal spoke gently. "Thoughts and words can affect your lives – your reality."

"In the beginning was the Word, which was made flesh." The Cardinal turned serious. "The Word incarnate. The Word becoming reality. Love incarnate. God becoming human. That's the Magic of Incarnation! For every loving act, you incarnate and manifest the Love of God – our God of Supreme Miracles. Our God of Divine Magic!"

"What is a Miracle?" Cardinal smiled at the twins.

"Divine Magic!" Luck interjected.

The Cardinal chuckled, observing that Luck caught on fast.

"You see, my child, a Miracle is an event ascribed to God through His divine providence and not to human power or the laws of nature. When a Miracle occurs, it is as if the laws of nature are interrupted. Some attribute statistically unlikely outcomes as miracles, such as being the sole survivor in a horrific plane crash. Some coincidences are deemed as Miracles."

The brothers listened attentively, taking in his words. It was rare for youngsters to have a private audience with the Cardinal.

"You see, we are primarily spirit and secondarily flesh." The Cardinal paused, picking his words carefully. "Our souls live forever. We live in a world of spirits and of forces – with certain given sets of circumstances – each wishing to incarnate into this world and connect with each one of us. They have their agendas and vendettas."

Chance's eyes were brimming intensely. "Father, are you implying that we are avatars of the spirits and the forces in the universe? Are we spirits with bodies?"

"You are sharp." The Cardinal snapped back, deeply impressed by Chance's acumen.

Luck's mind was racing to keep up with the Cardinal's exposition. "They're here to play out the unfinished business of the forces out there."

Impressed, Augustin moved on. "Right on! The roots of Good and Evil in this world are supernatural. Various opposing spirits and forces are struggling to dominate each and every person. How each of us deals with the spirits and forces will determine our character, disposition and actions – ultimately, our destiny.

"Each of us is a battleground of different spirits and forces. Unwittingly, each of us is influenced by an amalgam of these, influencing the character of each soul. In turn, each person will influence the other. Then, one family will push to dominate another. Groups will influence other groups. One nation shall press upon the other... and so on. History is the end result. It all starts with the individual – you – followed by myriads of feedback loops through the many people you come across over a lifetime. This is the society we live in. This is the universal reality."

There was silence.

"Do you understand? These are the Mysteries of the ages and will continue to be. Our invisible God manifests our visible world. Conversely, our visible world informs us about the invisible world and our invisible God. So, what game do you want to play? Are you for the forces of Good or of Evil? For what is right or wrong? Are you for the forces of Light or of Darkness? Are you for God or for the Devil? How will you play the game?

"The battles between Good and Evil are about to intensify: within each of us, within our communities, within our world."

The Cardinal paused; then, he continued: "The days of reckoning will soon unfold. The man of sin shall appear in the Antichrist, leading mankind to perdition. I don't like what I see." His brow furrowed, he looked deeply disturbed.

"Why, Father?" Luck was taken by the deep sadness on Cardinal Legazpi's face.

"The struggle will be rough, treacherous, beguiling and nasty. There is an ongoing struggle between God and the Devil." The Cardinal replied hesitatingly, shaking his head. "That's why, I ask each of you: Are you a believer?"

The Cardinal looked intensely into the two youngsters' eyes. "A maelstrom is coming! I fear a lost generation ensuing from chronic turmoil, where people rise up against their nation, with nations pitted against nations, resulting in the gnashing of teeth for many." He sighed.

The pair looked uncomfortable.

"Today is your Day of Confirmation. Today, each of your spirits is marked by the Divine with an indelible mark for remarkable missions. As a believer, you'll be confronted with issues and struggles. Some will not be pleasant. No one is exempt. We are nomads in this secular world. We all have to rise to our occasions. God, help us! "

"Why is this important?" asked Chance.

"Because, the reckoning of this age is at hand. As a believer, you'll be better equipped. Then, you'll soar above the mundane, above the ordinary, beyond yourselves, beyond the Realm of Wisdom."

Not to cause undue concern, the Cardinal tried to sound more upbeat. "You'll do *great* things! Live a *hero's* life. Live with conviction." He urged.

"Are you a believer?" Cardinal Legazpi queried the two.

There was a pregnant silence.

"In what, Father?" Chance finally blurted out, still quite puzzled.

"In God and in Humanity." Through the people he had come across, the Cardinal had seen the face of God.

"What are we to do?" Luck asked.

"Love God and Humanity. Focus your minds on God. To love thy neighbor is to see the face of God. In time, you will be one with Him. Events will happen. Intentions will manifest. You will know what to do. There'll be surprises – lots of them. Expect the unexpected." The Cardinal affirmed.

A long silence.

"Remember this paradox: the more you give, the more you receive. Happiness is the giving of yourself to humanity for its greater good. Giving is difficult. But it is in giving that you encounter greatness. Giving is divine. Ironically, the more you pursue happiness, the more it escapes you. In serving humanity, happiness *comes* to you.

"Be faithful to your *true* passion. Then, you will be able to live out your *true* destiny. You will find *true* fulfillment, peace and joy. Be a force for Good. And history will be in good hands."

The Cardinal looked deeply into the eyes of the twins. "Salvation. It's all about the salvation of the world. First, save the world; then, you will save yourself."

The Cardinal paused, then, smiled. "Welcome to the timeless Mystery of Mysteries! Welcome to the joyful Miracle of Miracles. Believe in the God of Supreme Miracles. Welcome to this *Mysterium Magnum* – where the secret of ultimate reality is revealed. This will be the most incredible and breathtaking journey you both will be taking in your lives. Experience the Magic in your lives.

"Learn to recognize, read, decipher and follow the signs of your daily lives in this great journey: the Journey of Dreams. *Be the idea you want to be.* The signs – note and follow them, and your dreams will come true. With today's confirmation, you are each an Ambassador for the Light."

The Cardinal was practically whispering. "Most important, always believe in yourselves. Believe in the Magic within yourselves. Trust your guts and you will most likely do the right thing! It's most amazing: your body and your spirit instinctively know the Truth. Truly, you will manifest yourselves in your very personal Journey of Dreams." Then, in a loud voice, he concluded with a smile: "But first, you must be a believer! Believe in yourselves! Live fully and be the Word – in your body and in your soul – because the Truth is in you!"

With a mischievous wink of an eye, the Cardinal took out two velvet boxes. Inside each box was a multicolored seven by seven Rubik's Cube: a V-Cube 7.

Seven by seven Rubik's Cube: V-Cube 7

He gave one to Luck and one to Chance. "Master this V-Cube 7. It's going to be *very* daunting. But it can be done. And your lives will be easier!" Augustin laughed.

The pair broke into radiant smiles. "Awesome!" Luck exclaimed – wide-eyed. They had *not* seen a V-Cube 7 – ever.

"Each time you solve the V-Cube 7, it will play this tune." The Cardinal was scrambling his own V-Cube 7 and re-assembling it again. "There! Do you hear the tune?" The twins strained their ears and heard this tune:

Row, row, row your boat;

Row it down the stream.

Merrily, merrily, merrily,

Life is but a dream.

The twins were enthralled by the enchanting music.

Then, the Cardinal gently exhorted them, saying: "Watch, observe and learn! Get a fantastic education at ISBS! You both will be great and famous!" With that, the Cardinal gave them his final benediction. "Go, be the Soldiers of the Light. Present yourselves to God as instruments for righteousness. Make Jesus Christ the *centrality* of your daily lives within the Church. Be on the lookout for signs of Divine Magic. *Dominus vobiscum, nunc et in secula seculorum!*"

The Cardinal took out a business card and handed it to Chance. "When you arrive in America, visit with Professor Michael Paige. He is the Professor of Mysticism. He was my professor in Comparative World Religions at ISBS. Tell him I sent you. He will be delighted to meet you. He is a fascinating fellow. I learned much from him. He *changed* my life."

Chance looked at the business card. Very classy. The cream colored card had this logo printed on it: the symbol of INFINITY (∞), an eight, resting horizontally. Underneath the symbol were embossed the initials of ISBS.

Augustin stood up to take his leave. With tenderness, he

134

gently hugged each of the twins. "When will I see you again?" He was going to miss them. Fighting to steady his emotions, he looked at each of them in the eyes with this promise: "I will try my best to see you when I visit America."

*   *   *

Ah, Infinity! From Infinity, we come. To Infinity, we go. This is the cosmic journey we all partake. Quo vadis?

It is a far, far away destination we are headed for – beyond any realm we can fathom.

What cosmic forces are within us?

We all have the kernel of Infinity in us, as much as Luck and Chance have.

How will we evolve and transform? How will we play in this cosmic drama? What role will we each play? For good or evil?

What is true? What is false? How can we know the difference?

So often we have gone astray. Yet, each day, we struggle and fight to reach Infinity.

*   *   *

CHAPTER 19

THE ANGUISH OF THE CARDINAL

MUSIC INSPIRATION

ALWAYS
BON JOVI

YOU GIVE LOVE A BAD NAME
BON JOVI

HOW CAN YOU MEND A BROKEN HEART
BEE GEES

WHEN I WAS YOUR MAN
BRUNO MARS

HERE WITHOUT YOU
3 DOORS DOWN

SHE BELIEVES IN ME
KENNY ROGERS

FAITHFULLY
JOURNEY

NE ME QUITTE PAS
(DON'T LEAVE ME / IF YOU GO AWAY)
(FRENCH)
JACQUES BREL

LA MALADIE D'AMOUR
(THE MALADY OF LOVE)
(FRENCH)
MICHEL SARDOU

LET HER GO
PASSENGER

FIREWORKS
YAN HUO
烟火
(CHINESE MANDARIN)
MICHAEL WONG / 光良

QUIÉN DE LOS DOS SERÁ
(WHICH ONE FROM THE TWO OF US)
DIEGO VERDAGUER

HIGIT SA LAHAT TAO
(MOST OF ALL A PERSON)
(TAGALOG)
FREDDIE AGUILAR

PIE JESU
REQUIEM
(FAITHFUL JESUS)
(LATIN)
ANDREW LLOYD WEBER
SINGER: JACKIE EVANCHO

LARA'S THEME
DR. ZHIVAGO
MAURICE JARRE

*　　　*　　　*

Where does Compassion lead us? Does it liberate or entrap our very soul? We strive to do good – to do our very best. But at the end, we are confounded by its results. Because the results may not be what we expect.

*　　　*　　　*

Sick to his stomach Cardinal Legazpi barely ate his dinner. He had lost his appetite.

After dinner, he retired to his private study for quiet contemplation. Tonight, he would have the time to re-examine his old assumptions in his life as an ecclesiastic and as a man.

137

He was deeply troubled by Gul: why she would go to the extent of trying to *kill* the twins? Her attack on the twins was very much like an attack on him. It was personal – very personal.

Over the years, he had worked hard to cleanse his own karma by doing good deeds for others. He had vowed to God that he would try his best to have the twins well cared for at Misericordia de Dios Orphanage. He believed in his priesthood: to bring Hope to others who are dispossessed and hopeless or otherwise not cared for in human terms – for the greater glory of God. His was a mission of spreading Mercy – to unleash human compassion to the destitute. And now this. How could he rest?

Shortly after the twins were born, he had made a promise to Marcus Blundermore, his best friend while both were attending ISBS, that he would watch over his nephews at the orphanage. He thought of Luz, Blundermore's younger sister and felt sorry for her. She seemed *most* unlucky.

It looked like war had broken out between the two women: Gul and Luz. The sorrows of the Past had once again erupted. And he was here to bear witness. With a heavy heart, Cardinal Legazpi made this entry into his Mini-Myth Folio:

My Mini-Myth Folio

Cardinal Augustin Legazpi

June 20ᵗʰ. Dear Lord, help me understand. How did Maria Clara Prisma become Gul? Why have you given me such a cross to bear? Why would she inflict such cruelty upon Luck and Chance? Oh Lord, grant Your mercy upon her, grant her compassion and peace. Let her spare the twins.

Very soon, the twins will be leaving for America for their college education. Oh, Lord, be with them always as you have been with Vetruvian and Luz. Embrace their family in Your Love.

So I've reached out to Luz and the twins. Through them, You have granted me Wisdom for which I am most grateful.

Bless Luck and Chance in the years to come!

*   *   *

Later, Cardinal wrote an e-mail to Marcus Blundermore. He reported the latest sad developments involving the brothers, especially their near brush with death in the crazy hands of Gul.

*   *   *

Before retiring for the evening, he knelt in front of a miniature replica of Michelangelo's *Pietà* and meditated. "Oh, Jesus, let me partake in Your suffering! Purify my soul. Touch me with Your Mercy. Heal me with Your Love!" *Such is the Human Condition: his propensity to sin! Such is the Mercy of God: His propensity to forgive. We keep going forward, hoping that, in time, we shall overcome our frailties.*

"Oh, God! What makes a man? We are who we protect – to the least of our brethren." His lips moved in fervent prayer. "Oh, God! Where are you? How can I understand you? Do *not* forsake me! Deliver me from Evil."

*   *   *

CHAPTER 20

THE FINAL PREPARATION

SONG INSPIRATION

AS COLD AS ICE
FOREIGNER

ALL BY MYSELF
ERIC CARMEN

IT'S NOW OR NEVER
ELVIS PRESLEY

SUIT & TIE
JUSTIN TIMBERLAKE & JAY Z

NIGHT FEVER
BEE GEES

WORLD
BEE GEES

TONIGHT
WEST SIDE STORY
LEONARD BERNSTEIN & STEPHEN SONDHEIM
SINGER: GEORGE CHAKIRIS

SOMEWHERE
WEST SIDE STORY
LEONARD BERNSTEIN & STEPHEN SONDHEIM
SINGER: BARBARA STREISAND

*   *   *

The twins returned to Aunt Juliet's home late that evening.

"Any one home?" Luck hollered, as the brothers entered Aunt Juliet's bungalow house in Sta. Mesa District, Manila.

No response. No one was home.

A note from Aunt Juliet was taped to the refrigerator door: "Family at the carnival. Will be home after midnight."

*   *   *

For the past seven years, the twins endured the apathy of Aunt Juliet and Uncle Romeo. All these years, the twins got hand-me-down clothes from Nero Montago, the couple's only son.

Now eighteen, Nero's hair was prematurely gray, a stark contrast from his dark complexion. Rumor was: he was once struck by lightning as Mother Nature's curse on him. This was how he turned prematurely gray. His salt and pepper moustache looked like a thistle of misplaced armpit hair.

*   *   *

The twins' bedroom was a cramped storage room on the second floor of Aunt Juliet's house. With neither fan nor air conditioning, their room was suffocating. Its windows were often locked, seldom opened lest the mosquitos fly in. Over a hundred crates and boxes, big and small, old and new, filled the room. These boxes consisted of Nero's unwanted clothes and books, Uncle Romeo's merchandise, and Aunt Juliet's unused or unwanted household goods.

*   *   *

This evening, Luck felt a heavy yoke was about to be lifted. "After tonight, we don't have to suffer Nero's crazy antics."

141

Chance agreed. "I remember *that* time. Nero was about to lose a game of chess with you. He would suddenly point overhead and shout: 'Oh! There's a spider!' You would invariably turn around. He'd quickly steal a knight, a rook, or a bishop. Then, you'd lose the game. You *should* always keep your eyes on the chess board, dude."

Luck chuckled. "Now, he won't have anyone to play chess with."

Luck began to pack his stuff. "I remembered that night when Nero put *bricks* underneath your pillow. Later that night, as you crashed to sleep, POW!, you almost cracked your head."

Chance shook his head. "That was nasty. I thought I saw Uranus! Unfortunately, we have no one to complain to." He finalized his packing for the trip, placing Uncle Antiweetee's gifts neatly into his hand-carry black leather attaché.

For easier identification, Chance tied a yellow cord with his name tag by the attaché handle. "No more mean-hearted teasing from Nero. He used to say that we were picked up and brought home from the nearby garbage dumpster! He really wanted to dash our self-esteem. *'So where is your Missing Mama? So where is your Phantom Daddy?'* These taunts were uncalled for."

Luck finished Chance's sentence – imitating Nero's spoiled brat's voice. *"'No one wants both of you – hence, the orphanage!'* Absolutely disgusting!" After placing Uncle Antikweetee's gifts into his attaché, Luck tied a crimson red cord with his name tag by the handle. The twins tucked each of their V-Cubic 7's from Cardinal Legazpi into their suit pockets.

The brothers placed each of their two suitcases by the bedroom doorway.

They hung each of their rumpled hand-me-down suits from Nero on the two chairs in the room. With cheerfulness of heart, they laid out their white socks, shirts and pants on top of some low lying boxes in the storage room. They placed their new rubber shoes by the bedroom door.

*   *   *

Midnight came and went. No one returned. Aunt Juliet, Uncle Romeo and Nero were still out at the carnival. The twins were getting sleepy. They could not wait any longer. At 1:00 A.M., they climbed onto their bed-bug infested wood-planked bed, fell asleep and entered into the Realm of Dreams.

*   *   *

ONCE UPON MANY DREAMS

THE EARTH PRELUDE
(PIANO)
LUDOVICO EINAUDI

FLOWERS ON THE WATER
ANNA AND THE KING
GEORGE FENTON & ROBERT KRAFT

MOONLIT BEACH
ANNA AND THE KING
GEORGE FENTON & ROBERT KRAFT

MOONLIGHT
(PIANO)
YIRUMA

MOONLIGHT SONATA
LUDWIG VAN BEETHOVEN
PIANIST: VLADIMIR HOROWITZ

I AM ONLY SLEEPING
THE BEATLES

SWEAT DREAMS (ARE MADE OF THIS)
EURYTHMICS

FAIRY PRINCESS
(PIANO)
CARLY COMANDO

FAIRY TALE
ALEXANDER RYBAK
EUROVISION 2009 WINNER

PIANO CONCERTO NO. 2 IN F MINOR, OPUS 21
LARGHETTO MOVEMENT
FRÉDÉRIC CHOPIN
PIANIST: DOMENIC DICELLO

*　　　*　　　*

*O*nce upon a time, I, Chuang Tzu, dreamt I was a butterfly, fluttering hither and thither, to all intents and purposes a butterfly. I was conscious only of following my fancies as a butterfly, and was unconscious of my individuality as a man.

Suddenly, I awoke, and there I lay, myself again. Now I do not know whether I was then a man dreaming I was a butterfly, or whether I am now a butterfly dreaming that I am now a man. This is called the Transformation of Things.

Chuang Tzu (庄子)

*　　　*　　　*

*W*here was Chance in Time and Space? Did it exist in the Pre-Bang? During the Bang? Or did it come about in the Post-Bang? What about in the previous cosmic oscillations? What role did chance play in these cosmic cycles? How did Chance come about?

*　　　*　　　*

*C*hance had this incredible dream.

His world dimmed darker, darker and darker. Chance was floating amidst the wide expanse of nowhere. He was in the void. He was everywhere, for the void permeated all.

Chance was suspended and adrift in the void of outer space, freely adrift in the wide chasm of the universe. There were no stars yonder. There was no sun, no earth, no gravity. There was only Chance – adrift in the chasm of the void.

Outer space was in muted silence. Chance was pure consciousness: in total wakefulness and in heightened and full awareness of the universe.

For Chance, it was complete enlightenment. Silence filled the void. Chance was fully awake in the silence and in the void.

There was a deep cosmic hum. Above him, he saw a gigantic gray slab floating and slicing through pure Time and Space – beyond matter, defying physics. Silently, the huge gray slab traversed Time and Space, emanating this message: I AM THE PARACLETE. From the Paraclete came Wisdom. And Wisdom was with Chance.

Through Chance, the stars, the heavenly bodies began to appear. Chance smiled. The sun, the solar planets appeared. Chance nodded. He understood. The Earth appeared. Then the Moon. Chance was ecstatic in his understanding.

Through Chance, the cosmic sonata began.

*   *   *

Likewise, Luck hit the sack and had this watery dream.

It was high noon. The sun was blazing in the cloudless sky. Luck was walking all alone on a white sandy beach. The air above him and the fine sand underneath him were hot, hot, hot.

Suddenly, to his left, he saw a gigantic hundred-foot wave advancing toward him from the sea. Forebodingly, it rose higher and higher as it approached nearer and nearer. The raging emerald green wave approached in record time.

His instinct was to outrun the wave. Deep within himself, he sensed it would be the end of life: his life. Luck felt he was a goner. He tried to outrun the tsunami wave; but the tsunami wave would outrun him.

Luck was enveloped in the rising water of this billowing tsunami wave, over a hundred feet high.

Luck thought he would surely drown and die. Fully submerged, he held his breath, until he could not hold it anymore. Then he gulped, and to his surprise, he could breathe – underwater! He could swim effortlessly, breathing in, breathing out. Luck had no fear. This amazed him to no end.

The wave would sweep him to a white-washed sea-side town with red Mediterranean tile roofs. The waves would wash the narrow cobbled-stoned streets empty. There was no one on the street. There was no destruction. The whole town stood still; it had been swept clean by the tsunami wave into a time warp.

At a forked road, Luck encountered Missing Mama and Aunt Juliet. The two were chatting as they entered one of the white-washed houses on the seaside. Luck followed them into the house. The house inside was spacious, welcoming and pleasant but eerily empty. There was no furniture. There were no clothes in the closets. No one lived in this house.

In a blink, a gigantic tsunami wave smashed into the house and Luck was sucked out through the backdoor of the house into the bright emerald green sea which quickly turned light turquoise blue.

Voila! A great white whale approached him. It must have been over sixty feet long. Luck saw the whale blink, beckoning to Luck. Luck gripped and clung to the whale's dorsal hump, and was soon brought to the depths of the clear blue ocean.

The great white whale was soon met by other great whites. They formed a gregarious pod. These great whites had such nurturing behavior that Luck was at once at ease and full of wonderment at their elegance and gentleness. Luck was in sea heaven.

Luck felt that if he could be an animal, it would be: A Great White Whale.

*   *   *

In the next instant, Luck had this second dream.

The hotel room was enticingly elegant. Luck realized he had no money with him. He was heading for a faraway place – to America.

In his hotel room, there were other travelling companions. He somehow knew them but didn't know how that was so. They, too, had no money. Everyone was hungry with no money to buy food.

Luck happened to open the wardrobe closet door. And behold! There were packages of freshly made tuna sandwiches in cellophane wrap on top of the closet shelf. Luck distributed these to his companions, who erupted into cheers.

When Luck returned to the wardrobe closet, he saw a colorful carton box at the corner of the closet. Behold! Inside the box were: a lively little fat man and a tiny monkey.

The Fairy Godmother, in a brilliant white robe with a wand, appeared saying: "Luck, you shall have Buff the Monkey and Chance shall have Lotto the Pirate. You and Chance shall care for them and help them achieve their missions."

She proceeded to sprinkle the tiny creatures with magic dust. Bending slightly, the Fairy Godmother spoke to Buff the Monkey and Lotto the Pirate: "Perform your missions well and you will each find your soul leading you to a better existence in your journey toward immortality."

At this very moment, Luck cried out: "I can't believe it! It's true! THE FAIRY GODMOTHER IS REAL!"

*   *   *

As the two youngsters were reveling in their dreams, the alarm clock rang. 6:00 A.M. June 21. Summer solstice. The longest day of the year.

Today would be a most memorable day. A day for no turning back.

*   *   *

CHAPTER 22

BUFF THE MONKEY
AND
LOTTO THE PIRATE

<u>SONG INSPIRATION</u>

IT'S YOUR DAY
(PIANO)
YIRUMA

THE GAMBLER
KENNY ROGERS

C'EST LA VIE
(THAT'S LIFE)
(FRENCH)
CHAB KHALED

HERE COMES THE SUN
THE BEATLES

EUROPE'S SKY
ALEXANDER RYBAK

I'LL FOLLOW THE SUN
THE BEATLES

* * *

*W*hat is Destiny?

How do we dance with Destiny? Where is the Divine Will and where is our own will in this Dance with Destiny? What's the difference between Divine Destiny and human destiny? How do we make the distinction?

* * *

For the brothers, today, June 21 would be their rendezvous with Destiny – a day that would change their lives forever.

Luck barely slept. All night till dawn, in his excitement, he tossed and turned, drifting in and out of dreams.

*   *   *

With a startle, Luck awoke, only to hear himself scream: "THE FAIRY GODMOTHER IS REAL!" He barely heard the Fairy Godmother's last words: "These *Molidivans* will protect you. Take good care of them…"

Luck sat up, wide awake. Looking down his bed, he saw a colorful carton box on the floor. In it were: Buff the Monkey and Lotto the Pirate. With great care, he lifted the box onto the bed.

Excitedly, he shook Chance to wake him up. "Chance, you must see this!"

"Mmm…What?" Annoyed, Chance turned toward the opposite side of the bed to continue his sleep. "Ten more minutes! Let me sleep!"

"Wake up! We've got *Buff the Monkey and Lotto the Pirate*. I just saw the *Fairy Godmother*!" Luck was practically screaming into his brother's ear.

Chance jumped up, completely baffled. "What?" As his sleepy head came to focus, he gazed into the colorful carton box and marveled at what he saw. Yes! In the carton, there were: Buff the Monkey and Lotto the Pirate, a half-naked pot-bellied man with a protruding navel, a man not more than eight inches tall.

"You shall have Lotto and I shall have Buff." Luck relayed the Fairy Godmother's instructions.

151

With care, Luck picked up Buff the Monkey from the carton. He proceeded to give his new monkey friend a good cross-examination. "Who are you? Why are you sent here?"

Six inches tall, Buff laughed, scratching his head and fidgeting all over. Then, he spoke smartly in his Elizabethan British accent. "You see... I'm a monkey in search of a soul. If I proveth myself heroic and true in my service to you in the coming years, I hope to find my soul, to achieve immortality as I journey from this world toward Monkey Heaven. There, I shall be free to roam to wherever I want, jumping from tree to tree – happy forever! For now, I want to gain Wisdom through a purposeful Life. I don't want to return to *Moldivia* where I had to perform curious acts for my king and queen and their honored guests. That's pure silliness! Alas, I need your help. That's my deal with the Fairy Godmother."

"I'll do my best." Luck promised. Curious about Buff's past life, Luck inquired: "So, where are you from?"

"I was born and raised in the Misty Mountain of *Moldivia*, a British protectorate in South Asia. In my early youth, I was one of the naughtiest and wiliest monkey, stealing and eating fruits that belongeth not to me, causing trouble in a royal palace. I was a monkey *without* a purpose in life; this doomed me. I was cast out and imprisoned in the Caves of Rumination in *Moldivia* for the past four hundred years. Truly, I've done enough reflection. Today, the Fairy Godmother has given me another chance. I promise: I'm a rehabilitated monkey this time, a monkey in search of a great purpose for the Common Good."

"We shall see." Luck smiled at Buff's forthrightness and felt sorry for his long-time imprisonment within the Caves of Rumination. "Oh, Buff, no one should suffer so much. You are a glimmering shadow of man, so primal yet so earnest in your

152

search for honest sobriety. Ah, to survive. Perhaps to thrive. May you find your Monkey Truth when you least expect it!"

*   *   *

Chance picked up Lotto the Pirate from the carton and examined him closely. Shirtless, Lotto wore a ruddy pair of purple pants and wielded a pirate's pistol and sword around his enormous waist. Not more than eight inches in height, his pudgy face was covered by a thick black beard, complementing his bushy black curly hair. He had a pot belly.

"You don't look too happy, Lotto." Chance started the conversation.

"You're right, my lord. This huge round belly is the source of my discontent." Speaking in his awkward, stammering, broken Elizabethan British accent, Lotto sounded rather morose. He tried to make a deep bow, but couldn't, due to his enormous belly. "Master, I am at your service. Speak and I shall obey."

"What brings you here?" Chance was curious.

"I was an admiral pirate of the high seas, a-sailing the vast Indian Ocean and the South China Sea, in charge of a ten thousand sailors. But I love a-boozing and often went about a-pillaging coastal villages and a-doing bad things to innocent villagers and seafarers. As punishment for my piracy and evil deeds, the heavens a-cast down a terrible storm and a-caused a deadly mutiny in my flag ship. To a-save themselves, the mutineers a-squeezed me into a gigantic wooden barrel and a-threw me overboard to drown. In the high seas, I a-floated for four hundred years, a-bopping up and down until today. But the merciful Fairy Godmother a-gave me another chance."

Chance was mesmerized by Lotto's story and felt the admiral

pirate's deep remorse. "So, what are you going to do?"

"According to the Fairy Godmother, if I a-serve you well in the coming four years while you are at ISBS, I shall a-have the choice of becoming an immortal sage – a fine country gentleman, fit as a fiddle, wise in my ways and eternal in my joys, a-living out my destiny. Yes, I can be an expert in horticulture. No, I don't a-want to be the admiral pirate of the high seas. This I a-declare: I a-choose to be a country gentleman, an immortal sage with a good soul a-writing great books on horticulture – forever! That's my deal with the Fairy Godmother." Lotto spoke with sincerity.

"I shall do my best to help you in every way." Chance promised. "I suppose you're also from *Moldivia*?" He detected Lotto had the same Elizabethan British accent as Buff.

"Yes, my master, you've a-guessed right." Lotto was impressed by Chance's deep knowledge of geography. "How did you figure where I came from?"

Wanting to appear mysterious and wise, Chance just smiled. Then, he whispered. "It's an ancient Chinese secret." But Chance remained curious about Lotto. "So, tell me, why are you here?"

"In my past life, I a-ate, a-slept and a-drank most of the day away. I was lazy and greedy. I a-gambled and went after women. I was a wretched lecherous slob." Lotto paused, turning red, getting embarrassed with his true confession. "And for all that, I had to a-pay dearly: four hundred years in a barrel, tossing in the high seas. That's no fun. Can I a-change my *karma*? Master, a-teach me what it means to be a man: how to make the right choices, how to a-reconcile the irreconcilable, how to a-deal with my crazy emotions. I want to a-live an inspired life."

"That's a good starting point! You have great intentions. You want to fix your life. You have a great attitude." Chance consoled him. "Most importantly, you didn't drown and you didn't starve these past four hundred years."

"I'll do my best to do the right thing: a-eat moderately, be industrious and sober, a-treat women with courtesy and decorum, and be a gentleman. And if the chance a-presents itself, I a-want to be your hero." Lotto sounded penitent and determined. "That's my deal with Fairy Godmother."

Chance couldn't be more impressed. "Ah, Lotto, I can see a refined Adonis emerging from you, despite your current looks of a hideous pig. Four centuries of solitude in the high seas must be hell! Dude, I feel your pain!"

The twins were impressed with Lotto's and Buff's contriteness and their honorable quest for redemption and immortality.

Buff the Monkey clung onto Lotto's bulky shoulder, making them the oddest couple.

As a sign of friendship, Buff offered to find some lice on Lotto's hair.

*   *   *

Chance was now thinking about the next step. "How are we going to take them to America? I guess we'll just have to carry them in our rectangular leather attachés." Chance was assessing how to fit them into their bags. "My attaché is big enough for Lotto."

"Yes, I think so. Buff will fit into my attaché." Luck was confident. "There's enough room."

"We'll put them in our respective attachés when we are about to leave – lest Nero finds out and wants to keep them. Nero should NEVER know!" Despite his moment of joy, Luck was suddenly indignant at the thought of Nero, who would most likely make a claim on their newfound friends.

"We've got our new friends and they will be *ours* to keep! We need to keep our little friends quiet – here and on the airplane." Luck was firm on this idea.

"Yes!" Chance agreed. He bent over and spoke to Lotto and Buff. "You two must keep *absolutely* quiet during the whole trip to America. That's an order! We'll take care of you! You two will be comfortable and well fed!"

"I'll keep quiet!" Buff butted in, to the annoyance of Lotto.

The twins watched the interaction of the *Moldivian* pair with much amusement.

*　　　*　　　*

Except for the twins and their *Moldivian* friends, the whole house was still and silent as a church at dawn.

Meanwhile, Luck dashed downstairs to the kitchen. *Ah, they will need food for the trip!* He cut several chunks of leftover chicken and beef into very thin slices and wrapped them in aluminum foil. He tore off some grapes and bananas. Then, he stuffed all these and some crackers into two large-sized zip-lock plastic bags.

Then, Luck got two clean cloth napkins to keep his little friends cozy and comfortable for the duration of the flight. For additional safety, he unrolled a bundle of paper towels for their sanitation. After taking out additional large zip-lock bags, Luck scrambled back to his bedroom.

To test out their accommodations, Luck placed Buff into his

rectangular attaché; while Chance placed Lotto into his. Separately, they put the food and cloth napkins into a duffle bag. "This way, our little friends won't munch all the food at once." Chance looked teasingly at the *Moldivian* pair.

"I think we need to put our gifts from Uncle Antikweetee inside the large zip-lock bags, lest they ruined them. What do you think?" Chance, in his mind, was going through the whole checklist for their hand-carry items. *Brilliant idea!* The brothers proceeded to put their gifts from Uncle Antikweetee into the large sized zip-lock plastic bags. *Ah! Almost there!*

Suddenly, in a flash, Chance recognized what was happening. "These two *Moldivians* are SIGNS! Buff and Lotto are SIGNS!" He remembered the parting words of Cardinal Legazpi: *Learn to recognize, read, decipher and follow the signs in your daily lives in this great journey: the Journey of Dreams. The signs will make your dreams come true. Note the signs.*

"Signs of what?" Luck, likewise, recognized that Buff and Lotto were signs. But their significance and meaning escaped him. "Are these the SIGNS pointing to my own Mini-Myth? How so?"

*   *   *

CHAPTER 23

THE RED UNDERWEAR REVEALED

<u>MUSIC INSPIRATION</u>

EVERYDAY
(PIANO)
CARLY COMANDO

ALEJANDRO
LADY GAGA

A DANGLING CONVERSATION
PAUL SIMON & ART GARFUNKEL

A CLEAR DAY
QING TIAN
晴天
（CHINESE MANDARIN）
JAY CHOU / 周杰伦

WHAT ARE YOU WORRYING ABOUT
NI ZAI FAN NAO SHEN ME
你在烦恼什么
(CHINESE MANDARIN)
SODA GREEN / 苏打绿 & ELLA

IT'S MY LIFE
BON JOVI

*　　　*　　　*

Oh, Destiny, that sweet cosmic wind that drives our everyday lives! What do you know that we don't?

Shed your wisdom upon us so that we may know our true destiny. How do you reveal yourself? Through what signs?

How do we decipher your signs?

*Which direction should we turn? Right? Left? Forward?
Or, even backward?*

Wherefore? What for? Destiny, unveil your mystery!

*   *   *

For the brothers, today's breakfast at Aunt Juliet's home would be their last in the Philippines.

"You should have been at the carnival last night!" Cousin Nero was egging Luck on. "It was fantastic! There was this dare-devil motorcyclist, motoring inside a gigantic steel mesh egg-shaped sphere. 'Round and 'round he went. It was just awesome!"

Nero still couldn't get over last evening's show: a motorcyclist in black driving inside a huge metal egg.

Chance nodded lamely. "We had to finish packing."

*   *   *

The door-bell rang. Nero dashed to the door.

"Uncle Antikweetee!" Nero squealed as he opened the door. Uncle Antikweetee marched in with a new pirate's outfit.

"Hello! Chopsticks!" Jokingly, he greeted Nero, who got this nickname because he was thin like sticks and bones. He hated this nickname: Chopsticks.

Following the frying sound of the sizzling eggs, Nero stealthily headed toward the kitchen.

"HA!" He threw a slithering rubber snake at Luck. Startled, Luck almost dropped the skillet as the rubber snake landed amidst the sunny-side up eggs.

"Dang!" Luck practically jumped out of his skin. *Crazy eggs!*

Nero doubled-up in gut-busting laughter. "Hahaha!"

Luck was *not* amused. Inside, he was boiling. Seven years of suppressed anger was about to erupt. Gnashing his teeth, he hypnotically stared at the rubber snake on the skillet. *Nero is your man!* In a flash, the rubber snake leapt off the skillet toward Nero, who practically blacked out in fright.

"Awesome!" Luck could not believe his eyes. *Incredible! How did this happen?* Luck realized that his *ch'i* had just leapt out of him toward the rubber snake. In *this* instant, Luck discovered he had *telekinetic* abilities!

"Atta boy!" Uncle Antikweetee cracked up in boisterous laughter.

Coming to and in a daze, with the snake's tail still writhing around his neck, Nero let out a savage wail: "MAMA!" at which time, Aunt Juliet rushed to the kitchen.

She was a pale-faced nerve-wracked hag, moving with quirky jerks. At fifty-two, Aunt Juliet had lost her flamboyant youth and her debutante's passion – all gone with the wind. A mere shadow of her past beauty, she was now a grumpy old lady.

Her cup of coffee in hand, her hair disheveled, she was visibly annoyed at the crazy pandemonium in the kitchen. "What the hell is going on!" Her voice shrilled like the squeaking chalk on the blackboard.

For Aunt Juliet, the twins became an added inconvenience

arising from her relations linked to her older sister, Missing Mama. Whatever promises she had made to Missing Mama were long forgotten. By now, Aunt Juliet was sick and tired of the twins.

"Luck pulled this trick on me!" Shuddering in fright, Nero pointed at the snake lodged around his neck. "He made the rubber snake jump on me!"

Aunt Juliet gave Luck a brutish pinch on the ear. "How dare you, pulling pranks on Nero! Now, stop this nonsense!"

In his anger, Luck glared at Aunt Juliet's coffee cup and telekinetically ripped it off her hand. "Yaoooowww!" Aunt Juliet screamed. The coffee cup went flying, busting out a few light bulbs in the kitchen and the dining room. Then, it zoomed back and hit Nero on the head. Awwwwww! He screamed.

Likewise, Luck telekinetically yanked off Nero's belt. Nero's pants dropped to the floor, exposing his *red* underwear. Uncle Antikweetee could not stop laughing. "RED UNDERWEAR!"

Luck finally had his revenge.

*   *   *

Thuds boomed from the stairs as Chance dragged down his two suitcases to the kitchen. "Where should I park these?"

"By the main doorway." Aunt Juliet bellowed. "Use your coconut head, silly boy."

At this time, Uncle Romeo appeared at the kitchen, puffing his first cigarette for the day. At fifty-seven, he was a man of few words. His cigarette twitched to every syllable he uttered. An incessant smoker, he had a constant wheezing cough of emphysema.

This morning, Uncle Romeo wore only his briefs. His back and pot-belly were puckered with giant red acnes. His rough face looked like the dark side of the moon. Macho in demeanor, he grunted his orders at Luck and Chance. "Everything's ready?" He muttered between puffs. "Don't forget to sweep the floor and throw out the garbage before we leave for the airport."

Uncle Romeo had lost his youthful charm, his passionate heart, his magical eloquence for his undying love for the once sublime Juliet Blundermore. His chivalry had turned to sloth. His once handsome countenance was now but a faint memory. Young crazy love had dissolved to the pathetic monotony of middle age marriage. His Montago family still *hated* the Blundermore family. For him, dying for love was a totally alien idea; it would never happen. How Cupid could bring together this couple was an enigma.

*   *   *

As Luck finished cooking, Chance served breakfast. Everyone sat down to eat. With gusto, the twins quaffed down their porridge, mixed with sunny-side eggs, sausages and pickled vegetables.

While eating, Aunt Juliet gave out a weak sob. "We are going to miss you both so much! Do take good care of yourselves. If I was ever mean to you, it was done out of love... for your own good. I had to be strict. I've no choice. Please forgive me. You two have been so naughty!" A drop of tear rolled down her cheek. "A diamond does not shine until you cut and polish it. Its brilliance depends on how you cut it."

Uncle Romeo feigned sadness to see the twins leave. "Write us often, my dear boys. You've meant so much to our family." Incapable of acting, his words came out flat and insincere.

Uncle Antikweetee could not bear the chicanery of these false pretenses. He shook his head, rolling his eyeballs. *Hate this hypocrisy! I can't stand it! This is killing me! Let me out of here!*

Luck wanted no part of these theatrics. "We'll have to run. We are very late."

Like a diplomat, Luck said the obligatory "thank you's" to Aunt Juliet and Uncle Romeo for their seven years with them.

*   *   *

The twins chugged down their *café au lait*.

Nero interrupted. "By the way, did you receive your special deliveries two days ago?"

"What special deliveries?" Luck was puzzled and annoyed. "Why tell us at this last minute? We have no time to go to the post office!"

Nero protested. "Don't be rude, Chance. I was trying to be nice. I never had a chance link up with you."

"Who were they?" Chance asked hurriedly, concerned that they might be late for the airport.

"Two courier delivery men came, saying they have important and urgent confidential mail for you two. From ISBS. Hand delivery. These two were gigantic and bald! One, very muscular. The other, massively fat. Both were heavily tattooed! I told them you were at the Makati Shopping Mall to get some new shoes."

Crash! Luck dropped his coffee mug on the table, shocked at what he heard.

"How could you!" Luck hurled his fork at Nero, who ducked for dear life. An empty chair flew over Nero as it hit a wall, crushing the family photo.

"You almost got us killed!" Never this furious, Luck screamed at Nero.

In a split second, a deadly brawl almost exploded.

Uncle Antikweetee placed himself between Luck and Nero. "This is no time to fight! We'll be late for your flight. Tell me all about it on our way to the airport!"

On his part, Uncle Romeo shielded Nero from the twins.

A tense silence ensued.

Uncle Antikweetee was stunned at his discovery of Luck's telekinetic energy.

*   *   *

After breakfast, Chance threw the garbage outside. As he hurled the huge black plastic trash bag, the seven years of frustration and misery at Aunt Juliet's went with it into the trash can. "Good riddance!" In disgust, he slammed the trash can lid shut. *Why do I have such a nasty karma?*

He wept.

*   *   *

CHAPTER 24

A PRECARIOUS DEPARTURE

MUSIC INSPIRATION

TIME TO SAY GOODBYE
(CON TE PARTIRÒ)
(ENGLISH / ITALIAN)
SINGERS (ENGLISH): SARAH BRIGHTMAN & ANDREA BOCELLI
SINGERS (ITALIAN): FRANCESCO SARTORI & LUCIO QUARANTOTTO

GOODBYE KISS
WEN BIE
吻别
(CHINESE MANDARIN)
JACKIE CHEUNG / 张学友

EVERY BREATHE YOU TAKE
POLICE

SYMPHONY NO. 5, MOVEMENT NO.1
LUDWIG VAN BEETHOVEN
CONDUCTOR: HERBERT VON KARAJAN

THE YELLOW RIVER CONCERTO, MOVEMENT 1
SONG OF THE YELLOW BOATMEN
HUANG HE XIE ZOU QU, HUANG HE CHUAN FU QU
黄河协奏曲，黄河船夫曲
XIAN XINGHAI / 冼星海
CHINA PHILHARMONIC ORCHESTRA
中国爱乐乐团
CONDUCTOR: LONG YU / 余龙
PIANIST: LANG LANG / 朗朗

*　　　*　　　*

A journey of a thousand miles starts with a great dream.

*　　　*　　　*

In silence, the twins went upstairs to their bedroom and donned their hand-me-down business suits – which were clearly too tight for them. They put on their brand new rubber shoes. Carefully, they hoisted their respective attachés over their shoulders – with each *Moldivian* sequestered inside.

"Now, Buff and Lotto, be *completely* quiet – all the way to the airport and onto the airplane!" Chance commanded them. "Hush-hush!"

Steadily, the twins descended the stairs.

"Got to roll!" From the driveway, Uncle Antikweetee yelled for everyone to board as he started his jeepney engine.

Nero's pit-bull Demonio barked crazily at the backyard, as the dog heard the jeepney engine roar to life. Almost immediately, in a pandemonium, a deafening chorus of dog barking erupted throughout the neighborhood. Amidst the canine commotion, the twins loaded their four suitcases onto the back section of jeepney. Slowly, they boarded the front part of the jeepney. Squeezing tightly beside Uncle Antikweetee, the twins held their respective attachés upright on their laps. Chance also had the extra duffle bag on his lap.

Auntie Juliet, Uncle Romeo and Nero climbed onto the back section of the jeepney. Here, they could not see the twins' attachés and duffle bag.

In time, they were all heading to Manila's Benigno Acquino International Airport.

Uncle Antikweetee's jeepney was multi-colored in pastel violet and pastel pink, with gaudy decorative art surrounding the whole jeepney. Today, Uncle Antikweetee made his jeepney special for the twins. He adorned it with a big "Good Luck" header on top of the windshield.

The mood during the ride to the airport was somber. In a low voice, Luck narrated what had transpired two nights ago at Gul's.

Uncle Antitweetee listened attentively, shocked and horrified at what he was hearing. *Ugh! How did Nero get involved in this mess? A near disaster! All these ten years of kung fu training can just be for naught!*

*   *   *

At the international airport, Terminal One was jam packed with itinerants. The brothers took their spots along a winding snaking line toward Jet Orange's ticket and luggage check-in. They inched forward ever so slowly toward the ticket processing counter. They would be checking in for their direct flight to Newark, *New Joy Sea.*

Uncle Antikweetee lined up with them, making sure the twins' plane tickets, paper work and all arrangements were in order. "Always remember your roots. There'll be good times and rough times. In tough times, never ever give up. *Never!*" Uncle Antikweetee knew that this would be his last time in a long time when he could be with them again. "Believe in yourselves. Follow your true passion. And your true destiny will unfold."

"One believer is equivalent to a hundred thousand of interested bystanders. Between Chance and me, we have an army!" Luck declared.

*   *   *

Amidst the noise and chaos in the terminal, Uncle Antikweetee murmured this important message to the twins.

"At ISBS, if you are lucky, you will learn about the mystical and supernatural secrets of History. From mystic revelations to esoteric codes, you shall discover an alternative world history based upon *beliefs* over the ages up to modern times." By habit, Uncle Antikweetee pulled out his cigar.

"Uncle, you can't smoke here." Chance quickly reminded him.

"Oh! Where was I?" Uncle Antikweetee put his cigar back into his pocket. "You will find a radical *re-interpretation* of human existence and a perspective of History previously concealed from us. That will be a real treat! By linking humanity's mystical imaginings about how humans came to this Earth and its evolution over the millennia, you will gain a deeper insight into a richer pattern in human history, juxtaposed with the materialistic, scientific, economic and political narrative of conventional history."

Despite being unruly, with people shoving and pushing, the crowd did not bother Uncle Antikweetee. "Watch out for pickpockets. There are plenty of them here." Uncle Antikweetee strained his neck and surveyed the crowd.

"Let me continue. Your *discernment* will be trained to perceive and understand humanity's deepest secrets – secrets only a lucky few will get to decipher. You will learn what is meant in the secret teaching of the expulsion of Adam and Eve from Eden and the Great Fall, the mystery and necessity of human suffering and the promise of a path toward Redemption."

They were inching forward, getting closer to the check-in counter. Uncle Antikweetee checked his watch. "Another few minutes... Now, where was I? You see, in time, your consciousness will be enhanced, becoming aware of the patterns evoked by coincidences and synchronicities in the events of our lives and in the world. Hopefully, you will be able to discern the deeper laws that govern our very existence. Good luck to your attending the Mystery School that is ISBS!"

Chance gave Uncle Antikweetee an earnest look. "We will succeed."

"I'll be with you – even though I'm here in the Philippines and you're in America. In mind and in spirit, I'll be there with you. Just let me know your needs. E-mail me often." Uncle Antikweetee assured the twins. "You're never alone. Stay in touch. Don't be strangers, OK?"

Luck and Chance appreciated Uncle Antikweetee's kindness and graciousness for all these years.

Despite his outlandish pirate's outfit, Uncle Antikweetee was now feeling sad. "When will I ever see you again!"

But he kept up a happy front for the twins. "Make yourselves the strongest protagonists in your own lives! Don't let anyone tell you otherwise. Remember this: in this world, there are these types of people: johns and suckers; winners and losers. The choice is yours." Uncle Antikweetee was trying to impart some last words of Wisdom to his twin nephews.

"Uncle, we'll make you proud. We promise!" Luck assured him.

In time, the twins checked in their suitcases and got their seat assignments.

Maudlin and sad, Auntie Juliet hugged each of the twins, careful not to hurt their wounds. "When you arrive at ISBS, please send Uncle Blundermore my best wishes."

*   *   *

Suddenly, from the corner of his eyes, Chance saw two muscular menacing men, their heads shaven, making their way through the crowds, from the distance, approaching the check-in counter for Jet Orange. At once, he recognized them. They were the same two skull heads who had kidnapped them! Fear shot through his spine. Gul's goons were on the sprawl for them again!

"Luck, run! The skull-heads! Gul's after us again!" Chance grabbed Luck. "Uncle Antikweetee, got to go! No time to explain!" Chance yelled.

In distraught panic, Chance and Luck dashed off and raced toward the immigration check-point, got their passports stamped, and headed toward the airline boarding gate. All the while, they hoped that the skull heads had not discovered them.

*   *   *

Meanwhile, Uncle Antikweetee, Aunt Juliet, Uncle Romeo, and Nero stood at their spots, completely bewildered at the brothers' unceremonious and rushed departure.

A sadness fell upon Uncle Antikweetee, as he stood there dumb-founded by their hurried departure. *What is this? Why is it this way? Again? First, Vetruvian. Then, Luz. Now, the twins. Is this the same karma all over again – this karma of sudden disappearance?*

*   *   *

Terror gripped the twins. *No, not again!* Shaken, they did not want to re-live another kidnapping, another close encounter with Death.

"I'm finished with the Philippines!" Chance muttered, completely upset.

"Quick! Let's board now." Luck urged, his heart thumping. He took Buff gently out of his attaché and put him into one of his suit pockets. Chance did the same with Lotto.

Finally, they were processed at the boarding gates. As they boarded the aircraft, the twins turned back one last time to make sure that they were not being followed. They seemed to have out-run the skull-heads, believing that they were out of harm's way.

"Ugh! They couldn't get to us now." Droplets of sweat trickled down Luck's forehead as he entered the aircraft.

Chance's face was ashen. "I'm not too sure."

*   *   *

Soon, Johnny Dangerous and Double Trouble approached the airplane boarding counter, inquiring about the twins.

"I'm sorry, sirs. Under *what* authority do you have to inquire about them?" Undaunted, an airline stewardess struggled to stand her ground against the pushy Johnny Dangerous. "You've been here yesterday morning! Don't harass our passengers!"

Each of the skull heads flashed their fake police badge.

"This is a serious matter!" Double Trouble growled, his shirt completely soaked with sweat and stinky like a swine..

"We need to board the aircraft – and look for ourselves." Johnny Dangerous pushed his way toward the boarding walkway. "My job is at stake!"

"Show us a probable cause! You have no right – " The stewardess protested as Johnny Dangerous pushed her aside.

Double Trouble looked grumpily at Johnny Dangerous. "If we fail this time, Gul will not forgive us. We'll get the ax! My ten kids! How do I feed them?" Pale faced, Double Trouble was a nervous wreck. For him, this was a do-or-die moment. Everything hanged on their ability to capture the brothers. He dreaded Gul Diabolica's ruthless wrath. Today, he truly felt like a Broken Fridge.

*   *   *

CHAPTER 25

ONCE UPON A JOURNEY

<u>MUSIC INSPIRATION</u>

NOW WE ARE FREE
GLADIATOR
HANS ZIMMER & LISA GERRARD

IMAGINE
JOHN LENNON

HEART ATTACK
DEMI LOVATO

UP, UP AND AWAY
THE FIFTH DIMENSION

LAWRENCE OF ARABIA – MAIN THEME
MAURICE JARRE

MAN OF STEEL – THEME SONG
HANS ZIMMER

CHARIOTS OF FIRE
VANGELIS

FLY
(PIANO)
LUDOVICO EINAUDI

*   *   *

***D**oes one really have to jump through fire to cross over the threshold of Destiny?*

*   *   *

The aircraft interior resembled that of Captain James Cook's *HMS Endeavor* which traversed the South Seas in the eighteenth century. The faux-wooden-decked floors were festooned with maritime paraphernalia, including beer kegs (without the beer), hay, sawdust and peanut shells. The curvature of the bulkhead were adorned with sea masts, pulleys and thick ropes. Prints of eighteenth century maritime ships and maps decked the side walls. The aircraft ambiance screamed thrilling adventure above the friendly skies.

But the twins were oblivious to the décor and the banter of youngsters around them. Weak-kneed and shuddering uncontrollably, Chance took his designated seat by the window at the front section of the economy class of the aircraft. As he sank onto his seat, terror stricken, he felt he would die.

Luck comforted Chance by vigorously rubbing his back. "The gates will soon close and we'll be up, up, and away!"

Luck's words and backrub failed to register with Chance. He could feel Gul's evil approaching the aircraft. This threat of an impending abduction shook him to the core. "This is too much. I can't take it anymore!" Chance whispered to Luck nervously.

Moments later, an idea came upon Chance. "Let's do this. Let's each lock ourselves up inside one of the toilet cabins, until the aircraft doors are locked and the plane is geared for take-off. It will be much safer for us – hiding in the toilet cabins."

Luck nodded, as he turned around to assess the locations of the toilets on the aircraft. He was too agitated to notice the several big 3-D screens displaying the famous mysterious sites of the world: the Stonehenge, the Sphinx and the Great Pyramids of Giza, the terra-cotta army of Chin Shih Huang Di, amongst others. He rose and passed through the numerous youngsters milled around the computer tablet banks playing virtual games. His eyes were trained to the very last toilet at the tail-end of the aircraft.

Meanwhile, Chance headed toward the toilet in the middle of the aircraft, with his attaché strap slung over his shoulder.

Minutes seemed like hours, as Luck and Chance stayed locked within their respective toilet cabins.

"I can knock anyone dead if he comes near you!" Buff assured Luck. "He'll be sorry he was ever born."

Inside his toilet cabin, Chance held Lotto tightly. Every knock or swivel of the door knob would send shivers of terror up Chance's spine. "This, too, shall pass." Chance consoled Lotto.

"Don't a-worry, my Master. I'm here to a-protect you." Lotto showed his prowess by waving his antique pistol in the air. "Trust me, sir, one shot from my hot pistol and the intruder is a goner!"

*   *   *

Noisy rumblings sounded at the aircraft hallways. "We are looking for Winston and Brandon Blundermore Mann." A gruff and curt voice boomed.

Chance heard heavy boots stomping down the aisles and toward his toilet stall.

Tying Lotto to his tie, Chance clambered his way up toward the toilet ceiling. He outstretched his hands and legs against the four walls of toilet ceiling walls, his back pressed against the ceiling. Like a *ninja* in the spider position, he was ready to strike should the toilet door burst open. There, he waited as sweat trickled down his neck. Dangling in mid-air from Chance's tie,

Lotto had his pistol cocked, ready to fire.

There was a noisy bang against the toilet door as the knob was jiggered violently. "Anybody in there?" A rough voice thundered from the outside of the toilet.

"Oh, oh! Can't you a-leave an old lady alone? I'm a-doing my thing!" Lotto let out a holler in falsetto of an old scolding lady. "I'm a-pooping diamonds! Got constipation! My butt-hole a-hurts! Young man, why don't you try another washroom? If you a-come in, I'll a-shove my cane up your butt-hole and you'll *never* a-walk the same again. Do you want to walk funny?"

*　　　*　　　*

"AAAWWW!" A deathly scream thundered outside the toilet door. Then a heavy thud.

"Quick! Call the paramedics! Someone's having a heart attack!" A gruff voice hollered. There were mad scramblings on the aisles, with stewardesses shooting orders to one another.

"Dr. Acula! Come to the international airport at once! Double Trouble is having a heart attack!" A gruff voice was phoning a doctor.

Shortly thereafter, a team of paramedics rushed in and worked on the victim. Then, the paramedics were heard struggling to haul their victim. "This is one *heavy* dude! We'll need more than four strong men to put him on the gurney."

*　　　*　　　*

Inside the toilet stall, Chance felt the aircraft floor heave as the paramedics were lifting Double Trouble onto the gurney.

Lotto whispered: "Starting today, I'm a-going on diet."

176

Chance retorted: "Dude, you need to exercise, too!"

"Aye, aye, sir! Four hundred years in a barrel got me so out of shape!"

*   *   *

After some delay, the plane's captain announced over the loud speaker: "Welcome to the Jet Orange. You are aboard *Imagination*. This is Flight 99 to America: the Land of Dreams. This is a direct flight non-stop from Manila to Newark, *New Joy Sea*. Those *not* traveling to this destination *must* disembark now."

Luck could hear claps and boisterous laughter from the youngsters outside the toilet.

"I am Captain Fairsailing. Please head to your seats and fasten your seat-belts"

Chance could hear the youngsters outside the toilet cheer.

As he heard the aircraft gates slam shut, Chance let out a sigh of relief. He leapt down and stood on top of the toilet stall. He and Lotto gave each other a big high five. "Good grief! We've made it!"

Chance stared at the toilet mirror and was shock to see himself white as a phantom ghost. He proceeded to wash his face vigorously with hot water, hoping to restore some color back.

Then, he unlocked the toilet door a crack, peered out the toilet door to make sure everything was safe. Emerging from the toilet, he headed toward his seat, his knees shaking.

He noticed the flight attendants were dressed in pirate outfits of the South Pacific. Some had tattoos on their arms, others had eye patches. Some had buck teeth. They were now collecting plastic cups of left-over tomato juice and other exotic tropical fruit drinks from the passengers.

In time, Luck, too, emerged from his toilet and headed toward his seat. He was soaked with sweat, his legs wobbly.

Now, the twins each sat by a window seat. Chance was seated behind Luck. The plane windows were big and round.

"Those skull heads really tried hard to get us." Chance was incredulous that the skull heads went to this extent to find them.

The brothers pulled down their window shades, lest they be spotted by the skull-heads at the terminal.

At 11:55 A.M., Captain Fairsailing announced: "In five minutes, we will be taking off. Please fasten your seat belts."

As if on cue, a row of dancing flight attendants bounced their way down the middle aisle of the aircraft. In hip-hop cadence, they jumped, twirled batons, and break-danced, while demonstrating how to use the seat belt, the oxygen mask and other air-safety maneuvers. They tried to be funny, but only a few passengers seemed to be enjoying the performance.

"What happened a while ago?" Chance asked one of the flight attendants nearby.

"A super fat security guard collapsed with a heart attack. I'm not sure whether he'll make it or not." The flight attendant looked worried.

After the safety demonstrations, the passengers clapped half-heartedly. There were sporadic cheers. A few wild kids stomped their feet. A couple of teens hooted like baboons. One even barked! Bow-wow! Aaooww!!

At 12:00 Noon, the plane's engines roared to life. Slowly, the plane rolled down the tarmac. It turned onto the main runway. Then, it began to accelerate in speed. Faster and faster, it went. At last, the plane took off.

Luck and Chance gave each other an exploding fist bump. *Free at last. Bouyah!*

Moments later, Captain Fairsailing's voice came on the loudspeaker: "*Imagination* has taken off! We shall be ascending toward 33,000 feet cruise altitude. Lean back and enjoy the flight."

For the pair, this was their first time to be on a plane. The feeling was exhilarating.

On the other hand, Buff and Lotto were making irritating noises – because their ears were tightening up painfully. The air pressure was too much for them. Most importantly, they had no such flying machines in *Moldivia*. They had never flown in their lives and they were freaking out!

"Just keep swallowing. Keep opening your jaws!" The twins instructed them.

"My head is going to explode!" Buff screeched. "My monkey brain will be splattered all over you!"

*　　　*　　　*

As the twins peered out the window, they could see Manila Bay, receding smaller and smaller, as the plane headed north. Soon, they were looking down at jungles, a lake here, a river there. They were captivated by the ever changing landscape.

In time, they saw outlines of the famous Ifugao rice terraces of the Mountain Provinces. These were rice terraces farmers had carved out of mountain sides to make the land productive. These were rice terraces to heaven. The twins had seen these on land. Seeing them from the air was just breathtaking.

Soon, Captain Fairsailing's voice came over the loud speaker. "You may now unfasten your seat belts. You may roam freely. If you see the buckle seat belt signs turned on, please return to your seats. At times, we'll encounter air turbulence. Make sure you return to your seats and buckle up. It's better to be safe than sorry. Enjoy your flight."

Before long, the plane's shadow crossed over the Pacific Ocean, which was a majestic blue stretched to the very edge of the visions of the twins. This was the ocean that inspired Magellan's historic trip to prove that the Earth was round.

In no time, the flight attendants served Asian and Western finger foods: beef, chicken, and shrimp *satays, lumpia Shanghai (上海润饼),* various pork and beef buns, scallops wrapped in bacon; shrimp cocktails, liver pâté on crackers; various kinds of cheese. The finger foods were delicious – completely out of this world!

A wide selection of on-flight films were made available.

The youngsters would play all sorts of virtual board games with each other: Monopoly, Strategy, Risk, Scrabble, chess, backgammon, checkers, you name it. This was a youngster's magical flight come true.

Underneath the flight blanket was Buff, snuggled warmly in Luck's armpits. Likewise, underneath Chance's flight blanket, Lotto was snugged warmly inside his suit pocket.

Leaning back and relaxing, Luck felt how lucky he was to have come through the final hurdle in leaving the Philippines. *I can't be luckier!*

He took out his multicolored V-Cube 7 and began to play with it. "Merrily, merrily, merrily, life is but a dream!" He hummed to himself, trying to figure out this game.

*   *   *

CHAPTER 26

LOVE AT FIRST FLIGHT

MUSIC INSPIRATION

FIRST LOVE
(PIANO)
YIRUMA

HELLO
LIONEL RITCHIE

FUNNY LITTLE WORLD
ALEXANDER RYBAK

DON'T YOU REMEMBER
ADELE

WE FOUND LOVE
RIHANNA

LADY
KENNY ROGERS & LIONEL RITCHIE

ANGIE
THE ROLLING STONES

TO LOVE SOMEBODY
BEE GEES

HOW DEEP IS YOUR LOVE
BEE GEES

GIVE ME A REASON
P!NK & NATE REUSS

TE SIENTO
(I FEEL YOU)
(SPANISH)
WISIN & YANDEL

ALGO ME GUSTO DE TI
(SOMETHING ABOUT YOU)
(SPANISH)
WISIN & YANDEL & CHRIS BROWN & T-PAIN

OUR LOVE
WO MEN DE XIN
我们的心
(CHINESE MANDARIN)
F. I. R.

BECAUSE OF LOVE
YIN WEI AI QING
因为爱情
(CHINESE MANDARIN)
FAYE WONG / 王菲
EASON CHAN / 陈奕迅

STILL WANT HAPPINESS
HAI SHI YAO XING FU
還是要幸福
(CHINESE MANDARIN)
TIAN FU ZHEN / 田馥甄

MARRY ME TODAY
JIN TIAN NI YAO JIA GEI WO
今天你要嫁給我
(CHINESE MANDARIN)
JOLIN TSAI / 蔡依林
DAVID TAO / 陶喆

PANGARAP KO ANG IBIGAN KA
(TAGALOG)
REGINE VELASQUEZ

27 MAY
(PIANO)
YIRUMA

*　　　*　　　*

Love is from the infinite, and will remain until eternity.

The seeker of love escapes the chains of birth and death.

Tomorrow, when resurrection comes,

The heart that is not in love will fail the test.

Rumi

*   *   *

*F*ate. Oh, this cosmic force that defies logic and wisdom. Why do some people meet beyond all odds?

What debt do they have to each other, in this existence, in earlier existences or in later existences? Why do lives and events become intertwined the way they do?

Whose Wisdom is this? And for what purpose?

What is Fate? What can we do about Fate?

*   *   *

*O*ne day, Cancer the Crab rose to leave the shore, as she shrugged off the sand on her shell and on her shoulders. She waited patiently for the tides to drag her to the ocean, toward a different shore. "Life here hurts!" And the sea, in its soothing ways, took her to a far, far away land.

*   *   *

"*C*hance, please keep an eye on Buff. Make sure he doesn't jump around and get lost; or worse, go disturb other plane riders. We'll be in deep doo-doo!" Luck got up to fetch something to drink at the aircraft kitchen.

"When you return, don't forget to get me some snacks!" Buff shout out his order request. "Preferably salted peanuts!"

*   *   *

At this moment, at 33,000 feet above sea-level, their eyes met, crisscrossed and locked. She had the most beautiful scintillating eyes, the fairest angelic face that made Luck a true believer. Yes! There was such a thing as serendipity. His heart might have skipped a beat. Awkwardly, they smiled at each other.

Luck leaned over to introduce himself. "How should I call you?" Luck asked while offering her a glass of orange-mango juice, which was initially intended for Chance.

"I'm Sophia Angelis Deepthinker. Call me Sophie." She had long braided chestnut hair, pinned neatly up on her head. Seventeen and smart looking, she wore a knitted navy blue business dress, with a green silken scarf around her neck. She had a brooch in the shape of an elegant red rose, pinned to her lapel. She wore a pair of black high heels. She had long slender legs like that of a fashion model.

"Would you like a seat?" She offered cheerfully, with surprisingly good humor.

Sophie was surprised at her own openness toward a total stranger. *Oh, who gives a hoot? I'm all grown up now. And Dad is not around!*

Luck was instantly captivated by her warm smile and intense gaze. He sat in an empty seat beside her and began a blissful chat with her.

"So, what got you onboard?" Luck inquired. He was taken by her beautiful white teeth.

185

"I'll be attending the International School for Braniacs Squared. And you?"

"What a small world!" Luck exclaimed. "I'll be a freshman there." He could not believe his luck.

Luck felt like he had died and gone to heaven. It was love at first flight. It was love made in heaven, at 33,000 feet cruise altitude.

For Luck, this was a reckoning with the moment. An embrace with the Now. For a blissful moment, he was love incarnate.

After some time, Sophie asked gently. "Don't you remember me?" Sophie was a woman of Mystery, entailing all of life's yearnings and possibilities.

Luck looked at her queasily.

We have met before. A long, long time ago. Sophie remembered. She was seized upon a transcendent realization that life was fluid, that Life transcended the Past, the Present and the Future – that this very Moment entailed Time in its *totality*. There she sat, staring at Luck, in a timeless *presence* of the mind. She remembered her failings with Luck in the deep Past. At this moment, she decided that her time with Luck at ISBS would be her chance to rectify her failings with him. She resolved to love him persistently, with the hope that she could atone for her deeds.

"You may have forgotten." Sophie looked at him hauntingly. *We've made our promise...a long time ago...you and me. Don't you remember? How could you have forgotten?* Sophie's look became a soulful stare. Her piercing looks shot searing bolts upon Luck's very being, as if Cupid's arrows had smitten his very soul: he was love struck.

186

Luck glowered back playfully, oblivious to Sophie's thoughts or what she was saying.

"So what got you to the Philippines?" Luck asked.

"My Dad is Aristotle Angelis Deepthinker, a visiting Professor of Metaphysics at the University of the Philippines."

Right there, Sophie wanted to embrace him. *Once, I've kissed you and you've blossomed.* This was also the transcendent nature of Sophie's love for Luck: she wanted to seize this fluid Moment, and transport Luck and herself back to the reality of their Past, to that Past when she was wedded to Luck, into that blissful Past when everything was right, with both of them having the full capacity for wonderment and imagination – until all went wrong. As she looked at Luck, her heart throbbed in warm reception to the idea, that maybe, just maybe, she would be able to repair her Past and that of Luck. *This time, it will be different.*

"Luck, we'll be great friends – for a long time." She whispered gently. "For I'm a visitor from our Past." She smiled assuredly. *I'm a visitor from our Past – of the greatest order!*

So, she is Sophia Angelis Deepthinker. Luck was trying to figure her out. He did not seem to hear what she *just* said. "What's that?" Luck only picked up Sophie's mysterious word: Metaphysics.

"What?" Sophie raised her thinly arched brow. She was now entranced in this transcendent Moment – where the memory of the Past was melded to the Present – in the person of Luck.

"Metaphysics." Luck smiled at her. "Tell me more about Metaphysics." Luck wanted to strike up a conversation, hopefully a long one. *Metaphysics will justify a long discussion!*

187

Luck was delighted at his own brilliance. *This is perfect topic.*

Sophie could just totally *be*. Momentarily, she drifted deeper into her own thoughts. *We agreed that we would stay apart for a while. We will develop ourselves. Intellectually and morally. We will be better human beings. Then we would meet again… someday.* Her eyes betrayed the painful secrets of her being, now in a rendezvous with a Fate most unexpected – knowing she had a terrible Past seeking redemption. Remorse and sorrow streamed into her mind. In her heart, she was gently weeping. *It has been a long time. Hope we will be better this time. It has taken me a bit longer to get back to you. May Fate be kinder and gentler this time. Oh, Fate, give me another chance! This is my chance to rehabilitate myself for what I've done in my Past – in our Past.* Her spirit yearned to reach out to Luck but she seemed to lack the language or the experience to articulate her feelings, her memories and her renewed intentions. The good news was that she had come face to face with her Luck. *What a precious rendezvous! This must be a gift from heaven.*

"Hey, what's *this* Metaphysics thing?" Luck was getting impatient.

Sophie almost missed Luck's question. "Oh! It's a study in philosophy regarding the biggest problems in the universe and in our lives." Sophie pulled herself back to the Present. "It's the inquiry into the most fundamental nature of reality: Why do we exist? Who are we? Where are we going? The relationship of cause and effect. What is Time? How fluid is it? What is Space? How do we relate to Time and Space? How do we relate to the Past, the Present and the Future? What is naturally human and what is supernatural. What is karma? Cool stuff, aren't they?"

Luck was intrigued. "A metaphysician…" He was trying to register it in his mind.

"Yes. My Dad deals with the basic categories of being and how they relate with one another. He can discuss the fundamental notions of the world, such as existence, the issues of object, property, time, causality and possibility. "

"That's awesome!" Luck was fascinated.

"It's mind blowing. When I was ten, Dad would play games with me. He'd ask: 'Can the finite contain the infinite?' Isn't that so cool?"

Luck could only smile, while his brain was flying through a thousand miles.

Sophie expounded: "You see, bottom line, we are infinite by the fact that we can think of infinity – because only the infinite can contain the infinite."

The rhythm of the airplane engines hummed along, paralleling the rhythm of Sophie's headlong pursuit of a potential dream in a faraway land which was America at ISBS. All of a sudden, her upcoming ISBS education bestowed an added meaning: possible reparation of her past with Luck.

"I like that." Luck loved the conversation, without grasping the profoundness of Sophie's comments.

"Listen, in a few days, you'll meet my Dad. He'll be lecturing at ISBS. He has just joined as permanent faculty of ISBS. He's lots of fun."

"You're kidding!" Luck practically dropped his soda cup. Luckily, it was empty.

Luck was enthralled by Sophie's brilliance, her clarity of mind and her mysterious glances.

Hours later, the flight attendants began serving dinner. Luck suggested that Chance join them. You should meet my twin brother, Chance." Luck stood up to return to his seat.

"That would be lovely." Sophie agreed.

*   *   *

Luck found Chance knocked out on his seat, with Buff and Lotto asleep in each of his arms, snoring loudly like a choo-choo train. On his tummy was his pad of paper. On it was the first page of his Mini-Myth. On it he wrote:

MY MINI-MYTH

Chance

June 21. Today is my second birthday. A young man, full of dreams, just boarded *Imagination* toward America for an education.

Like a frog leaping out of a deep dark well, the sky is no longer one small circle but an immeasurable wide expanse.

God has lifted me to soar up in the skies. With joy, I thank God.

The gates of my heart are flung wide open,
my joy flying so high above the sea.

What is my destiny? Oh, Destiny, you are
wind of my sails! Now show me my Promised
Land.

Que será, será... Whatever will be, will be...
My night has ended. My day is about to
begin.

The rest was illegible. Chance did not last long in his writing.

The trauma of the past few days had drained him and he had quickly fallen asleep.

*   *   *

Tapping his shoulder gently, Luck woke his brother up. "Wake up!" Luck whispered excitedly. "I'd like you to meet a new friend of mine."

Luck gave Chance a quick update on his new acquaintance, Sophie. "Very interesting." Chance smiled in acknowledgement, as he stretched. "Come see! You will like her." Luck urged Chance, who politely rose to follow Luck.

Before leaving his seat, Chance gently placed Buff and Lotto into his huge rectangular attaché. Buff and Lotto were so groggy, they continued their up-in-the-sky slumber.

"Hey, keep an eye on Buff." Chance tapped Lotto gently on the shoulder. But Lotto barely budged.

Together, the twins walked over to where Sophie was sitting, whereupon Luck introduced Chance to Sophie.

The three dove into a free flow conversation as dinner was served. Chance could feel a warm camaraderie amongst the three of them. *Sophie is super smart, fun, and bubbly!* Chance, too, took a liking to Sophie.

Luck's eyes were sparkling with glee. "ISBS will be more fun with Sophie in the picture."

Chance teasingly glanced at Luck with this thought: *Luck, you are one real charmer!*

After dinner, the brothers retired to their respective seats for a few hours' sleep.

*   *   *

Hours later, *Imagination* shuddered due to air turbulence. "We're going through some air pockets. Take your seats. Please fasten your seat belts." Captain Fairsailing announced through the loudspeaker.

Luck and Chance woke up and looked out the window. The sky was still dark. But there was a streak of brightening dawn breaking at the edge of the horizon. And yes, they were now approaching America, this land of dreams, this land of possibilities.

*   *   *

The sound of clinking of silverwares and china could be heard traversing down the aisles.

"Coffee, O.J. or milk?" Queries from the flight attendants filtered through the sleepy heads of Luck and Chance. Other

192

heads began to bop up from the orange blankets throughout the aircraft. The aroma of coffee filled the air.

Soon, breakfast was served. Scrambled eggs, bacon and hash browns. This was the brothers' first *American* breakfast. Surreptitiously, the pair slipped some of their food to Buff and Lotto.

Breakfast was yummy!

"In another half an hour, we will be landing at Newark, *New Joy Sea*." From the loudspeaker, Captain Fairsailing announced *Imagination*'s impending landing.

As Luck peered out the window, he could detect a sliver of a skyline of Midtown Manhattan, New York City over the horizon. He could make out the miniature outlines of the iconic Empire State Building, the crowning spire of the Chrysler Building and the bladed silhouette of the Citicorp Tower. Yes, this was the city of the courageous and adventuresome, a city for those with dreams of greatness. Luck saw the crescent of the American Dream written on the landscape that was New York City.

The view was magnificent and mesmerizing. Four sets of eyes were glued to the circular windows: those of Luck, Chance, Buff and Lotto. As *Imagination* made its descent toward Newark, *New Joy Sea*, it made a few circles around Manhattan.

"Ah, Mad-Hat-On!" Buff was taking in all of Manhattan's glory in early dawn.

After a few minutes, *Imagination* began its final descent. The aircraft shuddered and roared like crazy as it was making its final descent. Finally, *Imagination* landed. The twins felt the thud of the rear wheels touch ground. The passengers clapped and cheered. The plane roared even louder as its thrust reversers deployed to further slowdown the plane. Moments later, after taxiing around the runway, it came to a full stop.

"Welcome to Newark, *New Joy Sea*! It is now 7:00 AM in the morning, June 21. Thank you for flying *Imagination*! It's been a delight to serve you." Captain Fairsailing announced.

Now that was Magic! For the hours Luck and Chance had flown half-way around the world, they were back on the same day of June 21st.

Today was the Summer Solstice. The longest day of the year. The beginning of summer. The brothers would live this day twice.

*   *   *

Morning has brought forth a new cycle of Time. The stars are re-aligning. T'is the Age of Aquarius! A new life has begun!

*   *   *

CHAPTER 27

VAROOM!

MUSIC INSPIRATION

PAPER PLANES
M.I.A.

SYMPHONY NO. 40 IN G MINOR, K. 550
WOLFGANG AMADEUS MOZART

COME SAIL AWAY
STYX

SAILING
CHRISTOPHER CROSS

A WHOLE NEW WORLD
THE LION KING
ALAN MENKEN & TIM RICE
SINGERS (A): BRAD KANE & LEA SALONGA
SINGERS (B): PEABO BRYSON & REGINA BELLE

ENVOLE-MOI
(FLY ME AWAY)
(FRENCH)
TAL & MPOKORA

INTERNATIONAL LOVE
PITBULL

LAUDATE DOMINUM
SOLEMN VESPERS, K 339
(PRAISE YE THE LORD)
(CLASSICAL GUITAR)
WOLFGANG AMDADEUS MOZART
GUITARIST: CHRISTOPHER PARKENING

NEW YORK, NEW YORK
FRANK SINATRA

EMPIRE STATE OF MIND
JAY Z & ALICIA KEYS

*   *   *

Fate and Destiny. They are opposite sides of the same coin – of Life itself. So similar yet so different.

Fate is a force inevitably predetermining events. It acts upon events with an assuredly inexorable outcome, which is unalterable.

Man against his fate: man would surely lose. For Fate has its own will upon which Life unfolds. Man has no choice. He has no exit. He is imprisoned in his own fate where there is no comfort, no logic, no escape. Such is the cosmos spinning its yarn upon events and human lives.

As distinct from Fate, Destiny involves human participation, with all his will and foibles. It is an evolutionary process involving probable outcomes – but requiring human participation. Self-participation is willful and essential. Through it, the person is transformed – finding meaning and inspiration in Life.

*   *   *

Luck and Chance had arrived in America – in *New Joy Sea*!

Moments later, *Imagination*'s main doors opened.

As the twins deplaned, they could not believe that they were in America – an idea, an aspiration actualized into reality upon

196

their disembarkation into the Liberty International Airport in Newark, *New Joy Sea*.

They joined the army of passengers, snaking through the cordoned serpentine lines, making their way through to the immigration checkpoints.

Finally, it was Luck's turn at the checkpoint. He gave his passport to the officer, who checked it and his F-1 Student Visa. There was a big stamping sound. "Welcome to America! Winston Odysseus Blundermore Mann." The officer smiled at Luck. "That's one long name! Your parents couldn't decide on which name to give you?" The officer joked.

Then, it was Chance's turn at the checkpoint. He handed his passport to the officer, who checked it and his F-1 Student Visa. There was a big stamping sound. "Welcome to America! Brandon Perseus Blundermore Mann. Another long name! You are *not* royalty, are you?" The officer chuckled, handing the passport back to Chance.

Voila! The twins were now officially in America – incredible but true.

Sophie Angelis Deepthinker was processed next. She soon joined the brothers.

As the three passed through customs gates with their luggage, they came face to face with a lady with a burgundy aviator's cap, reminiscent of the 1920's. Atop her cap was a pair of pilot's goggles. She carried an enormous bright red placard with their names on it.

"Welcome to Newark, *New Joy Sea*!" The lady stepped forward, greeted and embraced each of the newcomers. The twins made sure her hugs were real gentle, lest their chest wounds hurt. She had red auburn hair tucked under her cap, dark green sparkling eyes, with silky shiny fair skin. She wore loose khaki pants tucked inside her heavy pair of black boots. Despite her tough-looking attire, she came across feminine with her warm smile and wet-look lips. "Call me Lady Destiny!"

To be sure, Lady Destiny commanded her own law upon herself, exercising special considerations regarding her favored protagonists. At fifty, she possessed *the* Magic of managing and relating to the matching of characters, events and outcomes. With the dexterity of a weaver, she had a tremendous knack for timing and change – manipulating imperfect situations which yearned for sense and sensibility. Most importantly, she sought the Good, the True and the Beautiful in this world. She brought these about with her *initiative* as a skilled diplomat. She had an acute sense of fairness, and would attempt to bring favor to those less fortunate. With her intellectual acuity, she was a force to be reckoned with.

"I'm *Finnish* from Espoo, a city outside Helsinki. Now I'm living in New York City." She beamed at her guests.

"We've just *started*. Tell me more about Espoo?" Luck teased, picking up on her Finnish ethnicity. A wise-ass, he egged her on.

"Very funny," Lady Destiny winked at Luck. "And I'm not yet *finished* with you. If you don't behave, I'll send you to Espoo!." She pretended to be cross with Luck, pointing sternly at him. "You smart aleck, you!"

Luck gave her a laughing rejoinder. He liked the sound of "Espoo".

To the group of three, she said: "While being the head of the International House at ISBS, I'm also with the Experiment in

International Sensible Living. EISL! Its purpose is to give you a myriad of authentic and deep experiences while you are in the ISBS, by linking you up with host families. Through EISL, you will have total immersion in the wonkiest experiences. Are you ready for these?"

The three nodded eagerly.

"These EISL experiences will be amazing and unforgettable. Your lives will be forever transformed."

"I can't wait to be transformed!" Excited, Luck was trying to be funny.

"You'll be meeting your assigned host family soon." Lady Destiny assured Chance, who had a puzzled look on his face.

"So, shall we begin? I'm sure you'd like to see New York City – the Big Apple!" With that, Lady Destiny led the three out of the Newark Liberty International Airport toward the nearest curb, by Bus Stop Number 8. There stood a roofless magnesium alloy, cone-headed turbo shuttle van in loud violet. On its side was painted the word: *VAROOM!* Behind the turbo shuttle van was an orange ISBS SUV.

Lady Destiny introduced them to *Varoom!*'s chauffeur: Zeppelino Intello Lite. At forty-five, his eyes blood-shot and wild, he had on an old 1920's fighter-pilot's leather cap, with a pair of orange rimmed aviator's goggles cocked upon his forehead. His jet-black hair was tied back in a pony-tail. "Just call me Zep."

Having been raised in Pompei, Italy, Zep spoke with a heavy accent, making histrionic gestures with his hands. He was half Italian from his mother's side. His father was Irish, whose family emigrated from Dublin, Ireland, during the Great Irish Potato Famine of 1845 to 1852. Over a million died, reducing Ireland's population by a quarter. The Irish called this period the *"Gorta Mór"*, meaning the "Great Hunger".

To the brothers, he gave out a broad grin, exposing his gold-laden dentures. He was lanky tall with a broad frame. He wore a rough looking denim jacket, matched by a pair of dark paratroopers' boots. "All aboard!" Zep ordered in his deep throaty voice.

As the three lugged their suitcases, Speedy Gonzales, a twenty year old driver of the ISBS SUV, emerged from the vehicle to receive the suitcases and their hand-carries. He was an eager beaver where speed was everything. He was a man who would run first and ask questions later. Hence, his moniker: Speedy Rosales.

"Your belongings will go behind this ISBS SUV." Whereupon Speedy hauled the suitcases and the hand-carries into the back section of the ISBS SUV. Without wasting a minute, he quickly issued claim tickets to each of the three youngsters.

"Speedy will take your luggage to ISBS Admissions Office storage area. There, you will redeem your belongings later." Lady Destiny assured her newcomers.

A sense of awkward hesitation overtook Chance. He whispered to Luck. "Remember Uncle Antikweetee's advice: we should keep our gifts close by and *never* entrust them to strangers."

Luck nodded in agreement.

"Lady Destiny, I'm afraid we need to have our attachés with us." Chance made a polite request.

"Why?" Lady Destiny gave Chance a testy frown. "Your

belongings will be safe with Speedy." She assured them.

Speedy gave Chance a glassy glare.

"Per instructions." Chance responded. "From our Big Boss in the Philippines!"

"Is there extra luggage compartment space in *Varoom!* ?" Luck cut in.

"I believe so." Zep was trying to be helpful.

The twins were relieved and proceeded to retrieve their attachés. Accordingly, Speedy revised the items on their respective claim tickets – while pretending to give the twins a nasty look. "I'll give you boys a break – just this one time."

But the twins had a confession to make to Lady Destiny: they had their *Moldivians* inside their attachés.

"How do we manage these little ones?" Luck was practically pleading.

From inside their attachés, Luck took out Buff while Chance took out Lotto.

"Oh! They *are* lovely!" Lady Destiny was struck by their cuteness. "Now, now! Where did you get them?"

"From my Fairy Godmother!" Luck exclaimed.

Lady Destiny smiled sweetly as she showed the twins the luggage compartment beside Zep's seat.

"What to do with our *Moldivians?*" Luck was a bit lost. "We can't squeeze them in the compartment. They'd get dizzy and suffocate in there!"

"Good point!" Lady Destiny nodded in agreement, her mind racing for a solution. Then, she broke out with a foolish giggle. She bent over and fished out two strange looking bands from her bag in the luggage compartment.

"What's that?" Chance did not get it, examining the bands.

With a big laugh, Lady Destiny declared: "These are my daughter's training bras! You can put them on and strap your *Moldivians* with you during the ride! It will be one wild ride! And you will need these training bras to restrain them, lest they fly off."

Lady Destiny and Zep exploded in gut-busting laughter.

"Lady Destiny, your daughter's training bras will need fine-tuning." Zep pulled out a pair of scissors from his kit. "We need to cut four little holes for the *Moldivian's* limbs to extend out." Lady Destiny and Sophie were bending over in gut-wrenching laughter.

"OK." Zep did his job prepping the training bras with his scissors. Zip. Zip. Zap! "There you go!" Four tiny holes appeared in each bra.

Luck took off his suit. Grimacing with pain, he put on the training bra. The pain of wound inflicted by Gul was distinctly there. Carefully, he strapped in Buff, with his limbs sticking out the tiny holes made by Zep.

Likewise, Chance took off his suit. Cringing with pain, he put on the training bra. Gently, he strapped in Lotto, with his limbs sticking out the tiny holes.

Then, the twins donned their respective suits again.

By now, Lady Destiny, Sophie, Zep and Speedy were teetering

in laughter, as the twins looked on pathetically.

The brothers did not expect that within the first hour after landing in America, they would be wearing training bras! That was not in their playbook.

The pair slid their attachés into the compartment, whereupon Zep locked it.

"Now, are we all ready?" Lady Destiny inquired, making sure everything was in order. Then, she climbed up onto *Varoom!* and sat directly behind Zep. Sophie sat at Lady Destiny's right.

Directly behind Lady Destiny was Luck. Chance sat at Luck's right.

"What's the next program?" Chance was curious.

"You'll see." Lady Destiny gave Chance a sweet smile, exposing her deep dimples.

"Before we start, I need you all to empty your pockets and put the items into the plastic zip-lock bags I am passing out." Now, Lady Destiny acted like a school teacher. "Nothing should be in your pockets. No pens. No money. And by all means, no smart phones."

The youngsters emptied their pockets, eagerly anticipating what would happen next. Lady Destiny promptly put the zip-lock bags into the dashboard compartment.

Then, Lady Destiny produced three pairs of aviator goggles. "Put these on and make sure they fit. I'm sorry I don't have small ones for your little friends. They'll have to grin and bear it."

Chance proceeded to place the goggles over his eye-glasses.

"Now fasten your seatbelts." Zep spat out the tobacco cud he was chewing and got busy inspecting each newcomer's preparations.

"Ready?" Lady Destiny made a final inspection.

The three nodded enthusiastically, as each of them snuggled tightly into their seats.

"Now, some instructions." Over his microphone, Zep yelled out the basic hand signals. "A constant back and forth of your palm signifies 'Slowdown'. Keeping you palm up like a policeman means 'Stop'. A thumbs-up, like so, means: 'Higher'. A thumbs-down, like so, means: 'Lower'. Two forefingers crossed together like an X means: 'Let's go down. I'm feeling sick.' *Capiche?* Do you understand? Are these clear?"

"Yes." The three youngsters cheered.

"Now, fasten your over-the-shoulder restraint." Zep shouted. He walked to each side of the turbo shuttle van to make sure each youngster's restraint was securely in lock position.

"All right!" Thereupon, Zep locked-in the lap-bar, a restraint bar right above the lap area running across each row of seats.

"And I say: Are you ready?" Zep signaled, as he hopped onto his driver's seat.

"Yes!" came loud screams from the newcomers. The youngsters were aching for the thrill soon to come. Luck was vigorously signaling a thumbs-up.

With a loud roar of the engine, *Varoom!* sped toward the nearest freeway. As soon as it entered the freeway, *Varoom!* screamed and accelerated even more, and took off – up, up they soared into the air toward Newark.

For the brothers, this would be the most exhilarating ride they had had in their lives! Never in their lives had they dreamt to soar so high in a turbo shuttle van like this one. Despite having their suits on, the twins could feel the chilly blasts of wind. Enthralled, Luck gripped his shoulder restraint tightly.

Everyone was on cloud nine!

Chance looked at the azure blue sky. *Oh, what a lofty, limitless sky – so grand and yet so quiet; so receptive and so all encompassing!*

Varoom! headed north and took them for a brief sky-tour of Newark. Then quickly it swerved and flat turned to the right. Everyone was pulled toward the left.

"We're over *Joy Sea City!*" Zep yelled over his microphone. In less than a minute, the Hudson River appeared below them. Within seconds, *Varoom!* made a diving loop heading toward the water. "Now, hold on to your *Moldivians!*" Zep screamed over the microphone.

Yeeeooowww!! Everyone was screaming – including Buff and Lotto. The world was coming unglued and was turning upside down! They were now into a vertical loop! A three hundred sixty degree summersault downward!

Then, as suddenly, *Varoom!* rocketed up – shooting straight up to the sky! Yeeeooowww! This was insane! They felt being pulled back against their seats. The gravitational force exceeded one G! The force was so strong Chance could feel heavy pressure against his chest. Up, up, they rocketed up! Everyone's heads were pressed against the headrests. Everyone's cheeks were wind-blown, stretched flat, fluttering against the wind.

When *Varoom!* reached the apex of its climb, it turned toward Manhattan and into a free-fall! Yeeeooowww! Now, they were in a down free-fall with negative G force. Now everyone could feel air-time! Yes, they felt like floating on their seats!

Now *Varoom!* was racing toward the Statue of Liberty! At this time, Sophie was making the "Slowdown" sign. The thrill was too much! She could not bear it anymore! But she had an aching smile on her face.

Zep slowed down *Varoom!* as he fast approached the Statue of Liberty Enlightening the World. The morning sun was beating upon her green patina face. The colossal Liberty looked elegant, beaconing newcomers to America.

In a split second, Chance remembered the message of Lady Liberty:

Keep, ancient lands, your storied pomp!

Give me your tired, your poor,

Your huddled masses yearning to breathe free,

The wretched refuse of your teeming shore,

Send these, the homeless, tempest-tossed to me,

I lift my lamp beside the golden door!

Varoom! circled around the Statue of Liberty a few times.

Chance noticed the torch and the *tabula ansata* – a tablet evoking the law, with the inscription: July 4, 1776, the date of the American Declaration of Independence. He saw a broken chain by her feet. Once upon a time, *Libertas,* the goddess of freedom, was worshipped in ancient Rome, especially among emancipated slaves.

Chance was touched. He took this scene deep to heart. So he was entering New York City – the city for the ambitious and daring.

Next, *Varoom!* swerved over to Ellis Island, an immigration station, which once processed millions of immigrants into America, whose lives were forever transformed if accepted.

Within seconds, *Varoom!* zoomed forward, flying just above the water level, toward the tall buildings of the financial district in lower Manhattan. As *Varoom!* reached the southern tip of Manhattan, it surged forward in a corkscrew heading northwest, along Broadway to Times Square. Gigantic advertisements flashed by as *Varoom!* zipped through downtown Manhattan heading uptown. Luck was overwhelmed by the advertising bill boards he was trying to catch an eye on.

"MAD-HAT-ON!" Buff shouted at the top of his voice.

Sophie screamed, fearing that *Varoom!* might crash into the tall buildings.

Next, *Varoom!* cruised above Central Park. Doves and pigeons dove for cover.

They flew over the magnificent Columbia University campus – whereupon, *Varoom!* made a cobra roll with a double downward summersault and was suddenly heading southward back to New York City. *Varoom!* blasted over Central Park again, flying over the Metropolitan Museum and the Guggenheim Museum. *Varoom!* suddenly rocketed upwards. In a blink of an eye, they could see the bladed solar roof of the Citicorp Tower, the pointed antenna of the Empire State Building and the swirly curves of the Chrysler Building conical top. From there, *Varoom!* veered toward a diving loop, with all in an upside-down free fall. With twists and turns, *Varoom!* zoomed through the Arch at Washington Square.

Sophie shut her eyes. She thought she would die! When Sophie opened her eyes, *Varoom!* was passing through Little Italy and making a landing at Canal and Elizabeth Streets. Chinatown! Wow!

Varoom! landed and jerked to an abrupt stop.

Then as now, Manhattan was an island of dreams, dreams for commercial success, dreams for career and life success. For centuries, this granite island had beckoned millions to its shores for a better living, for higher purpose, for a deeper realization. Yes, Manhattan was the gigantic granite rock upon which many dreams were built, upon which many dreams were smashed. Manhattan was an island of Truth and Disillusionment: *one either makes it here or not.*

"Surprise! We'll be having *dim-sum (点心)* here! This is a popular Chinese tea-time snack!" Lady Destiny declared, confident that the twins would enjoy a Chinese meal – their very first one here in America.

As they got off *Varoom!*, the twins' hair was standing straight up – completely wind-blown.

Overwhelmed, Buff and Lotto were speechless. They did not have this kind of flying technology in *Moldivia*. This was more than what they had bargained for with the Fairy Godmother.

Everyone's legs were wobbly from the wild rollercoaster ride.

Zep had a big mischievous grin across his face, knowing everyone enjoyed the ride.

Lady Destiny pulled out two ponchos from her bag in the luggage compartment, handling them to the brothers.

"Here, flop the poncho over your shoulders and cover your front, so that you don't look silly. You can continue to wear your training bras." Luck and Chance appreciated Lady Destiny's humorous sensibility.

By now, Luck and Chance looked more like clowns than international travelers.

Like a scout leader, Lady Destiny led the youngsters to the best Chinese restaurant for *dim-sum* up at Golden Prosperity Pavillion. Luck and Chance were in for a gastronomic experience. Sumptuous shrimp dumplings. Tofu stuffed with minced beef. Spicy thinly sliced beef tripe. *Xiao long bao (小笼包)*. And more! Yummmmy! While eating, Luck and Chance cut up little *dim-sum* morsels and shared them with their *Moldivian* friends.

As Lady Destiny was settling the bill, the three youngsters were cracking open their fortune cookies and reading their fortunes.

Luck had this fortune: *"If you want to add value to your life, take care of NOW."*

Chance had this fortune: *"He who cannot endure the bad won't live to see the good."*

Sophie had this fortune: *"The only gold you'll see in your golden years will be the color of your pee."*

The three youngsters exploded into laughter.

Lady Destiny's fortune was this: *"Life must be lived forward, but can only be understood backwards."*

"Hmmmm... That's deep!" Luck snatched and read Lady Destiny's fortune.

*　　　*　　　*

Soon, they emerged from the restaurant and retraced their way back to the turbo shuttle van.

"This time, we're heading toward ISBS at *Lore County, New Joy Sea.*" Lady Destiny was walking briskly.

"Climb on in!" Zep hollered in his usual loud voice.

With that, everyone scrambled on board, fastened their seat belts and their over-the-shoulder restraints. Then, the lap bar was set in place, locking with a click.

Zep turned on the engine. Rrrrrrrrr! With a deafening roar, *Varoom!* blasted toward the Verrazano Bridge, one of the world's longest bridges.

In a corkscrew maneuver, *Varoom!* rocketed up the horizon and the youngsters could see the elegance of the Verrazano Bridge, an outstretched expanse connecting Brooklyn and Staten Island.

The brothers had never seen a bridge like this, a dazzling, eloquent arc announcing and displaying the majesty of the Atlantic Ocean yonder.

For the pair, this was their first taste of heaven. For them, this was a blissful rollercoaster ride beyond words, where speed, velocity and pure thrill were merged together into the Moment. For now, they completely forgot the pain of their chest wounds.

Like riding a rollercoaster, *Varoom!* did a fan-turn to the right. Everyone jerked to the left. From the sea, it cut into land, passing Monmouth County and headed straight into the wonderland of *Lore County, New Joy Sea. Varoom!* cork-screwed over small town rooftops, surged above brushed trees, toward thicker woods, over sparkling rivers and lakes. It buzzed through lush verdant hills until, alas, it fast approached Testament City on top of the *Moriah Mountain Plateau*, where the shimmering and jaw-dropping seven spires of the most extraordinary and majestic Testament Towers of ISBS suddenly emerged.

They had arrived at ISBS!

A whole new world would begin.

*   *   *

CHAPTER 28

EUREKA, ISBS!

<u>MUSIC INSPIRATION</u>

ARRIVAL AT THE PALACE
ANNA AND THE KING
GEORGE FENTON & ROBERT KRAFT

WINDMILLS OF YOUR MIND
NOEL HARRISON

HERE, THERE AND EVERYWHERE
THE BEATLES

HIGH SONG
HIGH GE
HIGH 歌
(CHINESE MANDARIN & ENGLISH)
ISABELLE LING / 黄龄

THE SOUND OF MUSIC
RICHARD RODGERS & OSCAR HAMMERSTEIN II
SINGER: JULIE ANDREWS

SUMMER
FOUR SEASONS
ANTONIO VIVALDI

*　　　*　　　*

*W*hat came first: the chicken or the egg?

This conundrum prevailed over the millennia, pondered by the greatest philosophers.

It is a question to which a definitive answer is elusive – like so many issues in life.

What do we default to when the inexplicable occurs?

Many times, we come upon a fork in Life where choices are mutually exclusive. And we have to make a choice. For better or for worse. We make our choice, only to wonder later whether we made the right one.

*   *   *

Varoom!, the turbo shuttle van, circled the ISBS campus area as it slowed down for a landing.

From the air, atop the wide stretching mountain plateau, the twins could see a wide moat snaking around the outer perimeters of the Gaudian stonewall fortification of ISBS. The campus was filled with verdant rolling hills entailing seven thousand acres.

At the eastern most edge of the school ground stood the massive East Gate, beyond which was a drawbridge. Made of steel, this eclectic eye-catching drawbridge arched over the wide mote, linking it to Testament City, a quaint university town. At the center of town was the bustling Testament Square, whose main economy and activities catered to the ISBS community through the myriad of colorful shops. From the Testament Square, any faculty or student could access the quaint red train station within three minutes' walk. By train, passengers could reach New York City or Philadelphia in one and a half hours' ride.

Being a university town of thirty thousand, Testament City prided itself to be established right at the dawn of the American colonial period. Testament City had featured prominently during the American Revolutionary War. The Battle of Testament City was the turning point of the revolution. From the City of Providence, Julius Blundermore led the Rhode Island Continentals to join up with George Washington's troops. Together, they smashed the British army and its Hessian mercenaries in *New Joy Sea*.

ISBS also contributed importantly to the revolutionary effort, through to the establishment of the American republic and all the way to the present American age. It started out as a divinity school, then evolved as a school producing statesmen. Now, its graduates filled the high ranks in government and corporations all over the world.

Varoom! landed and parked at the far end of the Grand *Piazza Rotunda*, facing the Testament Towers, the main ISBS building with its seven glorious towering spires. It gave the newcomers a breathtaking view.

At the center of the Testament Towers Piazza was a thick gray flagpole soaring up high, atop of which flew the blue ISBS flag bearing its insignia and its motto: MANY WORLDS IN HARMONY.

For the twins, the whole place looked ethereal – enchantingly otherworldly. Noticing the perplexing look of the newcomers, Lady Destiny gave them their first introduction to the campus.

"Welcome to ISBS – the *most* magical place on Earth!" Lady Destiny declared triumphantly. She looked intensely at the three newbies. "ISBS. This is *the* international school of dreams, of aspirations – a school for genuine striving for a magical world of achievement and realization.

"Here, the pivotal direction of human civilization was once fought and decided. This is *the* international school of transcendent History, without which human existence might have decayed and disintegrated into abysmal misery and meaninglessness. Yes, great battles were fought here because of the tenacity of its professors and students who held on to the tenets of their fervent beliefs which made ISBS what it is today. Over the years, many have suffered and died for the higher truths of humanity."

At this Moment, above the front entrance doors of the Testament Towers, the long hand of the circular bronze clock struck twelve, announcing high noon with its chime.

Under the noontime sun, the edifice of the Testament Towers exuded optimism and hope.

Shaking and weak in the knees, Luck and Chance disembarked from *Varoom!*. The twins and Sophie gave each other spirited high-fives, congratulating each other for having made it to ISBS.

Chance gazed up at the seven towering spires of Testament Towers, savoring this moment of triumph, this moment of arrival.

Turning to the opposite side, Luck stared at the East Gate, which was thirty-three feet in height. Outside, toward the right side the gate stood a colossal oculus, which was eighty feet in height.

Lady Destiny offered this explanation: "At night, this Oculus of the East guards the Eastern Front of the school perimeter. It sweeps its intense searchlights through the Eastern Front of the campus, guarding it from intruders."

The brothers nodded, giving themselves pause. The Oculus of the East looked intimidating. Wrapped around its rounded conical top was a strip of translucent glass, totally encircling its cone head. Its base was three times larger than its top, projecting a bastion of towering solidity

The twins took their respective attachés from *Varoom!*'s compartment as they said goodbye to Zep.

The pair carefully placed their *Moldivian* friends into their respective attachés. "Sorry, we can't afford to look like clowns in our first hour at ISBS." With that, Luck and Chance carefully slipped out of their training bras.

"Good luck!" Zep hugged his three student passengers. The twins did not enjoy the hugs.

"Lady Destiny, we'd like to keep these training bras. Is that OK?" Luck was thinking ahead. "These may come in handy in the future."

"Sure!" Lady Destiny was more than happy to oblige.

Chance was thinking long term. "In fact, we may need more of them. Can you bring us more next time we meet?"

Inside *Varoom!*, Zep was cracking up with laughter. "Oh, no! This is too much!"

"By the way, we would like to have the ponchos, too." Luck wanted the ponchos for their friends, especially in the evenings.

"American evenings are much cooler than those in *Moldivia.*" Chance did not want their little *Moldivian* friends to be cold at night.

"Not a problem! Those are yours now." On her part, Lady Destiny wanted to make sure they would not become the laughing stock on campus. "After all, you need to *save face* with your new college friends."

*   *   *

Lady Destiny led the way, as the three youngsters followed behind, fully distracted and engrossed by their new surroundings.

Entering the Testament Towers, the first thing they noticed was a gigantic planetarium dome above the expansive entrance rotunda displaying in 3-D the whole universe as mapped out by the Hubble Telescope. The Milky Way was just a tiny spiraling galaxy amongst the billions of galaxies. Suspended in the middle of the planetarium dome was a holographic projection of an enormous translucent human brain.

"Just in case you're wondering, that's called *The Mind Contemplating the Cosmos.*" Lady Destiny read the minds of her new arrivals. They were, indeed, blown away by the sight. It was an impressive sight: the mind and the universe.

Lady Destiny was tickled pink by her entourage's curiosity. "You see, in a scientific world, matter comes *before* the mind. From this perspective, the mind emerges through matter. Stephen Hawkins stated that God is not needed in the Big Bang. Some physicists claim that through the M-theory, the laws of quantum physics caused many universes, including our own, to have been created from nothingness!"

"What is M-theory?" Luck queried.

Without fanfare, Lady Destiny continued. "It is a construct to generalize the strings of string theory. Take your pick. M can stand for the dimensional *membrane* in our multiverse reality. Or M can stand for magic, or mystery, or mother-theory. Ah, M is the Missing Mama of Physics!" She chuckled. "M-theory will tie in everything."

"Now this is getting too deep for me!" For Chance, this was over his head.

But Luck was excited. He loved physics, mathematics and the sciences.

With a smile, Lady Destiny continued. "Not to digress, for a scientific materialist, the baby attains its mind only after years of growth and experience. In contrast, in a mind-before-universe perspective, the Mind of God willed the universe to exist. From this perspective, the cosmos is conscious and alive, responding to our individual needs. When you pass this rotunda, day in and day out, you'll be reminded of these two schools of thought: Are you a scientific materialist or a spiritual being yearning for maximum consciousness?"

"Awesome question!" Luck wagged his tongue, licking his swollen lips in the process, eager to delve into this question.

The twins and Sophie were deeply taken by the profundity of Lady Destiny's question.

Lady Destiny was beside herself. "To put it simply, which came first: the chicken or the egg?"

*   *   *

At the forefront of the hallway by the edge of the rotunda was a holographic sepia image of Leonardo da Vinci's Vitruvian Man facing *The Mind Contemplating the Cosmos*. The glowing image of the Vitruvian Man was life size, engulfed by a translucent sphere, and within the sphere, a yellowish transparent cube.

Lady Destiny smiled. "Do you know that the Vitruvian Man is one of the most referenced and reproduced images in the world? Such is the genius of Leonardo da Vinci. This image is called the *Canon of Proportions*; sometimes, it is referred to as the *Proportions of Man*. Do you know that the length of our outstretched arms is equivalent to our height? Amazing, isn't it?

"This image is an implied symbol of the essential symmetry of the human body and that of the universe. In this context, we have man face to face with the universe. Understand man and you will gain insight into the universe. At this stage, man has become the measure of all things."

The three youngsters were absorbed by the image.

Luck and Chance were fully taken in by the image since Phantom Dad's name was Vitruvian Mann, the source of their existence into this world. What a coincidence!

*   *   *

The floors were of white Italian Carrera marble. As they walked rapidly to the Admissions Office, they could hear the muffled echo of their footsteps, and those of hundreds others, as new and returning students were walking up and down the grand hallway, attending to their registrations for the school year.

Here and there, flashing every twenty seconds, they saw holographic projections of other famous statues in key spots of the hallway. Likewise, by the hallway walls, they viewed 3-D images of world renowned paintings from museums like the Metropolitan Museum of Art, the Louvre, the Tate Gallery, the Uffizi, the Prado and the Hermitage.

Just in front of the Admissions Office, at the middle of the hallway, was a dark-green holographic image of Auguste Rodin's *The Thinker*, with his seated pensive pose, declaring:

"I think; therefore, I am. I will, therefore, I am."

A symbol of knowledge and philosophy, *The Thinker* evoked a contemplative mood of deep thought. His hunched torso projected a powerful sense of brooding reflection.

But lo! Whom did they meet in the hallway?

It was Marcus Blundermore, the President of ISBS. Tall, Blundermore wore a magnificent midnight gray high collared, Lincoln long coat which reached down to below his knees. He had a pin of a rose crisscrossed by a golden key pinned on his lapel. With a Chinese high collar, his starched white shirt was adorned with black onyx buttons. He wore a thick belt whose buckle was that of a silver snakehead swallowing its own tail. He had long gray silky hair down to his shoulders. He had a matching long gray beard, tied by a tiny black bow near the tip. On his slender nose sat a pair of rimless spectacles. On his left ring finger was huge golden ring, imprinted with the ISBS Testament Tower logo. On top of the logo were the words: Society of Light. Underneath the logo were the letters: SOL.

At sixty-five, Blundermore exuded an ineffable mystical aura, displaying authority and grace which emanated from deep within. His excellence came from his attitude of performing his best at every moment, an attitude imparted to him by his father, Lucius Blundermore. He had the uncanny ability to read into the innermost of human heart and soul, in all its nobility and vices. Through his mother, Lady Hope, he learned the virtue of modesty and generosity.

The twins were thrilled to see him. Instantly, they ran forward and hugged him – just gently. "Uncle Blundermore!" Luck and Chance each hugged him lightly, given the wounds on their chest.

Blundermore was ebullient. "You two are the joys of my heart and soul!"

"Look Uncle Blundermore, we've got new friends!" Luck brought out Buff from his attaché. Chance brought out Lotto.

"They are wonderful!" Blundermore's eyes sparkled as he greeted Buff and Lotto.

"Fairy Godmother sent them to us!" Luck declared.

Blundermore laughed with amusement.

Over the years, the brothers had received Christmas cards and other knick knacks from Blundermore, from as far back as they could remember. Most recently, each had received from their uncle: crisp hundred dollar bills totaling US$800. A note read: "Please smell these bills. Such is the *sweet* smell of success. Wishing you success! Merry Christmas!" The money had helped in paying for their college application fees. Besides Uncle Antikweetee, Blundermore was a dear uncle to the twins.

Unfortunately, while Blundermore wanted to spend more time with the youngsters, he was approached by another school official on some urgent business matter.

Blundermore wanted to make sure they would meet again soon. "Let's have breakfast tomorrow! We'll catch up then!" With that, he headed off with the other school official. "Tah-tah!"

*   *   *

CHAPTER 29

THOMAS LEEDS
AND
THE NEW PEDAGOGY

MUSIC INSPIRATION

LIFE
(PIANO)
LUDOVICO EINAUDI

FOR THE WORLD
HERO – THEME SONG
TAN DUN / 谭盾
PERFORMED BY: LIU LI

LOVE SONG
BRUNO MARS

JUST THE WAY YOU ARE
BRUNO MARS

SUPERSTAR
(CHINESE MANDARIN)
S.H. E.

FRIEND
PENG YOU
朋友
(CHINESE MANDARIN / CHINESE CANTONESE)
WAKIN CHAO / 周华健

EXPERIENCE
(PIANO & DRUMS)
LUDOVICO EINAUDI

*　　　*　　　*

*E*xistence is the prerequisite to evolution, the portal to possibilities.

*   *   *

At the Admissions Office, Katya Athena Tolstaya, assistant to the Dean of Admissions, Mr. Thomas Leeds greeted the newcomers. She was a tall and captivating Russian belle from the Ural steppes, with long brunette hair. At twenty-one, her skin was fair and smooth. Katya stood at five feet seven. She expressed this disarming yet enchanting all-knowing look where nothing was hidden. She evoked a godly visage of Athena, her namesake.

Her brilliant blue eyes smiled greetings to the youngsters. "I've been expecting you!" She had a Russian accent. "Welcome to ISBS! Mr. Thomas Leeds will be out momentarily." She stood up, extended her long slim hands, and shook hands with each of them energetically while guiding them to the sitting area. "Your suitcases are at our storage area down the hall." "You can claim them after your meeting with the Dean or anytime, at your convenience."

Katya was instantly struck by Chance's good looks. His square glasses made him look so intellectual, so sophisticated. She smiled at him sweetly. *He is so handsome! He's got a nice tush!*

Meanwhile Lady Destiny took her leave saying: "I have to pick up Enigma and Choice – another of your compatriots from the Philippines. They will be arriving this afternoon at the airport. You should meet them, for sure! You'll see them this evening." Then she took off.

Minutes later, Mr. Leeds emerged, finishing up with two new students, wishing them good luck for the school year.

Excitedly, the twins and Sophie rose up to greet Mr. Leeds.

"It's so nice to see the three of you." Mr. Leeds welcomed them, giving each of them a firm hand shake.

He had met with them months ago in Manila, while interviewing the finalist candidates for ISBS. "The Admissions Committee have chosen each of you given your evidence of exceptional abilities."

At forty, Mr. Leeds's hairline had receded prematurely. He combed his well-oiled hair backward, displaying his shinny forehead. He wore a thick moustache, matching his bushy dark brows. He had an athletic physique. The curve lines on his shiny forehead betrayed a perpetually worried look.

"The incoming class will be terrific!" Mr. Leeds boomed, tucking each of his thumbs with pride by his pair of suspenders. Standing tall in his long sleeved starched-stiff white shirt, he appeared well quaffed. With his bow tie, he looked professorial.

Mr. Leeds saluted Sophie. "I am so proud you've chosen ISBS! I can't wait to see father and daughter discussing Metaphysics in the lecture hall! Aristotle Angelis Deepthinker was nervous that you would choose Harvard, Princeton or Yale. Or, you might choose Foxscabs, Rat-Hole Polytechnic or the Horsemeat School for Business. That would be a blow to your Dad's pride."

The newcomers laughed, with Luck laughing the loudest.

"I know ISBS will be great!" Sophie felt confident she made the right choice.

"Come in!" Mr. Leeds led the group into his office.

The shaggy beige carpet on the floor made Mr. Leeds' office feel instantly cozy.

On a wall was a genteel 3-D portrait of Albert Einstein, the patron saint of ISBS. Mr. Einstein seemed to be nodding as he uttered these words:

"Imagination is more important than knowledge.

"For knowledge is limited to all we now know and understand, while imagination embraces the entire world, and all there ever will be to know and understand."

Mr. Leeds directed the three youngsters to the sofa section of his office.

Gently, he shut his door.

After a few pleasantries, Mr. Leeds dove in with the latest news: "You will absolutely *love* this school year! Our whole curriculum has been revamped – approved just this past month in time for the new school year. It's a new, improved program – intended to be transformative!" Pride filled his eyes.

"The pedagogic format and approach has been changed. To start out, each student will be given solid grounding in the real world – as it really is. Mastery of reality is key. Each student will need to understand the physics of the world, both materially and metaphysically. Moving forward, each student will learn to think out of the box. Everyone will be trained to think and execute accurately. The course structure will now revolve more closely around each student's needs, desires and goals. Hence, with two thousand new entrants, we're talking about two thousand points of references. This is so because each student counts."

Mr. Leeds handed each of the newcomers the newest course catalogue. "You will love our new program." Then, he continued. "You see, each person is a cosmic necessity. Everyone born into this world represents a new hope, a step forward, an aspiration for a breakthrough in creation. Through each person, our world cries out for progress. With each new birth, our world seeks the next breakthrough – for solutions to its challenges. Each person is a new opportunity for this world to create that *ideal* person with personality and character: a complete person with humanity. Each of us represents a *unique chance* at which the world's phenomena intersect – now and never again – for perfection."

"Screen on!" Mr. Leeds ordered. Automatically, the wall screen lit up.

The newcomers were impressed by his gadget.

"Portrait of Nicolaus Copernicus." Mr. Leeds spoke facing the screen. A portrait of Copernicus appeared.

Luck shouted out Copernicus's most important work. "*De Revolutionibus orbium coelestium!* Expounding on his heliocentric theory! He published this right before he died on May 24, 1543." He gave Chance a fist bump.

Mr. Leeds smiled. "With Copernicus, succeeding generations came to adhere to a heliocentric worldview – that the Earth revolves around the Sun. He made a most significant contribution to the world. That was powerful. He revolutionized astronomy, cosmology, philosophy, and metaphysics – all in one stroke. Without him, man would not have been able to land on the Moon. Nor would spaceships be heading for Mars."

The newcomers nodded.

Mr. Leads returned to his main point. "Sorry for the digression. Who will be *that* person – or persons? Each person's journey is important, compelling and eternal. We need heroes: those who are willing to partake and make it against all odds. ISBS wants to play *that* leadership role in human evolution."

Mr. Leads gazed intently at each of the three. "Hence, each person needs to strive forward – toward making his own contribution to this world. By overcoming the vestiges of his own origin, he nudges himself out of his own unconscious and wakes toward a new self-consciousness leading to a new reality – a reality devoid of delusions, chaos and madness. In other words, each person is capable of creating a new world reality."

Chance was impressed with Mr. Leads' presentation. *Wow! This is deep. Is this what I signed up for?*

"Hence, each student's school year will be quite different from the next student's, in content, context, function and result." Mr. Leads expounded on the pedagogic points. Even Mr. Leads himself was getting excited. "The results will be amazing. We'll be dealing with real life projects, real world issues, in real time. We are lucky to have at our disposal the support of large alumni endowment and our links with various enlightened foundations, corporations, governments and multilaterals – on a global basis. First year students *can* intern with any of the enlightened organizations – assuming it accepts you."

"Booyah!" Luck exclaimed, his eyes beaming.

"On the schooling part, student projects will be graded for originality of concept, effectiveness in execution, and impact. There will be individual projects, group projects and class projects. This will be awesome!" Mr. Leads wiped the perspiration off his forehead. "ISBS is taking college education to the *next* level. Here, we encourage students to do work that makes a difference, producing outcomes of significance!"

The three were speechless.

Mr. Leeds stood up and pointed to the portrait of Albert Einstein. "He is our inspiration: Albert Einstein. He was the Millennium Man because he changed the world. This *one* person changed our view of the universe. Who will be the next? Hopefully, in our time, ISBS can produce the next GREAT ONE. That's why ISBS has *chosen* each one of you for admission. To be great, we must be willing to TRY – and really try hard in our endeavors.

"Remember, the Universe has conspired to bring each of you into this world, to this Moment. So, don't be a phony. Make your lives count. Live authentic lives. Live your own lives. Then, Life will be meaningful and fulfilling."

Mr. Leed's phone beeped.

"Got to take this call." Mr. Leeds apologized. "Let's meet again – soon. Good luck with your school year!"

As the three rose to depart, Mr. Leeds, once again, shook hands with each of the three. "I have high hopes for you!"

Meanwhile, inside the attaché, Lotto was finishing up his notes.

"I got Mr. Leeds's whole presentation in my head!" Buff bragged.

* * *

CHAPTER 30

THE MYSTERY WITHIN THE TESTAMENT TOWERS

<u>MUSIC INSPIRATION</u>

RIVER FLOWS IN YOU
YIRUMA

WIND, RAIN AND WATER
THE LAST EMPEROR
RYUICHI SAKAMOTO, DAVID BYRNE, CONG SU

GONNA GET OVER YOU
SARA BAREILLES

TAKE MY BREATHE AWAY
BERLIN

PROMENADE
PICTURES IN AN EXHIBIT
COMPOSER: MODEST MUSSORGSKY
ORCHESTRATION: MAURICE RAVEL
CHICAGO SYMPHONY ORCHESTRA
CONDUCTOR: GEORGE SOLTI

MAGICAL MYSTERY TOUR
THE BEATLES

CALL ME MAYBE
CARLY RAE JEPSEN

IF I FELL
THE BEATLES

LOVE YOU LIKE A LOVE SONG
SELENA GOMEZ & THE SCENE

*   *   *

So, what is Happiness?

Happiness is being loved by someone we love.

*   *   *

In the elapsing thirty minutes, one year of solitude lifted from Katya. A cheerful excitement swept through her. Once again, she wanted to give herself a chance for Love.

*   *   *

"So, how was your meeting with Mr. Leeds?" Katya was eager to strike up a conversation, especially with the twins. "I've heard so much about the two of you! The Office of Admissions was abuzz about your impending arrival, especially this past week. The professors can't wait to meet you!"

Luck felt content, comforted by the warm anticipation of the professors. "The meeting went swimmingly well. We've got a new *kick-ass* program."

Sophie had a puzzled and envious look. *Why is there so much fuss about Luck and Chance?* She wondered, slightly jealous of the brothers' popularity. After all, her father was a distinguished Professor of Metaphysics at ISBS. *I should get some attention, too!*

At this time, the pair wanted to help Buff and Lotto settle in but they did not know how.

"Katya, we need help." Chance confessed. He glanced at Luck for his permission. Luck nodded. Chance bent over, opened his attaché, lifted Lotto and placed him on the counter. "There! This is Lotto the Pirate. He needs beddings, clothing and eating utensils. Where can I find them?"

"Good gracious! What do you have there?" Katya could not believe her eyes.

Lotto bowed politely. "It is an honor to a-make your acquaintance. I'm here to a-serve Master Chance."

"He's adorable!" Katya never saw anything like this.

"The Fairy Godmother gave Lotto to me – the very morning we left the Philippines." Chance was proud yet embarrassed to admit. "The Fairy Godmother really exists."

"She appeared to me in my dream." Luck jumped in. He, too, bent over, opened his attaché, lifted Buff and placed him on the counter. "There! This is Buff the Monkey. Likewise, I need to get his beddings and his personal set-up."

"My, oh my! Isn't he something else!" Katya was amazed by Buff. "He'll be a show stopper!"

Buff bowed and declared: "I'm here to protect Master Luck. His word is my command."

Katya giggled with fascination. "He's a talking monkey!" She extended her pinky finger to shake hands with Buff.

"Listen, I'll show you around Testament Towers. Then, I'll take you to the Market District – otherwise known as the Market. There, I'm sure you'll find something for Lotto and Buff." Katya found her chance to be of assistance to the twins and to Sophie. Along the way, she grabbed a few campus maps for the newcomers.

Excited, Katya whispered eagerly to Daisy Parton, her assistant, a second-year student from Austin, Texas. "Please hold down the fort for me. I'll be back later." Katya winked at her, exuding excitement.

She was curious about Chance, because she saw something special in him: the melancholy of his soul.

*   *   *

Marshaling all his courage, Luck took out his training bra and put it on. Wanting Buff to benefit from the tour of the ISBS grounds, Luck placed him snuggly into his training bra.

Chance did the same with Lotto.

When pressed upon, the pain of their chest wounds remained intense.

Katya and Sophie bent over in gut-busting laughter, but the brothers did not care. The twins flopped their ponchos over their shoulders, so as to hide their training bras or at the very least, to make them less obvious.

"This is the right thing to do!" Luck declared firmly.

"You're a real pal!" Buff chuckled. "I love you!"

*   *   *

Katya started her tour for the newcomers: "These Testament Towers consist of seven towers, where the university administration and professors hold office."

In good cheer, Katya led the three youngsters further down the hallway toward the Atrium Arboretum, which was populated with a myriad of exotic plants of varied colors, resembling a miniature tropical forest.

There were seven ponds of different sizes, with mini-waterfalls separating them. Rippling waters cascaded down from one pond to the other, with hedges and bushes here and there.

From various nooks, the most captivating tulip blossoms bloomed, punctuated by vivid orange, red, yellow and purple. Then, there were the most enchanting purple and white orchids.

"I am digging this place!" Buff exclaimed.

"Me, too!" Lotto echoed. "This is one a-perfect playground for me!"

Invariably, the passing students could not help noticing the twins' funny gear, pointing at them teasingly with smirks on their faces or in hysterical laughter.

Starting to feel uncomfortable, Chance hated to look like a fool, especially on his first day in school. "Is there a bookstore or gift shop nearby? I'd like to buy a little trolley for Buff and Lotto."

"We have the Market just a stone's throw away from the Testament Towers." Katya looked understandingly at Chance. "With all sorts of quaint stores there, we can do some serious shopping for our little friends!"

*   *   *

Miniature oriental wooden bridges arched over running streams. The ponds were filled with red, white and golden carp, swimming past lotus leaves spread across the ponds. There were bulbous gold fish of red, white, orange and black.

"Can we have a picnic here?" Buff inquired, mesmerized by the soothing tranquility of the place.

Elegant pink lotus blossoms filled the ponds. A few large red-necked turtles rested atop rocks, enjoying the warmth of the sun.

"This is one gorgeous garden!" Lotto beamed. "I can a-pick up some gardening skills here in my spare time."

Male and female peacocks strutted around, doing their love dances. Some English sparrows chirped nearby. Grey squirrels bopped and leapt behind bushes and trees.

At the extreme edge of the Atrium Arboretum, there was a gigantic bamboo bird castle, rising over ten feet. Inside were numerous tropical birds contending for their spots.

Along two elongated bayou ponds, white herons and pink flamingos lingered. And there were white storks, ambling about for a new mission!

Seeing the storks, Chance chuckled silently, recalling Wawa's often told tale of the brothers' arrival into this world of Light and Darkness.

*   *   *

At this Atrium Arboretum area, Beethoven's *Moonlight Sonata* filled the air.

At the center of the Atrium Arboretum was the Gazebo Bar. It housed the Genius Café, with student *baristas*, dressed in orange shirts, serving coffee. For this whole week, coffee would be offered free.

At the coffee bar, the pair ordered *café-au-lait*, while Sophie had strawberry bubble tea. Katya got herself a double chocolate chip *caféccino*.

"Wait two minutes, and I'll organize your double chocolate chip *caféccino*." At eighteen, muscular and well built, Homer Iacocca gave Katya an energetic smile. Matching his hairy arms, he had long hair reaching his shoulders. His handsome face was made more striking with a black eye patch on his right eye.

"That's Anastassios Parnassós. Tassos for short. He's Greek. From Sydney, Australia. Speaks with an Australian accent." Katya whispered to Chance. "Australians love to use the word 'organize'. Even for a cup of coffee." Then, she added: "With one eye, he sees the world."

While Luck and Sophie were ordering their beverages, Katya and Chance found a table for the four of them.

As Chance took his seat by the table, Katya surreptitiously slipped him a small folded up note – sealed with a wink.

Discretely, Chance opened the note. Inside was *her* phone number, with this addendum: "If your little *Moldivians* need help, call me."

Then their eyes met. Chance smiled at Katya, as he put the note into his shirt pocket, his heart racing, his ears turning red. *Oh, no! What do I do?*

Katya ran her hand through her hair. "How are you liking it here so far?"

"Very much. This place is heavenly. Thank you for taking time out for us today." Chance responded shyly.

"Over time, I can tell you so much more about our school." Katya twirled her hair. "There are some *secret* places here that I can show you. Secret places. Secret stories. Secret adventures."

Katya waved at Luck and Sophie, who were approaching to join her at her coffee table.

"It's our turn to get our coffee." Katya stood up, signaling Chance to follow her to the coffee bar. "They call out our names when our coffee is ready – which will be any minute now. Come!"

His curiosity aroused, Chance followed Katya closely. "Tell me more."

As they sat at the coffee bar, in a low voice, Katya shared this secret with Chance. "You see, the Atrium Arboretum is at the middle of the Testament Halls, amongst the confluence of the grand hallways. From where you entered at the main hallway is called: PRESENT. It's also known as the Great Hall of the Present. To your left from here, you see the left hallway yonder. It is called: PAST, also known as the Great Hall of the Past. Toward the right hallway yonder: FUTURE, also known as the Great Hall of the Future. You see, TIME is all connected in the NOW. Time is fluid."

"I've got your *caféccino* organized!" Tassos handed Katya her coffee. "*Café-au-lait* for the gentleman." He gave Chance his coffee.

A mild mannered Greek, Tassos exuded sophistication and lyricism in his motions.

"Tassos, I'd like you to meet Chance." Katya introduced Tassos to Chance. "His first day here. From Manila."

Tassos gave Chance a firm handshake. "Nice to meet you, mate. Really busy today. We'll have to catch up, mate. Welcome!" With that, Tassos proceeded to cater to other students.

"Tassos is poetry in action." Katya whispered. "He is most fascinating. Oh, the tales he tells! So full of drama and action!" Chance nodded, taking a second glance at Homer.

"Now, where was I?" Katya wished to stay on topic. "Yes! The Testament Halls. You may *not* want to veer to the left away from this Great Hall of the Present, lest you enter into the Great

Hall of the Past. That's where the Realm of the Past pervades. *Strange* things happen in that Realm of the Past. Nor would you want to veer to your right away from this Great Hall of the Present, lest you enter into the Great Hall of the Future. That's where the Realm of the Future pervades. *Strange* things happen in that realm. When you stray to the Realm of the Past or into the Realm of the Future, that's when life becomes complicated. Save yourself some trouble, don't go there! If at all possible, stay within the Great Hall of the Present and dwell in the Realm of the Present! Remember that!"

Chance nodded. But he still wondered what those two other realms would be like. He saw the black metal railing gates sealing off the Great Hall of the Past and the Great Hall of the Future from the general public.

"You need *special* permission and faculty escort to enter into the Great Hall of the Past and the Great Hall of the Future. Get that!" Katya was emphatic.

*   *   *

Later, the four of them proceeded beyond the Atrium Arboretum, continuing down the hallway toward the expansive foyer of the Great Commons. At this spot was projected a holographic image of William Shakespeare declaring:

"To be or not to be? That is the question!"

As Chance peered into the Great Commons, he saw a huge and elegant dining hall.

The gigantic bronze doors of the Great Commons displayed the reliefs of the top forty-eight men and women who most influenced world events and the course of modern history.

Chance was fascinated. "The most famous ones seem to have the shiniest noses. Leonardo da Vinci. William Shakespeare. Albert Einstein."

"Can I touch Einstein's nose – for good luck?" Luck rubbed Einstein's nose – even before getting Katya's permission.

"You're too much!" Katya chuckled at Luck's naughtiness.

"Now, this is the main dining hall: the Great Commons." Katya declared. "And yes, please come on in." She invited the three to cross the entrance railing and enter into the Great Commons. "See, these hundreds of round tables here – they're set up with white cloth, with each plate setting accompanied with special silverware and a long white candlestick toward the right side of each plate setting. These are for this evening's dinner event: the Grand Welcome Dinner, which will be held here. It will be *unforgettable*!"

Katya gave Chance a wink. She was enamored by his mild manner, his gentle sensitivity and his pensive demeanor. *Ah, if only I can hug him!*

Noticing her flirty glances, Chance blushed, feeling flustered. His ears turned red.

Bright and airy, the Great Commons had a magnificently arched glass ceiling. Translucent light burst through its roof and glass windows. At mid-day, the place was expansive but relatively quiet.

Cutting through and going to the other end of the Great Commons, Katya showed them the Magnificent Vista: a Zen Garden of Meditation that doubled as a Holographic Projection Quadrangle.

238

"Our Japanese garden was designed based on a similar Kyoto garden which was constructed during the Tokugawa Period. I love this Zen Garden of Meditation. By day, students could pace through its serene paths for calm reflection and meditation. I come here to seek my peace." Katya enjoyed taking refuge here, away from the day's stresses, her oasis from troubles, her sanctuary for solace.

Katya was prepping the twins for what was to come. "From this Japanese garden, how would you like it to manifest virtual reality?"

"How?" Luck inquired.

"At dusk, this Zen Garden doubles as the Holographic Projection Quadrangle or HPQ for short. At that time, it can serve as a holographic platform from which to see anything projected into this HPQ. One can study archeology and ancient structures, bringing you to ancient times and ancient places, especially involving enormous monuments, like the Great Pyramids of Giza. Images can be adjusted to scale."

Now, Chance was getting excited. He could imagine all sorts of holographic possibilities.

Katya continued. "Take the human body. For those who want to study the muscle performance or the vital organs of the human body, the HPQ can provide tremendous insights.

"Or, new robotic inventions. Engineering students have a holographic dry runs here, prior to any 3-D printing or building the real thing. Isn't that great?" Katya observed Luck's keen interest on the subject.

"Or, one can do reiterations on astronomical bodies over time using holography. This is great for our space science program.

Astrophysics students can work with known astronomical variables to calculate space travel to Mars."

Sophie had often wondered about galactic oscillations over time and its impact on human evolution. "Can one reverse engineer the Universe back to the moment of the Big Bang?"

Katya was amused by the sophistication of Sophie's thought process. She continued. "Yes! Holography is the wave of the future! ISBS is really advanced in this field." She took pride in ISBS's preeminence in science. "At the edge of the Great Commons abutting the HPQ, there are two stalls. Each stall has three of the latest printers. The first stall has three black and white 3-D printers.

"The second stall has three color 3-D printers. For example, you can actually print out a miniature car model. Or an architectural building. Or any sculpture you fancy. In a specific size or scale."

*   *   *

"Oh, I've so much more to share with you." Katya cast Chance some loving glances, hoping to stir his heart. Chance was now the object of her affection. *Oh, Love! Give me a chance with him!*

Chance was now the object of her affection.

*   *   *

CHAPTER 31

THE ISBS PROGRAM

<u>MUSIC INSPIRATION</u>

IDEAL STATE
TAO HUA YUAN
桃花源
(CHINESE MANDARIN)
JOLIN TSAI / 蔡依林

SOMETHING
THE BEATLES

A WAY OF LIFE
THE LAST SAMURAI
HANS ZIMMER

SPANISH DANCE, NO. 4
VILLANESCA
CLASSICAL GUITAR
ENRIQUE GRANADOS
GUITARIST: CHRISTOPHER PARKENING

PASTORAL
SYMPHONY NO. 6, MOVEMENT NO. 1
LUDWIG VAN BEETHOVEN

*　　　*　　　*

***W**hat is Wisdom?*

It is the ability to act or not act to achieve the optimal result, to grasp the Truth of the Moment and deliver the correct outcome. It requires control of one's emotions and actions so that Reason prevails for the Good of oneself and others.

*　　　*　　　*

"Tell us, Katya, how does the ISBS Program work?" Luck wanted some tips to do well at ISBS. "What should we expect?"

Katya nodded collecting her thoughts. "First, as an initiate, you have four years of college studies and training. The Grand Masters and professors teach you how to think inside and outside the box. You develop a wide range of core skills. You do deep dives into critical and strategic thinking. You specialize in one or two areas of keen interest to you. Upon completing college, you'll become an *Adept*. That should be your goal." Katya looked encouragingly at the three newcomers.

"And then?" Smiling, Luck could imagine himself an Adept. "I'll be the smartest aleck around! – I mean, Adept!" He broke into a boisterous laughter.

Katya went on. "Then, you go to the next stage of your ISBS education – as a *seeker* in the Master's Program. These two years will be focused on: critical development and execution on your master's thesis."

"A master's thesis?" Sophie inquired.

"Yes. An *original* piece of research or project development for the *advancement* of humankind."

"I've never heard of that!" Luck wanted to ascertain he heard Katya right.

"Now you have." Katya asserted, slamming back a response like a ping-pong ball.

"And then?" Luck was egging Katya on.

"When you complete your Master's Program, you become a *Brainiac Knight*."

"That's a long time." Chance interjected. "Six years – to become a Brainiac Knight.

"There are exceptions, of course." Katya thought of some short-cuts. "If you perform a *super* heroic act – you can be a Brainiac Knight sooner. That is a decision made by the three Grand Masters."

"Oh…" Chance liked *that* idea. He could imagine himself a Brainiac Knight riding on a white horse in shining armor.

"Then, what's next?" It was Sophie's turn to ask a question.

"Well, there's the Doctoral Program." Katya chuckled. "The highest degree!"

A doctoral degree! Sophie wanted to go beyond the master's degree, beyond the Brainiac Knighthood. "I want to teach, be a specialist in my field – like my Dad, Professor Aristotle Angelis Deepthinker. To be a professor, I'll need a doctoral degree."

"What about the Doctoral Program?" Luck taunted.

Unfazed, Katya continued: "The seventh year is the empirical evaluation for the results of your original master's thesis which has become a doctoral dissertation. This includes a *post-execution* evaluation of your doctoral dissertation. Did your initial hypothesis produce the *intended* results? There is a thorough evaluation of the impact and effects of your dissertation. Empirical proofs are presented. The doctoral takes three years. You can pursue it concurrent with the Master's Program. During this doctoral period, you are a journeyperson. Like me!" Katya declared proudly. "I'm both a seeker and a journeyperson!"

"And then what?" Sophie was intent for an answer.

"You have seven years to finish your doctorate. Upon

completing the Doctoral Program, you get a Ph.D. and you become a Magi. A full-fledged Magician!" Katya broke into a triumphant smile. "Ah! A Magi! A Wizard Most Wise! The Wisest of the Master Magicians!"

"Huh! Ph.D. Permanent Head Damage!" Luck joked.

Sophie tugged sternly at Luck's sleeve for being disrespectful. "That's not very nice."

"Let's call *that* Pile Higher and Deeper!" Chance interjected, upping Luck's joke.

Katya frowned at Chance, surprised that he was also capable of cracking naughty jokes. "Now, you *know* all the programs. It's in the ISBS catalogue." To her, she was just stating the obvious.

"The catalogue is about to change." Sophie interjected.

"Right on!" Katya nodded. "Starting with your school year, everything is revamped! ISBS is rolling out a truly revolutionary program."

Sophie concurred. "Mr. Leeds just told us."

"I can't provide any insights into your *new* Bachelor's Program. I am still operating within the *old* Program – with extensive *required* courses." Katya clucked her tongue.

"But you can still advise us..." Chance was a bit disappointed. He thought he had a secret weapon at ISBS through Katya.

Fat chance! Katya read his mind.

*   *   *

CHAPTER 32

KATYA ATHENA TOLSTAYA

OASIS
(PIANO)
YIRUMA

MEMOIR OF A GEISHA – THEME SONG
JOHN WILLIAM

NOTHING COMPARES TO YOU
SINEAD O'CONNOR

**COURAGE
YONG QI
勇气**
(CHINESE MANDARIN)
LIANG JING RU / 梁静茹

THIS GIRL IS ON FIRE
ALICIA KEYS

WE FOUND LOVE
RIHANNA

BOHEMIAN RHAPSODY
QUEEN

*　　　*　　　*

Wisdom is the source of all virtues. It realizes what is of value in Life for oneself and for others. It is the superior ability to understand the nature of things, people and events and what make them tick.

*　　　*　　　*

Emerging from the Zen Garden, the group strolled through the grassy Knoll, heading toward the Wisdom Trail – a broad emerald-gravel pathway around the Enchanted Pond of Mysteries located at the heart of the campus. At specific intervals, the trail would branch outward with walkways toward each of seven academic buildings, the library and the performing arts building, all perched atop the rolling hills around the pond.

Blissfully lost in their own conversation, Luck and Sophie trailed behind Katya and Chance.

*   *   *

"So what got you to ISBS? Why ISBS?" Chance asked Katya, curious about her background and her choice.

"As you can tell from my accent, I'm a Russian immigrant, born and raised in Moscow. When I was five, my parents left Moscow and moved to Paris to live for a few years. There they divorced. When I was ten, my father and I immigrated to America for a better life. My father is Professor of Russian Literature at Columbia University. We settled in Brooklyn Heights here in New York. I'm their only daughter."

Rapt in attention, Chance got closer to Katya, straining his ear, not wanting to miss anything.

Katya continued: "My first two years in New York were challenging. I could barely speak English. It was tough to make friends and fit in. In high school, I worked hard on my English and Mathematics. So I was lucky to get a very high scores in my SAT Exams. I was also the Head our high school debating team and President of our school government. My extracurricular activities really *opened up* opportunities and choices for me. These were what got me into ISBS – my good grades in school, my high SAT scores and my leadership experience.

"Besides working at the Admissions Office, I also work for Mr.

246

Blundermore at the President's Office. These campus jobs cover my outlays. I've three or more years of schooling. Then, I enter the *real* world. Having just completed college at ISBS, I'm now an Adept." Katya declared triumphantly.

Chance brightened up, wishing to get some insights on how to excel as an initiate in his next four years in college at ISBS.

Instead, Katya focused on discussing her Master's Program. "Currently, my academic advisor is Mr. Ken Knowland. He is a world famous transhumanist."

Puzzled, Chance's brow went up. "A transhumanist?"

"Are you familiar with transhumanism?"

Chance shook his head. "That's a new to me."

"Well, transhumanism is a movement toward the fundamental transformation of the human condition by integrating emerging technologies – such as information technology, artificial intelligence, nanotechnology and biosciences – with the human body. Particularly with the human brain. The goal is to further expand human intellectual, physical and psychological abilities"

Chance nodded understandingly, digesting Katya's comments.

"For his own reasons, Ken is studying the potential effects of such technologies in overcoming fundamental human limitations." Then Katya whispered. "Ken has a disabled child. Adam is his name. He is fifteen years old. But he barely moves. He cannot even talk. All he can do is flail his arms and utter some *unintelligible* grunts. He needs to be spoon fed. He is all skin and bones. He cannot walk. Not even crawl. All day he lies in bed in his diaper. He has a serious case of cerebral palsy. Furthermore, his back is bent due to a severe case of scoliosis. His spine resembles a big "S". It is so sad." Katya's eyes reddened. She could not continue. A drop of tear rolled down her cheek.

"I'm sorry to hear that." Chance turned serious.

"You see. People with severe cerebral palsy have short life expectancy. So, Ken and I are working on a proto-type brain implant for him. For Adam to enjoy life – even for a little bit."

"Oh..." Chance was beginning to understand.

"Ken wants his son to have *some* quality of life. To be able to lift his arm and use his fingers. Perhaps to navigate his own wheel chair. Perhaps to feed himself. To learn to communicate more clearly. To enjoy TV. To read. To interact with Ken in some intelligent way... After all, WHY DOES HE LIVE?"

Chance nodded in empathy.

"So Ken and I are on this quest: to make Adam present and one with this world – through a proto-type brain implant. This is Ken's *prime* motivation! For him, this is urgent." Katya searched Chance's eyes. "This is the reason *why* I'm pursuing the ISBS Master's Program. To help Adam and others like him." After a brief pause, Katya added. "I'll introduce you to Ken very soon."

*   *   *

CHAPTER 33

DOLLY FOLEY'S DOLL HOUSE STORE

MUSIC INSPIRATION

LUCY IN THE SKY WITH DIAMONDS
THE BEATLES

DIAMONDS
RIHANNA

WORDS
BEE GEES

1000 WORDS
FINAL FANTASY X-2
(ENGLISH & JAPANESE)
KAZUSHIGE NOJIMA, NORIKO MATSUEDA, TAKAHITO EGUCHI
SINGERS
JADE VILLALON / SWEETBOX

EVERYTHING'S GONNA BE ALRIGHT
HOME GROWN REMIX
SWEET BOX

*　　　*　　　*

The opposite of Wisdom is Folly.　The lack of Wisdom causes Human Suffering and Death.

*　　　*　　　*

Soon, Katya led the newcomers to the nearest trolley car stop. "Let's take a ride. It's free!" Thereupon, they all boarded the electric trolley car named *Intention*. It was an inviting tiny trolley car that could take around twelve passengers at a time. Its main purpose was to provide short commutes between points within the campus. Such trolley cars roamed the campus till midnight.

It was not too long when the driver hollered: "Market District!" whereupon the group disembarked.

Being one of the older sections of the campus, the Market was a quaint shopping district whose winding cobblestone alleys led to myriad of colorful shops and restaurants. The Market's main entrance was festooned with flagpoles displaying the major currency signs of the world. The multicolored cobblestones were marked with various painted mathematical symbols from the simple to the very complex. The tight crowded alleys were bustling and swarmed with students and their parents. The students were doing last minute shopping, while using their parents' credit cards. Besides the main bookstores, there were micro-shops, ice cream parlors, beauty shops, antique stores, a wand shop, a café and a tavern.

"The café is called the Last Chance Café." Katya turned and smiled at Chance. "Someday, we can try the coffee there."

This amused Chance. Next door to Last Chance Café was the Wine Wise Tavern.

Katya recounted: "Rumor is: its wine could make a wine drinker wiser, making one score higher in exams, especially during finals. Drinking their wine will increase your chance of getting A's."

"You'll find me booking here at all hours. I will graduate *summa cum laude!*" Luck gave out his quirky burst of laughter.

At the end of the street was a doll house store.

*   *   *

Upon spotting Dolly Foley's Doll House, Chance got really animated as if he won the lottery. "Lotto, you're in luck! You've won the jackpot!"

"Today's my day!" Lotto got whacky, excited about what Chance would get him.

Dolly Foley's door chimed as the youngsters entered her store.

At forty, Dolly Foley was attractive, with bright rosy cheeks, and nicely proportioned. Since her divorce, she worked hard to stabilize her financial standing – but just barely. With a heavy mortgage load weighing her down, she almost went bankrupt. Scraping her remaining savings, plus some help from her business friends, she managed to open a shop here in the Market. Unfortunately, she was living her life to service her mountain of debt.

Dolly Foley's Doll House was more a personality projection of her own flight to fantasy. This Doll House represented her habit, her aptitude, her worldview and her tendency to daydream. Like her dolls, she had these wistful round eyes, with a perpetual smile, hoping someone would hug her and console her, telling her that everything would be alright. But her world was *not* alright. Behind her cheerful demeanor was a veil of secrets, which condemned her to her present state of financial uncertainty.

* * *

Chance felt awkward that he was shopping in such a boutique. *This place is for girls. Am I becoming a sissy boy? First, I got the training bra. Now this!*

"May I help you?" Dolly Foley greeted the four of them with a broad grin. Noticing her incoming shoppers with their training bras, she giggled with amusement. She marveled at Buff and

Lotto, who were snugged up against the training bras. "Coochie! Coochie!" She put forth her forefinger at Buff. "I can see your little friends. They may want a nice roof over their heads." Her high pitched voice betrayed her English-French accent.

Without hesitation, Dolly pulled Luck into the middle of the store, to show him the selection of doll houses.

"Can we look around first?" Chance wanted to check out the prices of the doll houses.

"Gosh!" Taken aback, Luck was having a fit of sticker price shock. "A small simple doll house costs over US$300!"

"Can you drop the price?" Chance bargained. "In the Philippines, almost everything in small shops was negotiable."

"I'm sorry, our prices here are fixed." While smiling ever so radiantly, Dolly remained firm.

"Here in America, we don't negotiate prices." Sophie whispered into Luck's ear.

"Hmm… What kind of a doll house do you fancy?" Dolly looked at Sophie charmingly, hoping to entice her into buying one. "A doll house brightens up the possibilities of life, adds cheerfulness, especially to your lovely doll, which I'm sure you brought one along. Otherwise, you can choose one from the many lovely dolls here. In a stressful day, you can always escape into the fantasy world of the dolls. "

"Oh, I don't need a doll house." Sophie gestured awkwardly to the twins. "My friends here, Luck and Chance… errr … they want some reasonable doll houses for their little friends." She pointed at Buff and Lotto, who were snugged up against the brothers' training bras, their tiny limbs sticking out.

"Oh, I have some sturdy doll houses just for them." Dolly lit up. "I'll be right back." With that, she quickly disappeared into a little entrance leading to the back of the store.

"What do we do?" Chance was desperate for advice. "These doll houses won't do. They're *too* expensive. It's way out of my budget."

"It looks like we just may need to share our beds with them. In no time, I'll be fleece infested." Luck burst out laughing. "Otherwise, Lotto and Buff may need to sleep on the floor."

Dolly reappeared with two big boxes. "Here, these are from Scandinavia, and you can assemble these doll houses yourselves."

"How much would each cost?" Katya asked, hoping to take the pressure off the twins.

"You all are in luck. These cost US$99.99 each. They are on summer sale! They are discontinued products." Dolly was all smiles. hoping to make a sale. "They were over US$150 each previously."

Morosely, Chance shook his head. He turned around, ready to head for the door.

Dolly teased: "What do you think this place is? The Salvation Army?"

As Chance turned the door knob, Dolly waved at him. "Hold it! Wait!" She had a brilliant idea. "Would your little friends mind sleeping inside little teepee tents?" Dolly could smell a deal.

Hoping for their approval, Chance looked toward the direction of Buff and Lotto, who nodded eagerly.

"OK. But how much would each cost?" Chance inquired, not wanting to be disappointed.

"Wait!" Dolly scurried to the back of the store and returned with a proud grin: "Your little friends will *surely* like these teepee tents. They can just crawl in, play Indians, and stay warm during the night."

"And how much are we talking about?" Chance was guarded. "Miss Dolly, don't let me down."

"You will like the price: US$9.95 each!" Dolly confidently cocked her hands by her waist, waiting for his response. "You can't beat that! What do you say? Deal or no deal?"

There were loud cheers. Lotto and Buff were elated.

"Deal!" Luck was happy, as he fished out a crisp US$100 bill. "I'll buy one. My brother will buy the other one."

Buff and Lotto were kicking their legs and waving their hands with excitement. "Yea! We'll live like little Indians!"

Majestically, Lotto folded his arms, declaring this to Buff: "I'll a-have the *bigger* tent. I'll be your Indian chief!"

"Both tents are exactly the same size." Dolly assured the two *Moldivians*. "You two surely *deserve* these teepee tents. You can just crawl into each of your tents, be the biggest Indian chiefs, and stay comfortable."

Chance reached for his wallet to settle his bill. "I'll get one of the tents. Separate receipts, please. We'll be going Dutch."

*　　　*　　　*

"I would like a nice outfit for Buff." Luck explored around

for something for Buff to wear. After a while, he found a navy blue soldier's outfit with gold trim for Buff.

"How do you like this?" Luck showed the outfit to Buff.

"It looks swell!" Buff nodded approvingly.

"How much would this cost?"

"Not much: US$14.95." Dolly gave Luck a broad grin.

"Ugh!" Luck was stunned at the price. "It's *more expensive* than the teepee tent!"

Sophie gave Luck a stern look. "No bargaining!"

Dolly noticed the distraught look on Luck's face and felt sorry for him. "I'll give you a break today. As a special favor." Dolly wanted Luck to leave the store happy. "US$9.95. Same price as the teepee tent. Final price. Take it or leave it."

Luck realized he could not argue. "Okay." He fished out another US$10 bill for payment.

"Sorry. The total is: US$10.65." Dolly chuckled. "There is a 6.5% sales tax. Remember this: As long as you live in America, there'll be taxes. Uncle Sam is your silent partner in any business. In America, there are two certainties: Death and Taxes!"

"Meow!" Luck looked stunned.

*   *   *

"What else do you have?" Luck was venturing more aggressively. "Do you have little blankets for our little ones?"

While ringing up her cashier, Dolly was thinking. "Hmmm... Let's see..."

As she was counting the change, she offered: "I've got some left-over linen. Will that work?"

Sophie jumped at this opportunity. "I can sew! I'll make the blankets for them. It won't be difficult." She volunteered. "This way, Lotto and Buff won't be cold at night."

Once again, Dolly disappeared into the little entrance leading to the inventory storage at back of the store. "I'll be back."

Moments later, she reappeared. "Here!" She flopped a roll of white cotton linen atop the glass counter. Underneath the glass counter were glass menageries of exotic and mythic animals, like the unicorn and the centaur.

"And how much is this?" Chance was guarded. "Don't scare us with your price."

Dolly cocked her hands by her waist and thought for a while. "Well... on *one* condition." She had her own issues, something *deeper* than just making a buck right away. Finally, Dolly said: "It's yours, free!"

A wild cheer broke out even before Dolly could continue. The four students were ecstatic.

"Wait – I'm not done, yet." Dolly wanted to be heard.

"Free" was a word Dolly seldom use. "*In exchange*, you all need to *bring* me customers! *Comprenez vous?* Do you understand?"

Dolly put the linen in a large plastic bag and tied it nicely. "You can use the linen for many other things."

Katya smiled at Dolly. "I think you just made some new friends. You've made the twins and their *Moldivian* buddies very happy." Katya was quite impressed, noting Dolly's sudden generosity.

"Oh! Do you have bags or baskets – with straps – for these little ones?" Luck gestured to Buff and Lotto.

"Without us looking silly with these stupid training bras?" Chance finished off what Luck was saying.

"Hee hee hee…" Then, Dolly thought for a moment. "Let me see." She looked underneath the cashier's machine and fished out two thermo bags. "Will this work? It's my niece's."

"That's fantastic!" Luck was ecstatic. "What do you think, Chance?"

Chance gave Luck a thumbs-up. "We can put a belt or a shoulder strap through the thermo bag."

"Good!" Dolly kept thinking. "Now let's see…" Her eyes brightened. "Wait!" Again, she disappeared toward the back of the store.

Not a moment too soon, Dolly reemerged with a squeaky red trolley cart. "How do you like this?"

"Wow! Perfect!" Luck couldn't be happier. Crouching slightly, he began to do an Indian dance in the store.

"But your niece will feel terrible for your giving it away." Chance was feeling reluctant to accept the trolley cart.

"Don't worry. She's already outgrown them. She just turned eleven. You may need to oil and readjust the trolley cart. Here, you take it." Having dusted it clean, she placed the tepee tents, the roll of linen cloth, the thermo bags on top of the trolley cart. "There you go! *Voila!*"

"How much are these – the thermo bags and the trolley cart?" Sophie was willing to chip in.

Dolly was feeling magnanimous. *"De rien.* Nothing at all. These will do your little buddies a lot of good! *Avec plaisir!* It's my pleasure!"

Dolly wanted to get rid of them all these years, but never did. *Today is a perfect day to give them away.*

The twins thanked Dolly.

Luck chuckled. "These training bras have served their purpose. Going forward, we don't need to look ridiculous. Yeehah!"

Gently, the twins placed their *Molidivian* friends onto the cart.

Then, very carefully, they removed their training bras and hid them in their attachés.

With a happy skip in his heart, Chance opened the store door, which let out a charming dingle. "We've got one less thing to worry about. Let's go!" With that, he pulled the squeaky trolley cart along with him.

With joy, Dolly bid her new friends goodbye. Deep in her heart, she knew she had done something good for her *karma.* She *desperately* needed to fix her karma.

*   *   *

CHAPTER 34

WHO-R-U
WONDER WANDS

MUSIC INSPIRATION

WHAT HAPPENS WHEN
YOU'RE GROUND UP?
PETER PAN
JULE STYNE & MARK CHARLAP
SINGERS
BETTY COMDEN & ADOLPH GREEN
CAROLYN LEIGH

DESCENDANTS OF DRAGON
LONG DE CHUAN REN
龙的传人
(CHINESE MANDARIN)
LEEHOM WANG / 王力宏

GRANADA
(CLASSICAL GUITAR)
ISAAC ALBÉNIZ
GUITARIST: JOHN WILLIAMS

*　　　*　　　*

What is karma?

Karma is the totality of our actions and of their effects in this and previous lives all of which determine our future.

*　　　*　　　*

"Since we're here in the Market, we may just as well get your wands." Katya suggested.

Thereupon, they entered *Who-R-U Wonder Wands,* a

259

decrepit and haunting shop, specializing in all sorts of wands. By the foyer of the store, numerous eerie looking wands of years past were displayed. Above each of them was a corresponding painting or picture of previous owners, the good or the evil wizard, long dead. Some of the wands looked darkly intimidating – if not outright foreboding.

Today, the shop was packed with student shoppers, being the first day of Freshmen Week.

Katya led her friends into the shop and went directly to Master Willy Sparks, an old bloke aged one hundred. He wore a long crumpled trench coat. He was no taller than five feet. Age must have shrunk him. A fabled centenarian, he moved rather slowly but with determination, with a set of *pince-nez* glasses sitting on his hooked nose. He could very well be one of the oldest men in ISBS. He was the only surviving master of Wand Works, operating his unique wand technology which surpassed all others. Furthermore, he knew ISBS well. Some considered him its in-house historian. With all his years, he knew Life and had eschewed Death many times like a cat with nine lives.

"Master Sparks, I want you to meet our new students: Luck and Chance and Sophie!" Katya announced proudly.

"Yes! I'm expecting your arrivals!" Master Sparks broke into a weird smile, displaying his dirty crooked teeth. He had a squeaky voice. "Each of your wands is ready." Whistling, he made his way to the back of the store. Moments later, he re-emerged with three long boxes. These, he laid on the counter for their inspection.

"Your ID please?" Master Sparks requested, extending his thin craggy hands. "For security."

After rummaging through their respective bags, the three newcomers produced their passports.

*   *   *

"Good!" Master Sparks exclaimed with satisfaction, placing each of the passports on the counter. Through his spectacles, he peered at each passport, matching it with the appropriate wand box. "Each of you has gotten your unique wand. Amazing! Through your wand, you will possess magical powers – magical *ch'i*. Through your wand, you will write your life. So, master it well. Each of your souls will be *irrevocably* linked to your respective wand – whether you want it or not. Take good care of your own wand. You and your wand are one."

Mysteriously, Master Sparks stared at each of the newcomers: Luck, Chance and Sophie. There was stunning silence from the three newcomers. Slowly, Willy bent over and reached for his own wand, which was nestled in a long sleeve pocket along the pant of his right leg. "I've lived many, many years. I've seen many people come and go. We never know whether it was by choice that we were born or not. But born we were and we have to live our lives. Unbeknownst to us, we've lived a thousand lives and died a thousand deaths." He showed them his wand made of yew.

"See, yew is the most pliable wood, resilient to pressure and stress. It does not break easily." He passed his wand to the newcomers, who examined it with curiosity. "The handle is made of jade. See, it is brilliant green. That means I'm very healthy…despite my age."

His words made a deep impression upon the newcomers.

After a pause, Master Sparks picked up and opened each of

the boxes. With the solemnity of a high priest, he breathed life into each wand. Then, he passed the wands out to their rightful owner.

"Your first wand is fully paid for – through your tuition fee. If it is broken or lost, your subsequent wand will cost you most dearly. Take good care of it. Protect it. Let no harm fall upon it. You will learn more about how to use your wand this week in school."

With fascination, Luck looked at his gnarly and elegant wand. Eighteen inches in length, the wand was shimmering brownish pink.

Noticing Luck's curiosity, Master Sparks commented: "Your wand is made from the sequoia wood of the West. Its handle is from a ram's horn. It's a powerful wand."

With studied seriousness, Chance lifted his wand. Eighteen inches in length and with rough crookedness, the wand exuded tough ruddy masculinity.

To Chance, Master Sparks commented: "Your wand is made from the pine wood of the East. Its handle is from a deer's horn. A most powerful wand it is."

To Sophie, Master Sparks gave her a gentleman's bow. "I know your father, Aristotle. How is he?"

"He'll be coming very soon. I can't wait to attend his lectures on Metaphysics. I'm so glad to finally meet you, Mr. Sparks. My Dad has spoken of you."

With rapturous nervousness, Sophie gripped her wand. Sixteen inches in length and with slender toughness, the wand exuded a feminine mystique.

"My young lady, your wand, like mine, is made of yew wood of Britannia. Its handle is made of onyx. A most enchanting and supple wand, indeed!"

"The three of you are getting the most powerful wands." Willy Sparks whispered. "To whom much is given, much is expected."

The three newcomers carefully placed their wands into their bags.

"I will see you all soon. Hehehe!" Willy's gave out a wry asthmatic laughter, which was at once weird and haunting. "I'll be giving you some Super-Hot Incredible Training on your wands tomorrow." He chuckled and shook hands with each of them. His jaundiced gaze penetrated into the newcomers' souls. "May you be one with your *ch'i*"

Chance suddenly remembered his day with Cardinal Lagazpi. *So, this is what the Cardinal meant: a journey to the Mystery of Mysteries; a journey to the Miracle of Miracles.* For Chance, receiving his wand was a good omen. A magical SIGN!

*   *   *

CHAPTER 35

MUNTAHA, THE ULTIMATE

MUSIC INSPIRATION

A SMALL MEASURE OF PEACE
THE LAST SAMURAI
HANS ZIMMER

HOLIDAY
BEE GEES

REFLECTION
MULAN
MATTHEW WILDER & DAVID ZIPPEL
SINGER: CHRISTINA AGUILERA

PARTY ROCK ANTHEM
LMFAO

SKYSCRAPER
DEMI LOVATO

MACARENA
(SPANISH)
LOS DEL RIO

RECUERTOS DE LA ALHAMBRA
(CLASSICAL GUITAR)
FRANCISCO TÁRREGA
GUITARIST: JOHN WILLIAMS

*   *   *

So, live the Moment. For in the Moment, we find Eternity.

*   *   *

The Prophet and Gabriel travelled once more

Until they reached the absolute limit of the created intellect,

Named sidrat al-muntaha:

"The Lote-Tree of the Utmost Boundary."

Koran 53:14

*   *   *

They resumed their orientation walk at the Wisdom Trail heading toward the Enchanted Pond which had a radius of seven hundred and seventy feet.

"Yonder, that's our famous Pond at the pivotal center of our campus. All the academic buildings have a view of the Enchanted Pond." Katya had spent numerous hours reflecting beside the pond. "The pond has profound cleansing powers. It can bring clarity to the mind. It eases your spirit from life's issues. It lightens your heart from burdens."

Katya continued: "This Pond was inspired by those in Soochow, China. Except this one is much bigger in scale. In the middle of the Pond are two islets. "The big islet is called Bodhi. That huge white Bodhi tree on the big islet is called: the Transcendent Tree of Awes. Legend has it that this is a direct graft from the very Bodhi tree where Siddhartha Gautama Buddha, at the age of thirty-five, gained Enlightenment."

Katya declared: "Under this Tree, candidates are knighted as Brainiac knights or anointed as Magi wizards. Special ceremonies are held on this islet. For the selected ones, they are ennobled, entrusted with higher missions and greater responsibilities."

"Incredible!" Luck took in the whole tranquil scene of the Pond and the Tree.

Sheets of lotus leaves crowded the banks of the Pond, with shoots of pink lotus buds and blossoms jutting here and there. Large carp of spotted gold, orange, white and black would bop their heads to intermittently catch dragonflies perched upon the lotus leaves.

There were frogs leaping from one lotus leaf to another. White swans squabbled amongst themselves over the pieces of bread or crackers students would hurl toward them. Then, there were weeping willow trees adjacent to the pond, whose leaves were gently swaying against the summer breeze.

*　　　*　　　*

As Chance watched a colorful swarm of butterflies flew by, he wondered whether he was dreaming. Or, was he the dream of the butterflies dreaming?

*　　　*　　　*

Luck and Sophie took delight watching some upper classmen lazing on the grassy Knoll surrounding the Pond, with patches of picnic blankets here and there.

Luck gave Sophie a wistful look. *Hope we can likewise lounge here – someday soon!*

Sophie giggled. She could almost guess what Luck was thinking.

*　　　*　　　*

"The smaller islet beside Bodhi is called the Dot." Katya liked the upcoming pun. "On the Dot is a gigantic multi-colored perpetual Newtonian clock – telling Time."

The face of the clock was displayed on each side of a translucent cube measuring seven feet per side.

"This Newtonian clock is linked to the center of natural forces, whose Time is tied to the dance of the universe. We call this clock 'Big Abe'. This clock does not lie. It tells the True Time. On the hour, it chimes out the most heavenly tune." Katya declared.

"Like the Big Ben of London." Luck was impressed.

"Except the Big Ben does not chime out any tune." Katya looked at Luck sternly. "You can observe Time from any point of the campus. My watch was calibrated to this perpetual Newtonian clock. This Newtonian clock is the final arbiter of Time here at ISBS. So you may want to calibrate your watches now." The three newcomers promptly adjusted their respective wristwatches.

"Now, we're all in sync." Katya felt she was being useful. "There are *no* more excuses for being late. When people say they want something to happen on the dot, they are referring to Big Abe on this Dot – the original Dot."

The newcomers laughed.

Beside the perpetual Newtonian clock was a colossal Oculus of the Interior, which was eighty feet in height. It very much resembled the Oculus of the East. Katya dropped her voice a notch. "This Oculus of the Interior watch over the whole campus at night. Unwanted outsiders are not welcome – especially after sundown. Its key task is to keep the campus grounds safe."

*   *   *

267

At 3:00 P.M., like clockwork, a thick fog of drowsiness descended upon the twins and Sophie, as the heaviness of jet-lag crept upon them.

Katya could see their eye lids drooping. Sensing this, she led her group to the last destination of their ISBS tour.

Soon, they saw the stunning view of *Muntaha*. There it stood, an elegant D, like a giant sail rising from the horizon.

Katya pointed at the building. "That is your dormitory, also known as *Muntaha* – meaning the Ultimate in Arabic. This is where all the freshmen initiates will be staying. Like a ship at full mast with the wind, your living experience here will be fantastic. How magnificent is this!"

***Muntaha*, the Ultimate**

Katya stood there, watching the three, Luck, Chance, and Sophie, astounded by the majestic elegance of *Muntaha*: a truly jaw-dropping sight!

Expressionistic in style, *Muntaha* was a thirty-three storied triangular building, with a fanciful glass-paneled roof deck. The three edges of the building were supported by thin steel braces like those of ice-skates. The sky-scraper's façade projected a full mast, fully stretched as if from the ocean's billowing winds, with soft structural curvatures so pleasing to the eyes.

*   *   *

"So, we'll be living here!" Chance exclaimed in disbelief.

"I feel like I've died and gone to seventh heaven!" Luck was taken by the sight.

"My Dad has told me no one is left unmoved and unchanged after staying in *Muntaha*. This is the place where the body and the mind would become one." Sophie declared to the group.

Katya nodded as they proceeded to *Muntaha*. "It has happened to me."

*   *   *

As they entered *Muntaha*, Peedle Doo, the first attendant, greeted the four youngsters, giving each of them hot towels.

"Welcome to *Muntaha*." Tall and princely, Titus Atticus, the second attendant, poured fragrant perfume on the palms of each of the four.

Bubbly and highly spirited, Bella Bellicheck, the third attendant, gave each of the four a long stem half-opened red rose. "Compliments of the house! Enjoy your stay here!"

*   *   *

Projected on the center of the lobby was the holograph of

269

Michelangelo's naked *David*, declaring:

> "My master liberated me from this marble rock. Now, I've got to kill the uncircumcised Philistine Goliath of Gath! Who will join me?"

Squeezing Luck's hand, Sophie giggled abashedly at the sight of the naked *David*. "Am I blushing?" She looked teasingly at Luck.

Katya smiled, feeling an explanation was necessary. "Do you know that Michelangelo was only twenty-six years old when he was commissioned to complete *David* in 1501? Here, you see a life size projection of the seventeen-foot tall masterpiece. *David* is standing, relaxed, in his famous *contrapposto* posture. You see, he is leaning to his right, as if his left leg is bearing no weight. So, what's the meaning of *David*? During his time, Europe had this medieval Christian worldview of the universe divided in two spheres: heaven, where perfection, happiness and truth permeated; then, there's the human world of imperfection, misery and falsehood."

"He is one impressive dude!" Chance enjoyed Katya's narrative.

Acknowledging Chance but without being distracted, Katya continued. "During the Middle Ages, the image of man was mainly embodied in the bloodied, tortured and crucified Christ, destined for a violent sacrificial Death. With the Renaissance, man started to be freed from the shackles of guilt from Adam's and Eve's original sin. Man was reborn to comprehend his world and his universe, in all its glory. Imbued with his rational mind, man realized that he was deserving of happiness and greatness.

270

He could choose to fight and win. Here, we see the furrowed frown of *David* at the moment of *conscious choice* to fight Goliath. *David* is amongst the most recognizable Renaissance sculptures in the world, a symbol of man's determination and courage. So here he stands guard at the center lobby of *Muntaha*, the Ultimate."

*   *   *

"Master Watchman, I want you to meet these newcomers." Katya was proud of her role as a tour guide. She led the three to the dormitory director, Stanley Watchman, who received them with a warm grandfatherly smile. Despite being one hundred and ten, this super-centenarian looked superbly well-maintained. As the watchman and with his thick monocle snugged in his left eye socket, he observed everyone who entered and left the building – without exception. When he glared at anyone, he gave them a *total* stare with one eye: he could *see* into people's heart and soul. He could fathom everyone's intentions and past secrets.

Standing tall and neatly trimmed, he greeted the newcomers with a slight dignified bow. "Welcome to *Muntaha*, Luck, Chance and Sophie. I'm Master Watchman." He had a raspy voice. Limply, he shook hands with each of them. "You will like it here. Now, let's get you processed."

Master Watchman gave each of them forms to fill.

Behind the reception's counter stretched a wall-to-wall mirror. Each of the newcomers could see themselves. In the full length, each of the newcomers saw their reflection. Sophie fluffed her hair, shooting a playful wink at Luck through the mirror. In turn, Luck flashed a peace sign toward her.

"This mirror protects us." Master Watchman noticed the

gigantic mirror had captivated the newcomers.

"How?" Luck asked.

"It assures us that we won't have evil ghosts entering and lurking in this building." Master Watchman spoke rather seriously. "When evil ghosts see their own reflections, they will be frightened out of their wits – they will turn right back out."

Chance nodded, acknowledging the grand mirror reflected all the entrance doors and the whole entrance area.

"The day this grand mirror crashes, our doom will be at hand." Master Watchman warned.

He watched the newcomers fill out the forms.

"After you have completed your forms, let me take a picture of each of you." He motioned the newcomers to have their backs on the blue screen while facing a biometric camera. "All your facial biometric features will be captured by this camera."

"I also need a set of your fingerprints. All ten fingers." Master Watchman proceeded to take finger imprints of the newcomers through a digital scanner.

Each of the newcomers took turns having their picture taken and their face scanned.

Master Watchman pressed a button, and three retinal scanners emerged from the counter. "I need each of you to look into the retinal camera. Set your chin on the chinrest, peer into the camera optics, and the machine will do the rest."

As the newcomers obliged, Master Watchman continued: "This instrument is taking a picture of the retinal wall in each of your eyes – taking an image of the blood vessel pattern on the retinal tissue. Each person's retina is unique. Each pair of retinal tissue is *impossible* to duplicate. Unchanged from birth to death, except for serious retinal degenerative disorders like glaucoma, the retina remains the most precise, reliable and unalterable biometric. DNA is another biometric, but it does not give you instant identity confirmation."

Master Watchman looked at the three newcomers, while nodding at the twins. "Even identical twins do not have the same retinal imprints."

The brothers laughed self-consciously.

"Now, each of you need to take turns stepping into our motion mapping holographic videotaping room." Master Watchman gestured the three newcomers toward a glass chamber beside the reception counter. "This is an eight feet by eight feet purple-ray laser chamber. Outside this glass videotaping chamber are three circular loops of red, blue and green. In each loop is a track of seventy micro laser pointers and camera heads, aimed at the subject within the glass chamber. Its purpose is to capture a high definition holographic motion picture and the voice pattern of each student."

"Wow!" Luck was awestruck.

Master Watchman continued: "This way, when you transmit e-mails or text messages, the receiving party can receive you with 3-D or high-definition holographic options. Our ISBS purple-ray technology supersedes the DVD and Blu-ray Disc technologies. Who wants to be the first to go in?"

Eagerly, Luck raised his hand.

"Make your movements slow. This way, the laser pointers and camera heads on the triple loops of red, blue and green can do their job: take a 3-D, three hundred sixty degree videotape picture of you." Master Watchman opened the chamber and motioned to Luck to enter.

Luck took off his suit and stepped forward.

Once he was inside the taping chamber and its doors were closed, he proceeded to do the Macarena dance in slow motion, while singing *Macarena*. All who saw him broke into hysterical laughter – including Master Watchman.

Meanwhile, the belt on each of the loops turned slowly, with the laser pointers and the camera heads doing their job.

"Very good!" Master Watchman was most amused.

After a minute, Luck's videotaping session was done.

Then it was Chance's turn to enter the holographic videotaping chamber. Thinking on his feet, he proceeded to do some cool Michael Jackson dance movements in slow motion, while singing *Beat It*, to the marvel of all who watched him.

"I did not know you are such dancer." Master Watchman complemented Chance.

Katya was thrilled. *Here's a dancer for me!*

Finally, it was Sophie's turn to enter the videotaping chamber. On her part, she did some *Wudang kung fu* movements in slow motion, while singing *Love Before Time*, the theme song of *Crouching Tiger Hidden Dragon*, to the astonishment of all who witnessed her.

Luck was mesmerized, deeply impressed. *You are one elegant Wudang kung fu master!*

Master Watchman could not help but be amused by the jests of three newcomers. He then proceeded to work on the gadgets. Thereafter, he placed three super-smartphones and three super-tablet computers on the counter for each of the three. "Now, let me download each of your facial biometric data, your 3-D and holographic imprints into each of these smartphones and tablet computers." He busied himself.

"This is incredible!" Luck was pleasantly surprised by the gadgets.

As he finished, Master Watchman gave out more instructions. "These are the latest models. Each of you, please take your super-jazzy smartphones and super-jazzy tablet computer. Indicate the serial numbers of your assigned smartphone and your tablet computer onto your registration form. These super-smartphones and super-tablet computers are yours while you are here at ISBS. They all have 2-D, 3-D, and holographic options. Press the '#' symbol and they will display in 3-D. Press '+' and they will display in holograms. Be careful when in hologram mode. It eats up your battery life much faster. For better holographic viewing, the mezzanine floor has a special holographic viewing room – and in each of the ISBS buildings." The newcomers were fascinated with these advanced gadgetry.

Master Watchman smiled. "Now, your virtual selves are in bits and bytes. When you send tweets, text messages or e-mails, the other party can receive them in 2-D, 3-D or holographic mode. When in holographic mode, you can actually speak to the receiver in your own voice. When you tweet, text, or e-mail to several recipients in this holographic mode, you are *virtually* in multiple places simultaneously – potentially all over the world – transcending Time and Space. At the end of each floor, there is a holographic viewing room."

Chance was flabbergasted. "You mean I can virtually multi-locate? Really? That's mind boggling!"

Sophie was thrilled. "Luck, I can always see you in 3-D or in hologram. You will never be far from me."

Stan raised his finger to emphasize one point: "Let me be clear. You *cannot* lend your smartphone or tablet computers to anyone. As a rule, only you can use your assigned equipment."

The newcomers nodded and busied themselves, jotting down their personal details onto their respective registration forms.

Master Watchman made sure each registration form was properly filled out, with the serial numbers noted on each form matching up with the proper smartphone and tablet computer. Then, he busied himself entering additional codes and other set-up protocols into the respective equipment of each newcomer.

"Now, each of the equipment is matched up to your individual fingerprints, facial biometrics and holographic imprints. Only you can turn on these machines. Is that clear?"

Nodding, the newcomers picked up their respective equipment.

Master Watchman continued his instructions. "It's hard to lose them and difficult to get hacked into, since they are biometrically programmed to each owner – and are traceable through GPS if lost or misplaced. Upon reported lost, the smartphone and the tablet computer will immediately be disabled. To operate the equipment, they require three factor authentication. When you fire up your equipment, just imprint your right thumbprint upon the screen or the pad of your gadget; then press the enter key. Then type in your passcode. But nothing is fool proof."

Master Watchman paused to make sure the newcomers got what he was saying. "The passcode requires twelve characters consisting of letters, numbers and symbols. Please do not put your nickname, birthday, or a smiley face as part of the passcode. At least two letter characters must be capitalized. Be smart!"

The three laughed as they eagerly set up their gadgets.

Master Watchman continued. "Now proceed with entering your password and imprinting your right thumb onto the designated pad or screen area of your equipment."

The newcomers were busy setting up their gadgets.

"*Voila!* You're there! Your machines are on. To activate and launch your computer operating system, just look into the computer camera and press enter. Now, you're in business!" Master Watchman nodded approvingly – with a smile.

Then, turning suddenly serious, Master Watcman declared: "Into your super-jazzy-tablet computer, you shall write your own Mini-Myth. Whether you know it or not, you will be writing new entries every moment, entailing both significant and insignificant events. By the phone calls you make. The e-mails or texts you write and send out. The pictures you take. The events you record into your camera. All the Internet searches you make. All these are recorded – as long as you own your equipment. In time, all your activities build a composite picture of your virtual self – and your real self."

Luck wanted to come across smart. "What if I lose my gadget? It is stolen? Or worst, my smartphone gets crushed by a truck, or it falls into the toilet or into the deep sea?"

The group laughed.

But not Master Watchman. "You see, as soon as your data is entered into your gadget, it is backed up and stored immediately in the cloud – our very *own* ISBS Cloud Nine – including all erasures and deletions. Hence, to answer your question, no data will be lost. You just come to me. I will incapacitate your previous gadget and re-issue a new one to you. But you will have to *pay* for the replacement. It will *cost* you."

Chance raised his hand. "What happens if our gadgets get a virus or worst, they get hacked?"

Master Watchman was impressed with Chance's question. He nodded as he collected his thoughts. "You can check your gadgets for bugs and hacks at any time. You can do it daily, weekly, bi-weekly or monthly. There are *three* firewalls to protect your data in your gadgets and those in the cloud. Update your antivirus software and your antispyware software whenever they prompt you to. Turn off your computer completely when you go to sleep at night – and also when you are not using it. Be careful with what you download, especially songs or movies. Don't open e-mails from unknown sources. Be cautious using other people's USB flash memory stick – especially from people you don't know very well, because it may contain viruses. To lower your chances of bugs and hacks, avoid sites which may be perilous."

Master Watchman paused and looked sternly at the twins. "Don't surf in *bad* neighborhoods. All dirty and unsavory sites have been filtered from your gadgets. Your equipment is shielded from these *bad* sites, which cause most of the bugs and hacks. However, hacks do happen. If so, just bring your equipment over and I will fix it for you. *Don't* try to do it yourself. It may make matters *worse*. Very good question, Chance." The group stirred in excited nervousness.

"Prior to sending out any e-mails or documents, press the

yellow encryption button. Once encrypted, you will see 'SOL' added at the suffix of your document title. You don't want anyone snooping into your communications. Our encryption system upholds the honor system within the school – so that nobody's work or communications fall into the wrong hands. This prevents cheating or piracy. Also, privacy is a human right we don't want violated. While you are matriculated here at ISBS, neither corporate entity nor nation state nor hacker group can compromise your virtual self. YOUR VIRTUAL SELF IS INVIOLABLE. There is no compromise on this issue. If you really have super-sensitive matters to communicate, I urge you *not* to use the Internet nor the any of your gadgets. Find another way to communicate. Ironically, a low tech means of transmitting or exchanging data may be more suitable in such circumstance."

Master Watchman paused, collecting his thoughts. "By the way, when you receive e-mails, a random number generator, also called 'RNG', will spit out an eight-number digit number series assigned to each specific e-mail for thirty seconds. You need to use that number series to open the e-mail. Otherwise, the e-mail remains locked. As you close your e-mail, your gadget will spit out its *own* RNG number series, linked with the first set of RNG. Hence, there is a double combination set of RNG locks to each of your e-mail: an incoming RNG combined with closing RNG. Each double combination is a key. Such keys are stored in a different security file, with its own separate firewall."

Master Watchman paused, as if he forgot something. "Ah, yes!" He went to a credenza and took out three portable hard disc drives. "I almost forgot these. Every night, prior to going to bed, download all data, including e-mails and their respective keys into your assigned portable hard disc drive – your portable HDD. You should store your portable HDD in your room safe. God forbids, our ISBS Cloud Nine should fail or get infiltrated and hacked! You will still have your own personal HDD as back-up. Redundancy is a safeguard mechanism in the high tech world."

Master Watchman resumed his comments. "Where was I? Hmm... Oh, yes. When you have a chance, write down the dreams and goals of your life and the actions you'd like to take to bring them to reality. Do you know that for those who *actually* write down their dreams and goals, they have a much *higher* chance of realizing them? That is a proven fact."

Raising her hand, Sophie commented: "Since I was a little girl, I've been doing that. Except my dreams and goals keep changing."

Master Watchman laughed. "Not to worry. We can dream all we want. We only stop dreaming when we are dead."

The group laughed.

Master Watchman paused, waiting for the group to quiet down. "We are what we do or don't do. Each night, before you sleep, reflect and write down what you did right and what you did wrong and what you can do to improve yourself. Write down what you are thankful for. Write down *how* you are getting closer to the dreams of your life. Write down *what* you plan to do tomorrow. You *are* the author of your own Book of Life. You are *solely* responsible for writing your own Mini-Myth. Be *truthful* in what you write. This way, you can live an *authentic* life. After all: WHY DO WE LIVE? There may be files you may delete. Really, *nothing* is deleted from your tablet computer or smartphone. You know that."

Chance recalled Uncle Antikweetee's mentioning about the Mini-Myth. Now, he was hearing it again today. He also remembered Cardinal Legaspi's comments regarding the Journey of Dreams. *This super-jazzy tablet computer and smartphone must be more SIGNS! I will note all these signs in my Journey of Dreams. Another good omen!*

Master Watchman gazed intently at each of the three newcomers, reaching for their souls, hoping that his words would register with each of them.

*   *   *

Master Watchman proceeded to give instructions. "Gents will be on even floors. Ladies will be on odd floors. Luck, you will be on the twenty-eighth floor. Here's your photo ID card key. While you're in the room, keep the card key in the card slot to keep the room lights on. Pull the card key out, and the lights will go out automatically in three minutes. It's one way for ISBS to be environmentally responsible.

"Chance, you'll be on the eighteenth floor. Here's your picture ID card key. Co-ed meetings occur only on the mezzanine floor and on the third floor where we have our computer / printer rooms, our media room, and two large holographic rooms for group projects. And by the way, There is a holographic room at the end of each floor for viewing holographic documents."

Master Watchman paused, collecting his thoughts. "Now, where was I? Yes, you'll notice several mini-conference rooms of different sizes on the mezzanine floor. These are rooms for group projects or meetings. Reservations are done through the concierge desk over there. Bella Bellicheck will help you.

"Sophie, you'll be on the seventh floor. It's the ladies' floor. Here's your picture ID card key."

Master Watchman stepped back from the reception counter and gave this stern warning: "Men are *not* allowed on ladies' floors. Likewise, ladies are *not* allowed on the gents' floors. Violation of this rule *will* result in suspension or expulsion, depending on the severity of the violation. There is *strict* observance of this rule – and I mean it: zero tolerance! Gents will use the blue elevators, which stop only on the mezzanine and third floor and the rest of the even floors. Ladies take the orange elevators, which stop only on the mezzanine and third floors and the rest of the odd floors. Any questions?"

There was none.

With that, Luck, Chance, and Sophie collected their respective equipment and photo ID card keys.

Katya smiled teasingly at each of the newcomers. "Now, all of you are in the system. You are now a *real* person in ISBS. The important thing is *not* being lost in the system." She waved goodbye to the newcomers. "Go rest. See you all later at the Grand Welcome Dinner."

With that, Katya proceed to return to the Admissions Office to rejoin with Daisy Parton.

Facing the facial scanner for identification confirmation, each newcomer had to swipe his photo ID card key on the entrance turnstile registry scanner to access the elevator lobby. The brothers headed for the blue elevators. Sophie headed for the orange elevators.

"ISBS is super high tech!" Chance whispered excitedly into Luck's ear, as the elevator doors closed. "My only fear is: someone might hack into our smartphones and computer tablets. There are so many bad people out there."

*   *   *

282

CHAPTER 36

THE FIRST DREAMS

<u>MUSIC INSPIRATION</u>

SILK ROAD
CROUCHING TIGER HIDDEN DRAGON
TAN DUN / 谭盾
CELLIST: YOYO MA / 馬友友

SET FIRE TO THE RAIN
ADELE

ENDLESS LOVE
DIANA ROSS

I DREAMED A DREAM
LES MISÉRABLES
CLAUDE-MICHEL
ALAIN BOUBLIL & HERBERT KRETZMER
SINGER: SUSAN BOYLE
(BRITAIN'S GOT TALENT)

PARADISE
STORY OF PI
MYCHAEL DANNA & BOMBAY JAYASHRI
COLDPLAY

THOSE YEARS
NA XIE NIAN
那些年
(CHINESE MANDARIN)
YOU ARE THE APPLE OF MY EYE
SINGER：HU XIA / 胡夏

WHAT BRINGS YOU TO ME
SHI SHEN ME RANG WO YU JIAN ZHE YANG DE NI
是什么让我遇见这样的你
(CHINESE MANDARIN)
BAI AN / 白安

OPEN OUR LOVE
BA AI DA KAI
把爱打开
(CHINESE MANDARIN)
F. I. R.

HUA DIE
LIANG ZHU HUA DIE
化蝶
梁祝化蝶
(BECOMING A BUTTERFLY)
(CHINESE)
PENG LI YUAN / 彭丽媛

CAMBRIAN AGE
HAN WU JI
寒武纪
(CHINESE MANDARIN)
FAYE WONG / 王菲

YI YAN WAN NIAN
一眼万年
（天外飞仙）
(ONE LOOK, TEN THOUSAND YEARS)
(CHINESE MANDARIN)
S.H.E.

MINSAN LANG KITA IBIGIN
(TAGALOG)
REGINE VELASQUEZ

SACRIFICE
ELTON JOHN

EDEN
SARAH BAREILLES

CAVATINA
(CLASSICAL GUITAR)
STANLEY MYERS
GUITARIST: JOHN WILLIAMS

*   *   *

284

As Luck entered his room, he noticed a freshly cut long stem rose in a vase by the window sill. He headed toward the window and casually placed his own rose – which Bella Bellicheck gave him – into the vase. A red tag was clipped onto the stem of Luck's rose. Upon closer inspection, he detected an inscription. It read: STRUGGLE.

The view from his room was breathtaking. Facing the East, he could see the rising spires of the majestic Testament Towers. *I'd be able to see beautiful sunrises.*

He wanted to savor the view more, but he was too tired.

* * *

The next thing, Luck crashed onto his bed and had this dream.

As he dozed off, he continued to feel the bobbing up and down sensation of Jet Orange's Imagination. As he bobbed up and down, he realized he was on camelback trudging through the billowing desert sandstorm of Arabia.

For a moment, he found himself in an Arab tunic, very much like Lawrence of Arabia, galloping ever forward on camelback through the blinding sand storms over the dunes. Except now, he was transported into the deep Past – into a timeless millennium.

As the sandstorm subsided, yonder, he saw the most dazzling gigantic tree shimmering in the desert. For Luck, seeing that tree was pure joy and translucence. The tree was in flames but it did not consume itself. As he peered closely, he quickly realized that it was the fiery Transcendent Tree of Awes, declaring: I AM.

As he got closer to the Transcendent Tree of Awes, he heard a hum which got louder and louder. Eventually, he realized that it was the unceasing ever-increasing pitch of a ram's horn filling the whole atmosphere, from all directions, expressing the hopes and aspirations of all of humanity.

In front of the Transcendent Tree of Awes, were three elegant white tents. In front of each tent was a gathering of nomads.

At the very forefront of the tents was the altar of Melchizedek, upon which was a burnt sacrificed lamb, being consumed by billowing flames.

In front of the first tent, Luck realized they were Sarah and Isaac, seated underneath the Tree. How interesting!

In front of the second tent, he recognized they were Hagar and Ismael, seated underneath the Tree. How curious!

In front of the third tent, he noted they were Keturah and her six sons, Zimran, Jokshan, Medan, Midian, Ishbak, and Shuah, seated underneath the Tree. How fascinating!

There was an elderly man hurrying from tent site to tent site, solicitously catering to the women and their respective son or sons, serving large chunks of the choicest mutton of the most delicious aroma. Upon closer look, it became very clear to Luck that the elderly barefooted man was Abraham.

And a great hunger descended upon Luck.

*   *   *

When Chance entered his room, he noticed a freshly cut long stem rose in a vase by the window sill. He went to the window and carefully placed his own rose – which Bella Bellicheck gave him – into the vase. A yellow tag was clipped onto the stem of Chance's rose. Upon closer inspection, he detected an inscription. It read: AMBIGUITY.

Facing West, his view was the redolent Black Forest beyond the Western Walls. *I'd be able to witness the most memorable sunsets.*

*   *   *

But Chance was too tired. So he crashed onto his bed. As Chance dozed off, he continued to feel the bobbing up and down sensation of *Imagination.* Then, he had this dream.

He was deep in thick clouds. For a while, he could not figure out where he was. All of a sudden, he realized he was flying on the back of a huge angel. Flap. Flap. Flap. He could feel the vigorous flapping of his wings. Chance gripped hard on the golden reins around the angel's neck lest he fall.

Then, he heard the angel speak: "We shall be gathering clay from the Earth for the Most High."

And the angel flew to the North and the South, to the West and to the East of the Earth, and together, from each end of the Earth, the angel and Chance gathered and scooped up much clay, which they put into a large orange bamboo basket. When enough clay was gathered, the angel took off again, with Chance riding on the angel's back. The large basket of clay was slung by Chance's side.

"From this basket of clay, many beings shall come to be." The angel gave Chance a mysterious gaze.

"Who are you?" Chance asked of the angel.

"I am Azra'il, the Angel of Death."

Once again, Chance was swallowed by the thick clouds.

*   *   *

When Sophie entered her room, she too noticed a freshly cut long stem rose in a vase by the window sill. She went to the window and daintily placed her own rose – which Bella Bellicheck gave her – into the vase. A blue tag was clipped onto the stem of Sophie's rose. Upon closer inspection, she detected an inscription. It read: REMORSE.

Facing East, she had the same view as Luck: the Testament Towers, segments of the Eastern Wall and Testament City beyond the school grounds. Except here, the view was from a much lower height. *This is heavenly! To be able to wake and embrace the sunrise!*

Blissfully, she wasted no time and wrote the following into her computer tablet.

MY MINI-MYTH

Sophie Angelis Deepthinker

June 21: Meeting Luck today is totally unexpected! I cannot believe it, but it is true! Once again, I've met my friend and my love – my eternal love!

For all these years, I've loved you, Luck.

But I didn't know where and how to find you.

How intriguing is Fate! And yet, I will not trade this day for any other.

Oh, Fate, you are my friend. My friend
you will be – always!

*   *   *

Later, Sophie crashed onto her bed and had this dream.

Sophie suddenly felt cold desolate winds billowing in the darkest of nights. The shrubs, bushes, and trees quivered and shuddered against the ravaging winds.

Outside, at the Spiritual Abyss, she found herself standing by the gates of the Garden of Eden, looking in. Softly, she called: "Where art thou, Luck?"

There were only whipping winds, punctuated by the howls of jackals, amongst thistles of thorns.

And the Goddess of the Night wept bitterly as endless sorrowful remorse descended upon her.

"From the same clay we were made, I beseech thee come... Come back to me..." She sobbed amidst the stormy winds, as a hooting owl flew over her. "If I only knew! My attitude has wronged me more than my actions. Hear me, Luck. I'm back. If only I knew ... we could have had it all!"

She wept bitterly. "Let the heavens not cast aspersions on me. For I have changed." She poured her heart out in sorrow. So she struggled on against the current of Time – only to be brought back ceaselessly into the Past – back to the Gates of Eden. There, she sat facing the unsmiling Cherubim, in her vain effort to recapture the lost moment of promise – a promise which might offer the Future.

*   *   *

CHAPTER 37

KA-CHING

嘉程

<u>MUSIC INSPIRATION</u>

MR. MOONLIGHT
THE BEATLES

LA PALOMA
(THE DOVE)
(SPANISH)
NANA MOUSKOURI & JULIO IGLESIAS

SUN WILL NEVER SET
RI BU LUO
日不落
(CHINESE MANDARIN)
JOLIN TSAI / 蔡依林

RAIN OVER ME
PITBULLS

JULIA FLORIDA
(CLASSICAL GUITAR)
AGUSTIN BARRIOS
GUITARIST: JOHN WILLIAMS

MY CHINESE HEART
WO DE ZHONG GUO XIN
我的中国心
(CHINESE MANDARIN)
ZHANG MINGMIN / 张明敏

THE YELLOW RIVER CONCERTO, MOVEMENT 2
ODE TO YELLOW RIVER
HUANG HE XIE ZOU QU, HUANG HE SONG
黄河协奏曲，黄河颂
XIAN XINGHAI / 冼星海
CHINA PHILHARMONIC ORCHESTRA
中国爱乐乐团
CONDUCTOR: LONG YU / 余龙
PIANIST: LANG LANG / 朗朗

*　　　*　　　*

What is synchronicity?

It is a non-causal connection between two or more events in meaningful coincidence beyond the probability of chance.

Synchronicities suggest that reality is a lot stranger than commonly acknowledged since events occur, defying random coincidences.

When synchronicities happen, the finger of God is at work in deeper reality to catch our attention, where the paranormal or supernatural are brought into human intelligibility.

*　　　*　　　*

As this true story goes…

It happened in Ohio. There, James Edward Lewis married a woman named Linda, but divorced her and married another woman named Betty, with whom he had a son named James Alan.

Edward Lewis had been adopted as a baby, and when he was in his late thirties, he tracked down and met for the very first time his twin brother, James Arthur Springer. Yes, they both had the same first name: James.

Interestingly, Arthur Springer also married a woman named Linda, but divorced her and married a woman named Betty, with whom he had a son named James Allan.

Now things got weirder. As kids, Edward Lewis and Arthur Spinger had dogs named Toy. They both liked math and carpentry in school but hated spelling. They both had jobs in law enforcement: Springer, a deputy sheriff and Lewis, a security guard. They both got headaches at the same time of day.

They were destined to meet. Welcome to the twilight zone of synchronicities.

*   *   *

Luck's phone rang. Sophie was on the line. "Wake up, sweetie pie. It's 7 PM." Her voice was sweet like that of a chirping cardinal. "Meet you downstairs by the lobby in five minutes. We need to retrieve our luggage from storage and head to our Grand Welcome Dinner."

As Luck rose from his bed, he noticed his new roommate by the window. He had just placed his own rose – which Bella Bellicheck gave him – into the vase.

*   *   *

Luck got out of his bed and introduced himself to his new roommate. "Hi, I'm Winston Odysseus Blundermore Mann. Call me Luck for short."

"And I'm Ka-Ching. Lee Ka-Ching! 李嘉程 in Chinese!" He broke into a broad winsome smile. He wore his high collared long morning coat which reached down to beneath his knees. As they shook hands, the onyx buttons on his long morning coat reflected brightly.

Ka-Ching was the personification of ambition. At eighteen, he was handsome, with a well sculpted face, signifying his high birthright. When he smiled, his perfectly aligned set of very white teeth would shine brightly. He had a nick of a small scar above his left eye. But he lacked self-consciousness to draw himself back.

He had the knack of doing precisely what he wanted because he was a man of means. His father, Lee Bai Yi (李百亿), commanded one of the highest personal net worth in the East to afford Ka-Ching the connections and the resources for his young ambitions.

His heart burned with the ever clarifying desire of the Chinese Dream. In him resided an excess of courage, hope and panache. Overall, he had a cheerful look, with the twinkle of wonderment and eagerness for the promises of life.

Ka-Ching's English carried a slight British accent. Ka-Ching came across as the quintessential cosmopolitan man, with his friendly and confident comportment. "You can call me *Da Pao (大炮). Da Pao* means 'big cannon ball' in Chinese."

"I know! I speak Mandarin, too. What a name!" Luck gave out an irrepressible laugh. *That's a funny name. He's got big cannon balls!*

Ka-Ching chuckled smartly. "Growing up, I was a Tasmanian devil. A fireball of energy – my Dad used to say. So, he called me *Da Pao.* And the name stuck with me."

"Me, too! Some of my friends call me a Tasmanian devil! Together, we'll do lots of mischief!" Luck shook Ka-Ching's hands again – this time, more vigorously. "We'll be partners in crime!"

Deep down, Luck felt lucky to have come across a sympathetic buddy. *With Ka-Ching, everything would be possible, here in ISBS and beyond.*

"I hope you don't mind my taking this bed on the right." Luck apologized.

"Dude, it's perfectly OK with me." Ka-Ching was *simpatico*.

"I crashed in the nearest bed I could get my head on. I flew in directly from Manila. I was pretty pooped out." Embarrassed, Luck explained himself.

"No excuses needed. I just arrived from Hong Kong myself. I feel like zonking out soon." Ka-Ching did not exhibit any dissipation of spirit. He appeared in full control of himself.

Luck's face brightened up. "Hong Kong? I've always been fascinated by Hong Kong!"

"It's a jewel of a city!" Ka-Ching exclaimed. "It's got the most amazing Chinese food in the world and more!"

Interrupting himself, Luck blurted: "Oh, talking about food, I need to phone my brother, Chance. We need to go to the concierge at the storage to retrieve our luggage before dinner. Then, we'll all head out for our Grand Welcome Dinner. You should join us!"

"Dude, can I help?" Ka-Ching offered, defying his aristocratic upbringing.

"Sure." Before Luck could finish the sentence, he was on the phone with Chance. "Chance, meet you downstairs in the lobby in five minutes."

Luck was impressed with Ka-Ching, and his impeccable manners.

Deep in his heart, he wished to emulate Ka-Ching.

*   *   *

Moments later, at the lobby, the four met: Luck, Chance, Sophie and Ka-Ching. Then, they headed to the Testament Towers to the storage station to retrieve their luggage.

Upon getting their luggage, they marched back to their rooms at *Muntaha* to drop them off. Thereafter, the four headed to the Great Commons for the Grand Welcome Dinner.

*   *   *

A blood-red Canadian sunset blanketed the whole sky to the West, as swallows flew back to their nestlings by the nearby lakes for a good night's sleep, uncaring about what tomorrow would bring.

A bluish comet with a pair of long twisted tails shot across the eastern sky, as if sheering the sky in half.

"Did you see that?" Excitedly, Luck pointed at the darkening horizon in the East.

Immediately, Sophie put one hand over Luck's mouth to shut him up; with the other hand, she grasped his hand. "Don't talk! Don't point! It's bad luck to do so!"

In silence, the four watched the streak of the comet against the sky.

For Chance, this was a SIGN. *But signifying what?* He walked silently, peering the sky, wondering the meaning of the passing comet. "What heavenly sign is this?"

*   *   *

CHAPTER 38

THE GRAND WELCOME DINNER

MUSIC INSPIRATION

PIANO CONCERTO NO. 1, MOVEMENT NO. 1
PYOTR ILYICH TCHAIKOVSKY
CHICAGO SYMPHONY ORCHESTRA
CONDUCTOR: GEORGE SOLTI
PIANIST: SHURA CHERKASSKY

PAPARAZZI
LADY GAGA

FUNICULÌ, FUNICULÀ
(FINIBULAR UP, FINICULAR DOWN)
(ITALIAN)
LUIGI DENZA & PEPPINO TURCO
SINGER: LUCIANO PAVAROTTI

I KNOW
WO ZHI DAO
我知道
(CHINESE MANDARIN)
BY2

WU SUO BU AI
无所不爱
(CHINESE MANDARIN & ENGLISH)
SHINING DIAMONDS
SD5 / HIT5

*　　　　*　　　　*

*F*ollow your luck; it will lead you to your destiny. Not taking chances and not making choices will leave you struggling with the enigma of your fate.

*　　　　*　　　　*

The Great Commons was noisy, buzzing with conversation amongst the freshmen students.

In the crowd, Luck spotted Lady Destiny approaching, this time wearing a tapered knitted crimson dress with a matching wide-rimmed red hat. On her lapel was a golden bee and beehive brooch, dotted with tiny diamonds. She was dragging two Asian beauties along with her.

"You must meet your compatriots." Amidst the noisy chatter of the crowd, Lady Destiny hollered, gesturing to Luck to come over. "Meet Enigma and Choice. Also from the Philippines. They just flew in from Paris."

As Luck cheerfully shook hands with them, Chance, Sophie, Katya and Ka-Ching showed up. "This is my brother, Chance." Chance nodded courteously at the young ladies.

A cacophony of chatter and background music drowned out Lady Destiny's voice. "These young ladies are also twins!"

Luck chuckled. "So are we!" He yelled toward the sisters.

Enigma and Choice were twins at the cusp of Magic. Both possessed keen objectivity of mind, with reasoning powers serving as effective foil to their deep emotions. One of their strongest motivations was the desire to learn, to develop, in the *best* way possible – and this led them to ISBS.

The sisters were daughters of Ernesto Reyes and Maria Clara Prisma. Over the generations, the Reyes family owned *Los Huevos Locos*, the largest egg conglomerate in the world. Crazy Eggs! Their eggs commanded premium prices. *Los Huevos Locos* produced the best eggs of the world, through its numerous hatcheries in various countries all around the world. Their eggs were the *most* widely consumed worldwide.

Tonight, like a prima donna, Enigma donned a purple netted veil hiding her face, rendering her less recognizable. She wore a pair of purple rimmed reflector glasses, matching her purple dress. Her outfit made her even more mysterious. With a standoffish glance, she cast a rather condescending look at Luck – especially after she noticed that he was wearing a pair of *white socks* along with his red rubber shoes.

"We just finished two months of mini-French course at the Sorbonne in Paris." Enigma's whole demeanor was nonchalant and haughty. She spoke with a French accent, with her chin half-cocked forward.

Luck proceeded to introduce Ka-Ching and Sophie to Enigma and Choice.

Likewise, Chance introduced Katya to the twin girls. "How do I distinguish between you?" Chance hesitatingly asked the sisters.

With cool reserve, Choice answered: "Tonight, it will be tough. By our outfits, I suppose." Her speech exhibited high-class gentility. Choice wore elegant silver rimmed glasses, hiding a pair of beautiful almond brown eyes, around which were glittering pastel blue eye shadows. Her eyeglasses matched her smartly tailored yet outlandish long *eau de vie* green dress. She had the fair skin of a Spanish-Filipina *mestiza* goddess yearning to be wild. She had on bright red glossy lipstick. She wore *l'eau de toilette verveine* which exuded a gentle lemony fragrance. Despite her ravishing beauty, there was a certain studied and subdued detachment and business-like manner about her. In ample portion, she was graced with the strength of understanding and the coolness of judgment. With much sense and sensibility, she was capable of a wide range of personal interaction, from casual friendship to full blown deep relationships of passion. Private by nature, she only granted a few people admittance into her inner world – only those with whom she held a sacred trust and admiration. For her, nothing was more important than love; this was her primary reason to live. The irony was this: though she had a deep capacity to give love, she could just as well withhold it.

Enigma had on a stunning midnight purple haute-couture dress, with a classy royal purple shoulder purse to match. As etiquette, she took off her veil, having flaunted her status. Then she removed her purple reflector glasses just for a moment, for Luck and Chance, who caught a quick glimpse of her mesmerizing eyes cloaked in long seductive mascara. She flipped back her jet black hair, saying: "Because of my weak eye sight, I wear glasses." With pride and prejudice, she gave Chance a vain look, taking the taunting stance of a flamenco dancer ready to pounce the floor. "Hey, young man, isn't your suit a tad too *tight* for you?" Then she placed her black reflector glasses back on.

Chance flushed with embarrassment. *That's a rather obnoxious comment!* With Enigma's cutting comment, he was made self-conscious.

"Come." Lady Destiny dragged Luck and Choice in each arm toward the reserved head table, as the others followed, busily chattering amongst themselves.

*   *   *

As was the ISBS tradition, the sophomore initiates served the Grand Welcome Dinner. Extra tables were laid out for upper class students out by the hallway and onto the Great Hall of the Present.

As everyone took their seats, Lady Destiny declared: "Tonight is indeed the Night of the Great Encounter. Also, today is the

Summer Solstice, signifying a Great Beginning."

The ISBS Glee Club serenaded the freshman class with medleys from the *Wizard of Oz*, such as: *Over the Rainbow*, *If I Only Had a Brain*, *If I Only Had a Heart*, *If I Only Had the Nerve*, and *We're Off to See the Wizard*.

The atmosphere was flamingly festive.

*   *   *

At this time, Mr. Leeds joined the group at the same table, sitting opposite Lady Destiny. Before sitting down, he placed his leather folder at the back of his chair. "This will truly be a great school year! We have a great harvest." He exclaimed with satisfaction. "At this table, we are doubly blessed: we have *two* pairs of twins. Luck and Chance. Enigma and Choice. This will be a momentous year. Enjoy this Freshmen Week!" Mr. Leeds proceeded to pass the bread around the table. "We're expecting great things from you all."

The table settings were elegantly laid out with special silverware. To the right of each plate setting was a brand new unlit candle stick.

Various fruit juices were served as openers. Students had the choice of orange juice or apple juice. *Hors d'oeuvres* entailed varieties of oven-hot mini-slices of thin-crusted pizzas: plain cheese; pepperoni; cheese with mushrooms and olives; cheese with pepper and other vegetables; cheese with shrimp and other seafood. There was French onion soup. Then, salad was served, with the following salad dressing choices: ranch, Caesar's, Italian and balsamic *vinaigrette* with olive oil.

Luck could not believe his lucky circumstance in this

Moment. He looked around, taking in the whole scene. The buzz of the Great Commons. The clinks of silverware. The sweet serenade of the ISBS Glee Club.

Sophie sat at his right, with the most loving smile gracing her face. Occasionally, she glanced at Luck, savoring every moment that she was with him. She beamed ceaselessly toward Luck. Underneath the tablecloth, Sophie warmly caressed his hand, happy to be with him. She decided she would be with him, through thick and thin. She would never let him go – ever again.

Chance broodingly observed the twin sisters, as they queried him, regarding his family origin, his classmates and his family connections.

Over the course of the evening, the brothers were the intermittent subjects of interrogation by these two *mademoiselles*. They were sizing up the male twins, in their unique high society ladies' attempt to determine whether to take the boys into their fold.

Later, the main course was served: grilled salmon, Cajun style with black pepper sauce, accompanied with white asparagus and mashed potatoes. "Eat your fill." Mr. Leeds teased the kids. "You will need all your energy once school starts. Also, expect to *gain* between fifteen to twenty pounds in the next twelve months. That's an ISBS tradition!"

Choice, in her cursory conversation with Ka-Ching, quickly determined that he was a man to befriend. She absolutely loved his Eaton accent. Most important, they shared the *same* culture – a culture of the enormously wealthy.

During dinner, Enigma asked Ka-Ching about his strengths, to which he jokingly replied: "My strong point is my *humility*."

When asked about his weaknesses, Ka-Ching had this to say: "I've got no vices, except I *lie* a lot." Enigma giggled at his wry humor.

*   *   *

CHAPTER 39

PARTY RIDDLES

MUSIC INSPIRATION

POKER FACE
LADY GAGA

CUANDO ME ENAMORO
(WHEN I'M FALLING IN LOVE)
(SPANISH)
ENRIQUE IGLESIAS & JUAN LUIS GUERRA

CAN YOU FEEL THE LOVE TONIGHT
THE LION KING
ELTON JOHN & TIM RICE
SINGERS (A): KRISTLE EDWARDS, JOSEPH WILLIAMS,
SALLY DWORSKY, NATHAN LANE, ERNIE SABELLA
SINGER (B): ELTON JOHN

NO REASON
MEI YOU LI YOU
没有理由
(CHINESE MANDARIN)
BY2

LOVING YOU
AI SHANG NI
爱上你
(CHINESE MANDARIN)
BY2

PAPAGENA! PAPAGENI!
DIE ZAUBERFLOTE, K.620
(THE MAGIC FLUTE, K. 620)
WOLFGANG AMADEUS MOZART
THE METROPOLITAN OPERA
CONDUCTOR: JULIE TAYMOR
DIRECTOR: JAMES LEVINE

*   *   *

As dinner came to a close, Enigma asked Luck and Chance this question: "How many nines are there between zero to one hundred? This is not a trick question and has only one correct answer."

Luck did some quick calculations. *9, 19, 29, 39, 49 ... ah, 99, should not forget that!*

"I'd reckon: *ten* 9's." Luck answered triumphantly. "Ten times!" He declared confidently.

Enigma and Choice broke out in smirking laughter. "Wrong!"

Many were stumped by this puzzle.

Chance diligently figured out Enigma's puzzle. He also counted ten 9's. *Hmmm... Now I have to reconsider.* He took out a napkin and started writing on it: 9, 19, 29, 39, 49 .... Aha! ...89, 90, 91, 92, 93.... 99!

Chance looked up with and answered hesitatingly: "Twenty times?"

Surprised, the sisters each gave Chance a high-five with an appreciative cheer! "You got it! Bravo!" Enigma congratulated Chance, impressed by his intelligence. For the first time in the evening, she *really* smiled at him.

Everyone at the table beamed. Some could have gotten it right; others might have gotten it wrong. No one was saying.

*   *   *

It was Choice's turn for the party games. "Do you want to take a dumb test?"

Warmed up, everyone nodded.

"What's twenty plus twenty?" Choice looked seductively into Ka-Ching's eyes.

"Forty." Ka-Ching felt obliged to answer.

"Correct!" Choice raised her brow approvingly. "Tell me: What's twelve times twelve?"

"That's easy. One hundred forty-four." Luck barked out his answer.

"Bravo! You're a genius." Choice clapped her hands. "What's the square root of ten thousand?"

Pause.

"I'll take that. One hundred." Sophie chimed in.

"Awesome! You're a super genius!" Choice nodded at her. "Oh, by the way, what was my first question?"

"Forty!" Ka-Ching jumped in, knowing he was the first one to go.

"Wrong!" Enigma threw a napkin at Ka-Ching.

"How come?" Ka-Ching was puzzled. "I was the first one to take your questions."

"My first question was: Do you want to take a dumb test?" Choice purred.

Everyone burst out laughing.

"That's a trick question!" Luck defended his roommate.

*　　　*　　　*

"Are you ready for another one?" Enigma was on the roll.

Everyone nodded.

This was Enigma's puzzle: "A clown wanted to cross a river on a boat with his rower friend with three items with him: an apple; a ball of cabbage and a bowling pin. The rower friend warned: 'This boat can ONLY bear *our* weight, plus a maximum of TWO objects – otherwise the boat will sink. One cannot throw any of the three items across the river – onto the other side of the riverbank.' The clown managed to get to the other side with his rower friend plus his *three* objects in a single crossing. How did he do it?"

There was silence as everyone at the table was thinking.

Now, Sophie was ready with an answer: "The clown ate the apple!"

Everyone laughed.

"Wrong!" Enigma declared.

Then, Katya answered: "The clown swam across the river!"

More laughter.

"Wrong!" Enigma declared.

Next, Luck answered: "The clown pushed the boat rower overboard and rowed the boat himself!"

Even louder laughter.

"Wrong!" Enigma declared.

Finally, it was Chance's turn to answer: "The clown juggled! The clown only had two objects in his hand at any one time.

"Brilliant!" Enigma gave Chance a classy exploding fist

bump, convinced of his brilliance.

Choice clapped daintily. "How do you know all the right answers?"

"Attention to detail, rigorous logical and clear thinking." Chance gave Choice a shy smile.

*   *   *

"Here, I've got another one!" Enigma was ready to shoot out another puzzle. "This is a one room house. And it's blue, blue, blue. The table is blue. And the chair is..."

"Blue!" Katya blurted.

"Correct! And the walls are..."

"Blue!" Sophie chimed in.

"Correct! And the window curtains are..."

"Blue!" Chance intoned.

"Correct! And the stairs are..."

"Blue!" Luck shouted.

"Wrong!" Enigma pounded the table, while bursting into laughter.

"Why?" Luck protested, looking puzzled.

"Because this is a one room house!" Choice screamed excitedly. "You *can't* have stairs in a *one* room house."

*   *   *

Now it was Choice's turn. "Who can tell me the nine

307

heavenly bodies going around our sun – in the order from nearest to the sun going outward?"

Luck jumped in by calling out the planet Mercury. "After Mercury is Venus. Uh, after Venus is Earth."

Choice was nodding approvingly.

Luck continued: "After Earth is Mars. After Mars is Saturn…"

"Wrong!" Choice gave Luck a vigorous thumbs down.

"My turn!" Sophie butted in. "Okay… There is Mercury. Then there is Venus. Then, Earth. Mars. Uhmm. Jupiter. Hmmm…" She hesitated, while all eyes were on her. "Then, there is Saturn." Again, she paused. "Let's see. Uranus. Neptune. Pluto. With Pluto being a dwarf planet!"

"Bravo!" Enigma cheered.

Choice couldn't help but be impressed. "Now what is your secret in getting these heavenly bodies in order?"

"There's this nursery rhyme that my Dad taught me – to help solve this puzzle: My Very Educated Mother Just Served Us Nine Pizzas! Remember this and you *can* get the answers in the right order. But you know, Pluto is *no* longer considered a planet." Sophie was beaming. She just scored with the crowd at the table.

*   *   *

Choice threw out this next puzzle. "Fill in the *blank*. And guess who coined the quote. She asked: 'The first one gets the oyster. The second one gets the *blank*.' Anybody?"

"Hmmm" Luck was thinking hard. "The pearl?"

"Good try. Wrong!" Choice purred.

308

"Was it Confucius?" Sophie interjected.

"Nope!" Choice was squirming delight.

Chance thought deeper. "The shell? Andrew Carnegie?"

"Wow!" Choice laughed. "Awesome! You got it. Correct! 'The first one gets the oyster. The second one gets the *shell.*' *Andrew Carnegie* said that." Choice nodded at Chance, deeply impressed. "Good job!"

*   *   *

"Now, who said this?" Choice was setting up her next quote. "Listen. 'Even a little lie is dangerous; it deteriorates the conscience. And the importance of conscience is eternal, like *blank.*' Who said that? Who wants to try?"

"Hmmm..." Luck wanted to be smarter this time. "Like the soul... by Edgar Alan Poe."

"Good try. But wrong!" Choice enjoyed stumping the brothers.

Luck really felt chastened. Tonight was not his lucky night.

"Errr..." Chance thought he got the most obvious answer. "Like the mind... by Carl Jung. That's my final answer."

"Wrong!" Choice stomped her feet with excitement. "Anybody?"

"Like *love.*" Sophie answered. "By *Pablo Casals.*"

"Correct!" Choice looked at Sophie, stunned. "Fantastic! 'Even a little lie *is* dangerous; it deteriorates the conscience. And the importance of conscience is eternal, like *love.*' *Pablo Casals.*"

Everyone clapped.

*   *   *

Dessert was strawberry ice cream.

Dinner was, oh, so yummy.

With friendly civility, Enigma and Choice warmed up to Luck and Chance. Likewise, both sisters took a *strong* liking to Ka-Ching.

*   *   *

While outwardly friendly, Ka-Ching was suspicious about the twin sisters' motives.

*   *   *

CHAPTER 40

STRETCHING THE CORD CEREMONY

MUSIC INSPIRATION

SYMPHONY NO. 9 IN E MINOR, MOVEMENT NO. 1
NEW WORLD
ANTONÍN DVORÁK

LUX AETERNA
REQUIEM MASS IN D MINOR, K 626
(THE ETERNAL LIGHT)
(LATIN)
WOLFGANG AMADEUS MOZART

WE ARE YOUNG
FUN

*　　　*　　　*

Wisdom is the Light which banishes Darkness.

*　　　*　　　*

"That which is Below,

corresponds to that which is Above,

and that which is Above,

corresponds to that which is Below,

to accomplish the miracles of the One. "

Hermes Trismegistus, The Emerald Tablet

*　　　*　　　*

311

After coffee was served, the Great Commons suddenly went dark. Pitch dark. Except for the moonlight which flooded in through the arched glass roof.

Bang! Bang! Bang! There were three thunderous knocking bangs against the door. The dining hall suddenly fell into sudden silence.

The bronze doors of Great Commons creeked open. There stood Marcus Blundermore, the President of ISBS, with a fiery torch in his right hand and a long crooked staff in his left.

Tonight, with a black bow-tie on, he wore a midnight black tuxedo, whose coat tails were beyond knee length. His signature rose-and-key insignia was sewn on left coat lapel. Over his white shirt, he wore a double-breasted vest. He was adorned with a ceremonial crimson red cape – marked with golden keys of various sizes, weaving ceaselessly on it.

At each of his side was a male runner, barefooted and bare-chested, wearing white mini-skirted Egyptian tunics and gold-trimmed headdresses.

Each runner had a bulk of corded rope swung around his left shoulder.

"Let the Stretching of the Cords begin." Blundermore raised his torch and his staff.

Softly, an ancient Egyptian chant in steady cadence rose amongst the numerous attendants in Egyptian tunics around the Great Commons: "Zep Tepi, Zep Tepi, Zep Tepi…"

Whereupon, from each of Blundermore's sides, the two runners stepped forward toward each other and tied a triple knot connecting the bulk of corded ropes each had slung over their shoulders. These were the Beginning Knots. These they laid them in front of Blundermore's feet.

(A bit puzzled, Chance texted Katya: "What's *zep tepi*?")

Each runner turned about-faced opposite each other and proceeded to the opposite ends of the Gates of the Great Commons. Each runner bent over at the edge of each side of the gate, pounded a big round plug upon their designated spots on the ground, and looped his rope three times over his respective plug.

(Katya texted back to Chance: "The First Time.")

The Right Runner at Blundermore's right turned right and proceeded to run toward each corner of the Great Commons, unrolling the corded rope on his shoulder as he ran, and at each corner, placing a hoop over the rope and fastened the hoop holder onto the ground, with the help of an attendant at each corner.

(Chance texted Katya: "What's the hap?")

The Right Runner made a full run around the Great Commons, unrolling his remaining corded rope and walked toward Blundermore's left side and there he stood.

(Katya texted back: "An ancient Egyptian sacred rite for pyramid building. Like modern-day cornerstone ceremony. An initiation rite.")

The Left Runner did exactly what the Right Runner did, except in the opposite direction. As he was doing it, with the cadence of the chant of "Tep Zepi", many ghosts of the past descended upon the Great Commons, including:

• Leonardo Da Vinci, floating around propelling his flying machine;

313

- Isaac Newton, juggling with apples; some of which fell here and there; while muttering: "These apples fall because of gravity!"

- Christopher Columbus, screaming: "Land, oh land!" while peering through his telescope;

- William Shakespeare, strutting about the Podium area, declaring: "To be or not to be…"

- Galileo Galilei, declaring: "The Earth goes around the Sun!", while pointing his refracting telescope toward the heavens;

- Benjamin Franklin, the Master of Electricity, flying his kite with a key strung on a kite string;

- Thomas Edison, the Wizard of Menlo Park, winking with his incandescent light bulb, muttering: "Let there be light!";

- Henry Ford, riding on his cranked-up Model T, honking his way around the Great Commons;

- Steven Jobs, showing off his iPhone and iPad, uttering: "Wow…oh, wow!"

There were many more ghosts flying, too many to enumerate here.

Alas, the *Left* Runner took his remaining corded rope and walked toward Blundermore's right side and stood there.

Likewise, the *Right* Runner took his remaining corded rope and walked toward Blundermore's left side and stood there.

In front of Blundermore, the two runners tied a triple knot involving the ends of their remaining corded ropes. These were the Ending Knots.

At this moment, the two ropes became *one*.

The Beginning Knots and the Ending Knots were laid in front of Blundermore's feet. Then, he handed his torch to the Left Runner, and his staff to the Right Runner. He stepped forward, raised the knots to himself. He held and kissed the Beginning Knots and the Ending Knots.

Then, he declared: "As above, so below! Likewise, let what is bound in the heavens be bound on earth! As below, so above! Let the Miracles of One unfold! May all our efforts be fruitful and enduring. Let Goodness abound. Go forth onto the Path of Learning!"

At this time, the Right Runner and the Left Runner helped Blundermore gently lower the Beginning Knots and the Ending Knots toward the ground. From each runner, Blundermore received back his torch and his long staff.

Slowly, he stepped over the threshold marked by the Beginning Knots and Ending Knots and headed toward the podium.

Facing the student body, Blundermore intoned: "Receive the Light!"

Choice happened to be the student seated closest to the podium. Lady Destiny signaled to Choice to head up to the podium. Choice stood up, raised her unlit candle and approached Blundermore. She reached out her arm. Her unlit candle touched Blundermore's torch fire. She turned to the audience and showed them her newly lit candle, eliciting applause from the audience.

Blundermore intoned: "Receive the Light! Share the Light! Be the vessel of Wisdom and Virtue!"

Whereupon, Choice returned to her seat and tipped her candle toward Luck's unlit candle. Likewise, Luck tipped his candle toward Sophie's unlit candle. Slowly, the points of candle lights started to spread throughout the Great Commons, its darkened expanse shimmering in gentle candle lights.

Then, Blundermore intoned: "Ascend to the Light! May the Light shine in your innermost being! Peer into the deepest Mystery within yourself; from here, you shall unlock the mysteries and secrets of this world."

Gradually, the Great Commons and the Testament Towers were filled with over two thousand points of shimmering candle lights.

As the audience clapped, each of the candles miraculously floated right above each student, illuminating each student's eager and hopeful face.

*   *   *

CHAPTER 41

ABIGAIL DANEUVE'S DISCOURSE

MUSIC INSPIRATION

COME SEI VAREMENTE
(HOW IT IS TRUE)
(PIANO)
GIOVANNI ALLEVI

SAFE PASSAGE
THE LAST SAMURAI
HANS ZIMMER

CABARET
CABARET
JOHN KINDER & FRED EBB
SINGER: LIZA MINELLI

EDGE OF GLORY
LADY GAGA

FOREVER FRIENDS
YONG YUAN DE PENG YOU
永远的朋友
(ENGLISH & CHINESE)
BEIING 2008
北京 2008
SINGERS (ENGLISH): COCO LEE / 李玟 & SUN NAN / 孙楠
SINGERS (CHINESE): SUN NAN / 孙楠 & A-MEI / 阿妹

HAND IN HAND
SHOU QIAN SHOU
手牵手
(CHINESE MANDARIN / KOREAN)
SEOUL OLYMPICS 1988
汉城 1988
COMPOSER: TOM WHITLOCK
SINGERS: KOREANA

**IN TERRA PAX HOMNIBUS
GLORIA**
(ON EARTH PEACE TO MEN)
(LATIN)
ANTONIO VIVALDI
OSPEDALE SANTA MARIA DELLA PIETÀ
ORPHANGE IN VENICE, ITALY
ALL GIRLS CHOIR

*　　　*　　　*

Tall, strong and in high spirits, Abigail Daneuve strode briskly toward the podium. At fifty-seven, her face remained strikingly beautiful and radiant. She wore a high-neck regal black gown with a the insignia of a rose crisscrossed by a golden key sewn on the upper left side by her chest. Her crystal blue eyes exuded steely determination and ebullient vitality. Above all, she commanded a winsome smile that could disarm the shyest student.

*　　　*　　　*

She began to address the student body:

"Peace to this house.

"As Dean of the ISBS Undergraduate Program, I welcome you, freshman initiates!

"We have *chosen* you. You have *chosen* ISBS. Let our partnership in Learning begin."

Abigail vigorously pressed a button. The walls behind her receded to expose the Grand Vista, an extension of the Great Commons.

Numerous plexi-glass poles emerged, ready to project holographic images at Abigail's command.

318

A holographic image of the globe with accompanying graphs was projected upon the Grand Vista.

"We are most fortunate to have such exceptional incoming freshmen initiates. Your group is two thousand in size, drawn from eighty countries." Practically the whole globe was lit up in various colors, representing the nationalities of the new entrants.

With her gleeful smile, Abigail was connecting well with the audience.

"Half of you are female; half of you are male. Admission rate is six per cent, very selective indeed.

"You are Americans, Europeans and Australians; Asians, Hispanics and Latin Americans; Afro-Americans and Africans. You speak over eighty languages. You are an incredible group."

Abigail was proud of this year's admission harvest.

"Learning here will be experiential and multi-dimensional. There will be group work and individual work. Remember, this is a *marathon*, not a sprint."

Applause from the audience erupted.

"This year, we are launching and implementing a new curriculum – starting with you. Welcome to a new world where academia, Main Street, Wall Street, America, Europe, Asia and the rest of the world come together here in ISBS."

More applause.

"ISBS is committed in providing you academic excellence and professional orientation – the best the world can provide. You will gain the disciplines of academia and your chosen professional career. This way, you will master the art of living and working –

and be the very *best* that you can be, preparing yourselves for *great* jobs and careers, into a life of prosperity, significance and fulfillment. In time, each of you will choose your major and possibly a minor, and be proficient in your fields of specialization. Each of you will master your unique craft and be inspired to live a life of achievement and service. Many of our graduates have gone on to become great entrepreneurs, inventors, innovators, bankers and investors. Some have made boatloads of dough."

The audience cheered.

"For your information, the vast majority of our college graduates – our Adepts – have joined the private sector, a third of them went to the government or multilateral sectors, with the remaining going to non-profit organizations. These are the soft-boiled grads."

Muffled laughter from the audience.

"Our Adepts who have chosen to continue their studies into the ISBS Master's Program will become, in due time, Brainiac Knights. For the few who will choose to pursue the ISBS Doctoral Program, they will become Magi.

"Brainiac Knights and Magi will become hard-boiled graduates. Later, you, too, will have the opportunity to decide what *kind* of an *egg* you want to be."

There was suppressed laughter from the audience.

"Upon completing your undergraduate studies, you become an Adept. To be a Brainiac Knight requires at least *one* heroic act during your time here in ISBS. To be a Magi, you need to perform at least *two* super-heroic acts during your matriculation here at ISBS. You will make a mark in building our Kingdom of New Magic!"

(Chance texted Katya: "R we gonna be eggheads?")

(Katya texted back: "ROFLOL!")

(Chance was puzzled. "???")

(Katya responded: "Rolling on floor laughing out loud!")

*   *   *

Abigail continued. "Now, on to more serious matters:

"The mission of the new curriculum is to raise your consciousness. We are more than our physical body. Through our consciousness, we reconnect to the deep Mystery at the center of our existence. Indeed, our consciousness *survives* physical death.

"Our consciousness is a human dimension which extends beyond matter, *beyond* the brain and more akin to the mind – a conscious mind. Consciousness is the essence of our existence. This is one key aspect you will learn to further develop in your years here at ISBS: cultivating beyond just your brain; we want to cultivate your mind. Your total consciousness.

"We are irrevocably connected to a larger universe, where our power of *belief* can facilitate 'mind-over-matter', a universe in its many dimensions.

"Through deep consciousness, we can explore the depths of our soul, the realm of the afterlife, the issues of reincarnation, the reality of God and Heaven. Through prayer and meditation, we can catch a glimpse of these truths which are often beyond the Realm of Wisdom.

"In our physical world, we use our senses, reason and religion to uncover and comprehend the paradox, pathos and catharsis of

321

our daily experiences. Here, we deal with our painful mundane realities, often times so baffling and so inexplicable. Paradoxically, it is through our physical existence and experience in this world that our consciousness is developed.

"The *best* gift we can give ourselves is being *true* to our own self – both on the conscious and subconscious levels: living an *authentic* fulsome Life.

"So freshman initiates, have fun discovering yourselves, your strengths and weaknesses, your likes and dislikes, and most important, your consciousness, for this will lead you to your ultimate destiny, here on Earth and beyond."

At this point, Abigail turned to Aurelius, the Dean of the Master's Program at ISBS, signaling him to speak.

With that, there was thunderous applause, cheers and hooting from the student body.

*　　　*　　　*

CHAPTER 42

STRUGGLES BENEATH THE TESTAMENT TOWERS

MUSIC INSPIRATION

CACHE-CACHE
(PIANO)
LUDOVICO EINAUDI

BATTLE IN THE FOREST
HOUSE OF FLYING DAGGERS
SHIGERU UMEBAYASHI

NIGHT FIGHT
CROUCHING TIGER HIDDEN DRAGON
TAN DUN / 谭盾
CELLIST: YOYO MA / 馬友友

BEAT IT
MICHAEL JACKSON

*   *   *

Hell must have exploded! Boom! A giant explosion at Basement Five of Testament Towers shook the whole structure.

Remus Goggles dove for cover, not knowing what had struck. His eardrums were almost torn by the deafening explosion. The ground shook violently, buckling his knees as he keeled over.

Remus had just completed his Z-Aster checkpoint, the most important one for the evening. A few minutes ago, he had chatted with Z-Aster outside his prison cell. The whole night had passed so uneventfully until now.

Z-Aster was the most prominent ISBS prisoner who had been

incarcerated for thirty years in the Chamber of Ordeals on Basement Five.

Aged sixty, Remus wore a pair of goggles, whose dark green lenses were thick as Coke bottles. These were special goggles, displaying digital data at the beckoning of the viewer.

Being the ISBS Internal Security Chief, Remus was meticulous in his observation of Reality. His view of the world was factual, un-burnished by sentiment or bias. *It is what it is!* This was the motto he lived by.

His twin brother was Romulus Goggles, the ISBS External Security Chief. Having been severely wounded in the Great Battle for ISBS Liberation some thirty years ago, Remus walked with a limp and needed the assistance of a cane. At sixty, he was highly regarded by the top leadership of ISBS, especially by Marcus Blundermore, for his heroic acts during the Great Battle. Without Remus, Marcus would have died. And ISBS would have continued in the Dark Age within the Realm of Darkness.

A second explosion followed. Boom! Sparks flashed as ceiling electricals and piping crashed onto the floor. Thick smoke filled Basement Five. Immediately, Remus's mind turned to terrorism. *We're being attacked. There is no mistake.* Over the years, this eventuality was discussed amongst the leadership of ISBS. And now, it looked like it was happening.

Choking and coughing through the ever thickening smoke and dust, Remus scrambled toward the dimly lit stairwell, where he saw a strange figure in a full black diving suit, with oxygen tank and mask, ambling down each step, each hand firmly gripping the bannisters. While not knowing who it was on the stairs, Remus instinctively knew a break-out was underway. This was the moment he had been trained for. Courage and reflex were key. Without a minute to waste, he lunged like a tiger toward the dark figure.

With the skill of a martial arts *kung-fu* master, the dark figure summersaulted backward to the lower steps – agile, despite his oxygen gear and contraptions.

Remus whipped his cane at the dark figure who parried with skill. With one lucky whack, Remus smacked the dark figure directly in the groin. Jackpot!

OH! OH! OH! OH! The dark figure recoiled in pain, keeled over, sucking for air.

Between blows and kicks, Remus quickly gained the upper hand, as the dark figure was weighed down with his oxygen gear and contraptions. Amidst the fight, Remus was dying to know the identity of the man in the black diving suit.

With all his might, Remus delivered a face blow and ripped at the dark figure's mask, banging his opponent's body head-on against the metal balusters, almost smashing them.

Like two crazed tigers in deathly struggle, they rolled down the steps. First to come off was the opponent's diving mask. Amidst the fight, the opponent's tight diving hood was also partly ripped off.

Then, between head-locks and wrestling maneuvers, there was a deafening shout: AAAOOOWWW! It echoed deafeningly through the stairwell.

*   *   *

CHAPTER 43

AURELIUS PRIMUS'S DISCOURSE

MUSIC INSPIRATION

GLADIATOR – THEME SONG
HANS ZIMMER

THE HOLY GRAIL
JAY Z & JUSTIN TIMBERLAKE

ONE WORLD, ONE DREAM
同一个世界，同一个夢想
FINAL VERSION / 完整版
(ENLISH & CHINESE MANDARIN)
BEIJING OLYMPICS 2008
北京 2008
LEEHOM WANG / 王力宏

LIBERA ME
REQUIEM MASS IN D MINOR, K 626
(FREE ME)
(LATIN)
WOLFGANG AMADEUS MOZART

*　　　*　　　*

My good blade carves the casques of men,

My tough lance thrusteth sure,

My strength is as the strength of ten

Because my heart is pure...

Galahad, Idylls of the King, Alfred Tennyson

*　　　*　　　*

Meanwhile, the welcoming ceremony continued at the Great Commons.

A bulky hulk, Aurelius Primus rose and approached the podium with the commanding presence of a man aged fifty-nine. A dark thick neatly combed beard covered his massive face. He wore a black beret, which tilted to the right, covering a scar on his right upper temple, reminiscent more of a birthmark. Along with a matching high collar Indian shirt, he wore a long tapered dark gray Nehru coat which reached down to below his knee. He wore a pair of black leather high boots. On his coat was a pin of a rose crisscrossed by a golden key. With a deep booming voice, he began:

"As the Dean of the Master's Program at the ISBS, I welcome you!

"The main task of the Master's Program is to prepare you to be Brainiac Knights of the Kingdom of New Magic, dedicated to the Great Task."

Aurelius pressed a button, and a humongous holographic image of Sir Lancelot, with his knightly tunic, was projected upon the Grand Vista.

"Behold Sir Lancelot du Lac."

For a second, a heavy and inexplicable sadness descended upon Aurelius, making him unable to speak – as the image of Sir Lancelot pervaded the Grand Vista. After a deep breath, he continued. "Sir Lancelot du Lac was the finest of knights in the court of King Arthur…entrusted to guard Camelot." With a tortuous frown, Aurelius paused, his esophagus constricting his breathing. Then, a zinging dizziness hit him. *Am I going to faint? No, no, this cannot happen.* Gripping the podium to steady

327

himself, he peered resolutely at the audience to maintain his balance. "Instead, Sir Lancelot betrayed his king in his dealings with Queen Guinevere."

Another pause. In a deep agonizing voice, he stammered: "Sir Lancelot was a knight trapped in his humanity…a victim of chance. And yet, he persevered… His was the tragedy of the heart…a tragedy of the soul."

No… Don't be Sir Lancelot! He could not understand why he was being seized with such negative feelings.

*   *   *

Just as Aurelius finished these words, there was a muffled blast underneath the subterranean level of the building, causing the glasses, the spoons and forks on the table to quiver. Chandeliers above began to sway back and forth.

Murmurs and stirs rippled through the audience. "What was that?"

With a puzzled and concerned look, Aurelius turned to Blundermore, unsure of what just happened.

*   *   *

At this time, Aurelius pressed a button, and projected upon the Grand Vista was a holographic image of Galahad, with his white shield with a vermilion cross. "Behold Sir Galahad, the greatest knight the world has ever known!

"Son of Sir Lancelot Du Lac and Elaine of Corbenic, famous for his gallantry and purity of heart, Sir Galahad was the knight chosen by God to attain the *Sangreal* – the Holy Grail, with the help of Sir Bor and Sir Perceval, two great knights of his time." He truly admired Sir Galahad.

Aurelius' breathing eased a bit.

"Despite being conceived in sin and deceit, Sir Galahad lived in the grace of our Lord and in his knightly code, to be lifted up to the heavens by God's angels – to be glorified forever. Sir Galahad embodied the quintessential virtues of knighthood.

"Emulate Sir Galahad!"

*   *   *

Once again, Aurelius pressed a button, and a holographic image of the Holy Grail was projected upon the Grand Vista.

"Behold the Holy Grail! This is the Grail of the Last Supper, the Grail which gathered Christ's blood after the Crucifixion. The Grail obtained by Pandoraph of Arimathea. Through this Holy Grail and the Sacred Blood of Christ, we attain healing, the forgiveness of sins and eternal life! Sir Galahad found the Holy Grail – because only the *most* worthy finds it. May you attain the Holy Grail! My mission is to instruct and train you to attain your knighthood – a knighthood of the soul and into a new realm of consciousness."

*   *   *

Aurelius felt a second muffled rumbling underneath his feet. It was softer than the first one. He knew something was very wrong. *This is not an accident. This is a terrorist strike! Dang! What do I do now? How do I keep calm?*

*   *   *

Straining to keep his cool, Aurelius continued: "You are here at ISBS to train your brain, your mind and your soul to make the right choices in the face of dilemmas in our lives and in our age.

"Why be moral? This deals with our karma and eternity. We are rational beings. We have to decide what kind of life we will lead. Selecting our fundamental character is our supreme challenge. Our eyes must be fixed on our karma and our eternity.

"We often ask: WHO AM I? WHO DO I BECOME? These will be questions we need to answer while we are here in ISBS. To ourselves be true. Choose a life that is in accord with our abilities and interest. Otherwise, we have chosen a *wrong* life.

"Finally, a life without love, friendship and personal fulfillment will lead to unhappiness.

"Now, it's my turn to ask: WHO ARE YOU? Be who you are destined to be! There's so much to do, my fellow initiates!"

*   *   *

Suddenly, there was an ISBS Internal Security Flash on Aurelius' computer tablet: "Z-ASTER HAS ESCAPED FROM THE CHAMBER OF ORDEAL!" With a worrisome frown, Aurelius strained his eye at his tablet to make sure he read it right. Aurelius's mind was racing. *With all the security precautions and systems in place, how can Z-Aster escape? This can't be!* Aurelius was seized by a sense of urgency.

He could not go on with his talk. He had to attend to Z-Aster, a *notorious* ISBS prisoner.

"Please excuse me," Aurelius apologized to the audience.

At this point, Aurelius turned to Marcus Blundermore, the Dean of the Doctoral Program at ISBS, signaling him to speak. As he dismounted from the podium, he approached Blundermore and shared a few words with him. "Z-Aster *has* escaped."

330

Very much bewildered, Blundermore approached the podium, as Aurelius left the Great Commons, very much in a hurry.

*   *   *

(Luck texted Sophie: "Heard the explosions?   Felt the shakes?")

(Sophie responded: "Yes! What the hell r those?")

*   *   *

CHAPTER 44

ESCAPE FROM
THE CHAMBER OF ORDEAL

<u>MUSIC INSPIRATION</u>

ARIA
(PIANO)
GIOVANNI ALLEVI

IN THE AIR TONIGHT
PHIL COLLINS

KISS FROM A ROSE
SEAL

THE DARK KNIGHT – THEME SONG
HANS ZIMMER

*　　　*　　　*

On Basement Five of Testament Towers, the screams barely died down when six commandos in black diving suits and six battle droids in black platinum burst forth from an opposite stairwell. The commandos threw stun bombs, with machine guns blazing. The droids in black fired their laser guns. It was all shock and awe.

"Z-Aster! We're here for you!" A cry from the dark burst forth. "Z-Aster! Hit the ground!" More machine gun fire and more laser bursts. "We're here to get you out!"

"Aye...aye..." Z-Aster's weak gasps came through from the dark between intermittent cracks of machine gun fire.

From the cracked window of his stairwell door, Remus peeked

out to see what was happening. "Holy smoke!"

Three commandos worked on Z-Aster's prison cell door, deactivating the lock. Three commandos stood guard, shooting non-stop, providing fire cover. The droids secured the opposite stairwell entrance.

"Professor? Are you there?" One of the commandos yelled.

No response.

In no time, the three commandos burst open the prison doors, dashed into the cell to rescue Z-Aster.

*   *   *

In the dark, Remus got the gist of what was happening and what he ought to do. The ISBS security team had prepared for this possible contingency. Into his watch, he murmured the dreaded words and pressed the emergency flash button: "Z-ASTER HAS ESCAPED FROM THE CHAMBER OF ORDEAL!"

Without hesitation, Remus gave his fallen enemy by the stairwell a smash in the face and a final blow on the head which practically knocked him unconscious. As he ripped open his opponent's diving suit, he was stunned to realize who he was dealing with. "Professor Scroogle! You *traitor*!" Never in a million years had he suspected Professor Brutus Scroogle could be a turncoat. Remus fumed with disgust. *"Et tu, Brute!"*

Moving quickly, Remus stripped Professor Scroogle of his diving suit, contraptions and oxygen tank and put these on. Upon uttering the spell *Transforma Corpus*, Remus transformed himself completely into the appearance of Professor Scroogle, whereupon, he opened the stairwell door leading back to Basement Five.

By now, most of the commandos were entering into the

opposite stairwell door – half dragging Z-Aster along.

"Wait!" Remus had to catch up. "Wait for me! Sorry to be late!" Remus signaled the last commando, pretending to be Professor Scroogle.

"As usual, you're late, Professor Scroogle! When will you ever learn to be on time!" The rear commando grunted with disdain. "It's a good thing, we have a Plan B. Without it, OPERATION POO could have unraveled. All because of you!"

"It's my fault!" Remus apologized. With that, he joined the commandos in black and disappeared behind the opposite stairwell door, which was shrouded in smoke.

For Remus, Z-Aster's escape was unfolding too fast. *Holy cow! Where is this all leading to?*

*   *   *

CHAPTER 45

MARCUS BLUNDERMORE'S DISCOURSE

MUSIC INSPIRATION

WE ARE THE WORLD
MICHAEL JACKSON& LIONEL RICHIE
QUINCY JONES & MICHAEL OMARTIAN
USA FOR AFRICA

EARTH SONG
MICHAEL JACKSON

A VERY GOOD YEAR
FRANK SINATRA

REX TREMDAE MAJESTATIS
REQUIEM MASS IN D MINOR, K 626
(KING OF TREMENDOUS MAJESTY)
(LATIN)
WOLFGANG AMADEUS MOZART

*　　　*　　　*

Seven blunders of the world that lead to violence:

wealth without work,

pleasure without conscience,

knowledge without character,

commerce without morality,

science without humanity,

worship without sacrifice,

politics without principle.

Mahatma Gandhi

*   *   *

Back at the Great Commons, Marcus Blundermore mounted the podium. Before delivering this evening's keynote speech, he surveyed the audience; then he spoke:

"As President of ISBS and Dean of the Doctoral Program, I welcome you.

"You are all here for one compelling reason: THE WORLD NEEDS YOU.

"Each one of you is universal necessity, sent to this world due to the Cosmic Behest. Without you, the world is incomplete. Each of you has a mission in this world. It is your personal responsibility to discover that mission.

"Recognize that brain power is the new currency of international competitiveness. Here at ISBS, we are committed to provide you just that and more. Wisdom is a scarce commodity. Remember that.

"So you've come to ISBS to pursue the American Dream – a dream for economic success on top of the heap, replete with the largest toys money can buy. It is based on this premise: work hard, take responsibility, pay your dues and you will get ahead.

"What's the ISBS value proposition? Our unique ISBS curriculum puts you all on a fast track toward a professional career, especially in the private sector, through our extraordinary entrepreneurship program. Our task is to create high-powered careers for our students which address today's and tomorrow's problems. We will equip you with the skill-sets needed for the new world economy, especially in the fields of science, technology, mathematics and finances. Critical and innovative thinking are our specialties. Opportunity is our essence. Our students offer the best value to society.

"With ISBS-*New Joy Sea* as the center, we provide our students access to a global education through its seven campuses: the others being ISBS-Beijing (北鏡), in the *City of the Northern Mirrors*, China; ISBS-Paris, in the *City of Lights*, France; ISBS-Moscow, Russia; ISBS-New Delhi, India; and ISBS-Cairo, Egypt; and ISBS-London, UK, the center of the British Commonwealth. Our seven campuses will give each of you unparalleled breadth and depth of education encompassing the bulk of our global economy and demographics. This is our strong suit which no other educational institution can even come close. Hence, our school motto: MANY WORLDS IN HARMONY."

The audience broke out in a thunderous applause, with some sharp whistling sounds shooting through the air.

Marcus Blundermore savored this Moment of recognition: the progress ISBS had achieved in advanced education during his Presidency these past thirty years. Such public adulation bathed his heart with satisfaction.

"Our leadership position in science and technology research, coupled by our core strength in finance and economics, gives ISBS innovation in entrepreneurship a new meaning. We are on top of the heap!

"I trust that your ISBS experience will make you relevant throughout your lives. Through our cutting edge educational program, may your lives have impact and meaning."

At this time, Blundermore pressed a button, and a humongous holographic image of the Great Pyramid of Giza in the Nile Country was projected upon the Grand Vista.

"The Great Pyramid of Giza! This monument has stood here for over four and a half millennia. At the first cusp of Time, it signified the frontier edge between the desert and the oasis, between pre-history and written history, a time when human thoughts, from being unwritten to a time when humans could transmit their thoughts to future generations. We witness this this great stone construction that is the Great Pyramid of Giza: a construction practically without words and hieroglyphics. And yet, it demonstrated great human wisdom beyond words through its near perfect alignment with the world's axes, expressing the Great Mysteries of Mathematics, Geometry and Astronomy, at the very dawn of human civilization. It is truly mankind's most magnificent ancient temple.

"Over the arc of time spanning the millennia, this Great Pyramid witnessed the advancing march of Civilization.

"Many aspects of human nature remain constants in the march of human history: Ambition and Greed, Courage and Cowardice, Confidence and Fear, Truth and Lies, Love and Hatred, and finally, Hubris and Catastrophe.

"The Pyramid of Giza stands, once again, at the edge of the other end of the arc of Time, about to witness our Civilization march from post-industrialization to transhuman history.

"We are at a new cusp of Time, where the human race is about to evolve to the next level – where technology and the human body will inextricably be welded together. Emerging technologies will *overcome* many fundamental human limitations.

338

"Over the millennia, humanoids have *walked* on this earth, unable to fly. In the twentieth century, within a span of around seven decades, man went from walking, to flying, to going to outer space, to landing on the moon. All because the Wright brothers ushered in the Age of Flight. They solved the Lift Equation. A major breakthrough. Opening the Magic of Flight to humankind.

"Now, let's look at computers. The 1947 introduction of the transistor revolutionized the field of electronics. This semiconductor device has become the fundamental building block of computers and is ubiquitous in modern electronic systems. Since the emergence of the electronic computer, its speed and capacity has doubled every eighteen to twenty-four months. The cost of computer chips has halved at this same period. This is known as the Moore's Law. Now, mathematical computations are faster than the human brain. Artificial intelligence has been evolving exponentially. Computers can beat chess grand masters in chess competitions.

"Technology has been improving exponentially, whereas our body is improving only linearly. For the body, we have an artificial knee here; an artificial hip there. An implanted tooth here; an artificial heart there. All these are linear progressions.

"Over time, the merger of technologies and the human body will transform the human condition, enhancing human intellectual, physical and psychological capacities.

"The age of Super-Intelligence is dawning. A new Omega Person is about to emerge. We are approaching the Age of Singularity. At that time, the ultimate merger of technology and the human body will occur. The human person will experience exponential growth in intelligence and in consciousness.

"Soon, the exponential progress of computer power will be able to reverse-engineer the human brain and be capable of human-level intelligence. Thereafter, with the ever accelerating progress in information technology, bioscience and neuroscience, artificial intelligence and nanotechnology, mankind will reach Singularity. At this stage, man and technology will be accelerating in faster velocities.

"This is the *next* step for humankind. Artificial intelligence will help us treat the effects of old age. Living to one hundred twenty will be more common. Truly, the intellectual brain is the most exciting field of study. In time, humans will be *super-intelligent!*

"We will be one step closer to *hyper-intelligence* – while adding a few more years to our lives. This is our serious hypothesis about the future of human life on Earth.

"IBSB wants to play a *leadership role* in fostering the Age of Singularity. Our school will be at the forefront in enhancing human evolution toward the creation of human-plus. H+!

"In this endeavor, our minds will pass through an extreme gradient in worldview, a hard shear that will separate us, Singularitarians, from ordinary humanity. We will become Magi in possession of this New Magic: EXPONENTIAL MAGIC.

"Our New Magic will overtake the magic of Hawkwurtz. Ours will be based on science and technology. Our incantations will be formulas, algorithms and sequencing. The right algorithms and sequencing will enable the computer to read a book aloud, understand human speech, cook our meals, drive and navigate a car through crowded city streets, anticipate and prevent a stroke or heart attack, react properly to stock market movements – and God forbids, fight our country's future wars, if

340

need be. Learning and technological progress will be ushering us into the Realm of Exponential Magic! Our New Magic is the ultimate game changer! Hence, our namesake: the INTERNATIONAL SCHOOL FOR BRAINIACS SQUARED! The future is here. Welcome to the Age of Exponential Magic!"

With electrifying applause, wild cheers and crazy hooting, the students gave Marcus Blundermore a standing ovation. He smiled at the crowd, basking at the approval rating of the audience.

* * *

"Within the context of the approaching Age of Singularity and the resulting Age of Exponential Magic, each one of us must reflect upon these issues: WHO AM I? WHY AM I HERE? WHERE AM I GOING? FOR WHAT PURPOSE?

"It is our responsibility to *exponentially* expand our minds: in mathematics and in the sciences; in business and economics; in history, philosophy and ethics; and finally, in our consciousness and our spirituality.

"We are here to be the Adepts, Brainiac Knights and Magis for the Kingdom of Exponential Magic – for the improvement of the world.   This Kingdom embodies *exponential* innovation and creativity, entrepreneurship and economic prosperity – for the fulfillment and happiness of the individual and for the benefit of society.

"Building our Kingdom of Exponential Magic is our Great Task. We will be pioneering the Singularity Culture. It will be achieved with audacity and nobility; wisdom and prudence; love and goodwill; integrity and truth. For this is our New Culture of Light.

341

"What role do we want to play in society? What contributions do we want to make to society? What legacy do we want to leave behind? How do we want to be remembered? These are questions for each of us to ponder.

"You can choose between genius and mediocrity. Or, just plain average. The choice is yours.

"Ultimately, our character defines our destiny. And what is our purpose in life? In three words: TO SERVE OTHERS. That is our noble cause. The challenge of our very being. Each of us is here because we are exceptional in our own right, daring to make a difference in this world. We are here because: THE WORLD NEEDS US."

He noticed his time was up. So, he wrapped up.

"These comments reflect the issues, the challenges and the opportunities I wish to convey. Be sensitive to the sufferings of the world. As you embark on the road of success, be mindful of your conscience: to strive for the betterment of all – including the poor and the disenfranchised. Be part of the solution to the world's problems. So, live out your dreams in action. Today! For, if not now, when?

"Ultimately, your philosophies will drive your attitude. Your attitude sets your action. Your action determines your results. Your results dictates your destiny.

"Following our true passions, let us march forward toward new frontier – that frontier beyond the Realm of Wisdom! For there lies our destiny."

The Great Commons burst with cheers and applause, drowning out Blundermore's remaining words.

Blundermore broke into a broad smile, satisfied that he had communicated his main message. Elated and exultant, he felt hopeful that he had inspired a new batch of freshmen initiates. Feeling triumphant, he felt like he was on top of the world. *Ah, I've come a long way. Dad, you should see me now!*

*　　*　　*

Blundermore hollered while gesturing to Abigail: "Once again, I give you: Abigail Daneuve, your Dean."

Mounting the podium and with a big smile, Abigail declared: "Initiates, enjoy this Freshmen Week! Let the Days of Learning begin!"

A thunderous cheer burst forth from the audience.

*　　*　　*

With a brilliant flash of light, a loud bang exploded outside. The audience looked toward the Grand Vista and through the arching glass roof. Streaks of fireworks shot up in the air exploding their bouquets of pyrotechnics.

Amidst the 'oohs' and 'aahs' from the audience, the fiery face of an aged Leonardo Da Vinci appeared on the sky, followed by a shimmering image of the Vetruvian Man descending in the black sky.

Then, the face of Isaac Newton exploded into view, followed by a big red apple floating down the horizon.

The visage of Christopher Columbus flashed above the sky. Then a sailing ship flittered through the air.

The cheery face of Benjamin Franklin splashed across the sky, followed by a kite and a key.

Thomas Edison's face exploded into view, followed by a flashing light bulb in the sky.

Henry Ford's bright face popped with a big smile. Then, a bright red cranked-up Model T banged into view.

A handsome face of Steven Jobs graced the night sky, followed by firework images of an iPhone and an iPad.

Wow! What an incredible feast for the eyes!

There were many other firework images, too numerous to mention here.

When it was over, thick smoke and the smell of fireworks filled the air.

*   *   *

Two MCs came forward, a gentleman and a lady, as the podium was being pushed to one side by other assistants.

"Let the dancing begin!" The MCs exclaimed. "Enjoy the Freshmen Week Party!"

*   *   *

CHAPTER 46

THE ALMOST NAKED PROFESSOR BRUTUS SCROOGLE

MUSIC INSPIRATION

THE ENCOUNTER
CROUCHING TIGER HIDDEN DRAGON
TAN DUN / 谭盾
CELLIST: YOYO MA / 馬友友

MY KRYPTONITE
3 DOORS DOWN

STARS
LES MISÉRABLES
CLAUDE-MICHEL
ALAIN BOUBLIL & HERBERT KRETZMER
SINGER: PHILIP QUAST

KAHIT ISANG SAGLIT
(EVEN FOR ONE SECOND)
(TAGALOG)
MARTIN NIEVERA

CAPRICHÓ ÁRABE
(CLASSICAL GUITAR)
FRANCISCO TÁRREGA
GUITARIST: TATYANA RYZHKOVA

*   *   *

"Where am I?" A few minutes elapsed before Professor Brutus Scroogle recovered from Remus's punishing head blows at the stairwell of Basement Five of the Testament Towers. The pain seared through his head, which felt like tons of bricks. He moaned. Blood was all over his right hand.

At sixty, Professor Scroogle was the preeminent Professor of Weird Magic, conjuring the *surreal* from the real. He was master of *unreality*. He was the Grand Illusionist – perverting reality into a magical unreality. His students loved him, because his classes were the most creative and most innovative, despite being the most perverse.

But tonight, he was completely *outwitted* by events, events that were beyond his control. Least of all, he did not expect to encounter Remus by the stairwell.

He did not know what had eventually transpired. Did OPERATION POO succeed or fail? He was clueless.

Professor Scroogle looked down; all he saw was: HIS RED THONG, which he wore for good luck – and for better aerodynamics. "How was I stripped down to my red thong? Where's my luck when I need it most?"

His head throbbed with pain. He felt blood streaking down toward the right side of neck. Most searing was the pain on his right ear. "Owww..." It dawned on him that his right ear was in deep hurt. As he tried to touch his right ear, he jerked back in numbing pain and panic. A big chunk of his right ear was missing! YEOOOWWW! He freaked out in a wild scream and then blacked out.

*   *   *

When he came to, he did not feel any better. He felt like a complete failure. Today was D-Day, and he botched it! *"What a dingbat am I! It's the most important day of my life, and I blew it – big time! What a klutz!"*

As he sat up, he watched droplets of blood trickled down, hitting the stairwell steps, dripping down the stairwell steps.

Dang! This is total madness!

Slowly, with great effort, he crawled toward the stairwell door. He struggled to open it. He pushed the door open, stuck his head out and surveyed the whole of Basement Five, which was eerily silent.

"Z-Aster! Are you there?" Professor Scroogle called out. No response.

He crawled across the basement. His heart was pounding. *Z-Aster has escaped!* This he kept telling himself, wishing it was true.

He crawled across the basement and came upon Z-Aster's prison cell. Upon seeing it was empty, he let out a sigh of relief. *Freed at last!*

*　　　*　　　*

Professor Scroogle had another big issue. *How do I get out of here? Undetected. In my red thong!*

In his confused state, he did not know whether he was to ascend or descend through the stairwell. *How do I escape from here without getting my butt kicked?*

*　　　*　　　*

CHAPTER 47

GANGNAM STYLE

MUSIC INSPIRATION

GANGNAM STYLE
(KOREAN)
PSY

OM SHANTI OM
(PEACE)
(ENGLISH & HINDI)
DEEWANGI DEEWANGI

A REAL MAN
(ENGLISH & CHINESE MANDARIN)
JOLIN TSAI / 蔡依林

GIRLS JUST WANT TO HAVE FUN
CYNDI LAUPER

DIRTY DANCING – TIME OF MY LIFE
FRANK PREVITE, JOHN DENICOLA, DONALD MARKOVITZ
SINGERS: BILL BEDLEY & JENNIFER WARNES

WHAT A FEELING
FLASH DANCE
GIORGIO MORODER, KEITH FORSEY, IRENE CARA
SINGER: IRENE CARA

YOU SHOULD BE DANCING
BEE GEES

BLURRED LINES
ROBIN THICKE, T.I. & PHARNELL

WE CAN'T STOP
MILEY CYRUS

PARTY IN THE USA
MILEY CYRUS

*   *   *

In the Great Commons, without any introduction, music blared: Opp. Opp. Oppan! Gangnam style! Gangnam style!

From the Grand Vista, Sigh!, a thirty-something a plump funny-looking Korean disco dude, appeared unannounced, dressed in his aquamarine tuxedo. He was doing his famous Gangnam style dance. In dark glasses, he shook his booty and trotted his way to the front of the Great Commons. He was accompanied by a six-year old boy in red pants, doing his own dance number – Michael Jackson style. In his white rubber shoes, Sigh! hopped and pranced around doing his lasso number.

Images flashed holographs of horses nodding at the barn stalls, as if in approval. Sigh! was joined by some dashing-looking up-town Gangnam girls in tight white hot pants and high-heeled boots showing off their sexy legs.

By now, most of the students had surged toward the front of the Great Commons doing the Gangnam style dance.

On the Grand Vista, the holograph projector beamed out the image of Sigh!, with two gorgeous lasses in white. Strong winter blizzard snow beat upon them, covering their faces, covering their hair, covering their mouths, covering their eyeglasses with flaky snow.

Now, Luck and Sophie, Chance and Katya, Ka-Ching and Choice, Mr. Leeds and Enigma were all horsing around: Gangnam style.

From the corner of his eyes, Chance noticed a tall and super thin African American, dancing the Gangnam style, his pelvis gyrating rhythmically. For a moment, their eyes met, at which time, the African American blew Chance a flying kiss, sealed with a playful smile.

349

On the Grand Vista, the holograph projected an image of Sigh!, covered only in a towel, in a hot sauna, leaning against a super-fat sumo wrestler. Meanwhile, a scrawny thin and fully tattooed gangster was stretching his limbs while showing off his rib-bones to nobody in the hot sauna.

Strobe lights of green, yellow, and blue were shooting here and there in the Great Commons.

This is one awesome party! Sophie gazed amusingly at Luck, as she hotly trotted beside him. *Keep on trotting! Don't stop!* She could not help laughing.

Then, Pan, another thin dude with a thick mopped head in a bright-yellow suit came out to join Sigh! in front of the Grand Commons, which had become a riotous dancing floor. It looked like Sigh! and Pan were having a dancing competition. It was hilarious.

On the Grand Vista, the hologram projected an image of Pan, wearing a pair of oversized dark glasses, emerging from a bright red car, swaggering toward Sigh!, who was dancing with four other graces in white.

By now, everyone in the Great Commons was grinding wildly and trotting around: Gangnam style, in one gigantic line-dancing formation, several layers deep. The dancing floor was pulsating wild with energy and zest! Everyone was having fun: Gangnam style!

*　　　*　　　*

CHAPTER 48

TOP SECRET INSIDE
THE TOILET STALL

MUSIC INSPIRATION

YELLOW ROOM
(PIANO)
YIRUMA

**THE SECRET GARDEN
THEME SONG**
ZBIGNIEW PREISNER

WHAT'S MY NAME
RIHANNA & DRAKE

NO ME DIGAS QUE NO
(DON'T SAY NO TO ME)
(SPANISH)
ENRIQUE IGLIESAS & WISIN & YANDEL

*　　　*　　　*

Chance's bladder was about to burst. Right after the Gangnam Style dance, he rushed for the loo.

*　　　*　　　*

Crowded, the men's room was elegantly classy, decked with black marble walls and floors, with high tech lights overhead. The full-sized doors of the toilet stalls were of dark burgundy mahogany.

Chance went into the toilet stall to pee. Just as he was zipping up his pants, his eyes caught sight of a black leather folder on one side of the toilet floor. He bent over and picked it up. As he opened the folder, he saw a yellow sticky atop the scribbles of a yellow pad. The yellow sticky had this message: TOP SECRET: Z-ASTER HAS ESCAPED THE CHAMBER OF ORDEAL! MAXIMUM ALERT!

Chance fumbled through the folder; behind the sleeve, he found some business cards bearing the name of Sir Thomas Leeds.

Chance frowned. *This is odd. What is happening?*

His first instinct was to look for Mr. Leeds. *Something is not right. But who is Z-Aster?*

In deep thought, he headed to one of the sinks to wash his hands and face.

At this time, from the mirror, he saw Luck entering the men's room. Chance quickly joined Luck and they conferred.

Chance opened Mr. Leeds's leather folder and showed the yellow sticky to his brother. "What shall we do?" Chance was worried.

"Simple. Return it to Mr. Leeds." Luck appeared to be enjoying his evening with Sophie and did not want to be distracted. "But first, I need to pee, too." With that, he dashed to the nearest vacant toilet stall. "I'm about to explode!"

*   *   *

Luck had a big smile on his face when he emerged from the men's room. "Boy! That felt good. I'm now twenty gallons lighter. Phew!"

"Good. Now let's get moving." Chance was eager to get going.

"But you know what?" Luck gave his brother a strange look. "My pee stinks! It's never been this bad!"

"It's the *asparagus* you ate tonight! Duh!" Chance gave Luck a tug by the arm. "Let's go!"

The twins surveyed and looked about the Great Commons, but Mr. Leeds was nowhere to be found.

"Mr. Leeds may be at the Admissions Office. This is our next best move." Luck ran toward the Great Hall of the Present, with Chance chasing from behind.

As they approached his office, Abigail's uncharacteristic shrill blared through the public announcement system: "Ladies and gentlemen, your attention please. ALL EVENTS HAVE NOW ENDED. PLEASE EVACUATE THE BUILDING IMMEDIATELY. ALL STUDENTS MUST RETURN TO THEIR RESPECTIVE DORMITORY ROOM <u>NOW</u>."

Abigail's voice over the loudspeakers sounded ominous, aborting the celebratory mood of the night.

*   *   *

Arriving at the Admissions Office, the brothers found the office door firmly locked.

"What do we do now?" Luck scratched his head. "Let's just slip this under the door."

Chance felt leery. "Our presence here looks suspicious, if not outright weird."

Luck grabbed the leather folder from Chance's hand.

But just before Luck slipped the folder under the door, Chance stopped his brother on his track. "Wait, Luck. We can't have that yellow sticky in the folder. This *is* top secret: only for Mr. Leeds's eyes. It may *not* be for the eyes of anyone else."

With that, Luck tore the sticky note from the folder and stuck it into his suit's chest pocket. Then he slipped the leather folder under the door.

Luck sensed something bad was unfolding.

Then, the brothers scurried back to the Great Commons, eagerly seeking their party mates.

*   *   *

From various unmarked doors of the dining hall, a dozen school security guards emerged and formed a straight row, blowing their whistles and sweeping the area with their flashlights, while corralling the crowd toward the exits.

The students begun to disperse through several exits.

No matter where he looked, Luck could not find his gang friends.

(Chance texted Katya: "Where r u?")

He was getting worried. *What does this portend? First day in school, and crap is already hitting the fan! What's going on?*

(Katya texted back to Chance: "@ ladies' room w/ girls. Will see u @ left exit doors.")

Again, Abigail came through the loudspeakers: "Ladies and gentlemen, your attention please. THE GREAT COMMONS AND THE TESTAMENT TOWERS ARE IN EVACUATION MODE. IN ANOTHER FIFTEEN MINUTES, *MUNTAHA* AND THE OTHER

DORMITORIES ON CAMPUS WILL BE LOCKED DOWN. ALL STUDENTS MUST REPORT TO THEIR RESPECTIVE DORMITORIES IMMEDIATELY. ANYONE NOT IN THEIR DORMITORY BY 9:30 P.M. RISKS BEING LOCKED OUT FOR THE NIGHT." Abigail's voice sounded tense.

The lights at the Great Commons and the Testament Towers were alternately dimming and brightening, conveying the urgency of Abigail's message.

Chance observed the school security personnel pushing the crowd to vacate the premises.

Chance was visibly anxious.

(He text back to Katya: "No time 4 ladies biz. School patrol in Great Commons. Am clearing out now. See u @ left exit doors.")

The brothers could feel the pushing and shoving as the crowd surged through the left exit doors.

*   *   *

Upon exiting the Great Commons, the twin boys joined the swarms of students gathered by the grassy Knoll.

Still, there were no signs of the ladies. "Do we let the girls know what we know about Z-Aster?" Luck whispered to Chance.

"Not for now. Let's see what happens." Chance was studying the situation, unsure what to do next.

"We can pick Katya's brain. She should know something." By now, Luck was bewildered by the anomalies of the night.

The school security on the Knoll steered the students toward the Wisdom Trail. Two dozen droids in white platinum guarded the trail. Security raced their electric patrol carts with their overhead alarm lights swirling and blinking, electrifying the atmosphere. Wearing night goggles, security hollered at the students to head back to their dorms – ASAP.

(Miffed, Chance text Katya again: "What's going on? Am outside now. Gotta go!")

The twins stood outside the Great Commons, mystified by the delay of the ladies.

Meanwhile, Ka-Ching excused himself. "I'm exhausted. I'd like to retire early. Dude, I'm heading back to our room." He bid Luck goodnight.

At this point, only the brothers remained near the left exit and security was heading toward them – looking menacing.

"What do you think happened to them?" Anxiously, Luck considered reentering the Great Commons.

*   *   *

CHAPTER 49

THROUGH THE KNOLL

<u>MUSIC INSPIRATION</u>

ROMANZA
(ROMANZA ANÓNIMO)
(CLASSICAL GUITAR)
ANONYMOUS

RHAPSODY IN BLUE
GEORGE GERSHWIN

COME AWAY WITH ME
NORAH JONES

PATIENCE
GUNS N' ROSES

GIVE ME EVERYTHING
PITBULL

WONDERWALL
OASIS

IRIS
GOO GOO DOLLS

WE GOT TONIGHT
KENNY ROGERS & DOLLY PARTON

NO ONE
ALICIA KEYS

FEEL THIS MOMENT
PITBULL & CHRISTINA AGUILERA

THE WAY
ARIANA GRANDE & MAC MILLER

ESTOY ENAMORADO
(I AM IN LOVE)
(SPANISH)
WISIN & YANDEL

RED BEAN
HONG DOU
红豆
(CHINESE MANDARIN)
FAYE WONG / 王菲

BECAUSE OF LOVE
YIN WEI AI QING
因为爱情
(CHINESE MANDARIN)
EASON CHAN & FAYE WONG
陈奕迅 与 王菲

STILL IN LOVE WITH YOU
YI RAN AI NI
依然爱你
(CHINESE MANDARIN)
LEEHOM WANG / 王力宏

SUDDENLY THINKING OF YOU
TU RAN HAO XIANG NI
突然好想你
(CHINESE MANDARIN)
MAYDAY / 五月天

PRELUDE IN G MINOR, OPUS 23
(PIANO)
SERGEI RACHMANINOFF

THROUGH THE BAMBOO FOREST
CROUCHING TIGER HIDDEN DRAGON
TAN DUN /谭盾
CELLIST: YOYO MA / 馬友友

*　　*　　*

358

From earshot, Chance heard Katya's familiar voice, and those of the twin sisters not far behind. *These prima donnas want to look pretty in the dark.* He was not amused by their dallying. "Now, what kept you so long in there?" Annoyed, Chance glowered at Katya. "So, what's the hap?"

"Girls stuff…" Katya chuckled.

Meanwhile the twin sisters joined up with Luck. "Where's Ka-Ching?" Choice was puzzled by his absence.

"He signed off for the day. He's knocked down by jet lag." Luck saluted one of the officers, indicating to him that they were now heading off.

As they approached the Wisdom Trail, Katya noticed the massive presence of security. "This is very odd. In my four years here at ISBS, this has *never* happened. Hmm…"

The super moon, now less full, reflected brightly on the Enchanted Pond of Mysteries, with clouds racing through the sky, blotting it out altogether from time to time. Frogs croaked in the darkness of the pond. Cricket sounds blanketed the Knoll, blending with the noisy chatter of the students heading toward their dorms. The emerald stones looked like ordinary stones, their luster lost in the night. Crunching sounds of emerald gravel made by walking feet reverberated from the pathway.

On the Dot, the Oculus of the Interior's searchlights swept ominously through the Knoll. At intervals, the light beamed and combed through the buildings standing at the elevated hills.

Some students held on to their candles, whose lights flickered in the wind. For others whose hands were otherwise engaged, their candles floated in the air, leading their owners through the dark.

Katya reached out for Chance's hand in the dark, feeling romantic. This was the opportunity she was waiting for. A moment for closeness. Her signal for romance.

Feeling awkward, a hot flush swept through Chance. She smelt like lilac of the night. Katya's hand felt silky smooth. He felt Katya's hand softly squeezing his. He was liking it. His heart pounded with excitement. *Wow! This is something new! So this is romance – when you least expect it.*

*   *   *

Chance could not stand his own ignorance on the matter of Z-Aster any longer. "So, *who* is he?" Chance finally blurted out.

"Who?" Katya was not sure of what she heard.

"Z-Aster..." Chance whispered.

Katya let go of Chance's hand, her mouth wide open. "How did you know?" Katya was startled that Chance knew *this* name. There was no mention of Z-Aster in any recent ISBS school catalogues. Any reference to Z-Aster was obliquely referred to as the "Nameless" to minimize concerns from students and more recent faculty members.

After a quick pause, she asked: "Chance, do you know *something* that I don't?"

Chance did not know how to respond.

"Nameless. You meant *Nameless.*" Katya tried to maintain her cool. She wanted his queries to just blow away to insignificance. "It's better that you don't know." She kept her voice low.

"What do you mean?" Chance was confused. "Who's Nameless?"

"Shh…" Katya whispered, not wanting to cause a fuss. "Nameless *is* Z-Aster. Mentioning Z-Aster is *verboten* in school."

"Can you *un-read* what you've read? Can you *un-know* what you know?" Chance got testy.

"Now, *what* have you read? *What* do you know? *What* have you seen?" Katya retorted.

Catching himself, Chance decided that he better be careful and not *push* too hard.

They continued to stroll without speaking to one another. The promise of a melodic night of romance had turned dissonant.

Katya spoke softly. "Nameless is *bad* news. He caused massive chaos at ISBS. His father is the worst: he is the Insidious One."

"What are you two talking about?" Now curious, Choice drew near, overhearing parts of the ongoing conversation.

Katya did not respond.

"What did he do?" In a hush-hush tone, Chance asked insistently.

When they were a few paces ahead of Choice, Katya continued: "Nameless was a usurper and a disrupter. He is known as the Prince of the Dark Age, a *very* dark period in ISBS history. Many lives were destroyed because of him." Katya was getting visibly stirred. "Many of our best professors and school leaders suffered much."

"What did he do? You haven't answered my question." Chance interjected.

Pause.

Katya's mind was racing. She could sense they were at the edge of a full blown discussion on Nameless.

"This is a question better addressed to the Three Grand Masters: Blundermore, Aurelius or Abigail." Katya was not sure how much to divulge to such newcomers. She did not know how much of Z-Aster was common knowledge amongst them. Most importantly, she did not want to get into trouble. *No, I better shut up for my own good. This can only lead to no good.*

A few steps behind, Enigma, Choice, Luck and Sophie were whispering to each other.

"I can also ask my Dad." From behind, Sophie volunteered, wanting to be helpful. "He could shed some light on this. He'll be here in a few days."

Oh, no. The genie is out the bottle. Katya was beginning to panic. *I've said too much.*

*   *   *

Soon, they came upon a fork on the path. The path to the right would lead to The Grange, the seekers' dormitory for the Master's Program students where Katya resided. The path to the left led to *Muntaha*. The Grange was only a short distance away from *Muntaha*.

"Sorry, guys, I've got to leave you here." Katya was relieved – to be off the hook from this awkward situation. "I'm heading to the Grange. See you next time, guys." She gave Chance a light kiss on the cheek.

Katya bade good-bye to her new friends. "And remember, *discretion* is the better part of valor. Don't let *curiosity* kill the cat. Don't be too nosy." With that, Katya proceeded on the path to the right toward the Grange.

Confused, the gang of five proceeded toward *Muntaha*.

*   *   *

At *Muntaha*, a line was forming. Six eye scanners were raised in front of the turnstile area. Each student had to have his retina scanned before proceeding further.

Master Stanley Watchman stood behind the reception counter with the sternest look.

Then, with each face scanned, each student swipe his ID card key over the entrance turnstile registry to access the elevators. Several intimidating school patrol officers were stationed by the turnstile entrance.

Two droids in white platinum stood watch at each of the elevators with laser weapons in hand.

The brothers headed for the blue elevators.

The twin sisters and Sophie dashed for the orange elevators.

*   *   *

The mood in *Muntaha* had turned somber. Rather than being welcoming, the ambiance of the lobby area had turned foreboding.

The scowl on *David's* face had turned ominously dark.

*   *   *

Inside the blue elevator, Luck and Chance were each deep in thought, wondering how to crack the mysterious case of Z-Aster.

*   *   *

CHAPTER 50

THE THREE GRAND MASTERS

MUSIC INSPIRATION

SYMPHONY NO. 9, MOVEMENT NO.1
LUDWIG VAN BEETHOVEN
CONDUCTOR: HERBERT VON KARAJAN

DON'T KNOW MUCH
LINDA RONSTADT & AARON NEVILLE

DOMINE JESU CHRISTE
REQUIEM MASS IN D MINOR, K 626
(TO THE LORD, JESUS CHRIST)
(OFFERTORY / OFFERTORIUM)
(LATIN)
WOLFGANG AMADEUS MOZART

*   *   *

*I*s *it within our power to alter our human condition? How do we deal with circumstantial error of events? The inadvertent mishaps? How can we fix the consequences?*

We can be at the wrong place and at the wrong time. Meanwhile, our lives are inexorably changed.

*   *   *

Around his round white alabaster conference table, the Three Grand Masters convened at Blundermore's office. It was dimly lit. The curtains were drawn closed, with the security shield turned on.

"How did this *all* happen?" Blundermore bellowed with agonizing frustration. "How did Z-Aster escape?" His brows curled, with his lips pursed. Outraged, he howled, as he whacked his staff on the round alabaster table. "Dang!"

"It *is* what it *is*." Across the table, Aurelius spoke quietly and determinedly in his deep voice. "This is a night of villainy. The truce of the past three decades is over. The gauntlet has been cast."

"There shall be no retreats, no hesitation and no forgiveness this time." Abigail looked exasperated.

There was only brooding silence in the room, except for the heavy heaving of the Three Grand Masters.

Quietly, Aurelius continued: "His rescuer or rescuers went to Basement Five and accessed the unmarked Chamber of Ordeal. The electronic lock of the Chamber was deactivated."

"How did Z-Aster escape?" Visibly upset, Abigail let out a big sigh. "This is dreadful!" The unknown method of escape sent a shudder of fear up her spine. "Has Black Magic returned to the very heart of ISBS? Has it penetrated through our security systems?"

"We have very little clues at this time." On this same point, Aurelius was also quite puzzled. "Several video cameras went blank right before the blast. Someone deactivated the laser monitor system for the whole Testament Towers – minutes before the person or persons began the rescue operation. Before then, Remus Goggles did not report any anomaly in the area. In fact, we haven't spotted or made contact with him all night – since his emergency news flash."

Abigail asked insistently: "Do we know *where* he is? Has he died during the explosion? The news flash his last words?"

Also at a loss, Aurelius could not find the right words. "We could not trace the location of the blast at this time. No blasts were detected around the Testament Towers, or on Basements One thru Five. I will do a more thorough inspection with Romulus and his team throughout the night. We will get to the bottom of this." Aurelius assured them.

Abigail scrutinized the images of the school grounds flashed on the screen. Abigail was rather resigned. "It's late. Make sure the alarms and security shields are set across the school perimeters and in each of the buildings. What else can we do? The horse has left the barn."

With his downcast look, Blundermore whipped out his wand and WHAM! – a strobe light flashed through, zapping an armored knight statue by the corner of the office. The statue came crashing down. With ferocity, he brandished a double X in the air. *How can this be? Who can be involved? What will happen now?* Blundermore was absolutely furious – furious at Circumstance and at himself. "Aurelius, you're right. The battle for the soul of this school commences once again. I feel it in my bones. The peace which held over the past three decades is collapsing."

"I feel ill winds in the air." Aurelius was sure a conflict was brewing. "There is no doubt about it."

"Are we going to see the return of the Dark Age?" Abigail muttered, defiant tears rolling down her cheeks. "Will this be a fight of life and death? Haven't we had enough suffering?"

*   *   *

CHAPTER 51

ALAM BIBI
AND
LITTLE PRINCESS INDIRA

MUSIC INSPIRATION

JAI HO + LATIKA'S THEME SONG
(ENGLISH & HINDI & URDU & PUNJABI)
SLUMDOG MILLIONAIRE
A R RAHMAN & GULZAR
SINGERS
SUKHWINDER SINGH, MAHALAXMI IYER, TANVI

TUJH MEIN RAB DIKHTA HAI
(IN YOU I SEE GOD)
RAB NE BANA DI JODI
(A MATCH MADE BY GOD)
(PUNJABI)
JAIDEEP SAHNI
SINGERS
ROOP KUMAR RATHOD & SHREYA GHOSHAL

CHOLI KE PEECHE KYA HAI
(WHAT'S BEHIND YOUR BLOUSE)
(HINDI)
KALNAYAK
LAXMIKANT-PYARELAL & ANAND BAKSHI
SINGERS
ALKA YAGNIK & ILA ARUN

ROYALS
(U.S. VERSION)
LORDE

YOU DON'T KNOW ME
NI BING BU DONG WO
你并不懂我
(CHINESE MANDARIN)
BY2

*　　　　*　　　　*

As Alam Bibi was enjoying the eastern view of the campus, her eye caught sight of the third rose in the vase by the window sill. A purple tag was clipped onto the stem of her roommate's rose. Upon closer inspection, she detected an inscription. It read: PARADOX.

*   *   *

Later, Alam stealthily went through Enigma's things strewn on the bed, while making sure to leave them in their proper place without showing any disturbance. *Hmm... Some rich princess!* She studied Enigma's family picture on the table. *How lucky she is! I wish I were from a family of means!* She envied her roommate.

Intrigued, Alam was drawn toward a surrealist picture, hanging over Enigma's bed. In the picture was the hatching of a man emerging from a giant egg, with his lower torso and legs still inside the egg. The map of the world was imprinted on a canvas behind the giant egg. From the tear of the giant egg was blood oozing onto a piece of white cloth underneath it. Floating above the giant egg was a suspended white canopy. This was Salvador Dali's *Geopoliticus Child Watching the Birth of the New Man.*

At the sound of the key card sliding into the slot and the door handle turning, Alam headed toward the door to greet her new roommate.

Enigma still had her netted veil over her face, with her dark glasses on. "Well, who do I have the pleasure of rooming with?" Her voice was tinged with haughty sarcasm. *My, my, we're from very different worlds!*

Alam stood there, for a moment immobilized by the extravagance of Enigma's outfit.

369

Enigma introduced herself. "I'm Andromeda Prisma Reyes. Call me Enigma, for short.

Then it was Alam's turn. "I am Alam Bibi. I was born in Afghanistan. Grew up in Nasir Bagh, near Peshawar, a Pakistani refugee camp by the Afghan border. My father is a taxicab driver in Manhattan." She wore a simple dress, with a blue Afghan *chadri* headaddress, presently partially lifted.

Enigma stood by the doorway, awestruck and dumbfounded. She looked at Alam's piercing sea-green eyes. Hers was a timeless haunting look of someone having survived a terrible war. Hers was an anguished look of loss: a look of someone from Hell and back to this world of the living – her soul seared by her life's incomprehensible sufferings. Hers was a look of a *disturbed* gazer.

Enigma looked over at Alam's side of the room. It was bland and empty – a stark contrast from her own side of the room. Yes, she realized Alam was from a different world. For a moment, she was at a loss as to *how* to deal with Alam. Enigma took off her netted veil and her sunglasses. She put on her regular glasses. "Errr... So how many years have you been in America?" Enigma gently asked, her class prejudice suddenly melted away in light of Alam's reality all etched on her roommate's face and whole being: the ravaging consequence of war.

"Ten years. Graduated high school year in Manhattan – with high honors. From Stuyvesant High School at Battery Park." Alam gave Enigma a quiet smile of pride. "I'm eighteen. And you?"

Without revealing her own age, Enigma nodded, visibly impressed by Alam's achievement. "You are an awesome learner. A great one, for that matter – especially in Math and Sciences."

370

"An *eager* learner." Alam corrected her.

"Did you enjoy our Grand Welcome Dinner?"

Alam nodded. "Very much so."

"How about the dance afterward?"

"I left early." Alam shook her head. "That was *not* for me."

*   *   *

There was a rustle on the bed. A tiny soft voice emerged from the bed sheets, in a distinctive Indian-English accent: "I'm thirsty and hungry."

"Oh, that's my Little Princess Indira of *Moldivia*." Enigma was quick to point out. With joy, Enigma lifted Little Princess Indira from her bed. "At early dawn this morning, the Fairy Godmother gave her to me as a gift – through a dream! Can you believe that? Little Princess Indira just appeared at my bedside inside a multicolored carton box."

Alam could only gaze at the Little Princess Indira – with fascination. She had *never* seen anything like this.

Enigma placed the Little Princess Indira on her study desk which was festooned with baubles and jewelry. Not more than seven inches tall, the Little Princess Indira curtsied toward Enigma and Alam – Indian style. *"Namaste!"* She gave them the sweetest smile. She wore a choli, cropped at the upper midriff. She was draped in a white sari, bordered with embroidered gold leaves. She was fair skinned, with a beautiful set of beaming eyes. She had the look of royalty and moved about with elegance. Her warm disposition took Alam's breath away.

"How can this be?" Alam was a bit puzzled.

371

"She came about through a dream. We'll let Little Princess Indira explain."

"I have not accomplished my life's mission in my previous life as a court dancer of the royal house of *Moldivia*. Most of my time was spent in dance practice and performance for the royal couple and during visits of dignitaries at the royal palace."

"So, why are you sent here?" Alam was curious.

"If I prove myself heroic and true, I shall have a choice of becoming a full-sized human and be an *eternal* princess. I don't want to be a court dancer with no specific responsibilities or duties – idling my days away. If I succeed in aiding my Lady Enigma during these coming four years while at ISBS, I can gain my independence and freedom to do what I enjoy doing in life and to make something of myself. I am tired of loitering in the imperial courts doing *nothing* significant. I can be *myself* – making significant contributions to humanity! That's my deal with the Fairy Godmother." The Little Princess Indira spoke with sincerity.

Alam was most impressed with the Little Princess Indira. For a moment, Alam's internal sorrows dissipated. Little Princess Indira's message resonated with her.

*   *   *

Before retiring for the night, Enigma looked out her window. Except for the searchlights of the Oculus of the East, the Eastern Front was dark. She noticed the third rose in the vase by the window sill. A white tag was clipped onto the stem of Alam's rose. She took a closer look. It read: MISUNDERSTANDING.

*   *   *

CHAPTER 52

CAMILLA MEDUZA GORGONIA
AND
MAGUS THE ELEPHANT

<u>MUSIC INSPIRATION</u>

JUST CAN'T GET ENOUGH
BLACK EYED PEAS

LE SENSE DE LA VIE
(THE MEANING OF LIFE)
(FRENCH)
TAL

ANGEL OF MUSIC
PHANTOM OF THE OPERA
ANDREW LLOYD WEBER
SINGER: EMMY ROSSUM

WRECKING BALL
MILEY CYRUS

ALONE
YI GE REN
一个人
(CHINESE MANDARIN)
JOLIN TSAI / 蔡依林

HEARD LOVE HAS RETURNED
TING SHUO AI QING HUI LAI GUO
听說愛情回來过
(CHINESE MANDARIN)
JOLIN TSAI / 蔡依林

BEAUTY AND THE BEAST
BEAUTY AND THE BEAST
ALAN MENKEN & HOWARD ASHMAN
SINGERS: CELINE DION & PEABO BRYSON

*   *   *

Camilla Meduza Gorgonia was enjoying the western view of the campus, her eye caught sight of the third rose in the vase by the window sill. A green tag was clipped onto the stem of her roommate's rose. Upon closer inspection, she detected an inscription. It read: REVELATION.

*   *   *

Later, Camilla took her time hanging up three Japanese ornamental masks above her study desk. The faces were painted in white, with full lips painted in red. Each of the faces had a unique expression. One exceedingly happy; another, a mysteriously neutral expression. The last one was a horrific gruesome facial contortion of Death. Above the three masks was a long intricately carved wooded speckled serpent.

She was looking contentedly at the masks when she heard the sound of the card key sliding into the slot and the door handle turning.

Gently, the door opened and Choice appeared.

Camilla turned and stared at her new roommate, Choice. With her deep blue-green eyes, entrancing and unblinking, she cast a mysterious hypnotic gaze at Choice, as if to uncover a secret. At eighteen, adorned with long jet black hair, Camilla had a most inscrutable stare. Her eerie beauty seemed to challenge Choice's uptown sophistication.

"Do you like my masks?" Camilla was proud of her wall decorations.

Choice nodded, as she introduced herself. "Most interesting! By the way, I am Elektra Prisma Reyes. Call me Choice for short." For some reason, Choice's introduction did *not* register with Camilla.

Choice examined the three masks with studied interest. Being captivated by the three masks, Choice wanted to know Camilla's preference. "Which of these three masks do you like the most? These are like the portraits of three sisters!"

Camilla never considered this question. "Hmmm… You see, these three masks reflect *our* reactions to Circumstance. What will be *your* reaction when certain events occur? You see, each expression represents a complete state of being." Camilla explained.

Choice peered deeply into each mask. "I'm beginning to see." She was riveted by the masks. "Of course! Yes, I like the happy face – if that is possible at all times. Let's say, for most of the time."

Camilla looked at Choice queasily but impressed by her conditionality. "You are *very* perceptive. We *can't* be happy all the time. How can we be happy with a *death* in the family, right?"

Choice nodded. "But perhaps our reaction to Circumstance is negotiable. Do we let Circumstance control us? Or do we control Circumstance?"

"This is a perennial question." Camilla was beginning to like Choice. "But do we have a choice? No *pun* intended."

"Great point!" Choice liked Camilla's dry humor. "Best to be *stoic*. In an eternal neutral state: neither happy nor sad. Then, we'll never be surprised; never be disappointed."

"How should one receive Death?" Camilla asked testily?

"Death is just a portal to *another* existence – inasmuch as birth is a portal into *this* existence." Choice said rather matter-offactly. "It's neither a reason for rejoicing nor for mourning."

Through this exchange, Camilla warmed up to Choice. With a smile, she greeted Choice and introduced herself. "I'm Camilla Meduza Gorgonia. I am Spanish. Spent the last ten years in Tripoli, Libya, the land of the late Muammar Qaddafi – a nation of Strife and Death."

They shook hands. "There, my father was a functionary at the Spanish Embassy. Our family left for Paris just as soon as the civil war broke out. Tripoli is a mess.

"Bien sur!" Choice was delighted to speak French with her. "I just arrived from Paris! In which *arrondissement* did you stay?"

"In the fourteenth *arrondissement*. At the *Cité Internationale*. At the *Maison de la Tunisie*. I studied at the Sorbonne for intensive French."

"Really!" Choice grinned broadly. "I stayed at the *Maison de l'Asie* these past two months to study Advanced French."

"Our paths must have crossed at the Cité." Camilla was likewise elated. *After all, we do have something in common.*

*   *   *

From Choice's wardrobe closet came a squeal: "I'm thirsty! I need a drink!"

"Oh, that is Magus the Elephant!" Choice giggled as she opened the wardrobe closet to let Magus out of his little pen. He was a miniature white elephant of not more than ten inches in height, draped with royal red silk. "My Fairy Godmother gave him to me through a dream! At dawn! This very morning! Can you believe that?"

376

Choice introduced Magus to Camilla, who was completely baffled at what was happening. Choice patted Magus by the head to calm him down.

"Let me get you something to drink!" Choice poured some bottled water into a plastic cup for Magus to drink.

"Thank you. It's delicious!" After sipping the water with his trunk, Magus quieted down.

"Now, why are *you* sent here?" Curious, Camilla asked Magus.

"If I prove myself heroic and true, I can become a full sized elephant of the great jungles of my choosing. If I succeed in *serving* my Lady Choice in the coming four years at ISBS, I won't be sent back to *Moldivia* where I was an imperial elephant, mainly for *show* during important holidays or when important guests visit the imperial courts. I want to be a *true* elephant of the great jungles. And *not* for show! I'm an elephant in search of a *higher* purpose: to seek the unity of man with divinity; for a drop of water to be one with the ocean; for the harmony of the microcosm with the macrocosm. That's my deal with the Fairy Godmother." Magus was sincere in his resolve.

Camilla was intrigued. "*How* can you help Choice?"

"I will make her *wise* in her studies. She will be the smartest student in her class. I will *dispel obstacles* in her life so that she will be free to do whatever she wants. I will help her *surmount* the many difficulties in life." Charismatic, Magus exhibited all the intellect and wisdom of an elephant.

"Likewise, I've promised to help Magus in anyway. He will be my friend forever. Doesn't he look wonderful?" Hugging her Magus, Choice tidied up the red mantle draped over his body.

377

Camilla was incredulous at what she was witnessing.

*   *   *

Before retiring for the night, Choice gazed out her window. Except for the searchlights of the Oculus of the West sweeping the landscape, the Western Front was dark. She noticed the third rose in the vase by the window sill. A black tag was clipped onto the stem of Camilla's rose. She took a closer look. It read: TRIBULATION.

*   *   *

CHAPTER 53

PEERING INTO THE DARK AGE

MUSIC INSPIRATION

THRILLER
MICHAEL JACKSON

LA LA LAND
DEMI LOVATO

IN MY LIFE
THE BEATLES

IS THIS LOVE
BOB MARLEY

DESERT CAPPRICCIO
CROUCHING TIGER HIDDEN DRAGON
TAN DUN / 谭盾
CELLIST: YOYO MA / 馬友友

EROS
LUDOVICO EINAUDI

*   *   *

When Chance entered his room, he saw a burgundy red envelope by the floor, addressed to him, slipped through the crack of the door.

Who can it be? Hurriedly, Chance tore open the envelope. Inside was a breakfast invitation card from Marcus Blundermore. Handwritten, it read:

Chance,

Welcome to JSBS. I'd like to invite you and Luck for

Breakfast at 8:00 AM tomorrow morning at the President's Dining Room beside the Great Commons.

Have a wonderful evening!

Uncle Blundermore

*   *   *

Then, looking up, Chance met his new roommate.

"Hi! I'm Norman Morpheus Twist." He was a skinny African-American – thin as a bamboo stick. Outgoing and hilarious, his eyes beamed mischievously beneath his well-defined arched brows. Those intriguing large eyes had an uncanny clairvoyance to see into people and into their world of dreams. His dazzling smile betrayed a hysterical personality within. With his hair was down to his shoulders, he projected a peculiar visage of an androgynous Venus wrapped in a man's body. The way he moved declared his natural flair for exuberance and entertainment – with flamboyance. "Welcome to America!" Morpheus was jovial in his greeting, displaying a boyish and quirky charm.

What a freakish voice! Chance was struck by Morpheus's girlishness. But he was immediately disarmed by his friendliness. "Hi, I'm Brandon Perseus Blundermore Mann. Call me Chance for short."

"I liked the way you danced the Gangnam Style at the Great Commons. You were awesome!" Morpheus giggled.

Chance remembered seeing him dancing there. "You, too! Your dancing is out of this world!"

"I'm from Los Angeles, also known as *Lala Land*." Morpheus

rattled off like a zinging machine gun. "It's the land of Hollywood. The land of pretense. The land of plastic. The land of celluloid film – with bigger-than-life images projected on the movie screen. A land governed by a philosophy: what have you done for me lately? Fakery infests people's lives. People get *old* in their cars while snarled in the eternal traffic to nowhere. People go there in pursuit of dreams for stardom only to learn it is a *sham*. One in a thousand makes it. Plastic surgeons make the most money because of facial jobs. Stars and wanna-be's demand to look young, to look pretty. Finally, they end up looking freaky with dreadfully mutilated faces! This is the city with drive-thru funeral homes, where the dead are tilted toward you for a last good-bye as you drive by, you rushing to your next appointment with the psychiatrist. It is a land of *Careless Feelings* in *A Material World*. A place for *Thrillers* and *Billie Jean* in Never Never Land, because you just can't *Beat It!* Do you get it? There's *Lala Land* for you! Do you dig that? Some say California will fall off the ocean. Arizona will become beach-front property! Booyah!" He laughed like a witch with a high pitched voice belonging to neither man nor woman.

For Chance, this was over the top. "You are crazy!" *Is this a self-confession or what? Morpheus has rhythm. He is the Man of Rap.* Totally engrossed, Chance was amused by Morpheus's verbosity, poetry and honesty.

Morpheus continued. "So tonight, we have a lock-down on campus. Ooouuu! The ghouls and the zombies will rise. With their dreary faces and deathly stares. Phantoms in the *Night of the Living Dead* come trudging down the streets. They march like Nazi's. Jump like monkeys. Shrieking their heads off in total anarchy. For tonight, the devils of the world will arise, singing in chorus to the *Music of the Night!*" Now Morpheus was grinding his pelvis, in a style that was part scarecrow, part rock-n-roll.

Chance was at a loss for words.

"This will be one *thrilling* evening." Morpheus grinned devilishly, as he turned on his computer tablet, now connected to its speakers – blaring Michael Jackson's *Thriller* at top volume. From his closet, Morpheus took out a Thriller Horror Mask and smacked it on his face. In a sudden shift of persona with the flair of a vaudeville performer, he gave a frightfully funny parody of Michael Jackson's *Thriller*. And so I personify the Lucifers who abound in every corner, in every nook. They conspire. They retire. In the shadows they grind. They moon-walk. Cuz tonight is the *Thriller's* night – with the King of Pop!" High kick here. High kick there. He huffed and puffed. He pranced. He thrust his pelvis, backward and forward. In full throttle, Morpheus shouted and screamed as he rhythmically ground his hips, while holding his crotch. He moon-walked. He thumped his feet, rocked his ankles and stood on the tip of his shoes. He cringed. With pleading gestures and swagger, he danced to the beat of the *Thriller*. For a moment, he brought Michael Jackson back to life.

Just as quickly, Morpheus shifted into break dancing, slithering on the ground in full-body contortions and twirling his whole body on his head. Later, he lunged into a *kung-fu* dance – still to the tune of the *Thriller*. Till the *Morning of the Night!*

Morpheus was a testament to the goofy funniness of life. *He'll make a great roommate.* Chance felt the magical chemistry palpitating between the two of them. "I'm gonna call you Lady Lala!"

Morpheus let out a joyful scream. "I love that moniker! I'll take that as a compliment."

*　　　*　　　*

And where was Buff the Monkey all this time? Inside the closet. He was sleeping in his tepee tent, with each of his forefingers stuck in each of his ears, sound asleep, oblivious to the raucous commotion outside.

*   *   *

It was very, very late when Morpheus finally retired to sleep.

Chance noticed a third rose in the flower vase at the window sill. He went over and saw a purple tag clipped to the stem of the rose. Upon closer inspection, he detected an inscription. It read: SURPRISE.

Chance proceeded to unpack his suitcases, putting his clothes into his cabinet.

From his black leather attaché, Chance took out the special gifts from Uncle Antikweetee: his lucky money in the red packet; his Magic Compass and his Oracular Dice of Life. Quietly, he chuckled. A sudden whiff of nostalgia swept through him – just thinking about Uncle Antikweetee and his kindness. He peered into his Magic Compass and confirmed that that his room faced West. *I'll be viewing the most majestic sunsets.* He nodded happily, as he placed his special gifts into the room-safe.

For Chance, practically forty-eight hours had gone by on this June 21, the longest day of his life, truly. Tonight would be his first full night sleep in America.

*   *   *

Meanwhile, upon entering his room, Luck likewise saw a burgundy red envelope by the inside of the entrance door. It was addressed to him.

Luck ripped the envelope open. Inside was a similar breakfast invitation card from Marcus Blundermore. *Fantastic!* Luck was ecstatic.

*　　　　*　　　　*

At this time, Ka-Ching was already in bed, sound asleep, knocked out by sheer exhaustion from the jet lag.

Luck noticed a third rose in the flower vase at the window sill. It was Ka-Ching's. He went over and saw a silver tag clipped to the stem of the rose. Upon closer inspection, he detected an inscription. It read: RISK.

*　　　　*　　　　*

Luck proceeded to unpack his suitcases, putting his clothes into his cabinet.

From his black leather attaché, Luck took out the special gifts from Uncle Antikweetee: his lucky money from the red packet; his Magic Map and his Head Band of Heightened Perceptions. He smiled as his thoughts wandered back to the Philippines, to Manila, to *Intramuros*, to AWE, to Uncle Antikweetee and all his goodness.

At this time, he recalled Uncle Antikweetee's warning: "For your sake, make sure to keep these gifts close by or at a secure place. And by all means, don't hand these to strangers. Yours will be the greater loss!" Judiciously, he placed Uncle Antikweetee's gift into his room safe.

After securing his special gifts into the room-safe, Luck quickly went to work. He booted up his computer tablet and googled: Z-Aster. But nothing showed up. In fact, his computer tablet mysteriously froze and went black. *Very strange.* He frowned. *First attempt at googling at ISBS and I'm stumped.* After a few more tries, Luck gave up on his super-jazzy computer tablet and his super smartphone.

*   *   *

Quietly, He unlocked his room-safe and carefully took out the tubular bamboo encasement of his Magic Map. He opened the encasement. Gently, he fished out his Magic Map, unrolled it over his study desk, laying his long Lucite ruler over it.

Gathering up his courage, he wrote with his finger over the Magic Map: WHO IS Z-ASTER?

This was what appeared on the Magic Map: "VERILY, T'WAS THE AGE OF CHAOS; MANY HEADS ROLLED DURING THE REIGN OF TERROR. WHEN SHALL WE HAVE ANOTHER?" Blots of blood appeared over the Magic Map.

Luck shuddered in fright and almost fell off his chair. *Awful!* He was terrified. This was more than he had bargained for. Frozen in fear, he could not go on. His heart pounded wildly. He felt the sinister malevolence in those words.

He stood up; rolled up his map; and stuffed it back into the bamboo encasement.

His legs shaking, he returned his Magic Map into his room-safe. There he locked it up.

By now, Luck was too frightened and scared to sleep.

Mystified, his mind would not shut down. *The Age of Chaos. The Reign of Terror. What was that all about?*

*   *   *

385

CHAPTER 54

Z-ASTER'S GREAT ESCAPE

MUSIC INSPIRATION

OLTREMARE
(PIANO)
LUDOVICO EINAUDI

DEMONS
IMAGINE DRAGONS

THUS SPRACH ZARATHUSTRA, OPUS 30
RICHARD STRAUSS

#Z21 AKA# ZEITGEIST21
SWEETBOX

READY OR NOT
THE FUGEES

BATMAN BEGINS – THEME SONG
BATMAN BEGINS
HANS ZIMMER

*   *   *

At ten in the evening, far beyond Testament City, Z-Aster and his rescuers – together with Remus Goggles, pretending to be Brutus Scroogles, were riding through the rough roads in a jeep, as part of a four car caravan. They were making a mad-dash for the meadows of the *New Joy Sea* shores. The commandos were still in their black diving suits, with their attached oxygen tanks. The thick fog by the shores blanketed the moonlight overhead.

Four battle droids in black platinum guarded the hovercraft at four sides, laser guns in hand.

In the dark, the commandos first hoisted Z-Aster onto the hovercraft. Then, the commandos and the accompanying droids climbed aboard – including Remus. The team aboard was also in diving suits with their oxygen tanks, prepared as back-up for all contingencies.

With stealth, the hovercraft motored out from the shores of *New Joy Sea* toward the Atlantic heading in the direction of Deception Hollows in *Lair County, Connect & Cut.*

*   *   *

Beyond the shores of Deception City was Deception Hollows of the Great Undersea, an extensive undersea urban complex. In the command center of Deception Galleria, banks of computers screens flickered, as operators communicate with hovercraft.

At ninety-five, Datu Villani stood in front of a gigantic monitor, watching the ongoing progress of Z-Aster's grand escape. Four droid soldiers in black platinum guarded Villani.

Villani leaned heavily on his cane. With his white hair protruding from his black Japanese headband, he had a grotesque frozen half frown on the left side of his vino red face.

Like an emperor, he wore a regal black Japanese kimono, whose back was emblazoned with a white flying crane, whose eyes exuded viciousness. The crane held a white chrysanthemum in his beak.

Datu Villani bent over and spoke into the microphone. "Welcome back!" Elated, he greeted the long suffering prisoner. "Z-Aster, today is your Day of Escape!" Villani's cracking voice filled the cockpit of the hovercraft carrying Z-Aster. "Welcome to Deception Hollows of the Great Undersea! It's been too long!"

"Thank you. I've come through..." Z-Aster muttered a few words, the rest of which were unintelligible garbled by the rotor noise of the hovercraft.

* * *

CHAPTER 55

INTO THE BOWELS OF TESTAMENT TOWERS

MUSIC INSPIRATION

LE ONDE
(THE WAVE)
(PIANO)
LUDOVICO EINAUDI

IN THE OLD TEMPLE
CROUCHING TIGER HIDDEN DRAGON
TAN DUN /谭盾
CELLIST: YOYO MA / 馬友友

SPECTER IN THE DARK
THE LAST SAMURAI
HANS ZIMMER

MUSIC OF THE NIGHT
PHANTOM OF THE OPERA
ANDREW LLOYD WEBER
SINGERS
MICHAEL CRAWFORD & SARAH BRIGHTMAN

DRACULA – THEME SONG
TOCCATA & FUGUE IN D MINOR
JOHANN SEBASTIAN BACH

*   *   *

Proceeding with their second sweep on Basement Five's dark and dusty cement floor, Romulus Goggles, the ISBS External Security Chief, brought in his investigation team, which included his personal assistant, Marcel Maladroit, and the chief school engineer, Gabriel Gaudi.

With Aurelius taking the lead, they combed for clues

throughout Basement Five, the floor where Z-Aster had been incarcerated.

With keen attention to detail, Romulus Goggles was a master of forensic deduction. Like Remus, his twin brother, Romulus had the piercing eyes of a hawk. He scoured every path and nook he passed. Endowed with a photographic memory, nothing escaped his gaze. His domain was external security of the campus grounds: to prevent crimes, sabotage and terrorism.

With him was Marcel Maladroit, his indispensable partner, a returnee from America's Afghan war campaign. Aged fifty-six, he was a military doctor turned university bio-science professor at ISBS. Now his main occupation was advancing nano-medical technologies, besides sleuthing with Romulus on important external security cases.

Then there was Gabriel Gaudi, the school engineer. Fifty years old, he exhibited a special genius in electronic surveillance. He was part of the FBI team that investigated the collapse of the World Trade Twin Towers many years back. His expertise was to prevent the future occurrence of such debacles. He wondered what caused the explosion tonight and who would be the most likely suspects.

On Basement Five, practically all the electricals were disabled. The electrical fuse box by the staircase was cut. The close circuit scanners were shot out.

"Look!" Marcel spotted drops of obvious blood on the floor. With great care, he collected the blood samples into his miniature hand carry test tube. He traced the blood tracks back to the stairwell. "Now, what is this?" Strangest of all, he noticed a bloodied inch-long cartilage – most likely human – on one of the steps in the stairwell.

"What can this be?" Marcel took out his tweezers, placed the cartilage into a tiny plastic bag and sealed it. "Looks like a brawl took place here!"

Aurelius strained his neck over Marcel's shoulder to take a good look at the cartilage in the plastic bag. "Let me see!"

Marcel placed the plastic bag into his waterproof belt pocket strung around his waist.

The team worked feverishly through Basement Five. On the dusty floor, numerous footmarks, smeared with blood, trailed here and there. Romulus promptly placed yellow tapes beside detectable foot marks.

Marcel took pictures, with a measurement indicator beside each foot mark. The footprints led to an unmarked fire escape area, which concealed a small fire escape compartment. At the extreme corner of the fire escape compartment was a manhole that was sealed *closed*. Clearly, the manhole led to fire escape rails going further downward. The footprints around the manhole told this much: *Z-Aster and his companion or companions disappeared through the manhole*. The shoeprints around the manhole were practically meshed together so as to be undistinguishable. However, some shoeprints indicated a return trace back leading to the staircases within Testament Towers.

Through the fire escape rails underneath the manhole, the inspection team went down, down, down, till the team hit Basement Nine.

*   *   *

For Aurelius, heading to Basement Nine was like a descent to Hell, once again, conjuring up the Age of Chaos at ISBS. *Those bloody days! Those horrible executions!* Aurelius's heart raced at the thought of the horrifying Past which occurred on this floor. His soul rebelled at the thought that he was now on this very same dreadful floor, revisiting the Dark Age of the Past.

On Basement Nine, Romulus discovered a huge blasted hole from which Z-Aster and his rescuer or rescuers escaped. Within the darkness of the blast area, Romulus measured the huge hole, which was large enough to allow one person to crawl through. He was surprised that the blast made it through a ten-foot thick wall. "Darn it! This is the blast that shook the Testament Towers. It was done very professionally."

A foul, atrocious, putrid whiff came through the blast hole, wreaking an unbearable stench on Basement Nine.

"The sewer!" Gabriel muttered. "Stinks like Hell!"

With his hard hat light, Romulus made out a chalked scribble on the wall: "GONE CHASING Z-ASTER! RG". Stunned, Romulus realized his twin brother, Remus Goggles, was already afoot on the chase. "Remus is giving us a heads-up! In no time, we'll know where Z-Aster has escaped to!"

Romulus made a few clicks to his smartwatch, to see if there were updated messages from Remus. There was none. "Looks like Remus might have turned off his smartwatch."

"What are we waiting for?" Whatever was beyond the blast hole of the ten-foot thick Testament Towers wall, Aurelius was ready to take the plunge.

Taking the lead, Aurelius crawled his way through it on his elbows, muttering to himself: "Holy crap! This is crazy! Absolutely crazy!"

Before long, Aurelius' head emerged at the other end of the

tunnel. He peered into utter darkness. The stench was overwhelming. Aiming his hard hat light into the darkness, all he could see were the black slimy sewer vaults and the sludge of slow-flowing muck in the ISBS sewer system.

Closing his eyes and holding his breath, his hands strained against the sides of the hole, Aurelius carefully dropped himself into the sludge of human feces. His feet touched the sewer floor. He stood up. The sludge was *chest deep*. "First day of school and I'm chest-deep in poo!"

Aurelius trained his hard hat light upon the blast hole. A while later, Romulus's face appeared. "We have to get to the bottom of this!" Aurelius was resolute. Reaching out, he helped Romulus and other members of the investigation team out of the sewage side of the blast hole. Slowly, the team waded eastward through the dark stinky chest-deep slush of human waste and muck. They passed through three protective railing gates, whose locks were smashed and ripped open.

Romulus examined the locks of the sewer gates. "It has been sometime since these gates were broken. Look at these rusted and corroded locks! "Z-Aster's escape was daring and masterful! Incredible!"

The Testament Towers sewage system cleared through under the East Gate, extending beyond the outer mote of ISBS, connecting with Testament City's main city sewer pipes.

Determining from which manhole in Testament City Z-Aster and his gang emerged was more difficult. The investigation team checked over scores of manhole exits, but there were no clues from which manhole the commandos exited. Any clues regarding their escape went cold. The infra-red heat-detectors of the investigation team seemed to be useless.

Aurelius and the whole investigation team were stumped. *How did Z-Aster escape?* This question haunted each of the team members as the first trains at the train station above-ground rumbled into service.

*   *   *

For Aurelius, this event was an unmitigated disaster on the part of the ISBS security team. *Where do we go from here?* He shuddered at the prospect of the looming crisis descending upon the ISBS leadership.

*   *   *

CHAPTER 56

DATU VILLANI

MUSIC INSPIRATION

SYMPATHY FOR THE DEVIL
ROLLING STONES

VIVA LA VIDA
COLDPLAY

FOOL ON THE HILL
THE BEATLES

NOWHERE MAN
THE BEATLES

FOR NO ONE
THE BEATLES

RADIOACTIVE
IMAGINE DRAGONS

EL MALO
(THE BAD ONE)
(SPANISH)
AVENTURA

BOLÉRO
MAURICE RAVEL

THE LAST SAMURAI – THEME SONG
HANS ZIMMER

*　　　*　　　*

As the hovercraft approached Deception City, it dove underwater toward the Deception Hollows of the Great Undersea.

With bated breath and his cold eyes peeled on the monitors at the command center, Datu Villani watched the hovercraft approach and park at the holding dock at the rear entrance of the galleria. He noticed Z-Aster disembarking from the hovercraft with some help from the rescuing commandos. In turn, six battle droids, in black titanium, with automatic laser weapons in hand, escorted the returnees into the Deception Gallery.

Having just turned ninety-five, Datu Villani remained the sum of all tyrants who ruled the American Atlantic – striking dreadful fear to foes and friends alike. Like molten steel, he was capable of morphing himself into any monster at will. Amorality was his essence. Decorated for his dark deeds deemed heroic by the general public, he reveled in his status in world history. He was a master of debt and financial sleight of hand, an art connoisseur and collector and a major conjurer of mirages in business and politics. His close friends called him a visionary. His enemies called him a fraudster.

His hunger for power was voracious. Patience was his strong suit, capable of outlasting any foes. While excessive wealth and power were his ultimate aphrodisiac, he also craved for the status of deity.

In polished aura, he was a man of utter connivance, a villain of gargantuan thievery. A plunderer of international wealth, he amassed vast fortunes through international drug trafficking cozying up with world terrorists and other tyrants. With his largesse, he ransomed and rescued the world's most notorious criminals and terrorists in the name of peace.

Despite his notoriety, he managed to get close with international royalty. A man of clout, he crafted his own financial empire, proud of its global reach like the tentacles of a thousand octopi. He participated in major international rescue efforts, such as the aftermath of the tsunamis in Indonesia and Japan and the earthquake in Haiti. These earned him respectability in the name of humanitarianism. For him, this was global politics by another means. But this was driven not by altruism but by pure selfish interest, securing him a polished standing amongst the who's who in the world. He envisioned himself to be the man to save the world as his namesake proclaimed him to be: Datu Villiani.

Datu Villani had his own undefinable brand of politics and machination with undeterred followings amongst disingenuous political leaders and their moneymen turned unscrupulous entrepreneurs.

Partnering with the world's most notorious global underworld cliques, Datu Villani was capable of cracking the world's hardest code systems, nabbing top conglomerate executives for ransom, and aiding shady governments in setting up prison and labor camps for profit.

For Datu Villani, money laundering had lost its meaning. His great wealth camouflaged his great crimes. His mastery was currency conversion *par excellence*. He had a good portion of his wealth in the indestructible currencies of rarified fine arts and antique gold objects. Such items were purchased legitimately from the most impeccable art auctioneers and brokers through unidentifiable offshore companies.

He understood the value of precious metals, especially gold. Through joint ventures with major gold mining conglomerates, he owned gold mines in China, Australia, U.S.A., Russia and South Africa.

With an unquenchable appetite of a gambler, he commanded untraceable interests in various global conglomerates, including gaming operations stretching from Las Vegas to Macau.

A first rate academic, he was a doctor of theoretical and applied mathematics, top promulgator of game theory optimization. As such, he was a prime mover in academia and in business. Notwithstanding his recent strokes, his mental faculties remained sharp. His personal doctor comforted him, saying that, while he might no longer be a genius, he was still "far above average" in intellect.

Datu Villani was a man of his own kingdom: the transnational State of Deception, in which he was *not* beholden to any jurisdiction – not even to the *State of Connect & Cut*. He possessed ultimate freedom in vice and virtue, to which many aspire. With his extensive and unbridled network of academics, scientists, politicians, entrepreneurs, financial operatives, thugs, hit-men, drug warlords and terrorists, he ran his own kingdom in this State of Deception.

On the surface, he was clean, a man beyond reproach. No evidence of malfeasance pointed to him. In his trade, he was on top of the heap, having sidelined and permanently silenced his enemies or future rivals. A ruthless schemer, he had cheated and bankrupted many of his counterparts – without them knowing he was behind their destruction. Such was his prodigious genius. His methods were most elusive so that he was also known as: The Man With No Fingerprints. A masterful hoaxer, he was a tantalizing enigma, cloaked in a mystery inside a mind-boggling riddle and a sick, dark joke.

He owned a big portion of the exotic Catalina Island off the coast of California, a resplendent castle in Monaco, major telecom companies in Southeast Asia, and mining companies in Africa.

He had a choice of leading a charmed life of an oligarch, filled with nightly soirees and parties with top socialites and entertainers of the day. But he was now seized with a mission: to

398

transform the world into his own image. And the re-conquest of ISBS was his top priority.

He believed that in the art of persuasion, honey was sweeter than vinegar. Numerous times, Datu had reached out to buy ISBS outright – but to no avail. Marcus Blundermore refused to negotiate with his ilk. To Blundermore, ISBS WAS NOT FOR SALE.

When diplomacy failed, Datu Villani defaulted to his last resort: intrigue and intimidation. If these didn't work, well then, there was murder. Ultimately, there was: ALL OUT WAR.

However, Fate was against him. He could not buy Time. He was getting old. His most recent stroke reminded him that he was mortal. He had to act fast before it would be too late. His fate was looming near. He wanted to realize his lifelong dream: to regain the Supreme Headship of ISBS.

Z-Aster would be his instrument of choice. Datu Villani had no other alternative.

*　　　*　　　*

CHAPTER 57

THE REUNION
AND
VILLANI'S DISCOURSE

<u>MUSIC INSPIRATION</u>

NUVOLE BIANCHE
(PIANO)
LUDOVICO EINAUDI

THE GODFATHER – THEME SONG
(CLASSICAL GUITAR, VIOLIN & STRINGS)
LARRY KUSIK & NINO ROTA

STRANGERS IN THE NIGHT
FRANK SINATRA

RED IMMITATION
HONG MO FANG
红磨坊

JAY CHOU / 周杰倫

DO YOU REALLY WANT TO HURT ME
CULTURE CLUB

SOMEBODY I USED TO KNOW
GOTYE

SMOOTH CRIMINAL
MICHAEL JACKSON

SWEET DREAMS
EURYTHMICS

CRAZY
AEROSMITH

ZOMBIE
THE CRANBERRIES

THE MUSIC OF THE NIGHT
PHANTOM OF THE OPERA
ANDREW LLOYD WEBER
SINGERS
MICHAEL CRAWFORD & SARAH BRIGHTMAN

SCHERZO NO.2, OPUS 31
FREDERIC CHOPIN
YUNDI LI / 李云迪

THE DARK KNIGHT RISES – THEME SONG
HANS ZIMMER

*   *   *

I swear—by my life and my love of it—that I will never live for the sake of another man, nor ask another man to live for mine.

Atlas Shrugged, Ayn Rand

*   *   *

*L*ife is a bitch, then we die.

*   *   *

Thirty minutes later, Z-Aster emerged, standing by the doorway. He was speechless, as he stared at Datu Villani, barely recognizing him.

Near the doorway was a large tank of carnivorous barracudas, exposing their rows of deadly teeth. As each guest entered, the barracudas' menacing eyes would signal: "Behave! Or else!"

In his regal Japanese robe, Z-Aster had his thick grey hair combed back, still wet from a thorough scrub down and shower. It was his first decent one in three decades. Aged sixty-five and displaying a neatly trimmed salt and pepper beard, his right eye was painted with golden rays of sunlight. He walked with an awkward shuffle – aided by an attendant, Consiglieri Mianus, a short elfish man, aged fifty.

Z-Aster surveyed Villani's dimly lit study. Three eerie death masks with horrific expressions atop the office credenza caught Z-Aster's attention. Theirs were faces evincing the tortures of gruesome deaths frozen in time. *They must have been executed.*

On the wall right behind the credenza, he recognized his once favorite masterpiece painting: Francisco Goya's *Saturn Devouring His Son.*

A large python slithered on a fake tree beside the credenza. It lifted its ugly head in the air and hissed, acknowledging the return of its master. That was his pet python Malas.

"Nakabalik ka na! You have returned!" Malas hissed, eliciting a smile from Z-Aster. *"Hindi mo ako nakalimutan!* You have not forgotten me!" Slowly, he crawled toward the returnee.

Z-Aster, once a notorious man of vanity and arrogance, was a man so very full of himself, but years of incarceration at ISBS deflated his ego to a God fearing man. He had suffered. In the Chamber of Ordeal, it seemed as if he had died a thousand deaths.

Tamed, he had returned with martyrdom as his badge of honor, reformed to a normal man through ISBS's reeducation program. He was Marcus Blundermore's reformed specimen of a hoodlum turned benign, like a poison snake defanged. It was still a mystery whether his conversion to apparent normalcy, per ISBS's current regime, was the result of torture, conditioning or free will – or a mixture of the three. Over the years, his criminal proclivities were subverted to a semblance of reasonableness and upright morality. But there was still justice to be served. Thus, his thirty years of incarceration at ISBS.

His return to Deception Hollows of the Great Undersea was at once familiar but eerily distant.

"Z-Aster…" Consiglieri Mianus declared in his squeaky voice, announcing Z-Aster's presence. In the dim gray shadows of the doorway stood Consiglieri, an extremely obese man of five feet. He had an aquiline nose, which dominated his face. In tuxedo and tap dance shoes, he was Villani's butler since time immemorial, going back to the Dark Age. The clicks of his tap dance shoes resonated against the marble floor. At sixty, his energy and agility remained undiminished.

Z-Aster stood by the doorway, absorbing the scenery of Villani's study. Then his eyes rested and focused on the old man.

Over the years, Villani's countenance had changed beyond recognition, now dreadful vino red in complexion, emanating the color of blood red roast beef, with a frozen half frown on the left half of his face. The two men stood transfixed, studying each other.

Z-Aster was shocked by Villani's contorted face. "Pops…" He was stunned by how much his father had aged. *Nasty Pops. He's suffered a stroke.*

"Are you now a sissy boy – after these thirty years? What are these sun rays around your right eye?" Villani limped forward with his cane to get a closer look.

"Welcome back, Chaos!" He squeezed his son's cheeks. Casting a hypnotic look from his bloodshot eyes, he gave his son a cold ghostly stare, attempting to read his mind. Villani's voice was raspy, betraying his advanced years. He gave Z-Aster a wry grin, combined with a firm hug. "For thirty years, I've waited! Finally, you're back!"

"Pops…You're looking good yourself for an old chap!" Z-Aster lied.

"*You* are the best gift for a ninety-five year old man. I need you to carry on our fight toward the New World of Disorder. A PERFECT WORLD IS A CRAZY WORLD!" He burst out laughing, displaying his practically toothless mouth, waving his cane in the air, accidentally smashing a lamp. He had one upper front tooth and one lower front tooth. "And you are flesh of my flesh; my only begotten son!"

"Happy birthday, Pops!" He thanked his stars for being rescued tonight. In some ways, he realized his karma was tied to his father's. "Such is the *affinity* of karma!"

*　　　*　　　*

"Did I hear something?" At this time, her white hair disheveled, a drunken and shriveled Lady Pandora staggered out of her bedroom, which was next to Villani's study. "All day today, I've over-indulged myself. After all, it's your birthday, my Datu Villani."

"You're always drunk." Villani looked at Lady Pandora with icy contempt.

"Who do I see?" She squinted at Z-Aster, not recognizing him.

Villani gave Lady Pandora a pathetic look. "Chaos is back. You cannot even recognize your own son."

"I have a son?" Lady Pandora struggled to emerge from her stupor. At eighty-seven, senility had contributed to Lady Pandora's bad case of amnesia aggravated by years of hard liquor consumption. Also, Alzheimer's had made serious inroads into her brain, calcifying its synapses. "Am I having a senior moment?"

404

Z-Aster embraced Lady Pandora and pecked her on the forehead. "Mom, I'm back!"

She had forgotten him. Now, she could only pretend to recognize him, preferring to play along. *It may be true that I have a son. This is stranger than strange.*

*   *   *

Father and son walked toward the dining area, while the scurrying Consiglieri was setting up the table.

"Mianus! Make sure to serve Z-Aster's favorite meal: *huevos rancheros* with eggs from *Los Huevos Locos. Con jalipeño muy picante!*" Villani ordered. "Only the *best* eggs for Chaos!"

On the dining table was a tall vase of fresh white chrysanthemums.

The old man chuckled. "Z-Aster, you are my *best* birthday gift."

Right on time, Consiglieri served Z-Aster his favorite *huevos rancheros con jalipeño.*

With zest, Z-Aster devoured his first decent meal in three decades.

For his part, Consiglieri did a few tap dancing numbers to entertain Z-Aster, confident of his captivating power to ensnare his audience with his theatrics.

"On the night of the Great Battle, I managed to escape, but barely." Datu Villani wanted to catch up with events. "Too bad you did *not* make it."

Crestfallen, Z-Aster felt he paid the ultimate price – serving time for his father. "In the chaos of the Great Battle, you managed to escape from ISBS. Trying to protect you from enemy attack, I was severely wounded in the process. I was captured by Lucius Blundermore's forces. Subsequently, I was tried, received the death penalty, which was later, commuted to life imprisonment. I had to pay for participating in *your* crimes against humanity. I was not as devious as you. This led to my unfortunate karma."

Z-Aster peered into Villani's large dark eyes, which were icy cold like those of a dead fish. *The old beast hasn't changed his stripes.* Sentiments from the Past awakened in him – this feeling of being abandoned and left to rot in the Chamber of Ordeal. The long suppressed anger of the past decades seemed to seep through his mind. "Pops, you betrayed me while saving your own skin."

"I've always been craftier." Villani was proud of his craft in deception and dissimulation. "Son, I had to sacrifice you to the enemy to save my own skin. Who said life is fair?"

"I've spent half of my life in the dungeon. And I've learned to be good." Z-Aster confessed. "I don't want to be part of your shenanigans anymore."

"Stop right there, Chaos!" Villani could read his son's thoughts. "They've brainwashed you into a sissy boy! You've been lobotomized!"

"I don't want to play this game." Z-Aster realized his efforts to emulate his father had led to much suffering during the Reign of Terror at ISBS.

"Son, in the world of Villani, there is a great equalizer: CHANCE. It levels the playing field. Now that you are free, you have a *chance* to get back at the world that punished you. We shall have another *chance* to liberate ISBS! Game's on, my son!" Villani

406

gave his son a murderous grin.

Uncertain, Z-Aster laughed, not knowing what to make of his father.

"Deft, my son. Deft. That's what will be needed." Now, Villani felt optimistic.

*   *   *

Z-Aster noticed the zombie that was Lady Pandora. "Mom, how goes your world?" Z-Aster reached out and gripped Lady Pandora's hand.

She just gave Z-Aster a dazed smile. "Darling, pour me a glass of merlot. I'm thirsty." Her words seemed slurred.

"Her mind's wasted." Over the past decade, Villani had witnessed her inexorable deterioration. "She belongs neither in this world nor the next."

Z-Aster did not know how to react. He was confused. Yet bit by bit, he recalled his dysfunctional family of old. *Nothing has changed. Some things never change.*

*   *   *

Villani's face turned contemptuous at the thought of having lost ISBS some thirty years ago to Lucius Blundermore's forces. "So, Marcus Blundermore took over the reins of ISBS. So, for these thirty years, what has Marcus Blundermore delivered? Has he brought prosperity for many? Neh... Son, what have his ideas of hope, faith, and love delivered to this world? Have these ideas brought us a *kinder* world? There is no room for the warm and fuzzy. There's no room for hope. It only brings despair and disillusionment. There's no room for faith. For it is baseless and lead us astray. There's *no* room for LOVE. Because love only brings

407

pain and suffering! Do you know the THREE RINGS OF LOVE? First, there's the engagement ring. Then, there's the wedding ring. Finally, there is SUFFER-RING!"

Villani burst out laughing at his own corny joke.

"Forget about feelings. Forget about hope. Forget about faith. Forget about love. This world *cannot* survive on self-righteous proclamations and the hypocrisy of false pretenders the likes of Marcus Blundermore! What is his morality? He is pure BS!

"Is the world better today than thirty years ago? Are the common people faring better? My son, the answer is clear: NO. Material scarcity is true immorality. There are more homeless people than ever before. There is more despair and hopelessness.

"We must restore our former regime of scientific materialism and objectivism back to ISBS. We live in the universe of matter. In the beginning, there was matter. And matter begat the mind. And *matter* is all there is. Life is a bitch, then we die. When we die, we will be no more. Show over! Our mind dies. Son, we only have *this* life. So, make the most out of it!

"Truly, it's all about putting food on the table, clothes on people's backs, shoes on people's feet. Employment and prosperity for all. That is *true* freedom. Do you understand? It's all about the mechanistic objective reality of well-being for all. Economic abundance is true morality.

"Selfishness is the *crux* of human motivation. This is what makes the world go 'round. Self-interest is the central mechanics of reality. Whoever masters this *truth* will be the winner. He will be rich! He will rule over his reality. He will be merrier.

"Son, this is why you've been rescued: We need to take back ISBS – to give this world another CHANCE – for its Salvation –

through the mechanism of self-interest. The world will belong to us. Power will return to us! And *you* will lead this effort!"

"Pops – no!" Z-Aster protested. *I can't stand this anymore!* A sudden migraine hit him like a ton of bricks. Grandiose thoughts of his father. These got him into deep trouble in the first place. Now, he discerned the stark difference between Marcus Blundermore and Datu Villani.

"Shut up! Rest for a few days. Let the scum of Marcus Blundermore blow off. His Age of Farce at ISBS will soon be history. His days are numbered. Remember, nice guys finish last. In this world, there is no room for altruism. Always look out for number one. I have to make you a *man* again. Restore your vicious self!" Villani had spoken. "I have great plans for you! Game's on! Let the Age of the *Illuminati* come forth! May the Dictatorship of Mephistopheles reign!"

* * *

Ding! Ding! Ding! Ding! Midnight struck. The Time of Reckoning was approaching.

* * *

CHAPTER 58

BLUNDERMORE'S NIGHTMARE

MUSIC INSPIRATION

INCEPTION – THEME SONG
HANS ZIMMER

YESTERDAY
THE BEATLES

THE IMPOSSIBLE DREAM
MAN OF LA MANCHA
MITCH LEIGH & JOE DARION
SINGER: JOHNNY MATHIS

NESSUN DORMA
(NOBODY SHALL SLEEP)
(ITALIAN)
TURANDOT
GIACOMO PUCCINI
SINGER: LUCIANO PAVAROTTI

IPAGLABAN KO
(I WILL FIGHT)
(TAGALOG)
FREDDIE AGUILAR

MEMORY
CATS
ANDREW LLOYD WEBER
SINGER: ELAINE PAIGE

UNCHAINED MELODY
EVERLY BROTHERS

LA VIE EN ROSE
(LIFE IN ROSY HUES)
(FRENCH)
ÉDITH PIAF

INA
(MOTHER)
(TAGALOG)
FREDDIE AGUILAR

AFTER ALL THESE YEARS
JOURNEY

FAITHFULLY
JOURNEY

WAKE ME UP
AVICII

END OF THE WORLD
SHI JIE MO RI
世界末日
(CHINESE MANDARIN)
JAY CHOU / 周杰伦

KAPAG AKO AY NAGMAHAL
(IF I LOVE)
(TAGALOG)
JOLINA MAGDANGAL

CONFUTATIS MALEDICTIS
REQUIEM MASS IN D MINOR, K 626
(THE ACCURSED SILENCE)
(LATIN)
WOLFGANG AMADEUS MOZART

*   *   *

When I had journeyed half of our life's way,

I found myself within a shadowed forest,

For I had lost the path that does not stray.

The Divine Comedy, Inferno, Canto I, Dante Alighieri

*   *   *

In dreams, the real, the subconscious and the surreal

411

converge. In this murky twilight zone of the soul, the subconscious comes alive, perhaps to reminisce, to foretell, or to forewarn.

*   *   *

It was a tortuous sleepless night for Marcus Blundermore. He was caught in the dilemma of the Past which left him in perpetual guilt. He tossed back and forth, unable to shut his mind down to sleep.

Between dreadful half-wakefulness and sordid half-sleep, if ever he slept, these dream images would overtake him.

*   *   *

This was young Marcus Blundermore's moment of condemnation. He was thirty-five. Emaciated and weak, he was dragged out of the Chamber of Ordeal in chains and shackles by two muscular guards toward the Court of Justice at Basement Nine of the Testament Towers.

Outside the Court of Justice, he could see the guillotine, its blade gleaming menacingly in the dark. Trepidation seized the young Marcus.

A menacing furnace was raging beside the guillotine platform.

"All was for naught!" Young Marcus thought, feeling for the worst. "I'm going to die!"

Inside the Court of Justice, a boisterous street crowd broke into cheers upon the entrance of Marcus Blundermore.

On the bench was the sixty-five year old Datu Villani with a white wig on. He sat there as Judge, his grotesque face painted with thick white powder, his lips smeared with red lipstick.

412

"Bring in the Accused!" A young man of thirty-five, Z-Aster, the Prosecutor, commanded.

The guards pushed forth young Blundermore, who stumbled onto the Defendant's Box.

"The crime of the Accused?" Datu Villani hollered.

Z-Aster screamed out the accusation: "Love, sir. He was caught in act of LOVE."

"How do you plead?" Datu Villani sneered at young Blundermore.

"Not guilty, sir." Blundermore looked disoriented and lost.

"Do you know our laws? Statute 10 states: THOU SHALL NOT LOVE!" Datu Villani thundered. "Present the evidence."

Escorted by court attendants, two witnesses came forth, each squabbling with the other.

Z-Aster declared: "These two witnessed Marcus Blundermore's love act."

Raucous laughter burst forth from the court gallery. Their faces were, likewise, caked in white, with weird, eerie make-up and lipstick. They wore late eighteenth century attire of the French Revolution.

"QUIET!" Datu Villani screamed, hammering his gavel. "Order in the court!"

"Present the First Witness!" Z-Aster ordered the court attendants.

The First Witness mounted the Defendant's Stand. She was a fat woman, with a dirty, red petticoat.

413

Z-Aster demanded. "What is your name?"

"Babushka."

Raucous laughter.

"SHUT UP!" Datu Villani threw a water bottle at one of the laughing ladies in the audience.

"Occupation?" Z-Aster queried.

"Trash lady, sir." She smiled.

There were smirks here and there.

"What did you see the Accused do?"

"Sir, three nights ago, I saw the Accused caress a mother hen."

Crazy laughter exploded in the audience, punctuated by razor sharp whistles.

"What's the mother hen's name?" Z-Aster snarled.

"Gallina Loca, your honor." Babushka broke out in a broad smile, exposing her two teeth – one was an upper front tooth; the other a lower front tooth.

Muffled laughter from the audience. "Crazy Hen! What a name!"

"Proof please!" Z-Aster barked.

From her bra, Babushka produced a wrinkled picture. "I took this picture, sir." She gently passed the picture to Z-Aster. Upon giving it a quick look, Z-Aster presented the picture to Datu Villani, who, in turn, examined it closely.

"Hmm... Marcus Blundermore caressing Gallina Loca.

Okay... Proof accepted. Ten U.S. dollars of meal tickets for Babushka. NEXT WITNESS!" Datu Villani hollered, banging his gavel on his desk.

"The Second Witness, please." Z-Aster The Prosecutor commanded.

The Second Witness limped up the Witness Stand. He had a club foot.

"Name?" Z-Aster queried.

"Dizzy, sir."

Hesitant laughter from the audience.

"Occupation?"

"Falling on the ground."

Laughter. A few whistles from the audience shot through the air.

"What is your testimony?"

"I saw the Accused kiss a mother hen."

Z-Aster requested the incriminating photograph from the Datu Villani and brought it in front of Dizzy. "Did the Accused kiss this mother hen: Gallina Loca?"

"Yes, sir."

"Proof please." The Prosecutor barked.

Dizzy fished out a video cassette tape from his coat pocket. This he gave to Z-Aster, who placed it into a VCR machine. Pressing a button, the projector light flashed a video sequence on the screen.

There, young Marcus Blundermore was shown caressing a cackling mother hen, which appeared to have just delivered an egg. With a smile, Marcus caressed the hen and kissed the mother hen by the head, saying: "Through you, I will have lots of 'huevos locos'! Most of all, I love 'huevos rancheros' for breakfast!"

"There, your honor! Marcus Blundermore kissed Gallina Loca on her head! CAUGHT IN THE ACT OF LOVE! You can see it with your own eyes." Z-Aster concluded triumphantly. "What is your verdict, your honor?"

Datu Villani peered hard at the screen. "Please give me a replay in slow motion."

The VCR was rewound and replayed – to the consternation of Marcus Blundermore. He watched his guilt displayed for the whole gallery to see.

"Marcus Blundermore, I see your act is done with forethought and conscious decision. You know exactly what you were doing. You did this with your own free will, knowing full well that you are violating Statue No. 10: THOU SHALL NOT LOVE. You know full well this is a capital crime – punishable by Death! Marcus Blundermore, this is your BIGGEST HUMAN BLUNDER.

Datu Villani paused. "Blundermore! This is your namesake. Blunder is your destiny! And you cannot stop making blunders. These lead you to your death!" Datu Villani burst out in laughter, as the whole gallery of audience joined in.

Do you understand? Do you know why love is forbidden here? LOVE CAUSES PAIN. LOVE CAUSES SUFFERING. LOVE CAUSES MURDER! LOVE CAUSES DEATH TO MANY! That's why we have this law. Do you have anything to say? Speak now or forever hold your peace."

White like a piece of Carrera marble, Marcus Blundermore gave Datu Villani a catatonic stare.

"Any comments? Any last words?" Datu Villani gave Marcus a taunting look.

Silence.

"Going once. Going twice. GUILTY AS CHARGED!" Hollering, Datu Villani hammered his gavel upon his bench. "Punishment: DEATH BY GUILLOTINE!"

Trumpets blared as Datu Villani rose and marched out the court toward the execution area outside.

"How about my pay-off, your honor?" Running with a limp after Datu Villani, Dizzy pleaded for his payment.

"Okay! Proof accepted. Twenty U.S. dollars of meal tickets for Dizzy for his video tape." Datu Villani bellowed as he exited the Court of Justice.

"Why is Dizzy getting paid more than me?" Babushka protested loudly from the court gallery.

*   *   *

Outside, the drums rolled.

This was young Marcus Blundermore's moment to die. He was dragged out of the Court of Justice by two muscular attending guards to the Guillotine Square, situated at the very center of Basement Nine – the lowest and scariest level of the Testament Towers.

Young Marcus saw the guillotine, its blade gleaming an evil smile in the dark. He lost all hope. He was going to die. Death would be young Marcus's fate.

"All was for naught!" Young Marcus could feel Death fast approaching with the remaining count of his footsteps to the guillotine platform.

As he approached closer to his death, beside the guillotine platform, he saw a groaning furnace filled with coal fire blazing inside it. Several long branding iron handles were sticking out of the furnace's mouth.

Then young Marcus was violently gagged and blindfolded into darkness by his attending guards.

The drums rolled louder.

"Let this be your last memory in life!" Datu Villani screamed. "KNOW THAT I'M THE LAW, THE JUDGE AND THE EXECUTIONER!"

Violently, he ripped off Marcus Blundermore's shirt.

Young Marcus legs wobbled in shock as he felt the white heat of an iron rod dangling in front of his blindfolded face. "My end is near! WHY DO I DIE?" He believed he had only moments to live.

"Marcus, you'll wish you were never born!" Datu Villani murmured into young Blundermore's ear.

The next thing young Marcus felt was searing heat exploding into a blinding pain onto his chest. Marcus let out a muffled screamed. AAAOOOWWW!

There was a wild hissing sound of burning flesh.

"Let this be your last memory in life!" Datu Villani growled in contempt.

Just as suddenly, there was a pandemonium. Young Marcus heard guns firing and bombs going off. His eardrums practically ruptured. Thick choking smoke filled the air. Then he heard his father's commanding voice: "It's not your time to die. Get him out of here!"

Amidst the wild scuffles, young Marcus was dragged away by the rough handlers of Lucius Blundermore's commandos. He heard his rescuers say: "You're safe, Marcus! You're safe!"

*   *   *

Falling out of bed, Marcus's head hit the floor with a thud, waking him up. His head was throbbing in excruciating pain. Sweating profusely, he clutched his left chest which was throbbing with pain, as if an onset of a heart attack.

This was a recurring nightmare. A nightmare without an ending. He sat up, panting. *I cannot escape my fate! Nor could my father!* Tonight's dream was particularly vivid. Trickles of sweat rolled down his forehead onto his eyebrows. This was his guilt-sweat.

*   *   *

Marcus turned on his night lamp on his bed table. Wishing to read himself to sleep, he picked up Dante Alighieri's *Inferno*, the first book of three in *The Divine Comedy*. As he read, his mind meditated on God's justice.

For Marcus, sin was human failure to live up to his true responsibility. Betraying his true responsibility on this Earth, the sinner never fully lived. Sidetracked by secondary priorities, the sinner passed his years without being true to himself and his loved ones. Betraying the central principle of his existence, the sinner condemned himself into oblivion, into insignificance, into

419

meaninglessness, into self-destruction and to Death itself. He realized that the sinner *was* himself: Marcus Blundermore. He had perverted his own consciousness into thinking he had done his utmost. For these past thirty years, deep inside, he harbored his biggest sin – his darkest failure. This guilt, this state of mind became Marcus's *Inferno. Oh, Time! You giver and devourer of Life! How Fate dances upon Time playing its tricks upon human lives! And we are powerless! We live by the Damnation and Death of others.*

*   *   *

Later, not being able to sleep, Marcus rose from the bed, wore his slippers and trudged his way to the kitchen to heat up some milk for a midnight snack. This would help him go back to sleep.

He could hear the tick-tock of the grandfather clock in the living room.

As he was preparing his snack, he caught sight of his mother, Lady Hope, sitting in the dark by the family room, knitting an orange scarf.

A lady of modesty and affection, Lady Hope had raised Marcus, Antikweetee, Luz and Aunt Juliet. At eighty-seven, she remained the Lady of ISBS through good times and bad. She commanded a steely humility and faith, which made her unyielding in times of trials and tragedies. She had the regal visage of a Chinese matriarch, being the product of the Soong family, which was renowned in contemporary Chinese history.

Marcus was startled to find her there. "Mother, what's keeping you up?"

420

"Knitting this large orange scarf for your dad. He deserves a birthday gift. June 21 is almost gone. I wonder how your dad passed *his* birthday?"

Marcus's heart sank. What could he tell her? Dutifully, Marcus went over and joined Lady Hope on the sofa.

"One day, he'll return." Lady Hope smiled. "This will be a nice belated birthday present, reminding him all that is good in his life."

What should he tell her? Marcus touched the unfinished woolen scarf with tenderness. His heart was pounding.

He confessed. "Mother, tonight, there was a break-out in the Testament Towers. *Z-Aster escaped.*"

There was a deafening silence – except for the tick tock of the grandfather clock in the family room.

Stunned, Lady Hope dropped her woolen ball of yarn to the floor. It rolled halfway across the room, stopping near the picture counter. Above it was the faded wedding picture of Lady Hope and Lucius Blundermore. Beside the picture was a faded and dried-up long stem rose named Heartbreak. This was Lucius's last rose to Lady Hope, given to her on *that* fateful day when he was captured by Datu Villani's forces – thirty years ago today.

Immediately, Lady Hope knew the implication of Z-Aster's escape: whatever chance of rescuing Lucius was now in jeopardy. She stared at Lucius's photograph. *My heart is empty with sorrow. This photo memorializes the proof of your presence and what you stand for. Nevertheless, you remain in my mind and in my soul. Time has not moved. Nor will it ever.*

At once, Marcus realized he misspoke.

Ding dong! Ding dong! The grandfather clock in the living room struck twelve midnight.

*   *   *

Thirty-five years ago, on the Day of the Great Insurrection, Datu Villani, then sixty, began his reign over ISBS, confident that his edict of atheistic materialism would free humanity from emotional and mental neurosis and propel society toward material progress. Devoid of mushy sentimentality, dubious Faith and Love, Humanity would conduct itself with efficient practicality. Apostasy was his creed. Five years' Reign of Terror subsequently plunged ISBS into the abyss of the Dark Age. It was a period where Hope, Faith, and Love were banned at ISBS, under the pain of Death.

*   *   *

However, Marcus Blundermore's eventual retaking of ISBS through his father's forces brought no breakthrough or relief with regard to Lucius's own captivity. So, three decades passed. He was never sure whether Lucius was alive or dead. *This* was the cruelest cut of all. Despite all efforts, direct or indirect, there was no progress in knowing Lucius's condition or whereabouts. No news. Over time, this limbo of *not* knowing his father's fate corroded Marcus's moral fiber and conscience. His only comfort was that Lucius's forces had captured and imprisoned Z-Aster at the bowels of the Testament Towers, a firm insurance against any rash measure against his father – if he were alive.

Tonight, he lost this insurance for his father's safety, if that ever meant anything. Tonight, the balance of terror was broken. Tonight, the conflict of Mutually Assured Destruction (MAD) was set in motion.

*   *   *

422

CHAPTER 59

REVISITING THE NIGHT OF TERROR

MUSIC INSPIRATION

UNA MATTINA
(ONE MORNING)
(PIANO)
LUDOVICO EINAUDI

THE FIRST MORNING
DI YI GE QING CHEN
第一个清晨
(CHINESE MANDARIN)
LEEHOM WANG / 王力宏

ANNA RETURNS
ANNA AND THE KING
GEORGE FENTON & ROBERT KRAFT

PHANTOM OF THE OPERA – THEME SONG
ANDREW LLOYD WEBER
SINGERS
SARAH BRIGHTMAN & MICHAEL CRAWFORD

*   *   *

Marcus Blundermore, dressed in a black cassock, sat at his breakfast table in the President's Dining Room. With a heavy heart, he read the morning's ISBS internal security reports from Aurelius Primus. They were not pleasant.

The wall clock struck eight when Luck and Chance arrived at the President's Dining Room. Despite his heavy worries, Blundermore was nonetheless happy to see his twin nephews.

Putting down his computer tablet, he stood up and hugged each of the twins. The pair made sure they were not hugged too tightly. Their chest wounds still hurt.

"Please make yourselves comfortable." Gesturing toward the table, Blundermore directed Luck to sit at his right and Chance to sit at his left.

"How you two have grown!" Blundermore stared at the two lads – proud to have his two nephews here at ISBS. "How's your Auntie Juliet? Your Uncle Romeo? And my nephew Nero?"

"Fine." Luck was not thrilled to even think about Auntie Juliet's family.

"They were nice enough to take you both in for seven years." Blundermore smiled. "They were not that bad."

There was no reaction from the brothers.

Noticing his nephews not too thrilled with their past with Auntie Juliet, he let the subject drop.

He rang the table bell.

"O. J. or coffee?" Blundermore asked the twins.

At this time, Jose Valdez, the student attendant for the President's Dining Room, emerged to take orders. Handsome and friendly, he had a nicely trimmed moustache. He made friendly eye contact with the twins.

"Coffee for me." Luck needed coffee for a boost. He had not slept well last night.

"I'll have both. O.J. and coffee. With cream and sugar." Chance gave Jose a friendly smile.

"Any breakfast, sir?" Jose inquired.

425

"Yes, later." Blundermore nodded at Jose. "I'll have coffee. Black, please."

Jose bowed politely and left the room.

"Just to be sure, who's who? Forgive me. I'm getting old." Blundermore chuckled at his own awkward quandary. He had not seen them for two years.

"Not a problem, Uncle. I'm Luck. I have this mole by the right side of my forehead. Remember?" Luck brushed back his hair, pointing to the right side of his forehead, revealing a good-size mole. "More important, I'm the optimist."

On his part, Chance broke into a broad grin. "And I *wear* this pair of silver-rimmed glasses. Most important, I'm the perpetual skeptic."

"We wear our red stringed necklaces, each with our unique medallion." Luck fished out his golden medallion from underneath his shirt.

"See, mine has this gold medallion, embossed with a triangle." Luck showed it to Blundermore. "It's real gold. Look at the brilliant white pearl embedded in the middle!"

Quickly, Chance took out his medallion from underneath his shirt. "Mine has a gold medallion embossed with a circular laurel." Chance practically pushed his medallion under Blundermore's nose. "It's pure gold with a brilliant white pearl embedded in the middle!"

Blundermore looked at each of the medallions pensively. *Yes, I have seen these before!* He recalled seeing these medallions each time he carried the kids in his arms over at Misericordia de Dios Orphanage in the Philippines. *These were the medallions of the*

426

white wizards. At last, he was now witnessing the *return of the white wizards* back to ISBS. His eyes brightened up.

Upon seeing these medallions, a wave of hope and consolation descended upon Blundermore. *Luck and Chance...they are truly the sons of Luz! Now, there is hope!* This much the Prophetess of the White Mountains had told him once upon a time – a long, long time ago.

Then, with deep seriousness, Blundermore whispered: "Guard and cherish each of your medallions. It represents your bloodline. And the pearl within your medallion encapsulates the mystery of your soul experience. See, each of your pearls shines so brilliantly!"

Slowly, from within his black cassock collar, Blundermore fished out a thick red stringed necklace from which hung a similar gold medallion. It had a big "M" embossed on it and with a big white pearl embedded in the middle of it. "You see, we are from the *same* sacred bloodline ordained from time immemorial." Blundermore put his gold medallion back into his black cassock. "We share the same special calling."

The twins were silent, each trying to digest the significance of what they had just witnessed and to figure out what was the special calling.

At this time, Jose Valdez returned with a pitcher of O.J. and a silver pot of coffee.

*   *   *

Gently, Blundermore said: "You two have tugged my heart from the first time I saw you since you were babies. Each year, I visited you at Misericordia de Dios as your birthday approached. Do you remember?" Blundermore was especially close to Missing

427

Mama. While she was still in the Philippines, he made sure he visited her and his favorite nephews each May, showering them with gifts.

The twins nodded. They remembered getting gifts from Blundermore through Wawa, when they were toddlers and through Aunt Juliet after Missing Mama left the Philippines.

"In you are my love and my hope!" Blundermore could feel the love he had for the twins surge throughout his being. He could feel his face flush with joy. "I'm so happy for today — seeing you both here!"

After a moment of silence, Blundermore chuckled good-humoredly. "Do you think I'm a fool? You two can swap necklaces or something and stir up *pranks galore* here at ISBS. Your professors will not know any better!" Blundermore's eyes were sparkling with mischief behind his rimless glasses. "Very clever! I'm anticipating some kind of wild stunts from both of you here at ISBS in the coming years! I won't be surprised."

"No, not so." Luck was not in a humorous state. On the contrary.

"We're marked men." A deep sadness descended upon Chance. "There is no escaping this *truth*. But we really don't understand why…"

"What happened?" Blundermore frowned.

"This dreadful thing." Without any introduction, Luck took off his suit, undid and removed his shirt. He carefully removed the long gauze wrapped several rounds around his chest. *There it was!* On the left side of his chest, there was a grotesque dark red-bluish wound, the letter "L", seared into his flesh.

428

Likewise, Chance took off his suit, undid and removed his shirt. He gingerly removed a long gauze wrapped several rounds around his chest. And lo! On the left side of his chest was a repulsive dark reddish wound, the letter "C", seared into his flesh.

"Holy crap!" Blundermore turned pale with terror, as he gripped his own chest. "These wounds are heinous!"

*   *   *

Tick tock! Tick tock! The eerie tick-tock of Time from the wall clock was the only audible sound in the room.

At this moment, the dining room lights flickered, throwing the room into an eerie darkness, dimming the room into a twilight zone of Hell – with the twins' brandings emitting evil energies. A whiff of evil wind swirled in the room, warping Time and Space within the dining room. Then, just as suddenly, the atmosphere in the room returned to normal again.

A putrid smell of rotten egg permeated the air.

*   *   *

"Oh, what *curse* hits our family!" Blundermore gasped.

"You see, we can't hide our identity," Luck confessed with dismay.

"When did this happen?"

"Three days or so ago." Luck was scared yet defiant. "We barely escaped Death!"

"Who did it?" Blundermore braced himself.

"A monster of a woman from hell: GUL!" Both twins cried out in desperation.

"Gul..." Blundermore remained shocked, despite being forewarned by Cardinal Legazpi's most recent e-mail report. "Gul..." His mind slipped into the deep past.

*   *   *

Blundermore shuddered at the eerie similarity of his wound with those of his nephews. *Are our karmas linked in some inexplicable way – linked through our affinities?*

CHAPTER 60

THE FOREBODING

MUSIC INSPIRATION

NO WAY OUT
HOUSE OF FLYING DAGGERS
SHIGERU UMEBAYASHI

THE ONLY LIVING BOY OF NEW YORK
PAUL SIMON & ART GARFUNKEL

ALL I ASK OF YOU
PHANTOM OF THE OPERA
ANDREW LLOYD WEBER
SINGERS
MICHAEL CRAWFORD & SARAH BRIGHTMAN

THE LONG AND WINDING ROAD
THE BEATLES

*   *   *

Marcus Blundermore remembered decades back when he had finished his Doctorate Program at ISBS. Young Augustin Legazpi was working on his Master's. Young Maria Clara Prisma was just a freshman initiate. For a while, all three were being actively courted by the *Illuminati* recruiters. Given their outstanding leadership qualities, the *Illuminati* recruiters deemed them to be attractive candidates. However, as the recruiting process progressed, the required rituals for continued candidacy got weirder and weirder. At some point, Augustin and Marcus withdrew their candidacies. Maria Clara chose to continue with the whole recruitment process. In the end, she was initiated into the *Illuminati*.

*   *   *

"Each of you has been touched by Evil of the most malevolent kind – wounding not only your body but also your soul." Blundermore groaned, as searing pain seized his own chest. "I can feel the hatred simmering in those wounds. Worst of all, this is the work of an *Illuminati*! You have the *Illuminati* signature. This is the *Illuminati* way vis-à-vis its enemies: branding its victims and then, killing them. In cold blood."

"The *Illuminati*?" Luck never heard of them.

"Yes. The *Illuminati*... It is a global conspiratorial group whose goal is to rule the world. Initially founded with good and noble intentions, it was formed in 1776 by Adam Weishaupt in Bavaria, Germany. It started out as anti-Catholic Church and anti-monarchy. So, in 1785, Charles Theodore, the Elector of Bavaria suppressed and wiped out the secret society. Some survived the suppression and became the masterminds behind the French Revolution and the Reign of Terror. Later, its members infiltrated in German Masonic Lodges. Then the Scottish Masonic Lodges. Subsequently, the *Illuminati* also spread to America through the Freemasons. Now, they are worldwide. They have *infiltrated* the upper crust collegiate fraternities such as the Skull and Bones in Yale, gentlemen's clubs such as the Bohemian Club and think tanks like the Council on Foreign Relations and the Trilateral Commission. This small group wants to bring about a world government – to rule the world. Their goal is to create a New World Order. *Novus ordo seclorum!* This is their mantra. Just look at the backside of your American dollar bill."

Luck quickly pulled out a U.S. dollar bill and stared at its backside. Sure enough, below the pyramid were the words: NOVUS ORDO SECLORUM.

This he passed to Chance to look.

Chance could not believe his eyes. *The Illuminati mantra is in front of everyone to see.*

Quietly, Chance asked. "What have we done – to be a target of the *Illuminati*?"

"Gul... " Marcus Blundermore whispered. "She is an *Illuminati*...going after both of your necks! She means business."

"What have we done? Why did this happen to us?" Chance pleaded for an answer.

"CRAZY LOVE! So much suffering results from crazy love!" Marcus gestured the twins to be still. "Now don't move!"

With grim determination, Blundermore stretched out his forefinger and touched Luck's wound, intoning the Healing Charm: *"Remedio corpus!"* Once again, he repeated the Healing Charm, this time, upon Chance's wound: *"Remedio corpus!"* Within minutes, to the amazement of the twins, their wounds began to heal. But dark grey scars remained.

"I'm afraid these wounds cut too deep, wounding beyond your flesh, so deep they have scarred each of your souls..." Blundermore understood the permanence of such wounds.

Confessing, Blundermore unbuttoned his cossack and revealed a nasty scar on the left side of his chest. "I, too, suffered a terrible ordeal – for different reasons." He laid bare his chest wound to the twins: a grotesque "M" branded on the withered skin of his aged chest.

The twins leaned forward and closely examined Blundermore's scar. Luck, with some daring, reached out his index finger and gently touched Blundermore's scar.

"Oh, God bless your soul, Uncle!" Luck was aghast, as he ran the tip of his forefinger on the contour of the scar on Blundermore's left chest. "What happened to you?" Luck muttered mournfully.

"The fallout of the ordeals during the *five* years during the Reign of Terror in the Dark Age at ISBS." Flashbacks of his own tortures gripped Blundermore into a horrifying glare. "Thirty years ago. This mark was given to me moments before my appointed death. It was meant to be my last memory here on this Earth. Mine was the mark of Datu Villani – himself an *Illuminati*."

Chance was aghast. "Are we damned?" What kind of Evil has cursed our family and our fates?"

"Every day, our fates hang in balance in the high heavens. DO WE LIVE OR DO WE DIE?" Blundermore could not find a good answer. "We are victims of heaven's whims. At any given moment, things happen in the most inexplicable way. I don't know what will happen to us. How do we deal with Fate? It truly tries men's souls. I dare not think of the consequences. Slowly but surely, the wheel of Fate turns. Are we its beneficiaries or its victims?"

After a brief paused, Blundermore confessed: "Gul wants both of you dead. What morbidity!" He sank to his seat, mortified and defeated. The hopeful joy that was with Blundermore just a few minutes ago had turned to foreboding gloom. *Oh, Datu Villani! You are out to liquidate the whole Blundermore family! Why? Why now?*

With resolution brimming through his eyes, Chance decided that he would struggle and triumph over Fate. "Uncle Blundermore, I have been through Hell and back. But I am resolved to walk through Hell with a smile on my face and my head held high. Despair will *not* be my lot. I will not let my situation define who I am. I *will* define the situation. I don't want to be

434

consumed by hatred and vengeance. I shall not flinch. I shall not cry. No more tears. No more regrets. 'I AM THE MASTER OF MY FATE. I AM THE CAPTAIN OF MY SOUL.'"

"Well said, my boy!"

*   *   *

"Gul…" Blundermore remembered a nightmare he had a few nights ago – before the super-moon.

He frowned. This was his dream.

It was an eerily evil night. He saw the lurching shadows of an old hag…the Old Hag of the Catacombs, descending toward a darkened dungeon with two branding irons. In the dungeon, there were two hooded youngsters chained against the forbidding walls. The Old Hag of the Catacombs ranted obscenities as she plunged her branding irons onto each of the hooded youngsters' chest, amidst delirious screams and shrieks.

*   *   *

"It's not your fault." Blundermore motioned the youngsters to wrap their wounds with gauze. "Button up. Never make our accursed wounds known to others. Yours and mine. Yes, I regret to say: you two are marked men. So am I. Fate has put a curse in each of our lives. Not a word of this to anyone." He looked at them with a heavy heart.

*   *   *

Marcus Blundermore was deeply troubled. *Has Datu Villani also consulted with the Priestess of the White Mountains?*

CHAPTER 61

FAMILY ROOTS REVISITED

MUSIC INSPIRATION

MEI AND LEO – THEME SONG
HOUSE OF FLYING DAGGERS
SHIGERU UMEBAYASHI

HURT
CHRISTINA AGUILERA

DON'T LOOK BACK IN ANGER
OASIS

SECRET
BU NENG SHUO DE MI MI
不能说的秘密
（CHINESE MANDARIN）
JAY CHOU / 周杰伦

PARLER À MON PERE
(TALK TO MY FATHER)
(FRENCH)
CELINE DION

VIVIR MI VIDA
(TO LIVE MY LIFE)
(SPANISH)
MARC ANTHONY

*   *   *

Marcus Blundermore rang the table bell again. "Now let's have breakfast."

Shortly thereafter, Jose Valdez appeared to take orders. This time, he gave Luck and Chance a warm smile.

Still shaking his head from what he had just witnessed, Blundermore asked the twins: "What would you like for breakfast?"

"Whatever you recommend, Uncle Blundermore." Luck was sure his uncle would order the right breakfast for them.

His face markedly darkened by the horror he just witnessed, Blundermore looked at the menu and ordered for three of them.

"We'll each have *huevos rancheros – con jalipeño.*" The joy in his voice dissipated.

*   *   *

Later, as they ate breakfast, Luck inquired: "We want to know where are our Missing Mother and our Phantom Daddy."

"Why did each of our parents leave the Philippines all *so suddenly*...with no apparent reason?" Luck was choosing his words carefully.

"Why didn't they take us with them?" Chance complained.

"Why did they just disappear? With no explanation?" Luck was downright depressed.

Blundermore stopped eating.

Silence.

Gravely, he relayed his sentiments: "Foolish love and inexplicable misfortunes. Besides affecting his own life for better or for worse, one's actions have a way of turning another person's life upside down – with unforeseen and unintended consequences over time."

"So why did Phantom Daddy have to leave the Philippines?" Luck persisted.

"CRAZY LOVE! Sheer stupidity on his part." Blundermore felt sorry for the boys.

"What do you mean?" Chance pushed on.

"Phantom Daddy was a loose cannon...a misguided soul. He could not control himself. Lust is poison that ruins the body and the soul to its core – with its tragic *karmic* consequences and other collateral damages." Blundermore felt the boys were too young to understand. But he found himself in an awkward quandary. "Phantom Dad stepped on too many toes, crossed too many people. He had to flee the Philippines in the nick of time."

"And then?" Luck straightened up in disbelief.

"Missing Mama was left to fend for herself." Blundermore loved his younger sister Luz dearly and felt angry at the raw deal she got. "Life dealt her a deck of bad cards. Since then, her life became miserable. Unhappiness became her lot."

"So, Phantom Daddy cheated..." Luck felt disgusted. Completely devastated! All these years, he had held Phantom Daddy in high regard: on a pedestal. Now, he felt betrayed and sick to his stomach. *How could he! How selfish! How immoral!*

There was silence in the room, except for the clinking of knives and forks, and the tick-tock of the wall clock.

"And the two of you bore the brunt of your Phantom Daddy's foibles and mistakes... All because of his crazy love! That was the unforeseen consequence of his act: a peccadillo turned into a family tragedy. Overcoming his *lust* was his challenge." Blundermore felt uneasy having to share such dirty laundry with his twin nephews on this first meal with them at ISBS. "You see, human shortcomings have their price – wreaking havoc on people's lives, affecting both the guilty and the innocent."

These words cut like a twisted knife into Luck and Chance.

"So why did Missing Mama have to leave so suddenly, too?" Chance wanted to know.

"It was due to the insidious fall-out caused by Phantom Daddy's initial indiscretions and misadventures. This much I was able to surmise: the first incriminating act causes disturbances beyond what we can imagine; the effects of which are unpredictable and can be totally heartbreaking." Blundermore felt sorry for Luz. "And your Missing Mama was on the receiving end of your Phantom Daddy's unholy deeds."

"But that is *not* fair! Life is so *unfair*!" Chance's eyes burned with anger.

"Who's to say?" Blundermore felt sorry for his twin nephews. "And who said the world is *fair*? Who said *life* is fair? Cosmic justice works itself out in wily ways beyond human comprehension over the expanse of Time and Space." Blundermore had been trying to understand this perturbing Mystery over the years. "Is there justice in this life?" He muttered in dismay. "For the sins of one, many are damned."

"Are we damned?" Chance burst out in anger. "Damned by the sins of our Phantom Daddy?"

"Anger is useless." Blundermore understood anger, because he, too, had been there. "Do not feed it. Anger is like a curse that will eat you alive. Banish your useless anger! Banish your dark past!"

*　　　*　　　*

439

"Where is Missing Mama?" Chance inquired.

"She has disappeared from the face of this Earth – heartbroken. A broken soul. Not a trace. She hasn't maintained contact with me for years." Blundermore, too, was mystified by her silence for all these years.

"Is she alive?" Chance asked the dreaded question.

Silence.

Blundermore felt helpless. "From time to time, she would send me post cards. No return address though. Like you, I missed her very much."

"Can we find her?" Chance asked.

"If she wanted to be found, she will let us find her. The question is: Does she want to be found?" Blundermore stared resignedly at the twins.

* * *

"How about Phantom Daddy? Is he alive?" Somewhat curious, Luck asked.

"Phantom Daddy is a brilliant man, a man with tremendous potential – but with two fatal flaws: poor judgment and reckless behavior, with an over-abundance of testosterone. He could have had a great future in the Philippines, but he blew his future – big time." Blundermore shook his head sadly. "He's one rotten egg!"

After a brief pause, he continued: "Interestingly enough, last I know, he was teaching Business Ethics at the *Dogscabs School for World Leadership.*" Blundermore gasped in utter disbelief.

"Maybe, he has changed." Chance was hopeful.

440

"It's hard to change the spots on a dog." Blundermore knew better. He stared deeply at the two youngsters, partly pleading, partly hoping that generational sins would not be repeated by his twin nephews. "You two, promise me this: gird your groins! Otherwise, I'll crack your nuts and squeeze your boobies. Is that clear?"

Luck nodded earnestly, letting out an impish smile.

Chance was quick to interject. *"Do we have a choice in our birth? What are our choices in life? Are we just condemned to live this life? WHY DO WE LIVE?"*

Blundermore stared at his nephews, now more seriously. "Do me a favor: Don't look back. You have everything in front of you here in the Present. You've got a whole Future ahead of you. Nothing good comes from dwelling in the negatives of the Past!" Blundermore stroked his beard in deep thought. "One more favor. Go visit your Grandma Hope. I've told her the two of you have arrived. She'll be delighted to see you both. She lives with me at the President's House."

*   *   *

Suddenly, there was an e-mail alert on his tablet: EMERGENCY EXECUTIVE COMMITTEE MEETING ON Z-ASTER AT 9:30 A.M.

Blundermore's countenance darkened. He was visibly worried. "Oh, my…"

Chance sensed something foreboding.

"What happened last night?" Chance could tell from Blundermore's anxious look that things were awfully wrong.

Blundermore paused, seriously considering whether to share the events from last evening with his twin nephews.

441

Intuitively, he trusted them, inasmuch as the twins had confided in him with their ordeal with Gul – and they were his blood relatives.

*   *   *

"This is top secret and for your eyes and ears only: Nameless escaped last night. We suspect there was an inside job involved." Blundermore's voice was tense, his look worrisome.

"Some thirty-five years ago, the Insidious One and his son, Nameless, wreaked terror for five long years at ISBS. Together, they enforced the murderous Reign of Terror upon ISBS. During the Great Battle of Liberation for ISBS, the Insidious One managed to escape while young Nameless was captured. Nameless was tried in court and was subsequently imprisoned – for crimes against Humanity and Civilization."

Blundermore felt depressingly sick to the stomach from the thought that Nameless had escaped last night. For Blundermore, the very thought of his own survival, the school's survival and everything he held dear haunted him. *Will all my efforts over my lifetime come to naught?* Blundermore shuddered at the thought.

"Truth be told, the Insidious One and Nameless cast ISBS into its darkest period." Blundermore admitted this much. "The Insidious One and Nameless undermined the very tenets of ISBS, ravaged its core beliefs and principles, wreaking the very spirit of ISBS citizenry and threatening to change world civilization as we know it. Those five years were the darkest of all – a period of annihilation. Hence, the Insidious One became known as the King of the Dark Age and his son, Nameless, was known as the Prince of the Dark Age." Blundermore's face turned ashen white as he remembered the dark days of Datu Villani and Z-Aster. "Both are the worst *rotten eggs* of our civilization! Please remember:

Nameless's break-out is to be treated as *top secret.* This campus is effectively on lock-down." Blundermore paused, still in deep thought.

"Uncle Blundermore, what will happen to ISBS?" Chance asked worriedly.

"That is the question that will test our souls to the very core. I mean that sincerely." Blundermore rose and hugged Luck and Chance tenderly. "I've to go. Come to my house anytime. Your Grandma will be very pleased to see her two grandsons. We'll meet another time. Meanwhile, be careful – *very* careful!"

Dread descended upon Marcus Blundermore as he headed out of the President's Dining Room.

*   *   *

CHAPTER 62

EMERGENCY EXECUTIVE MEETING

<u>MUSIC INSPIRATION</u>

FEARLESS – ENDING THEME
SHIGERU UMEBAYASHI

THE RED WARRIOR
THE LAST SAMURAI
HANS ZIMMER

AGAINST ALL ODDS
PHIL COLLINS

TRAGEDY
BEE GEES

WHO AM I?
LES MISÉRABLES
CLAUDE-MICHEL
ALAIN BOUBLIL & HERBERT KRETZMER
SINGER: COLM WILKINSON

I'M A LOSER
THE BEATLES

THE REASON
HOOBASTANK

*　　　*　　　*

*E*ach of us performs, hoping for an optimal outcome. Who's to say whether we did well or not?

The cumulative acts over a lifetime mark the final measure of our lives.

*　　　*　　　*

"Gone without a trace!" Marcus Blundermore exclaimed exasperatedly. Dazed and feeling lost, his reality was suddenly transformed into a potential tragedy.

Besides Blundermore, everyone gathered in his secure room was silent. Around the alabaster table were: the Three Grand Masters; Romulus Goggles, the ISBS Exterior Security Chief; Marcel Maladroit, his assistant; and Gabriel Gaudi, the chief school engineer. Each was grappling with the mystery of Z-Aster's escape.

Romulus had examined Z-Aster's cell completely for fingerprints, clues and other evidence. "His electronic leg bracelet was cut and left behind inside his cell. This much I can say: Someone from *within* ISBS helped him escape. The culprit or culprits are familiar with the secret lay-outs of the school."

A Scotsman with an impeccable pedigree, Romulus was a man who paid extraordinary attention to details. At sixty, he was the master of deduction and king of sleuth. He had solved myriads of criminal cases with cool detachment. "The timing was uncanny. It occurred right at the start of the school year, when the school grounds are open to the general public." Disheveled and unshaven, Romulus was at a loss just as much as the others in the room. Famed for his cool-headed forensic acumen and insights, his reputation, would once again be on trial. Indomitable in spirit, nothing could stop him – especially now, as Z-Aster was his "Most Wanted" person. There would be no compromise for this scientific master of cause and effect. Looking much younger than this age, Romulus tapped his unlit pipe against his palm in deep contemplation – trying to figure out how Z-Aster escaped. "It is my sincerest desire to see Z-Aster re-captured and returned to the Chamber of Ordeals. Nonetheless, we still don't know exactly how events have transpired. Preliminary deduction leads me to suspect that Z-Aster's escape involved an insider. But who the perpetrators

445

were, we cannot determine at this time. The five Oculus Towers at the four corners and at the center of ISBS showed no outside intruders. Right now, we have only a few clues to go by. First, the footprints. We have one diver's footprints of an insider accomplice mixed with stinking footprints of outside commandos. One set of footprints belonged to Remus. Dr. Maladroit will tell you the other clues we've picked up."

Marcel stood up, displaying the test tube of blood samples gathered from the site. "These blood samples were collected from the stairwell leading to Basement Five. These will be analyzed in the laboratory for further identification." Marcel paused and lifted the small transparent Ziploc bag. "Second, in this bag, we have a cartilage of someone's right ear. Looked like there was a serious fight in the same aforementioned stairwell. We don't know whose ear cartilage this is. I hope it's *not* Remus's ear. We need a few days of DNA analysis to confirm the potential identity."

Romulus stood up, displaying a picture on his smartphone for everyone to see: "GONE CHASING Z-ASTER. RG." Firmly, he declared: "Here's my brother Remus off chasing down Z-Aster."

Now it was Marcel's turn to speak. "Two years ago, when I did an appendectomy on Z-Aster, we implanted and attached one nano-GPS pin onto his outer stomach. Hence, we can trace his whereabouts through our tracking system. As of now, he is at Deception Hollows of the Great Undersea."

Romulus concluded: "In due time, I should hear from my brother Remus. He has a secure transmitter on his person. I'm surmising that he is at the Deception Hallows. Now, we have to engineer our own commandos to meet up with Remus there – to rescue Lucius Blundermore, assuming he is still alive."

*　　　　*　　　　*

Abigail could not hide her determination to defend ISBS. "Effective immediately, we should put *all* ISBS campuses worldwide on *highest alert*: that means including campuses in China, France, Russia, India, Egypt and the UK. Romulus will be in charge of this task. This means, *all* outside visitors must have background clearances before gaining entry into all school grounds. Permitted outside visitors will be escorted by security personnel at *all* times. No exceptions!"

Meanwhile, Romulus stood up to propose his dragnet. "All protocols for the highest alert will be activated worldwide within the next twenty-four hours. No time can be wasted. Attendance of students and faculty shall be closely monitored for absences – *today* and for the duration of the highest alert. My team will scour the computer print-outs of the attendance sheets of the students, administrative staff, the faculty members, and *all* ISBS staff – including our cleaning and security personnel, here in *New Joy Sea*. Any absences will be treated as a red flag." Romulus was setting the net to narrow down the identities of the perpetrators and accomplices. "To expedite discovering and capturing the perpetrators of Z-Aster's escape, I want to submit to the Three Grand Masters to approve these recommendations: the tapping of all phone calls and the surveillance of all communications – written or otherwise, such as e-mails, mails, phone calls, text and tweet messages, *et cetera*. One addendum recommendation: to turn on all ISBS cameras and microphones – including all those in the classrooms, libraries, the Great Commons, the dorm rooms, and toilet stalls."

Abigail's brows arched. "Why the toilet stalls? Are you going to listen to people's farts, too?"

Romulus bowed. "With all due respect, Ma'am, we don't know what people will be uttering from the other end of their mouths."

Gabriel and Marcel broke out laughing – but not the Three Grand Masters, who remained deadly serious.

"We shall put your recommendations through a vote." Thereupon, Blundermore stood up and went to his credenza. From one of its drawers, he took out three identical sheets of slates and three pieces of chalk.

Aurelius stood up and brought back a yellow Ming Dynasty imperial bowl of water and placed it at the middle of the conference table.

Abigail stood up and brought back a large towel and placed it at the middle of the conference table.

When Blundermore returned to the conference table, he gave Aurelius and Abigail each a sheet of slate and a piece of chalk. "In silence, we hereby vote upon the recommendation as submitted by Romulus Goggles. To tap or not to tap? Let this be on record."

Silence descended upon the room as Blundermore took his seat.

The only sound that could be heard in the room was the gentle tapping of Blundermore's wand on the round alabster table. *To tap or not to tap?*

When each of the Three Grand Masters had voted, each slate was laid on the table for everyone to see. It was a unanimous vote: NEGATIVE.

Blundermore spoke: "Romulus, as you well know, ISBS hold every individual's privacy sacrosanct. EVERYONE'S VIRTUAL SELF IS INVIOLABLE. PRIVACY IS A FUNDAMENTAL HUMAN RIGHT. ISBS LAWS PROTECT EACH PERSON'S RIGHT TO PRIVACY."

Romulus protested. "But this is a serious matter relating to the *existential* survival of ISBS!"

Abigail spoke: "Privacy *underpins* human dignity, autonomy and other values such as freedom of speech, assembly and association especially in this modern age of sophisticated information technology. This is all the more important as Civilization progresses to the next level of the Digital Age."

Auelius spoke: "There should be valid *demonstrable* probable cause for anyone to be subject to tapping and surveillance. The end does *not* justify the means. Adopting your recommendation will violate and seriously undermine the tenets upon which we have rebuilt ISBS. We are supposed to be the protectors of this right to privacy; for us to violate this right will undermine every social norm and principle of ISBS. GENERAL SURVEILLANCE AND TAPPING IN ANY SHAPE OR FORM IS FORBIDDEN. OTHERWISE, WHY DO WE LIVE?"

Blundermore looked at Romulus sternly. "You have heard from the Three Grand Masters. Privacy matters. It assures freedom of thought, expression, and assembly in our daily learning and living. We have spoken in one voice. Your recommendation for general surveillance and tapping is denied. Your recommendation is the ultimate Trojan Horse of the Enemy. Case closed."

The Three Grand Masters placed their slates into the yellow imperial bowl of water. With the towel, Abigail wiped each slate clean. Thereafter, Aurelius poured out the water in the sink area. Blundermore returned the slates into his credenza drawer.

Romulus was stunned and insulted by the decision, unable to speak. *This is only making my job all the harder! And to imply that I am in cahoots with the Enemy? This is too much! There must be another way!*

*   *   *

Taciturn, Gabriel Gaudi was a comprehensive operator, having fought in the Great Battle for Liberation.

"Gabo, what can you tell us?" Aurelius wanted a report from Gabriel.

Diminutive in stature, Gabriel confidently spoke with a heavy Spanish Catalan accent. "The structural integrity of Testament Towers remains intact and sound. No worries. The three sewer gates will be repaired and reinforced. Laser motion detectors and infra-red heat monitors will be installed at each sewer gate area – and at all strategic areas of this campus and all campuses worldwide. With the highest alert in effect, we'll install remote-control laser gunneries and drones at all strategic points on this campus and all campuses worldwide. Lastly, we'll patch up the blown out walls with reinforced concrete. We'll fix all the electricals from Basement Five though Nine. We'll check for any other secret tunnels around the Testament Towers and around the school perimeters."

"Why didn't we discover the break-in sooner?" Blundermore wanted answers.

Marcel took the question. "Our security system – especially those related to the laser monitor systems – was hacked. Someone overrode the security monitors at the control center and planted exogenous data and superimposed fake images. This was a sophisticated scheme engineered and executed by a cabal of conspirators – assisted by first class hackers."

In his gut, Aurelius felt the worst was yet to unfold. "A dark foreboding Evil is threatening to descend upon this school. Let us not kid ourselves. Knowing what happened during the Great Battle, the upcoming struggle will be an all-consuming struggle for all of us – if not more so." Aurelius spoke determinedly.

Blundermore could not agree more, noting the scars that marked him – physically, mentally and spiritually. "The cold truce which held so well for these past thirty years has now been broken. All the progress made at ISBS is once more at risk with the escape of Z-Aster. His incarceration here within Testament Towers for these past three decades was the insurance of peace within ISBS. Sadly, last night, we *lost* our insurance with his escape." Blundermore did not mince words.

"My soul is heavy with sorrow." Deeply troubled, Blundermore struggled to collect himself. "But we must carry on. The Days of Learning should continue. Meantime, let us ponder how we can make ISBS more secure for its students and faculty." With that, the meeting was adjourned.

* * *

Inside the President's washroom, Blundermore stared at his reflection in the mirror. "How can it come to this? What have I done? What's next? Oh, Father, I have *failed* you! I'm such a loser!" All he saw was a haunted face in the mirror. Refreshing himself, he proceeded to wash his face. But he could not absolve his feeling of guilt. "Does it have to come to this – unleashing a conflict with no solution? Oh, what will happen now?"

* * *

CHAPTER 63

PROFESSOR BLISS'S LECTURE ON HAPPINESS

MUSIC INSPIRATION

ODE TO JOY
SYMPHONY NO. 9, MOVEMENT NO.4
CHORAL
(GERMAN)
LUDWIG VAN BEETHOVEN
CONDUCTOR: HERBERT VON KARAJAN

OH HAPPY DAY
SISTER ACT
CHORAL

DON'T WORRY, BE HAPPY
BODDY MCFERRIN

HAKUNA MATATA
(DON'T WORRY)
(ENGLISH & SWAHILI)
LION KING
ELTON JOHN & TIM RICE
SINGERS
JIMMY CLIFF & LEBO M

PROBLEMA
(PROBLEMS)
(TAGALOG)
FREDDIE AGUILAR

HALF SUGARISM
BAN TANG ZHU YI
半糖主义
(CHINESE MANDARIN)
S.H.E.

*   *   *

Thy magic power re-unites
All that custom has divided,
All men become brothers
Under the sway of thy gentle wings.

Whoever has created
An abiding friendship,
Or has won
A true and loving wife,
All who can call at least one soul theirs,
Join in our song of praise.

Ode to Joy, Beethoven, Symphony No. 9, Fourth Movement

*   *   *

What is Reality?

What is the ephemeral?

What is the eternal?

*   *   *

The lecture auditorium was filled with freshmen, all eager for their first lecture at ISBS.

Exactly at 10 A.M., Professor Felicia Bliss walked onto the lecture platform from a side entrance on the stage. She wore a multi-colored outfit with stripes of the rainbow, with a purple sock on one leg and a yellow sock on the other. At forty, she looked more like a clown than a professor, especially with her summery rabbit hat adorned with long peacock feathers.

On her shoulder was a bulky bag, from which she grabbed candies, chocolate bars, lollipops, strawberries and bananas. These she hurled toward the students who instinctively lurched forward to catch them in wild excitement. For a few minutes, the auditorium was pure raucous. Dignified, she stepped down from the stage and walked toward the audience, showering the students with sweets and fruits, moving around the auditorium, as if Halloween has arrived early and she was the Fairy Godcandy.

She returned to her lectern, and with a big smile, addressed the students: "Are you *happy*?"

A chorus of "Yes" roared from the student audience.

Luck was amused by the pedagogic approach of Ms. Bliss, the Professor on Happiness. He had not expected nor experienced a lecture starting this way.

"It is a universal truth that Happiness is pursued for itself, unlike health, wealth, honor and friendship. A happy life is a good life. Half of life's battles are already won with Happiness. You see, just by being happy, your student career can be considered half successful!"

An enthusiastic applause from the students erupted.

"Even silly Happiness counts! It lifts the spirit. It beats taking anti-depression pills and going to psychotherapists. Silly Happiness saves money; saves lives. With Happiness, there will be less fights; less injuries; less bad endings. Have you ever seen two happy persons wanting to kill each other?"

Another loud applause.

"For Life is to be lived in the simple joys of the moment in small things. You've just experienced Happiness by the sheer delight of catching some sweets from thin air. Isn't that priceless?"

Chance never expected this: a Course in Happiness; a required course for all freshmen.

"Happiness is a universal experience that transcends nationality, gender, race, creed and social class. It binds us in our humanity. It's an everlasting reality found in the happy moment. Why do we take so many pictures while on vacation? It is to capture those happy moments which we hope will live forever in our memories."

Enigma was thinking whether one could be happy despite experiencing pain.

"Laughter and smiles are universal manifestations of Happiness, requiring no translations. Yes, a smile, a laugh – they transcend language. Cherish the happiness of each moment. Happy moments are building blocks of creating a beautiful life. Happiness provides the essential aesthetics of life."

Choice nodded, noting that happiness was a decision.

"Money cannot buy happiness. Focus on building lasting friendships and close relationships and you'll be happier than those whose lives are focused on building big bank accounts. Get close and personal with your fellow students and your experience at ISBS will be enriched in many ways. Get close and personal with your family members and loved ones – the nexus of Happiness."

Ka-Ching could not agree more. Watching his father's numerous multi-billionaire friends in Hong Kong and China, he wondered how many of them were truly happy – as many of them were mired in corruption and tax evasion investigations.

"Living a good life leads to Happiness. Cultivate a good character for it fosters happy endings; inasmuch as a bad character leads to sad endings. Character is *destiny*. For me, I enjoy comedies much more than tragedies. Comedies involve good characters; whereas, in tragedies one tends to find some bad apples that foster bad endings and tip the apple cart into a bloody mess."

Inside Luck's attaché, this statement caught Buff's attention. His *stealing* fruits in the palace got him imprisoned in the Caves of Rumination for four hundred years. Indeed, his naughtiness got him into deep *doo-doo*.

"Fill your everyday life with wonder by injecting it with a vision of freshness and of the miraculous. Fantastic thoughts produce fantastic outcomes. What a deal! Who would not like that? Fantasy is what makes Life *magical*."

Luck *wanted* his world to be magical. *How do I make this happen? A magical Life! If only I can harness the Magic!*

"Through achieving a quest or a great purpose, you will find your bliss. Look at the athletes, the artists, the scientists and the inventors. They are committed to their tasks and performance. Through them, humanity has progressed, hopefully for the greater happiness of all. Happiness is essential for a sustainable future for all."

Chance wanted to find the *meaning of his life. But how? My life seems so haphazard, like chop suey in a frying pan.* The escape of Z-Aster haunted him. *What if war breaks out with Datu Villani? What if …*

"But there will be days when nothing seems to go right. What can we do? One remedy is to make light of our troubles. Don't take them seriously. *Laugh* at our problems! Stay calm. For we are *bigger* than our problems. Our troubles can be worse – much worse, if you think through it. That is our only consolation. Sometimes, there are very little we can do to affect the outcome. But we can control our reaction. Truly, laughter is the *best* medicine; the *best* cure."

For Luck and Chance, these words were like an elixir of comfort to their miserable lives.

"Invest your heart and time in happiness; and you shall harvest boat loads of happiness. Remember, you reap what you sow!"

Inside Chance's attaché, this statement resonated with Lotto, who nodded vigorously in agreement. *Through horticulture, I shall find my bliss!*

"So now, this is the first spell you shall all learn: the Happiness Spell. When you are down and lonely, exclaim: *In excelsis vita!* – while conjuring up a happy thought or a happy moment. This Happiness Spell will dispel your sadness and call forth your happy thought or happy moment. The atmosphere around you will turn from negative to positive. And all will be fine. This will be your first homework of conjuring happy thoughts."

Sophie loved this lecture, especially how this applied to the concept of Mind over Matter: that the mind can affect its surroundings, turning a negative atmosphere into a positive one, at the very least.

"Most important, to be happy, you must *be* happiness: *the full embodiment of happiness.* You have to go *inward* to find it. You have to bask in the full idea and essence of happiness where you and happiness are *one.*"

For Chance, he interpreted this as: *the idea becoming reality through the flesh. How can that be?*

"Any questions?"

Sophie's hand shot up. "If we are happy now, how can we be happier?"

"Hmm… How to be *happier?* That's a great question."

"Any comments?" Professor Bliss looked for volunteers.

She paced to collect her own thoughts.

"Develop a short memory. Let go of the rotten Past. Cauterize your negative Past. It sounds counter-intuitive but it works. Forget the hurts. It serves no purpose. Cut your losses. Dwelling in the negativity of the Past does not work because the Past is dead.

"Avoid toxic people; they bring you down. They are poisonous people who will only *poison* your mind and your soul. There are so many good and healthy people out there. Why get stuck with toxic people who are already *dead in spirit?*

"Forgive. But remember, forgiveness is *not* approval. The only person who can change in the act of forgiveness begins with *you*. Gandhi said: 'Let *me* be the change I want to see in the world.' You must meditate on forgiveness: forgiveness of self; forgiveness of the other.

"It is in forgiveness that truth arrives – when you *least* expect it. Truth is the fruit of forgiveness. In humility, we embrace truth as reflected in its many facets. You need to see truth from many angles to understand it.

"Seeing truth leads to understanding. With understanding, you will appreciate many situations. With the understanding of truth, you are set *free*.

"Count your blessings! Be thankful to yourself and to others. Thank someone who has enriched your life. You will be amazed by the sparks that makes. Keep a 'Gratitude Journal'.

"Do what you love. Love what you do. Live in Love. Love your Life. *Love is the ultimate elixir of Life! Love and Happiness become one.* Happy Love is eternal!"

"Finally, surround yourselves with happy people, with the people you care about. You will achieve Happiness Squared or more. Make lots of friends. The more, the merrier. Happiness to the power of plenty! Hehehe!

"Remember: Your state of being defines who you are. Be Happiness and you will be happy. Happiness is within you. All of us have the capability to be happy. Through happiness, you will live Life more fully and more honestly. *Let everything you do be wrapped in bliss.* After all, WHY DO WE LIVE? In conclusion, all's well that ends well."

With that and with a broad smile, Professor Bliss gathered her stuff amidst enthusiastic applause from the students.

*   *   *

CHAPTER 64

PHILOSOPHY OF THE WAND

<u>MUSIC INSPIRATION</u>

DIVENIRE
TO BECOME
(PIANO)
LUDOVICO EINAUDI

OH, OH, OH, IT'S MAGIC
SELENA GOMEZ

YOU'RE WRITTEN IN MY SONG
NI BEI XIE ZAI WO DE GE LI
你被写在我的歌里
(CHINESE MANDARIN)
SODA GREEN / 苏打绿 & ELLA

*　　　*　　　*

*W*hat is Myth?

It is a metaphor for a mystery beyond human grasp. It is an expression of our mysterious selves, where profound truths abound, holding true over a long, long time. Through myths, we live – keeping the essence of our life events forever alive.

*　　　*　　　*

Master Willy Sparks trudged to the podium at the center of the stage in his rumpled trench coat. "I want to *make sure* each of you has your own wand." He peered through the whole gym, where all the freshmen were dutifully assembled. "Do you all have your wands?"

460

Gently, Master Sparks tapped on the mini-microphone fastened to his lapel. "I need your attention. Your life depends on it."

The student body quieted down.

By the walls of the gym were rows of target board, with different kinds of flowers and funny objects, such as a small balloon, a flashing bulb or a little bell, pinned at the center of each target.

Master Sparks surveyed the assembly of students gathered in front of him. "Interestingly, your wand has chosen you. What will you do? Why are we here today? To master your wand. Through your wand, you will manifest Magic in your lives. In the meantime, go figure out who you are and what you want to be. Is that clear?" Master Sparks cleared his throat. "Any questions? Today, your journey of magic begins – here at ISBS."

"Take good care of your own wand. And your wand will take care of *you*. *You and your wand are one.* Your wand is your life. You've now learned the Philosophy of the Wand – POW. Through POW, a whole magical world is open to you."

Once again, Master Sparks cleared his throat and paced the stage. Everyone was in rapt attention. He bent over and reached for his wand, which was nestled in his long sleeved pocket along the pant of his right leg.

"First we start with the 'Pledge to our Wand'. Hold your wand firmly with your right hand, and raise it up in the air – like Lady Liberty, like so." Master Sparks demonstrated the posture to everyone. "Place your left hand on your left bosom, like so and pledge yourself to your wand. Now, repeat after me:

MY WAND AND I ARE ONE

"My *chi* is my intrinsic life energy. Through my wand, my *chi* flows, manifesting my life. Through my wand, I write my karma – for better or for worse. Through my wand, I live or die. Today, I must figure out who I am and what I want to be. This is my responsibility. And mine alone. My journey starts now. I pledge to live in the NOW and be one with my *chi*.

"My soul is linked to my wand. Through my wand, I traverse my life, through triumphs and perils. I pledge to take excellent care of my wand. And my wand will take care of me. My wand is my life. Through my wand, a whole magical world is open to me. Afterall, WHY DO I LIVE? My wand and I are one.

After the pledge, everyone clapped and cheered. Master Sparks smiled and intoned: "Welcome to the Magic of the Wand!"

* * *

Master Sparks continued. "Today, you receive the First Lesson of the Super-Hot Incredible Training of the Wand – SHIT of the Wand."

Laughter broke out amongst the students.

"Without mastering this SHIT, you are in deep doo-doo. And I mean it. This SHIT is nasty business. Your life depends on it."

More laughter from the students.

"The first lesson you have to learn is to aim, focus and shoot straight, like so..." And WHAM! A streak of light flashed through the gym and hit the bull's eye of one of the targets in the back of the gym. That was a long distance. Master Sparks hit a little bell. Ding! Everyone heard it and was awed.

"Remember this: Salvation is in *your* SHIT. So get on with it. To survive, you have to go through your SHIT."

With that, the students lined up in front of all the targets around the gym and started doing their SHIT.

*   *   *

CHAPTER 65

PROFESSOR MICHAEL PAIGE

<u>MUSIC INSPIRATION</u>

SOUND OF SILENCE
PAUL SIMON & ART GARFUNKEL

LIKING LONELINESS
XI HUAN JI MO
喜欢寂寞
(CHINESE MANDARIN)
SODA GREEN / 苏打绿

NOTHING TO MY NAME
YI WU SUO YOU
一无所有
(CHINESE MANDARIN)
CUI JIAN / 崔健

*　　　*　　　*

The Kingdom of God is inside of you, and it is outside of you. When you come to know yourselves, then you will become known, and you will realize that it is you who are the sons of the living Father. But if you will not know yourselves, you dwell in poverty, and it is you who are that poverty.

Gospel of Thomas, 3

*　　　*　　　*

Self-knowledge is the quintessential reawakening of oneself toward the path of responsibility, performance and higher consciousness. It is the key that opens us to the knowledge of Truth, to discover what is magical in us and in the world. And we marvel at this discovery.

The most valuable experiences are the results of personal and mystical journeys of the soul which lead to Magic. A genuine self-discovery is the fruit of the mystical dimension of faith, which in turn opens up a new world. Into this deep ocean of the Great Self, we get connected to All. We become a citizen to oneself and to the world. This is the Magic: we achieve a relational consciousness of self by self, the core of the True Now.

*   *   *

At his office door was a name plaque:

MICHAEL PAIGE

PROFESSOR OF MYSTICISM

Gently, Luck knocked at Professor Michael Paige's office, not wanting to be rude.

"Come in!" A welcoming holler from the professor rang out.

As Luck and Chance stepped into his office, they were overwhelmed by the numerous archeological artifacts and ancient books, big and small, strewn all over his office.

"Let me finish this sentence." Professor Paige was in the midst of feverish typing. An hourglass served as time keeper and as paper weight to his pile of papers in front of him. At seventy, Professor Paige appeared extraordinarily fit and muscular.

Chance chuckled observing a worn-out Panama hat and a netted bag filled with archeological tools – picks, brushes and a magnifying glass – hanging on the wall. Next to the bag was a six foot long bamboo pole, which he used in his expeditions. Ancient maps of the Middle East were tacked on a nearby board. They were dotted with red pins, green pins, and blue pins. *He is one daring adventurer!* It was Chance's first encounter of a *real* scholar at work. A famous one, for that matter. On the shelves, there were several books bearing Professor Paige's name.

Chance gleamed with an eagerness of possibly learning much from him. "Cardinal Legazpi recommended that we visit with you when we arrive. We are from Manila, Philippines."

"We are Luck and Chance, sir." Luck was amused by Professor Paige's high energy. He was all charged up typing away with zest with his two forefingers, his eyes glued to his computer screen. With fire still in his belly, he had numerous important projects ahead of him.

"Ah, yes! Take a seat. Let me finish my trend of thought lest I forget these nuggets of Wisdom in my head." Professor Paige sucked his pipe vigorously without looking at them. His office was wreaked with the smell of tobacco.

Chance gawked at Professor Paige. *He is not the mystic I am expecting from a Professor of Mysticism!* In no way did Professor Paige look like a mystic. But looks could be deceiving.

The professor's office was unruly. Copies of ancient papyrus texts were spread around his conference table abutting his office desk.

Suddenly, he stopped typing, turned toward the twins, stood up, and offered his hand of friendship. He wore a Donald Duck watch on his left wrist. "Over the years, Augustin Legazpi has mentioned the two of you. *Cardinal* Legazpi, he was my finest student! How is he?"

His handshake was firm and strong. Fit like a safari hunter, Professor Paige had a dark tan. "I know he would go far. He has an amazing mind. One of my finest students. One day, he'll be pope. But what do I know?"

Luck and Chance were now intrigued.

"Just before we left the Philippines, he administered the sacrament of Confirmation to us." Chance volunteered.

"I would be the *last* person to guess that Cardinal Legazpi would go into the priesthood. He was every female's heartthrob. Exceedingly handsome and from a distinguished family, I thought he would enter into business or politics. How *wrong* was I!"

"How so?" Chance remembered Cardinal Legazpi, always a priest, visiting them over the years. "He used to visit Luck and me when we were at Misericordia de Dios Orphanage. Occasionally, we would visit him at the Manila Cathedral during special occasions."

Professor Paige recalled the Past. "During his last year at ISBS, he met a freshman gal named Maria Clara Prisma – a beauty. So much in love, they were inseparable. I thought, surely, they would get married! They were so well matched. Of course, Fate would *outwit* me!"

"He was the most loving to us!" Luck interrupted.

"Years later, Maria Clara and Augustin would break-up. Subsequently, he entered the seminary, a broken soul."

"What happened to his sweetheart?" Chance wanted to know

the full story.

"Maria Clara would go on to marry Ernesto Reyes. Together, they have become the world's richest entrepreneurs in the poultry and the egg business through their world renowned *Los Huevos Locos*. Now, she is the Queen of Crazy Eggs! Most of the eggs you've eaten most likely came from their poultry farms. Likewise, for the chickens you've eaten." Professor Paige gave the twins a mischievous grin and shrugged in resignation.

"Is that so?" Luck was incredulous.

*   *   *

"What are you working on?" Chance was curious what was keeping Professor Paige so engrossed this afternoon.

"Do you know about the Nag Hammadi scriptures?" Professor Paige poured orange juice into two Donald Duck cups and offered them to the twins.

Luck noted the Donald Duck image on the side of the cups. *Very funny! I think he is a kid at heart – a perpetual adolescent!*

Chance seemed to remember reading about the Nag Hammadi scriptures while researching on various strands of early Christianity. "Yes! These were ancient scriptures retrieved in 1945 in Egypt…"

"Bingo!" Professor Paige pointed approvingly at Chance. "I'm working on a book right now: *Secret Teachings over the Millennia*. Specifically, I'm in this section of the book about the secret teachings of Jesus. I'm deep into the Gospel of Thomas. Some would say that this is the fifth gospel."

"Tell us more!" Luck was well versed on the four synoptic gospels of Mark, Matthew, Luke and John. These gospels were

468

considered synoptic because they were very similar and drew materials from each other regarding the life of Jesus. He did not know much about the Nag Hammadi scriptures.

Professor Paige gave the brothers a knowing smile, confident that they would like this tid-bit. "According to Syrian tradition, the apostle Thomas was the *twin* brother of Jesus. He was the Doubting Thomas – Didymus Judas Thomas. Thomas is "twin" in Aramaic; Didymos also means "twin" in Greek. Thus, we have "twin of twin" or "twin squared"! According to the Acts of Thomas, Jesus and Thomas looked very much alike – like the two of *you*! According to Gnostic beliefs, Thomas served as the *twin*, not only within their family context but also as a metaphor for the relationship between a person and the spiritual counterpart of the person. Their twinship was highlighted in Gnostic literature – with Jesus being the *spirit* and Thomas being his *alter-ego in the flesh and blood*. The Gospel of Thomas was about the hidden sayings of Jesus: 'Whoever discovers the interpretation of these sayings will not taste death.' Now, how do you like that?"

"Very interesting!" Luck nodded approvingly.

"The Gospel of Thomas focused on Jesus's sayings – without alluding to His crucifixion or to His resurrection. Hence, the rub to the early orthodox Christian Church. It did not qualify to be included into the New Testament since it did not touch on Jesus's death and resurrection. Some scholars would attribute the early, oral form of the Thomas's Gospel back to 50 – 100 AD, almost contemporaneous to the four synoptic gospels. But nowhere did it espouse Gnostic precepts either: the death and the resurrection of Jesus Christ. Hence, the controversy: is it Gnostic or not?"

"What's the meaning of '*Gnostic*'?" Luck was a bit puzzled.

"Very good question! *Gnosis* means knowledge, specifically the knowledge of spiritual truths. Biblical scholars doubt that the Gospel of Thomas is Gnostic – except that it was found with a bunch of other books deemed Gnostic in the Nag Hammadi area. His gospel consisted primarily of secret sayings of Jesus. It's like guilt by association. In fact, Thomas Christianity is prevalent in Kerala, at the southwestern tip of India – because that was where Didymus Judas Thomas dedicated most of his life until his martyrdom near modern-day Chennai. Thomas Christianity is accepted within Christendom, with close affinity to the Eastern Churches. Because of Thomas's resemblance to Jesus, there were rumours that Jesus himself spent some time in India."

Chance nodded. "Yes, I've heard that."

Professor Paige continued: "Gnosticism is a whole different matter. The early orthodox Christian Church condemned Gnosticism as heresy due to its vastly different cosmology and theology. Since you ask, I'll give you a *brief* synopsis, otherwise we'll be here all day. Gnosticism is related to Platonic and Neo-pythagorean schools of philosophy, where virtue and perfection dwell in the spirit, whereas matter is considered impure, imperfect and evil.

"It presents a distinction between the highest and unknowable good God and the Demiurge "creator" – the not-so-good God – who created the material world. The Demiurge is antagonistic to the will of the Supreme God. Demiurge's act of creation occurs in the unconscious semblance of the divine model – except that it is fundamentally flawed due to his malevolent intention of entrapping divine aspects in materiality. The Demiurge explains the existence of Evil in the world.

"In simple terms, Gnostic Christianity has been deemed as heretic by the orthodox Christian Church. Since Gnostic Christians considered matter as Evil, Jesus, being the Son of God – the good

God, *cannot* dwell in the matter of human blood and flesh, which is impure and evil. Thus, His appearance on earth was an emanation of His spirit.

"As such, Gnostics claimed that Jesus *never* died on the Cross – since Jesus was pure spirit. Gnostics believed that His resurrection was deemed as the enlightenment of the spirit. They believed that it was Jesus's emanation that was crucified on the cross. Hence, the heresy – per the orthodox Christian Church, which believed that *no* crucifixion means *no* resurrection. Thus, *no* salvation."

"Wow! This is far out!." Chance was fascinated.

"The orthodox Church upheld that Jesus was *fully* human in the flesh and blood and *fully* God in the spirit. This is declared and affirmed each time we recite the Nicene Creed – which dated back to 325 A.D. resulting from the First Council of Nicaea, also known as the First Ecumenical Council. This council was ordered by the Roman Emperor Constantine the Great to settle the issue of Jesus Christ's divinity. Thereafter, whatever Christian strands which were not in concordance with Church orthodoxy were considered heresy. Orthodox Christology reached a major milestone: Jesus Christ is one true eternal God in deity with God the Father within the Trinitarian Godhead."

Peaked with interest, Chance could not hold back his enthusiasm. "Do you need help in your research?"

Chance wanted to be involved. *Secret Teachings over the Millennia. That's really cool!*

"I can be your research assistant." Chance was surprised at his own boldness in requesting to work with Professor Paige.

"Let me see if I have the budget." The professor looked at Chance, amused.

"Professor, I can work with *no* pay!" Chance did not want to be misunderstood.

Professor Paige continued more seriously: "I hear you. Isn't it interesting that the Gnostic Gospels were discovered in 1945, the *darkest* year of human history? The year we discovered the monstrous concentration camps, such as the ones in Auschwitz, Buchenwald and Dachau. The year when America dropped two atomic bombs on Japan." Professor Paige paused, letting his own words sink in. "I'm sorry. But I have to run to my first lecture. I'm late."

After putting on his tweed jacket, Professor Paige tidied his lectures notes and thrust them into his lecture folder and headed for the door.

"What's your class on?" Luck inquired, as he tugged behind.

"Comparative World Religions."

Chance straightened up, remembering that Cardinal Legazpi had mentioned attending this very course during his years at ISBS — a course that changed *his* life.

"How did the course *change* Cardinal Legazpi's life?" Chance was pacing quickly, trying to keep up with Professor Mike Paige.

With a wry smile, Professor Paige turned to Chance. "I taught him the secrets to the Magic of Belief."

At this moment, Luck's smartphone vibrated. Taking out his phone, Luck saw a message flashing: "MEET ME AT THE PRESIDENT'S OFFICE SOONEST." It was from Marcus Blundermore.

*   *   *

472

CHAPTER 66

CALL TO ARMS

MUSIC INSPIRATION

THE WAY OF THE SWORD
THE LAST SAMURAI
HANS ZIMMER

YEARNING OF THE SWORD
CROUCHING TIGER HIDDEN DRAGON
TAN DUN / 谭盾
CELLIST: YOYO MA / 馬友友

ASURA
A XIU LUO
阿修罗
(CHINESE MANDARIN)
FAYE WONG / 王菲

FIGHT
斗
(CHINESE)
HIT-5

FINAL BATTLE
ZUI HOU DE ZHAN YI
最后的战役
(CHINESE MANDARIN)
JAY CHOU / 周杰伦

WORLDLY TAVERN
HONG CHEN KE ZHAN
红尘客栈
（CHINESE MANDARIN)
JAY CHOU / 周杰伦

DO YOU HEAR THE PEOPLE SING?
LES MISÉRABLES
CLAUDE-MICHEL
ALAIN BOUBLIL & HERBERT KRETZMER
CHORAL SINGERS

DANS LE PORT D'AMSTERDAM
(IN THE PORT OF AMSTERDAM)
(FRENCH)
JACQUES BREL

HOSTIAS
REQUIEM MASS IN D MINOR, K 626
(SACRIFICES)
(LATIN)
WOLFGANG AMADEUS MOZART

*   *   *

What are the dynamics of our lives? How can we overcome the enigmas in our lives by making the right choices for a better karma, a better Destiny?

Is there such a thing as making the right choice? When will we know?

*   *   *

When Luck and Chance entered the President's Office, the three Grand Masters were already assembled around Marcus Blundermore's round white alabaster conference table in serious discussion.

The pair quietly sat by the chairs abutting the wall at the corner of the room near the door.

Curtains drawn, the executive office's window panes were fogged up for privacy and security. Sounding resolute, Blundermore declared: "We should set Operation Lightning Bolt in motion as soon as it is feasible. Lest Lucius dies."

474

Acknowledging the twins, Aurelius stood up and paced the floor.   "With Nameless's escape, your grandfather, Lucius Blundermore, is in dire risk – if he is alive. As you know, he has been held captive by the Insidious One for the past thirty years. Our imprisoning Nameless and Lucius's captivity by the Insidious One guaranteed a cold peace in a delicate balance of a potential Mutually Assured Destruction of both camps. A MAD strategy. A MAD outcome. With Nameless's escape last night, the cold peace was shattered. The age of MAD-ness is upon us. This is the world we live in. We will have to rescue your grandfather as soon as we get affirmative logistical details from Remus Goggles. He is our ISBS Internal Security Chief.   We believe he is in Deception Hollows."

Looking grim, Blundermore gestured the twins to approach the conference table.

Standing by the conference table, the brothers realized the gravity of the situation.

Blundermore's face was drawn. "Lads, we will soon mobilize our commando forces to free your Grandpa Lucius. I want the two of you to be part of my commando team."

Bewildered, the twins did not know how to respond.

Abigail came over to the twins to support them. "You *don't* have to join if you don't wish. You *have* a choice. There's *no* face lost if you decide not to be part of the commando team."

Blundermore continued. "I *want* to rescue your Grandpa Lucius. It is *my* obligation as his son. This is a sacred family matter. After thirty years, the moment has come to this: to save or not to save Grandpa Lucius. Should I or shouldn't I? *Now* is the moment of decision. I have decided."   Blundermore's many thoughts and considerations over the years melded together into this moment – a merciless moment presented by Circumstance.

Directing his attention to the twins, Aurelius delivered this instruction: "Your mission is to protect your Uncle Blundermore from both sides – as he leads the commando team."

With sadness, Blundermore stared at the brothers. "I've called both of you in because this is now our sacred family mission..." Blundermore heaved a big sigh, unable to continue.

"If you decline, we will understand." Abigail assured the twins. "You are free to say no."

Aurelius leaned at the edge of Blundermore's desk. "The reason you will accompany Uncle Blundermore, is to provide him with tactical cover and moral support and additional assistance to physically rescue your grandfather, Lucius. Your grandfather had led ISBS over twenty glorious years – until the Dark Age came upon us. During the five years' Reign of Terror, we all went underground, except for your Uncle Marcus Blundermore. He was captured and imprisoned on the Day of the Great Insurrection by the Insidious One. During the Reign of Terror, your Uncle Blundermore languished in the Chamber of Ordeal."

Blundermore cleared his raspy throat. "Lads, that's why you are being called in here. Over the past ten years, your Uncle Antikweetee has trained you in the *kung fu* martial arts – for the main purpose of rescuing your Grandpa Lucius. He has informed me that you have both achieved very high skill levels. As Abigail indicated, you don't have to decide until – "

Interrupting, Luck stood up and in a loud voice, declared: "Uncle Blundermore, I've chosen. Count me in. To die for a righteous cause is glorious."

Deep in thought, Chance did not respond. *Is this now my destiny: to live or to die? Nothing in between?* He bit his lip. *It looks like Death is claiming me – once again – whether I want it or not. I've barely lived. WHY DO I DIE?* "Our martial art skills did not spare us from Gul's goons..."

Blundermore stood up and rested his hands on Chance's shoulders. "You *don't* have to go..."

"Can I make a difference?" Chance was not sure. He felt inadequate. But on the other hand, he loved Uncle Blundermore. Over the years, he had heard bits and pieces about Grandpa Lucius from Uncle Antikweetee. *I won't be able to live with myself – if Uncle Blundermore and Luck die in this mission. What is there to live for? WHY DO I LIVE?*

Abigail tugged at Chance's arm. "You can sleep over this matter. We have time. Whatever decision you make will be a correct one. It is *your* life. The decision is yours to make."

Blundermore turned toward a wall portrait of Lucius Blundermore hanging at one side of the wall. Filled with conflicted emotions, he stared at his father's portrait. *Father, I've wronged you... Shame on me!*

*   *   *

Marcus Blundermore beckoned the twins to join him – as he stood in front of Lucius Blundermore's portrait at the far end of his office. In a near whisper of a tormented man, he made this confession:

"Thirty years ago, on the Day of the Great Battle, just moments before my execution, your Grandpa Lucius led a rescue commando raid to free me. In the melee of the fight, I was rescued and freed – with Grandpa Lucius being captured instead. At the same instant,

477

Grandpa's forces captured Nameless as prisoner.

"In that brief and furious struggle, I heard Grandpa's groans at the Moment of his capture. I screamed a promise to Grandpa: 'DAD, I'LL COME BACK FOR YOU! DON'T EVER, EVER GIVE UP! I'LL COME FOR YOU!' This was a promise that would *haunt* me for the rest of my life. That scream was etched into my soul up to this very day. Someday, I will *free* Grandpa. Someday. But, that someday never came. Shame on me! I have only myself to blame for my lack of courage, lack of deft, lack of knowhow, lack of determination.

"How does one negotiate with terrorists, with Fate, with Evil?

"Grandpa Lucius was whisked to Datu Villani's headquarters in Deception Hollows, never to be heard from anymore. That was thirty years ago – yesterday."

Marcus stared at the life-size portrait of his sixty-five year old father. His soul in turmoil, Marcus could not go on.

In his mind, he had failed his father: For these past thirty years, Lucius Blundermore had remained imprisoned in Deception Hollows in his stead. *I have not done enough to liberate my father. How have I lived my WORD? Where is my INTEGRITY?*

*   *   *

After regaining his composure, Marcus placed his father's portrait on the floor. He proceeded to unlock a secret door, sliding it open. There, in front of everyone present, were three racks, upon which were mounted a wand, a steel rod and a steel sword.

"These are Grandpa's Maven's Wand, Maven's Rod and Maven's Sword. The rod and the sword were forged in Mount Inspiration ages ago."

The Maven's Wand was of thick burgundy yew, with its handle made of green jade. Circular nodules, some rising, some sunken into the steel, pocked the Maven's Rod. Likewise, nodules of different sizes, some rising, some sunken into the center vein of the Maven's Sword.

With two hands, Marcus respectfully lifted his father's wand from the rack.

"Look at the Maven's Wand. Look at its jade handle — so vibrantly green. This signifies Grandpa Lucius *is* still alive. If he is dead, the jade will be pale green – lifeless to the eyes. This is how we *ascertain* his current state."

After the twins examined the Maven's Wand, Marcus carefully returned it to its rack.

*   *   *

One at a time, Blundermore lifted the Maven's Rod and the Maven's Sword and carefully laid them on the alabaster table. The jade in the handles of the weapons were aglow in deep brilliant green.

"Behold the `Maven's Sword and the Maven's Rod. These weapons belong to ISBS. But they are still bestowed to Grandpa Lucius – since we *know* that he is still alive. He remains the Chancellor of ISBS...*in absentia.*"

Blundermore wiped each of the weapons for extra shine.

"These two weapons have always been held together through one person: your Grandpa Lucius. Here at ISBS, the Chancellor wields these during his term of office. These are powerful weapons."

To the twins, Blundermore continued to recount that fateful night thirty years ago. "I was supposed to die that night. Grandpa Lucius was greatly outnumbered – being in the bowels of Testimony Towers. In the confusion of my rescue, Grandpa Lucius got himself very badly wounded. The Maven's Wand, the Maven's Rod and the Maven's Sword were covered with his blood as they were strewn on the ground of Basement Nine. Then, he was captured – ALL FOR MY SAKE."

Overcome with remorse, Blundermore broke down and started weeping. "Ever since, he has disappeared into the Great Unknown. We believe that he is imprisoned in Deception Hollows. We really don't know his fate – except that he is alive."

The brothers remained silent, absorbing the sad tale of their Grandpa Lucius Blundermore.

*   *   *

Aurelius lifted the Maven's Rod, giving it a close inspection. "For our commando raid, these weapons will be *lent* to the two of you – specifically for the rescue mission. But, since there are the two of you, one of you will use the Maven's Rod and the other will use the Maven's Sword."

Abigail took out a pair of translucent Oracular Dice of Life – very similar to the ones Uncle Antikweetee had given Chance. "Let the Divine Augur speak." She let the dice touch the Maven's Rod. "Luck and Chance, each of you call out one number from zero to twelve. The person with the number closest to the sum of the pair of Oracular Dice of Life gets the Maven's Rod. The other person gets the Maven's Sword."

The twins nodded.

Abigail placed a large orange-enameled Ming Dynasty imperial porcelain bowl on the alabaster table. The images of two dragons graced the outer surface of the bowl.

The Chinese character *yi* (意) was embossed at the inner base of the bowl, signifying "meaning" and "intention".

"Now, call out each of your number." Abigail closed her eyes, breathing into the Oracular Dice inside her palms.

"Nine." Luck uttered.

"Three." Chance whispered.

"I cannot hear you." Aurelius muttered.

Chance straightened up and, once more, called out his number. "Three, sir."

"That's a square root of Nine." Blundermore noted.

After a silent incantation, she shook her palms and cast her Oracular Dice of Life into the bowl. 'Round and 'round the Oracular Dice rolled until it stopped.

"A Double Six. Twelve! Well, Luck, you get the Maven's Rod." Abigail declared. "Luck, your training will start tomorrow. At six in the morning. From Monday to Friday. Aurelius will train you personally. He will take you to the next level of the Magic of *Ch'i*. It will be more amazing than the Magic of Physics in *kung-fu*."

Marcus Blundermore leaned over to Luck and declared: "Luck, the most important day of your life is the day you *formally* take possession of the Maven's Rod for battle for the first time. At that fateful moment when you grip the Maven's Rod, witnessed formally by your elders and peers, your life and your world will change forever. At this moment, you become a man, and your boyhood is

481

irrevocably discarded for all time. On the Day of the Glorious Rescue, your commitment to take up the Maven's Rod is the last and most sublime rite of passage across the gulf between the boy and the man."

Abigail looked at Chance with loving kindness. "Chance, your training will start only *after* you've decided to join the commando rescue team. You will use the Maven's Sword. Aurelius will train you. And on the Day of the Glorious Rescue, your commitment to take up the Maven's Sword will be *your* passage across the gulf of boyhood to manhood."

Respectfully, Chance bowed, expressing concurrence. "I'll give this some good thought." Deeply troubled, he pondered how his future would turn out. "How much time do I have to decide?"

"Twenty-four hours." Marcus Blundermore's voice was firm.

Chance was stunned. *How can this be? How did I get into this situation?*

*   *   *

CHAPTER 67

LADY HOPE AND THE TWINS

<u>MUSIC INSPIRATION</u>

COMPTINE D'UN AUTRE ETE
AMELIE
(NURSERY RHYME OF ANOTHER SUMMER)
YANN TIERSEN

THE LAST EMPEROR - MAIN TITLE THEME
THE LAST EMPEROR
RYUICHI SAKAMOTO, DAVID BYRNE, CONG SU

PICKING UP BRIDES
THE LAST EMPEROR
RYUICHI SAKAMOTO, DAVID BYRNE, CONG SU

STAIRWAY TO HEAVEN
LED ZEPELLIN

KARMA CHAMELEON
CULTURE CLUB

AT LEAST I HAVE YOU
ZHI SHAO HAI YOU NI
至少还有你
(CHINESE MANDARIN)
LIN YILIAN / 林忆莲

SOMETHING GOOD
THE SOUND OF MUSIC
RICHARD RODGERS & OSCAR HAMERSTEIN II
SINGER: JULIE ANDREWS

JE NE REGRETTE RIEN
(I DON'T REGRET ANYTHING)
(FRENCH)
ÉDITH PIAF

*　　　*　　　*

We are all fated to die. So shall our luck and our chance come to an end. One day, our luck and our chance will dissipate into that terminal day, that terminal night. The moment shall come when we shall confront Fate: our death.

Then, what? How do we overcome this last barrier called Death?

*   *   *

For Luck and Chance, the meeting with the three Grand Masters was a heady one.

Gripped with gloom, Chance was *not* at all happy. Once again, his life was at stake. "What is this all about? First day of class and I'm being recruited to join a commando rescue mission! This is *not* what I signed up for when I accepted ISBS's admission letter. We're *not* even sure whether Grandpa Lucius is alive. Uncle Blundermore is risking a lot of lives for an uncertain rescue mission." The deathly ordeal of a few nights ago flashed before him. "Luck, I have so much to live for. I'm not sure I can do this. This is too much to ask for. THIS IS A CRAZY LIFE!" He shook his head. His eyes welled up in frustration. "Why me?"

Luck felt remorseful. "You have a point there. I *rushed* into volunteering to join the commando. Now, I'm stuck. What do I do? I cannot retreat on this one. Or, can I?"

"Where is your Integrity?" Chance asked. "Remember what Uncle Antikweetee said? Nothing works without INTEGRITY. You have given your word to Uncle Blundermore. You cannot take it back. Not now. Oh, you Reckless Luck!"

Luck was despondent. "You have a point."

Chance commiserated with him. "I'm not any better off. I've

got a big decision to make in the next twenty-four hours."

With a heavy heart, they discussed their dilemma as they walked to the President's House to visit Lady Hope, their grandmother.

*　　　*　　　*

"Hello! Hello!" Poirot the Parrot screeched excitedly as Lady Hope led the twins to the living room. *Who are these two strangers?*

Excited, the white cockatoo danced from one side to the other of his perch – with his crest spread wide. *"Mon ami! Oy!"*

"Hello, Ling Ling! Hello, Ling Ling!" Ling Ling the Myna greeted the twins, with her friendly intonation, while jumping gleefully back and forth on her perch. A jet-black glossy bird, she flew around her five feet high palatial cage, displaying a playful behavior. She would preen herself exposing her white patches on the outer primaries and the underside lining of her wings. Her cage was mounted on a low oriental coffee table. Ling Ling had an orange bill, with a yellow patch behind her eyes and on her nape. She had bright yellow legs. *"Ni hao! 你好！"* She tilted her head to the left and then to the right, inquiring about her new guests.

*　　　*　　　*

"It's so nice to *finally* meet the both of you!" Ecstatic, Lady Hope hugged her two grandchildren. The twins were surprised that there was no sting on their chest. "Come, make yourselves comfortable."

"Who R U?" Poirot hollered in his low cockatoo voice.

Lady Hope introduced the parrot to the twins. "This is Poirot the Parrot. He is a riot! He is one well-traveled cockatoo. He grew

485

up in the rain forests of Costa Rica, where he learnt Spanish. He was bought by a French professor in linguistics and philosophy. When the French professor returned to France, he took Poirot with him. There, Poirot picked up French. For that matter, Poirot learnt Parisian French! That professor must be a really patient teacher.

"One day, Uncle Blundermore visited the professor's home. At first sight, your uncle became fascinated with Poirot. As a gift from the professor, Blundermore brought him to America where he learned to speak English. Now, Poirot speaks *New Joy Sea* English! Poirot is tri-lingual! I often wonder whether he knows what he is saying."

*   *   *

Ling Ling made a funny sound of an ignition key starting a car engine. *"Varoom! Varoom!"* It sounded as if a big van just took off. "Screech! Screech!" Now, it was a sound of a big van screeching to a sudden stop.

Lady Hope was all smiles. "Don't mind Ling Ling (玲玲). She is the most gregarious greater hill myna bird you'll ever meet. She is of the *Gracula religiosa* lineage. But she was in *no* way religious. That screech sound he just made is the sound of a van screeching to a halt. Sometime back, she must have been traumatized riding *Varoom!*, our school van."

"We rode on *Varoom!* yesterday." Luck blurted out.

"Once, when *Varoom!* came to an abrupt stop, Ling Ling almost fell off her traveling cage. The screeching sound of the van must have been imprinted permanently into her speech memory! She is a character!" Lady Hope laughed heartily in her elderly genteel manner.

"Ling Ling was raised in Hong Kong, where she learnt Cantonese, a local Chinese dialect spoken in Guangdong Province and in Hong Kong. She belonged to a technology and philosophy professor who taught at HKUST – the Hong Kong University of Science and Technology up in the Hong Kong Northern Territories. She lived in a luxurious flat at the Repulse Bay in Hong Kong Island, whose window faced the South China Sea. Ling Ling's cage was outside by the balcony, taking in one of the most breathtaking view in Asia.

"From her balcony, she picked up the Cantonese spoken by the guards downstairs and all the car sounds emanating from the driveway leading to the main street. From clicking sound of car doors opening and closing, to the sound of car engines jumping to life, to the honks and screeches of buses from the main road. Ling Ling is hilarious!"

The twins laughed.

Ling Ling guffawed!

"Wow!" Luck was beside himself. "What a laugh from Ling Ling! And I thought I have the craziest laugh!"

Lady Hope continued: "In Hong Kong, she also picked up Tagalog from the professor's Filipino domestic helper. Anyway, the professor took a position with our ISBS-Beijing, in the City of the Northern Mirrors in China. Well, guess what? She picked up Chinese Mandarin – with a Beijing accent – my Chinese friends tell me! One day, Uncle Blundermore was visiting our school there. The technology and philosophy professor invited him home for dinner. There, Uncle Blundermore met Ling Ling and immediately fell in love with her. The rest is history. The professor gave Ling Ling to your Uncle Blundermore, who brought her here. Over the years, she picked up English. Now she speaks English with a *New*

Joy Sea accent – like Poirot."

"You bet!" Ling Ling chimed in.

"So, Ling Ling is effectively quadro-lingual – if not more, given all the automotive sounds she picked up over time. She is one of the most talkative birds. A world champion in mimics! A research student reckons that Ling Ling commands *eight hundred* words and various sounds."

"Wow!" Chance was taken aback, really impressed.

"Meow!" Luck gave out a boisterous laughter – joined with a guffaw from Ling Ling.

Beaming, Lady Hope laughed along. "Luck, you can feed Ling Ling some bird seeds from the bamboo scooper. You'll become instant friends!"

Ling Ling jumped around her perch as Luck fed her.

Not to be outdone, Poirot danced on his perch, leaning to the right and to the left, brightening Chance's spirit. *"Buenos días!"*

"He's a most special bird." Lady Hope joined Luck admiring Poirot.

"How so?" Luck did not know what she meant.

"I'll show you." Lady Hope was most cheerful. Turning to Poirot, she asked: "Who are you?"

"The Boss!" He chirped.

*   *   *

"Welcome to Camelot! This is the name your Grandpa Lucius called this place that is the *heart* of ISBS. Enjoy your time here. Now, can I get you boys something to drink?"

"I'll get it, Grandma." Chance volunteered as the twins followed Lady Hope to the kitchen.

"What do you like?" Lady Hope's eyes were bright like Christmas bulbs. "I've heard so much about the two of you from your Uncle Blundermore."

"Orange juice, Grandma." Chance just realized how thirsty he was, having sweated profusely on this oppressively hot and humid summer afternoon.

"I'll do it." Luck rushed ahead of Lady Hope and opened the refrigerator.

"Ah, it's never been so hot and humid! Let's open the windows. It's so stuffy inside." With a glass of lemonade in hand, Lady Hope trudged back to the family room and opened the window panels to let some fresh air in. For a moment, the cheer of Life returned to Lady Hope. She read the arrival of her grandsons as a SIGN – a sign from her dearest Lucius! Lucius had given her his birthday joy. His birthday love! *He must be alive! There is hope! Oh, Lucius! You've given me such a wonderful gift!*

Tears of joy streamed down her cheeks. "You are my little pearls sent down from heaven!" With tenderness, she caressed her grandsons with her loving gaze. They gave her Hope that Lucius Blundermore, her one true love, was still alive.

With drinks in hand, the twins sauntered to the family room. Their eyes led them to the picture counter where Lady Hope displayed the significant photographs of her family.

At the center of the picture counter was the faded wedding picture of Lucius Blundermore and Lady Hope. It was a picture of just the two of them: young, happy, confident of the Future.

"Grandma, you are beautiful!" Luck exclaimed.

Lady Hope smiled.

"And Grandpa is one handsome gentleman!" Chance did not miss a beat.

"You know, beauty fades over time. Outer beauty is only skin deep." Lady Hope was being modest. "What remains is the heart. At the end of the day, the heart is what is important. The heart is what counts."

Then, there was the family picture: Lucius Blundermore, Lady Hope and their four children, aligned in a staircase formation: Uncle Marcus, Uncle Antikweetee, Missing Mama and Aunt Juliet.

"This was taken on your Uncle Marcus's sixteenth birthday. Those were the happy days!" Lady Hope beamed with obvious pride.

Uncle Marcus, chest out, projected a genteel gaze, announcing to the world he was of age.

Uncle Antikweetee, around ten, had his unmistakable mischievous smile, his front teeth showing.

And there was Missing Mama, around six years old. Her hair trimmed short, she stood straight like a little girl scout.

Embracing her doll, Aunt Juliet, around three, looked lost and clueless.

*   *   *

With a gasp of amazement, their eyes settled on the wedding picture of Phantom Daddy and Missing Mama. This was the *first* time the twins had set eyes on Phantom Daddy. Before this, they had *no* inkling how their father looked like.

"This *was* Phantom Daddy!" Luck could not believe his eyes.

"Yes, your Phantom Daddy is one handsome man." Lady Hope spoke with love.

"Missing Mama looked awesome!" Chance was fascinated with her stylish big rolling curls of hair.

"Who do you think you two resemble?" Lady Hope was playing devil's advocate with this question.

"It's hard to tell..." Chance was not so sure.

"Neither!" Luck blurted out. "It seems we look distinctly ourselves. We got the genetic traits of both. But that's about it."

"You both look exquisitely handsome. There's really no need to compare yourselves to your own parents. Right?"

*　　　　*　　　　*

Beside the picture counter was a Ming Dynasty imperial table. On it, encased in a glass case, was a white plaster cast mask of an old man. Displaying a strong square jaw and hollowed out cheeks, it was a face of a solemnly serious man, with the cranial forehead of an intellectual. The deeply set eyes accentuated the protrusions of the orbital eye bones. Also, he wore a beard. The mask exuded the equanimity and confidence of a soldier going to war. It harkened on the viewer's sense of mission in life. Frozen in time, the visage had a gaze of Eternity.

"Wow!" Luck was taken aback by the mask. "Who is he?"

491

Lady Hope turned sad. "That is your Grandpa Lucius's life mask, made on the eve of the Great Battle of ISBS Liberation."

"The image is so clear. So lifelike." Intently, Chance studied the face.

Lady Hope's voice turned heavy. "He thought there was a chance that he might die. So, for posterity, he sat for the life mask."

"Look. I can see his facial lines so clearly etched. The creases on his cheeks, so deep." Chance noted.

"I can see a few actual eye lash hairs on his left eye." Luck's face was inches away from the mask. "Look. I can see nose hair sticking out his nose. Wow! I can even see his pores."

Lady Hope did not mince words. "Yes. That life mask is like a twin. A near perfect copy of the real man at sixty-five that was Lucius Blundermore and for everything he stood for. His life mask held the truth and the answers to his life's issues. Here's the real man behind the myth. For us all, he's held captive at Deception Hollows of the Deep Sea these past thirty years. This life mask was his last birthday gift to me."

The room fell silent, except of the tick-tock of the grandfather's clock in the family room and the funny chatter of Poirot and Ling Ling.

*   *   *

With loving kindness, Lady Hope invited the twins to sit at the living room. "Come! Let's settle in the living room. It's more comfortable there. Let's catch up with the lives of the living! Moreover, Poirot and Ling Ling are getting lonely!"

As they sat down, Chance innocently asked Lady Hope. "Do you think Grandpa Lucius is still alive?"

492

Crash!

Lady Hope dropped her glass of lemonade, shocked by the dreadful question coming from her grandson. *What do they know that I don't?*

*   *   *

CHAPTER 68

AN OMINOUS PACKAGE

MUSIC INSPIRATION

A HARD TEACHER
THE LAST SAMURAI
HANS ZIMMER

TO KNOW MY ENEMY
THE LAST SAMURAI
HANS ZIMMER

IT WILL RAIN
BRUNO MARS

BRIDGE OVER TROUBLED WATER
PAUL SIMON & ART GARFUNKEL

DIES IRAE
REQUIEM MASS IN D MINOR, K 626
(THE DAY OF WRATH)
(LATIN)
WOLFGANG AMADEUS MOZART

*　　　*　　　*

We *struggle through Life seeking to make a name for ourselves. Each morning, we can stand before the person in the mirror and say: What face am I going to show the world today? What face will the others see?*

We are masters of our own mask. We keep a poker face. We project a cool demeanor. This way, no one knows how we feel. No one sees the tears behind our mask. We try to live strong. We smile bravely at the world – wearing our mask.

*　　　*　　　*

A one foot by one foot package arrived at the ISBS guardhouse, which was beyond the East Gate, across the mote of the campus, contiguous to Testament City. At the face of the package appeared the following:

TO: MR. MARCUS BLUNDERMORE - PRESIDENT

INTERNATIONAL SCHOOL FOR BRANIACS SQUARED

STRICTLY PERSONAL AND CONFIDENTIAL

TO BE OPENED BY ADDRESSEE ONLY

Alex Lagarde, the Patrol Leader, aged forty-five, had strangely moussed-up spiked-up hair – like a mini Eiffel Tower atop his head. He had a high forehead, with a broad jaw and a thick beard. His nick name was: T-Rex. Being a French-Scot, he wore a traditional knee length plaid kilt and high knee socks. He had a leather sporran hanging down his belt buckle. Its frontal flap had the face of a two-horned antelope impressed upon it. Alex looked outright peculiar. Students called him: Weirdo.

Upon receiving the package from the postman, he examined it carefully. Protocol dictated that he had to run it through the metal detector. This he did.

Today, the drawbridge was shut down, with a railing sign which read: BRIDGE CLOSED.

Alex Lagarde's patrol car was parked at the foot of the drawbridge, right behind the railing sign. Casually, with the package under his arm, he entered his patrol car. Away he drove onto the drawbridge, crossing the moat.

He entered the East Gate into ISBS proper. Turning sharply to the right, he headed directly to the main school post office.

Alex gave the package to Gary Mailer, the ISBS Postal Chief, for further processing. "Gary, be careful with this package. It has no return address."

At forty, Gary was a plump and jolly postal chief. Of Irish ancestry, he had red hair with a red face to match. With the package without a return address, it immediately aroused Gary's suspicion.

Henceforth, he placed it through the X-ray machine, had it chemically tested for explosives and biohazard materials. While the tests came out negative, a nagging suspicion kept Gary uneasy. He decided to place it in the bomb-proof room made of reinforced steel located at the far end of the postal office. *I'm not going to take any chances given the highest alert we're now in. Better be safe than sorry!*

At the center of the bomb-proof room was a transparent explosion proof encasement, wherein he placed the package, with the robotic opener set ready to go. *Well, what do I do now? Better give the Big Cheese a call. Who can possibly send such a package?*

Gary left the bomb-proof room and phoned Marcus Blundermore. "Boss, we just received a mailed package addressed to you. It's marked *strictly* personal and confidential. We've checked it out for explosives and biohazard materials. It passed. But it has no return address. We don't know the sender. I don't want to take *any* chances. You may want to swing by. I can assist you in opening it *safely*."

*   *   *

496

Later, in that wickedly hot and muggy afternoon, Blundermore appeared at the postal office, perspiring profusely. Katya was with him, since she was also his Executive Assistant.

Gary came to greet them and took them to a separate remote viewing control room – some twenty yards away.

"See. The package has no return address." Gary manipulated the remote camera for a close-up view of the package.

"Let's open it." Blundermore wondered what he was about to see.

Gary activated the robotic mail cutter which neatly opened the box from one end. The robotic arms tilted the box. Slowly, a wrapped up package in dark violet paper slid into view.

"Mr. Blundermore, you've got a gift!" Smiling wryly, Gary pressed a button and a pair of mechanical tweezers started to tear open the violet wrapping.

From the torn wrapping, a strange and undistinguishable object which seemed to be an antique mask appeared on the television screen. With better focus and upon closer viewing, it became evident to the three that it was a gory blood-stained contorted face of an old man with a golden bullet in his mouth.

Katya let out a gasp. It took a full minute for the image to register with Marcus Blundermore, whose face turned ashen. He keeled toward Katya, whose gaze was glued to the screen, while Gary was trying for a close up.

"What the hell is that?" Shuddering in fright, Gary could not make sense of the dead man's gruesome face on the screen.

"Turn off the T.V." Blundermore steadied himself. "I'll retrieve the package myself."

Blundermore trudged across the postal office to the far end, with some help from Katya, who was shuddering with fear. Gary followed not far behind. The three of them walked over to the bomb-proof room. Gary helped opened the door with his pass key. Blundermore motioned that he alone should get in.

Moments later, he reemerged, with the package in both hands. The foul smell of Death was detectable.

Blundermore instructed Gary: "*No one* should know the content of this. Nor *what* has just happened. Top secret. Under the pain of Death." With that, he and Katya left for the Knoll.

"Let's head toward the President's House." Blundermore was white as a sheet, deeply shaken, barely holding up. He was confounded by the coded message of a ripped-off face with a copper jacketed bullet stuffed in the dead man's half-opened mouth. *What does it mean?*

As they approached his doorsteps, Katya gently asked: "What happened?"

Grief stricken, with barely enough strength, he said: "They've *killed* my father, Lucius. They've *ripped* his face off!"

In shock and disbelief, Katya grimaced. "Are you *sure?*"

"Yes. Now, they are after *me!*"

"How do you know?" Incredulous, Katya tried to calm Marcus Blundermore.

"The number 399 is clearly written on the bullet stuck in Lucius Blundermore's mouth!" Marcus gave out a tortuous heave.

*   *   *

CHAPTER 69

IN THE THROES OF AGONY

<u>MUSIC INSPIRATION</u>

KISS THE RAIN
(PIANO)
YIRUMA

I'VE GOT A MESSAGE TO YOU
BEE GEES

WHO AM I?
CASTING CROWNS

ACROSS THE UNIVERSE
THE BEATLES

SI NO TE HUBIERAS IDO
(IF YOU HADN'T LEFT)
(SPANISH)
MARCO ANTONIO SOLIS

NOVEMBER RAIN
GUN N' ROSES

YOU'LL NEVER WALK ALONE
CAROUSEL
RICHARD RODGERS & OSCAR HAMERSTEIN II
ANDRÉ RIEU & SOLOISTS

HEY JUDE
THE BEATLES

ANAK
(CHILD)
(TAGALOG / ENGLISH)
FREDDIE AGUILAR

MY IMMORTAL
EVANESCENCE

END OF THE WORLD
SHI JIE MO NIAN
世界末日
(CHINESE MANDARIN)
JAY CHOU / 周杰伦

CANDLE IN THE WIND
ELTON JOHN

KHUMBAYA
(COME BY HERE / SOMEONE'S WEEPING, LORD)
(ENGLISH / MANDINKA)
SOWETO GOSPEL CHOIR

WHISPERING HOPE
J. C. BLAKE
SINGER: MARY DUFF

LASCIA CH'IO PIANGA
(LET ME WEEP)
(ITALIAN)
RINALDO
GEORG FRIEDRICH HÄNDEL
SINGER: HAYLEY WESTERNA

PIANO CONCERTO NO. 2, MOVEMENT NO. 2
IN C MINOR, OPUS 18
SERGEI RACHMANINOF

LACRIMOSA
REQUIEM MASS IN D MINOR, K 626
(WEEPING)
(LATIN)
WOLFGANG AMADEUS MOZART

*   *   *

Yet some there be that by due steps aspire
To lay their just hands on that Golden Key
That ope's the Palace of Eternity.

John Milton

*   *   *

Can we know anything? Can we know the world? Our destiny? Ourselves? Our reality? Our God?

Why do we live? Why do we die? So we keep on striving, searching for answers to these questions of the mind and of the soul.

*   *   *

Stumbling into the foyer of the President's House, Marcus Blundermore was devastated by the thought that his father, Lucius Blundermore, was murdered, with his face ripped off. It was as if someone has driven a wooden stake into his heart. All life seemed to have left him. His spirit dissipated, a sense of total defeat overtook him.

Lady Hope was knitting by the living room, carrying on with the twins. She was astonished by his ashen face.

Poirot the Parrot hollered: "Welcome home! Welcome home!" To his surprise, Blundermore did not bother to greet him. *That's strange. He usually gives me a few kernels of corn.* "Oy! Oy!"

Ling Ling the Myna jumped back and forth on her perch. "Hello, Ling Ling! *Kumusta ka!*" She was surprised *not* getting a friendly whistle from Blundermore.

Tears of grief blurred Blundermore's vision. He was oblivious of his two pet birds. He headed straight to his bedroom, weeping in grief. Inside, between groans of sorrows laced with guilt, he placed the package into the inner safe within the huge and thick steel vault hidden within his wardrobe closet. There, in the inner safe, he deposited his father's mangled face. He locked the safe and the vault, in coded combinations only he knew. There, within the safe of all safes, he would lock his shame and his disgrace.

All these years, he had planned and initiated attempts to rescue Lucius from Deception Hollows of the Great Undersea, but to no avail. Diplomatic efforts were attempted but went nowhere. And now this.

Crashing on his bed, Blundermore felt sorry for his father and for himself. The thirty years' struggle to rebuild ISBS had cast its toll on everyone. Today, the toll on him was the heaviest and the most devastating. *All was for naught.* Once again, he surrendered to the idea that this was an *ugly, vulgar and evil world.* All the efforts to rebuild ISBS, based on *Hope, Faith, Love and Optimism,* seemed to be truly for naught. He gravely doubted whether he could truly overcome Evil. *Is God drunk? Has God gone mad?*

"Oh, God! Where are you now that I need you?" Now, his deepest need was to reverse Time, to negate his tardiness in executing a heroic rescue of his father. *Can Time be reversed? Can I recapture my chance to rescue him?* He struggled with the idea that his life was one of *total failure* due to his inability to distinguish the terms demanded of Life and the terms offered and his inability to successfully negotiate with Datu Villani for his father's release over these past three decades. *Thirty years! That's a long time! I've failed you! Oh, Dad, forgive me!*

He could feel the tremors of self-destruction pounding in his head. "Oh, God, let me die! Why should I live? I'm lost!"

In his sorrow and in his pain, he was suddenly seized by a realization that, for all these thirty years, Reality was *not* perfect and would *never* be perfect: that Reality was convoluted, contorted, and oftentimes, unmanageable. He realized that on many occasions, he was living a *lie,* a life of false pretense amongst those he loved dearly – pretending that events would turn out all right, when in fact he harbored the deepest doubts.

502

I am a farce – cloaked in my own false heroics! I've no guts! No spine! Blundermore felt like an impostor to those who looked to him for Hope. He could not bear this realization: the possibility of the futility of Life and its meaninglessness, which at the very end, would lead all to Death. A lonely Death. And for *what? What can we know? Over the years, I've searched for a path toward Reason, toward Wisdom and what have I found? What is there beyond the Realm of Wisdom?* "I've sold my soul for this? What makes a man?"

*   *   *

When Blundermore awoke, it was raining relentlessly outside. The suffocating afternoon humidity had given way to a heavy late summer night rainstorm, with intermittent flashing lightning and grumbling thunder punctuating the night. It was a necessary rainstorm to vanquish the oppressive humidity.

There was a soft knock at his bedroom door. Blundermore realized that he must have wept himself to sleep. His bedroom door crept open. He opened his eyes. His room was dark. He heard the shuffle of Lady Hope's slippers. He knew his mother had entered his bedroom. The lights came on. He felt her weight sink on the side of his bed and her gentle hand rested on his back. He turned, sat up and looked at her with profound guilt and sadness.

Blundermore did not notice the twins, who followed Lady Hope into the room and were standing at the opposite side of the room. Quietly, they stood at the corner of the room, observing the solemnity of the Moment.

"My soul is bereaved unto Death." Grieved, Blundermore struggled to control himself. Lady Hope hugged him and patted him on the back, not saying a word. She had lived in a state of limbo these past thirty years not knowing whether Lucius was dead or alive. She preferred silence. Silence provided neutrality. Silence provided possibilities. Silence provided oneness with the Moment where Truth resided.

*　　　　*　　　　*

Tick tock! Tick tock! Tick tock! The faint distant tick tock of the grandfather clock in the living room ticked away, until finally – Ding Dong! Ding Dong! Ding Dong! It announced the onset of midnight.

"Mother... WHY DO WE DIE?" He asked her. "Are we given a choice in dying?"

"Marcus, many things happen which we don't understand. Paradoxically, without suffering, we will not know ourselves. Hence, we suffer, so that we may know ourselves deeper." Lady Hope heaved a sigh. "Now, Death is a dilemma and a dilemma has no solution...since time immemorial. Let me tell you a story.

"When you were born, a storm was raging and lightning filled the sky – very much like tonight. When you entered this world, you barely budged; you made no sound. Your lips and your tiny finger tips quickly turned blue. I cried, giving you up for dead. Between sobs, I mourned and called you a Child of the Storm. I wrapped you in swaddling cloth and put you by the fireplace to keep you warm.

"Minutes later, your father returned home and asked to see you. I only shook my head and wept all the harder, pointing to the fireplace. He went over and picked you up and you cried your lungs out. At that moment, your cry was the *sweetest* cry, banishing my despair. That was how you were named Marcus, because you are such a fighter – so soon after your birth. Your father called you the Child of Light.

"I hope this story answers your question about Death. Did you have a *choice* to die? I don't know. Did you *choose* to live? I don't know. All I know is that your coming to this world is a *necessity*. For what, I don't know. Except that you are a necessity."

With her kerchief, Lady Hope wiped the sweat from Blundermore's forehead. "So I've lived for your very existence and for all your siblings. I've raised a family. I've lived for your father – for his happiness and the happiness of all of you. Mine is a wonderful life. I've lived for the happiness of us all.

"Everything happens for a purpose. For me, your living gave meaning to the dilemma of Death. But there is no solution to Death. It is a dilemma. We can only extract meaning out of a dilemma – where we try to make sense out of it. Only you can give meaning to your life and to your death. We create our own lives. We define our own deaths.

"At the first moments of your life, you were already a fighter. And a fighter you are! I gave life freely to you. Whether you live or die, that was up to you. I took your living as a sign – a sign of ETERNAL HOPE. Of all the days in the year, you were born on April Fools' Day! You played the wildest prank on me! Thank you for gracing me with your life."

Blundermore did not have anything to say. With all his love, he squeezed her hands. "Mother, you have me here."

She understood what he was saying. "God gives; God takes away." She said with equanimity.

Wanting to be sure, she asked: "Has Dad died?" Blundermore nodded as he wept, overcome by emotion and guilt.

*　　　*　　　*

Dumbstruck with disbelief, the twins gaped at Blundermore and Lady Hope. *First day of class at ISBS and Grandfather Lucius dies.*

Luck thought that by coming to ISBS, he could be freer, eager to pursue his studies. Instead, he had arrived to witness the deep sorrows of his family. *Am I a harbinger of bad luck?* Then, as quickly as a twinkle of an eye, he felt himself lucky – very lucky! *With Grandpa Lucius's death, am I now off the hook from Operation Lightning Bolt? I WANT TO LIVE!*

*　　　*　　　*

Chance hesitated to believe that Grandfather Lucius had died. *What are the facts? Where is the proof?* He wanted to see concrete evidence – one way or another.

On the other hand, his heart lightened. *Maybe, Operation Lightning Bolt is now called off. I don't have to make that dreadful decision tomorrow. I DON'T WANT TO DIE!*

*　　　*　　　*

In his anger mixed with sorrow, Marcus muttered: "This act shall not stand! Father shall not die in vain. Datu Villani shall have his day! THIS IS WAR!"

Crestfallen, Lady Hope recited the following: "So Lucius, you've now stepped from the realm of Myth into the realm of History. Facts will determine your story, written by others, imposed upon you without your input – for better or for worse – as retold by allies and foes. Manipulated. Distorted. Compromised. Until Truth is no more."

*　　　*　　　*

REACHING FOR ETERNITY

MUSIC INSPIRATION

TIME FORGETS
(PIANO)
YIRUMA

MY HEART WILL GO ON
TITANIC- THEME SONG
SINGER: CELINE DION

I WILL ALWAYS LOVE YOU
WHITNEY HOUSTON

YOU LIGHT UP MY LIFE
DEBBY BOONE

L'HYMNE À L'AMOUR
(THE HYMN OF LOVE)
(FRENCH)
ÉDITH PIAF

ON MY OWN
LES MISÉRABLES
CLAUDE-MICHEL
ALAIN BOUBLIL & HERBERT KRETZMER
SINGER: LEA SALONGA

SAY SOMETHING
A GREAT BIG WORLD & CHRISTINA AGUILERA

FAREWELL
CROUCHING TIGER HIDDEN DRAGON
TAN DUN / 谭盾
CELLIST: YOYO MA / 马友友

IDYLL'S END
THE LAST SAMURAI
HANS ZIMMER

SYMPHONY NO. 7, MOVEMENT NO. 2
LUDWIG VON BEETHOVEN
CONDUCTOR: HERBERT VON KARAJAN

FIREWORKS COOL EASILY
YAN HUA YI LENG
烟花易冷
（CHINESE MANDARIN)
JAY CHOU / 周杰伦

A LOVE BEFORE TIME
月光爱人
(ENGLISH & CHINESE)
CROUCHING TIGER HIDDEN DRAGON
TAN DUN / 谭盾
SINGER: COCO LEE / 李玟

TOO MUCH HEAVEN
BEE GEES

INTROITUS
REQUIEM MASS IN D MINOR
(INTRODUCTION)
(LATIN)
WOLFGANG AMADEUS MOZART

AVE MARIA
(HAIL MARY)
(CLASSICAL GUITAR)
FRANZ SHUBERT
MICHAEL LUCARELLI

ETERNITY - MEMORIES OF LIGHTWAVES
(PIANO)
FINAL FANTASY X-2
NORIKO MATSUEDA & TAKAHITO EGUCHI

*　　　*　　　*

I believe in one God ...

I confess to one Baptism

For the forgiveness of sins.

And I look forward to the resurrection of the dead,

And the life of the world to come. Amen.

The Nicene Creed

*   *   *

"*I cannot be grasped in the here and now, For my dwelling place is as much among the dead, As yet the unborn, Slightly closer to the heart of creation than usual, But still not close enough.***"**

Tombstone of Paul Klee

*   *   *

509

How many times will we face the dilemma of Death and the promise of Eternal Life? How do we deal with these two extremes?

The secret lies in the beliefs deep within each of our souls. Herein dwells the Secret of Magic.

*   *   *

"**C**luck! Cluck!" With this, Piaf the Stork took a deep breath and sighed. Leaning back, she put her plume down. "This has been a long, long narration which I will never tire of telling. But I've got to sleep. It's very late. I have more babies to deliver tomorrow!" She stretched both her wings and yawned. Then she picked up two kerchiefs. On one kerchief was sewn the word: "JOY". On another kerchief was sewn the word: "SUFFERING". "This shall be for tomorrow!"

*   *   *

From across the room, her candle drifted closely above her, casting its gentle light upon her sepia parchment. It was late in the night. At her age, Death ceased to bring forth the terminal resignation Lady Hope once dreaded. She understood that Death was a portal to the next life. Instead, in sorrowful tenderness and yearning, with tears falling on the parchment, Lady Hope made this entry into her Mini-Myth Folio:

My Mini Myth Folio

Lady Hope

Today, June 22, a chapter of my life has closed.

Lucius Blundermore, my dearest friend, you have moved on to Eternity. Where are you? When will I see you again?

510

We've been the happiest together in this life. Why do we have to die?

You've become so much a part of me, our souls together. I long to touch you, to embrace you, to be with you.

So you die to go to a far, far better place, where no earthly worries follow you, where you become one with the Light, shining ever so brightly, beyond the Realm of Wisdom, into the realm of Eternity.

Somewhere, I know you live, leading the way for us.

When shall we be together again?

And so I run, my eyes locked onto the future, my eyes locked on you, hoping against hope, wishing that we shall someday run into each other out there in Eternity.

Forget me not.

I kiss you with all my love, now and forever,

Lady Hope

*   *   *

END OF BOOK ONE

TO BE CONTINUED

ABOUT THE AUTHOR

Elliot B. Addison obtained his B.A. in History from Rutgers University. He obtained his M.A. in International Relations from the Paul H. Nitze School of Advanced International Studies (SAIS) at Johns Hopkins University. He speaks five languages and has lived in six countries. He enjoys literature, music, history and art. He lives in Stamford, Connecticut, USA.

E-Mail: elliottaddison@yahoo.com

Visit his website:
WWW.ELLIOTTADDISON.COM

Made in the USA
Charleston, SC
09 February 2014